All That

and

a Bag of Chips

All That
and a
Bag of Chips

Darrien Lee

A

PUBLICATION

A Strebor Books International LLC Publication

Published by
SBI

STREBOR BOOKS INTERNATIONAL
P. O. Box 10127
Silver Spring, MD, 20914
http://www.streborbooks.com

ISBN 0-9711953-0-7

LCCN

COVER ILLUSTRATION: © *André Harris*
TYPESETTING & INTERIOR DESIGN: *Industrial Fonts & Graphix*

Manufactured & Printed in the United States
10 9 8 7 6 5 4 3 2 1

A Strebor Books International LLC Publication

Distributed by Simon and Schuster

This book is dedicated to all the people who touched my life in college. Especially my dear friends of Wilson Hall (The Zoo).

Tracy Dandridge, Shirlene Goodman, Lanetta Coleman, Buanita Ray, Cheryl Dean, Toni Britt, Teresa McElrath, Janice Talley, Esperonzia Noble, Angelic Thompson, and Dollie Morrison. Thanks for the memories.

Acknowledgments

First, I give thanks to God from whom all blessings flow.

To Daddy, I know you're looking down from Heaven with a big smile on your face. Thanks for watching over me. I miss you.

A heartwarming thanks to my Mother, Ines, who gave me life and love. You always knew I had a vivid imagination and adventurous nature.

To my loving husband, Wayne, who has supported and stood by me on this magical journey.

Thanks Sweetheart, I love you!

To my daughters, Alyvia and Marisa, you are so precious and the joy in my life. May you grow up to understand that your dreams can become a reality. Remember as long as you have God on your side, you can accomplish anything.

To my brother, Edward Jr. and sisters, Phylishia and Emily, you always knew I had it in me.

Thanks for the memories and the love.

Vanessa Harris Maston, your inspiration and encouragement help make my dream a reality; None of this would have been possible if not for you. I will always cherish the many memories we share. Never forget the green raincoat!

Devoted friends, Brenda Thomas and Tracy Dandridge, your

friendship is priceless! Over the last two decades, we've laughed and cried together as well as shared secrets we know are safe. Thanks for being in my corner.

I can't thank all my other friends and co-workers enough for the motivation. I appreciate all the critiquing you did to keep me focused and on the right path.

Andre' Harris, you are a talented artist and I am indebted to you for bringing my characters to life for this cover. You created them exactly as I envisioned. You are dangerous with a paintbrush! Stay Cool!

Romance Novelist, Carmen Green, thank you for your kind words of advice and encouragement.

Romance Novelist, Deirdre Savoy, I also thank you for your guidance and inspiration.

Finally, Zane, I had to save the best for last. I would like to thank you for taking a chance and believing in me. You motivated me when I need to be motivated. You encouraged me when I needed encouragement. I hope to make you proud!

All That
and
a Bag of Chips

One

The summer afternoon seemed just like many others. The mother was working on dinner in the kitchen while the father watched *Sanford and Son* reruns in the den. Venice, the baby of the Taylor family and the only girl, was about to leave for college. She was a natural beauty with smooth, cinnamon skin. Track was her sport of choice so she had the body of a typical sprinter. She was five-foot-six with well-conditioned, athletic legs. Her naturally long, thick hair dangled three inches past her shoulders.

Her two brothers, Bryan and Galen, were somewhat protective of her since she was their only sister. Bryan, the oldest of the three, was married with his own family. Sinclair, his stuck-up wife, was decent most of the time. However, she could turn into a real bitch when she didn't get her way. Bryan and Sinclair had an eight-year-old daughter, Crimson, who could be a brat from time to time. She had an attitude like her mother when things didn't go her way. Crimson did have her sweet moments. She inherited that quality from her daddy.

Bryan was quiet and passive, almost too passive. For the most part, he went along with the flow of things. Bryan was a handsome man: tall with the build of a former pro football player. His paper sack brown, smooth skin complimented killer bedroom eyes. He was constantly grooming his mustache and goatee into perfection.

Bryan was a sports agent for professional athletics. He'd met Sinclair, a florist, after rear-ending her car. A year and a half later, viola! They were married. A couple of years after they were married, Crimson entered their lives.

Galen, on the other hand, was closer to his sister's age. They'd been inseparable most of their lives. However, in high school, they'd had their own things going on. While Venice was running track, Galen was on the football field. Galen had a slender build, but also carried well-defined muscles on his tall frame. To describe him, most would say he was high yellow like their mother and had all the women at his feet.

The good thing about Galen was that he wasn't a player, player! He was entering his junior year at Dawson University. Venice was about to be a freshman there. She was supposed to go to the University of Michigan, but the administration had misplaced her paperwork. By the time they found it, Venice couldn't get in so she decided to join her brother at Dawson instead and nevertheless remained excited. She was hoping Galen wouldn't try to be an on-campus daddy to her; assuming he could tell her what to do. After all, Venice was about to meet college men and Mommy and Daddy were going to be six hours away. *Hey!*

Since the big day had finally arrived, Bryan felt he had to come over to give Venice a lecture on studying. He cautioned her about getting mixed up with the campus freak-a-zoids and dogs. This was kind of flattering, but little did Bryan know that Galen had told Venice that those were the exact kind of women Bryan had dated in college. Luckily, he didn't let them ruin his goal of getting his education. Now it was Venice's turn to remember to stay focused. She knew the fine men she was about to meet might be a slight distraction, even though her heart still belonged to the only man she'd ever loved.

Mr. Taylor, a retired police officer, didn't have much to say except, "Baby girl, call me if you need anything and Galen, you better look after your sister."

Galen nodded in acceptance of the task bestowed upon him by his father.

Mrs. Taylor had fried chicken packed for both of them. Brain food is what she called it. She said, "All black folks need a little chicken to nibble on when they're studying."

While Galen and Bryan were putting the last pieces of the luggage into Venice's car, Crimson asked, "Where are you going?"

Venice explained to her that she was moving into the college dormitory and would come visit her every chance she got. After hearing this, Crimson became very silent as if she were analyzing the situation. Then she asked if she could have Venice's room.

Venice told her, "No way!"

She chased Crimson out into the yard and around the house. Crimson was a pretty child with long, silky pigtails and dark chocolate skin. Her eyes were light brown and she had a smile that would con anyone. Her long legs had all the markings of a future track star.

Venice's closest friend in the world, Joshua, also came down to see her off. They'd grown up together and Venice regarded him as her third brother. They went practically everywhere together. A lot of people didn't understand how a sista and a brotha could be so close without having any sex between them. Venice's boyfriend understood their closeness with no problem, but Joshua's girlfriends always felt threatened by her. All of them except for his present girlfriend, Cynthia. She was cool and Venice really liked her.

Joshua was going to stay home, work the first year, and then join Venice at college later. They planned to share an apartment the following summer while they attended summer school. Venice was going to miss him more than anyone. Oddly enough, he was the one that she shared all of her secrets with. She had another friend, Chanelle, that she hung out with, but she wasn't like Joshua. He cared a lot about Venice. They were each other's rock.

Sinclair, Bryan's devilish wife, drove up in her forest green SUV. She couldn't even say hello because she was too busy scolding Crimson for running around like a wild child.

Venice hurriedly butted in by telling her, "She was playing with me!"

Sinclair gave Venice that "don't start with me look" and asked Crimson where her daddy was. As Crimson was responding, Sinclair's cell phone began ringing. She glared at Venice as she walked past her into the house.

"Skank!" Venice mumbled.

Two

At last, Venice could finally pull out of the driveway. Everyone came out onto the porch to exchange hugs and say their good-byes. Galen was still in the house feeding his face with his mother's chicken when Venice gave everyone a hug and kiss.

Joshua walked her to the car. "Girl, you'd better call me and don't go down there and get mixed up with any thugs."

Venice laughed. "Josh, you know I'm not going to do anything like that. I'll call you and let you know what's going on. Don't forget you're coming down for homecoming. Okay?"

He smiled, leaned into the window of her car, and gave her a kiss on the cheek. "I'm going to miss you, Niecy. I love you."

Venice got out of the car and gave him another hug. "I love you, too!"

This was going to be the first time they'd been separated since preschool and it already felt weird. Joshua lived one street over and during their years growing up, if Joshua and his brother weren't at the Taylor home, Venice and Galen were down at their house. It was hard to realize that they'd grown up and were moving on to *hopefully* bigger and better things.

Venice pulled out of the driveway and waved as she drove down the street. She had to make one more important stop. She had to say her final goodbye to her sweetie, Jarvis Anderson. He was also going to be leaving for college the next day. He was lucky to get both academic and football scholarships. He planned on majoring in Criminal Justice and figured if he didn't make it to the pros, he could work for the FBI or some other government agency.

They'd been dating for the past four years and had been through hell and high water together. It was going to be especially hard to say goodbye to him. Venice still loved him, but their parents felt they should cool it since they were getting ready to go in two different directions. They'd shared a hot love affair over the years and had just spent their last night together before heading off to school. They vowed that if fate put them back together after they graduated, they would get married.

Venice had dated a few guys when they were going through one of their temporary breakups. But, she never found anyone she liked as much as Jarvis. Only one incident seriously tested them and they'd found themselves back together again in no time. Joshua once told her that Jarvis was born to be her husband. Venice always thought Joshua was trippin' when he said things like that, but she listened to him anyway.

When she pulled up in front of Jarvis' house, he immediately came out to meet her. Venice got out of the car and sat upon the hood as he approached.

Jarvis asked, "Are you getting ready to hit the road?"

"Yep! Daddy wants me to get there before dark."

"Where's Galen?"

"He's leaving in a little while."

He stood in front of Venice and wrapped his arms around her, pulling her toward him. "I had a good time last night, Niecy. I just wish there were some way we could…"

"Don't go there, Jarvis. This is hard enough for me."

He hugged her, rubbing her hips. "I know, Venice. Damn, I'm going to miss you. Make sure you call me. You know your stuff will *always* belong to me."

Venice giggled and gave him a kiss on the cheek.

Jarvis went on to say, "I'm not playing, Venice! If you hook up with some buster down there, just remember that. I'm just loaning you out until I graduate. Then I'm coming back for you."

Venice had tears in her eyes. "Do you think we did the right thing?"

"I don't know, Niecy. My mind says we did but my heart says we didn't. We can't dwell on that now. What's done is done."

"I guess you're right."

Venice got down off the car slowly, wiping away her tears.

"What's wrong, Niecy?"

"I'm sore! You know what you did to me last night!"

Jarvis gazed at her with his devilish, seductive eyes. "Are you having regrets now?"

She pressed her body to his. "My only regret is that I don't have time to show you just how much I love you before I leave."

He held her against his strong, muscular body. "Baby, if you show me any more, I'm not going to be able to walk myself."

They held their embrace as they laughed together. Silence followed as they gazed at each other's lips and into each other's eyes. He held her face tenderly and gave her another sultry kiss.

"Niecy, you taste so sweet. I'm not going to make it without you."

"I'm going to miss you, too. Everything will be okay. You'll see. Well, baby, I'd better get going. I'll see you at homecoming."

"Without a doubt, but I need to see you before then."

"Same here, Jarvis."

"I'll get with Pops and see what he can work out."

She held onto him for a moment before they exchanged a series of toe-curling kisses. Venice went numb and lightheaded at the same time. She felt the warmth from his body and saw the devotion in his eyes.

"Lord have mercy, Jarvis!"

"You do the same to me, girl. Too bad I can't take you up on your offer."

"Don't tempt me, baby. I really better get going. Oh, don't go up to that fancy college and get something you can't get rid of. Better yet, don't become somebody's baby's daddy. I know you're a big football star and all, but I'd be pissed if you let something like that happen. "

Jarvis opened the car door for her. "I'm not going to take any chances with those chickenheads up there. You know where my heart is."

"Me too, baby. Love you and I'll call you when I get in."

Jarvis gave her another kiss and then waved to her as she backed out of the driveway. He hollered, "Don't be speeding!"

She blew her horn at him and was out of sight within seconds. Jarvis stared at the ground for a moment before mumbling, "We did do the wrong thing, Niecy."

Three

Venice had a six-hour drive to college, which she hoped she could cut into five. As she drove, she reminisced about the previous night with Jarvis. He definitely knew how to please a woman and Venice was really going to miss that. He made sure he sent her off to college well-satisfied. They'd been through a lot together, more than most people their age. Jarvis was definitely her boo. Venice was a little unconvinced that she wanted college to open new doors for her. She was also slightly nervous about possibly dating someone else since she'd been with Jarvis for so long. She knew she'd have to cross that bridge when she got to it.

When she finally made it to the college, Venice was exhausted and ready to settle in. She hoped that her roommate would be friendly and easy to get along with. Venice saw all the hustling freshmen coming into the dormitory parking lot. Some were pulling trailer hitches full of school necessities. It took Venice about an hour to get her things to the room. There were boxes in the room marked "Monique." Her roommate had obviously arrived.

Venice plopped down on one of the beds. "I hope she's not a nut case."

Venice called her parents and Jarvis to let them know that she'd arrived safely. After she got off the phone, she started hanging her clothes in the closet nearest to the bed she'd selected. By the time she made the bed, two hours had elapsed and her stomach was growling. It was eighty-thirty and she hadn't had a bite to eat. She still hadn't heard from Galen or met her new roommate. Venice decided to page Galen to make sure he'd made it in okay. It wasn't long before the telephone rang.

"What's up, baby sister?"

"Don't call me that! Why didn't you let me know you were here?"

"I was going to call you, but I've been kicking it with my boys. What are you doing?"

"I've finished putting up all my stuff and now I'm starving."

Galen laughed. "Look, I'm going to meet some of my boys over on the band's practice field in a minute. Look for me over there and I'll take you to get something to eat."

"How am I going to find the band field?"

"Follow the music!"

"Funny, Galen."

"I'm just playing. It's over behind the track."

"Oh, I know where you're talking about now. I'll see you after I change."

She hung up the phone and called her girlfriend Chanelle. She gave Chanelle her phone number and told her that she hadn't met her roommate yet. They talked a few minutes more and Chanelle informed Venice that it appeared she was going to be joining her after all. The dormitory had an unexpected opening and Chanelle was next on the waiting list. Chanelle told Venice that she'd see her in a couple of days. After they'd said their good-byes, Venice changed into a pair of royal blue shorts and a white tee, wrote her roommate an introductory note, and left out to meet Galen.

Venice took note of all the activities for incoming freshman as she walked across the campus. A vendor was selling Dawson T-shirts and baseball hats. Venice paused long enough to finger through them. Young men were trying to flirt with her, obviously sensing some "fresh meat." Venice's mind was on Jarvis, though. She missed him already. Only time would tell if they were doing the right thing by cooling it. Finally, Venice heard the band's music in the air.

Venice reached the field and saw the majorettes, flag corp, and band members on the field going through their routines under the glaring lights that had come on automatically at sundown. As she walked along the fence, she could see Galen and a group of guys across the field. She took her time, stopping occasionally to watch the band's dance routine.

Galen and his friends were hanging over the fence near the majorettes, checking them out.

One of his friends said, "Damn, look at the booty on that one! I'd love to get with her."

Galen didn't have much to say because he was spoken for. He'd been dating his girlfriend, Sidney, since freshman year. He did, however, laugh at the comments his friends were making. Galen hadn't talked much about Venice during his years at Dawson. It was going to be somewhat of a surprise to his friends to find out that he even had a sister. Galen didn't talk much about his family *period* to his friends because he was private like that at times. He was a little uneasy about Venice coming to college there and had tried to keep it on the downlow. When they were in junior high and high school, there were several times he had to get in the face of guys that he felt disrespected Venice. He had a pretty bad temper, but he was doing better controlling it.

As the guys continued to yell at the majorettes, one of the guys hollered out, "Lawd! Here comes another one over there! Damn, she's fine!"

Another one of his friends said, "Man! That one's going to be my baby's momma."

When Galen and his friend Craig turned to see who they were trippin' out over, Galen realized that it was Venice. He dropped his head and smiled as Venice approached the group. She noticed everyone was staring at her and it made her feel a tad bit uncomfortable.

She walked over to Galen and put her arm around his waist. "Hey, bro! Are you ready to go?"

Galen laughed as he saw his friends' mouths drop open.

One of the guys mumbled, "Don't tell me Galen's trying to be a playa."

"Nah, you trifling fools! This is my sister, Venice."

One of his friends said, "Negro, you ain't got no sister!"

Venice interrupted. "No, he's telling the truth. Can't you see the resemblance?"

Craig leaned against the fence, looked her up and down, and said, "Galen wished he looked like you."

Venice smiled and thanked the extremely handsome friend of Galen's. Venice sensed that he was checking her out and wondered what he was thinking. A tingle ran up her spine as he continued to ogle her.

Craig felt a familiar yearning start to build in his gut. While he was accustomed to being aroused, a woman had never stirred him to the core like Venice did. He thought to himself, *This woman is absolutely gorgeous! But...she's Galen's sister. Damn! Why me!* Craig noticed he wasn't the only one instantly attracted to Venice. *I want to get to know you, Venice Taylor!*

Galen told his partners he'd catch up with them later. As they walked away, Galen looked back to find every last one of his friends' eyes on Venice. Under his breath, he said, "I hope I won't have to kick none of their asses."

Venice asked, "Who was the guy in the gray shirt?"

"That's just Craig."

"A friend of yours?"

Galen unlocked the door of his car. "Why do you want to know? Aren't you still spoken for?"

"Sort of...we just decided to chill a little."

"If you two were chillin', I'd hate to see what you thought being together was like."

"You just don't understand, Galen. Our relationship's complicated."

"Whatever! Really, why do you want to know about Craig? You wanna hook up with him or something?"

"I think he's cute, that's all. He seems nice." *He is soul-stirring handsome, sexy and unbelievably fine,* Venice thought secretively.

Galen started up the car and pulled off. As he drove down the street, he looked at her and said, "Don't be rushing into anything because I know how you and Jarvis are. *But,* I guess if you hang out with any of my friends, Craig's the coolest one."

"Thanks for the 4-1-1, Galen."

Galen smiled and pulled into a local soul food restaurant. "Let's grub, girl!"

Venice laughed. "You're silly and thanks for the advice because you're right. I do still have a serious thang for Jarvis." *Then why was I shivering from being in the same air space with this Craig person?* she wondered.

"Are you listening to me, Venice?"

"Huh?"

"Never mind. Go slow, Venice."

"Thanks, Galen."

Four

When Galen dropped Venice off at her dormitory, he told her that he'd talk to her later.

She gave him a punch on the arm after thanking him for dinner and said, "I love you, Galen."

"I love you, too, girl. Now goodbye!"

Venice laughed because Galen didn't like to expose his soft side much.

As Venice got on the elevator, she wondered if her roommate was back. When she entered the room, it was still empty, but she could see this Monique person had read her note. Venice was sleepy and decided to lie down and take a nap. She didn't want to miss any of the happenings her first night on campus. She saw a sign in the lobby about a block party in the courtyard at midnight. This gave her time to take a catnap. Lying there, she wondered what she was going to wear. Most importantly, was Craig going to be there? It wasn't long before she'd drifted off the sleep.

Venice was startled awake by someone opening the door giggling.

She sat up. "Hello, you must be Monique."

Monique walked into the room and threw her purse on the bed. "Hey, Venice! Girl, we finally hooked up! It's been a wild day! Are you going to the block party?"

Excited, Venice answered, "I want to. Do you want to go together?"

"Yeah! There are some fine men out here!"

Monique was about five-foot-eight and was wearing some type of designer short set. She was thumbing through her closet trying to decide what to wear to the party. Venice got up and thought to herself, *I think I'm going to like her.* The two women selected their outfits. Venice chose a burnt orange, mini skirt set with her midsection out and matching sandals. Monique chose a red midriff blouse, which showed off her washboard stomach. She also put on some tight white jeans. Monique looked like a runway model. She was very pretty and had her hair put up in a stylish French roll. They continued to chitchat as they got dressed for the block party.

Midnight rolled around quickly and the two women headed to the courtyard. They could hear the music filling the air. It was a warm night and thankfully not too humid. Venice was a little nervous, but glad that she had Monique with her. Once they made it to the courtyard, it was hard to see faces. Some people were dancing while others were getting their mack on. Venice scanned the crowd looking for Galen and wondered if Craig was there. Monique found someone to dance with in a hurry, which left Venice standing alone feeling vulnerable.

As she continued to scan the crowd, a couple of guys came by and asked her to dance. She decided to take them up on their offer. After a few dances, she was no longer feeling like the new kid on the block. The guys she danced with wasted no time trying to get Venice's phone number, but she wasn't ready to give it out. About that time, the DJ slowed the music down. Just as another young man was about to ask her to dance again, she heard a husky, yet silky voice call out, "Venice!"

When she turned, she saw Craig. He took her by the hand, all six-foot two-inches of him and told the young man, "I got this one, partner."

The young man could do nothing but stand there with his mouth open. Craig led Venice out into the dance area through the crowd. Venice knew she was looking good in her skirt and Craig was definitely admiring her. Her hair was blown straight. It had so much body that it moved every time she turned her head or the wind blew.

Venice was a little shocked, but it was a good shock. She realized she'd been blind-sided and it was scary. Her hand in Craig's sent a heated tingle up her arm. They finally reached a good spot where Venice was able to really check him out.

Craig was wearing a nice pair of jeans and a white button down shirt and he smelled like heaven. The way his jeans were formed to his muscular thighs and buttocks should've been against the law. Venice felt herself trembling slightly but tried to keep her composure when Craig pulled her into his warm body and they began to dance. Chills started running all over her body as their bodies molded into each other. She could feel his gaze, but she dared not confirm it. She thought she would faint.

What is wrong with me? I haven't felt anything close to this since I met Jarvis, Venice pondered.

She glanced over and saw that Monique was still dancing. In fact, Monique hadn't sat down all evening. Venice tried to keep her mind focused, but it was hard. She felt his warm hands caress her bare back as they danced. Once the song ended, Craig once again held her hand and led her back through the crowd to find a seat.

Once they sat down, he asked, "How long have you been out here at the party?"

Venice surveyed the crowd, trying not to make eye contact. "Oh, not long."

Craig sensed her nervousness and smiled. "Do you like it here so far?"

Venice finally looked into his warm, brown eyes. "Yeah, it's nice here. Have you seen Galen?"

Craig pointed off to the left. "I saw him and Sidney over there a few minutes ago."

There was a moment of silence and Venice noticed Craig was once again staring. He discreetly whispered, "Venice, you're definitely wearing that skirt."

She crossed her legs and replied, "Thank you."

In a weird way, Venice felt like she was cheating on Jarvis. They'd been together for so long that it felt strange hanging out with another guy. Especially one who was making her body loose control the way Craig was.

Galen and Sidney found them not long afterwards. Monique also finally came over to take a breather. A few minutes later, Galen's other friends, Spoonie and a couple of other guys, joined them. Venice introduced Galen, Sidney, and Craig to Monique. Galen also introduced his friends to everyone. As they talked, everyone began to get to know each other better. They danced and laughed together and Venice felt great that her first night on campus was so cool. Galen's other friends seemed to admire Venice and Monique very much. Craig knew them and, in a sly way, made sure they didn't get too friendly with Venice in particular. He didn't mind them dancing with her. He just made sure there weren't any one-on-one conversations. He'd made up his mind that he wanted Venice for himself.

A couple of hours passed and the party began to wind down. Sidney told Galen that she was tired and ready to go. Monique was still macking with several of the guys. Craig socialized with several friends who'd returned for the new school year. Galen asked Venice if they needed a ride back to their dorm. It was about two-thirty and getting a little cool.

Craig spoke up. "Galen, if Venice doesn't mind, I'll drive her and Monique back to the dorm."

Venice was taken aback by his forwardness.

Galen asked, "Is it okay with you, Venice?"

"It's fine with me." She glanced at Craig. "I don't want you to have to go out of your way."

Craig stood up and said, "I don't mind."

Monique was talking to Spoonie and the other guys. She seemed to be having a great time with them. She came over and said, "Roomie, I'll see you a little later. I'm going to hang out a little longer."

Venice responded, "Okay, Monique. I'm headed to the room. I'll see you later." She stood and turned to Craig. "Well, I guess we can leave."

Galen and Sidney walked in the same direction as Venice and Craig. When they reached the parking lot, Galen leered at Venice. "Page me when you get to the room."

Craig laughed. "I'm not going to kidnap her, man. You don't have to worry about her. I'll take special care of Venice."

Galen jokingly said, "Don't make me have to put a cap in your ass."

Sidney hollered, "Galen, unlock the door! Venice, don't pay your brother any attention. You know he's crazy. See you later, Craig."

Craig opened the door for Venice and said, "Goodnight, Sidney."

Venice was feeling nervous once again. She realized that she was going to be alone with Craig. She wanted to act mature and not make a fool of herself. Craig had a very nice sports utility vehicle. Venice complimented it by saying, "Your truck's very nice."

Craig pulled out the parking lot and grinned at her. "Thank you." He reached down to turn on some music and slightly brushed her leg. "Excuse me."

She smiled at him. "No harm done."

"Do you like jazz?"

Venice looked straight ahead and answered, "Yes, it's my favorite."

"So, Taylor, are you hungry?"

Venice shyly said, "Not really."

He turned down one of the streets on campus. "If you are, I don't mind taking you to get a bite to eat. There's a place just a few blocks from campus that stays open all night."

"Maybe another time. I'm a little tired tonight, with the long drive and moving in the dorm and all."

"I understand."

The rest of the ride was silent. It only took about five additional minutes to reach her dorm. When he pulled into the parking lot, they noticed people sitting outside socializing. Most of them had also just left the block party.

Craig turned the truck off and got out to open Venice's door. "Do you mind if I walk you to your door?"

Venice blushed. "No, I don't mind at all."

Craig walked slightly behind Venice to admire her beautiful figure as she walked ahead of him. Her outfit looked as if God Himself had made it especially for her shapely curves. Venice could feel Craig's eyes, along with a weird stirring in her stomach. He finally got beside her and they walked slowly toward the entrance to the dorm.

Once they reached the porch, Venice turned to him. "Thanks again for dropping me off."

He touched her on the arm. "No problem." His touch was hot and fiery. "It was nice seeing you again, Venice Taylor. Maybe I'll see you again soon."

"That would be nice."

He gave her a quick hug and walked back to his truck. *What is this woman doing to me?* Craig thought as he started his ignition.

Venice's heart was still pounding when she arrived in her room. When she looked at her arms, there were goose bumps. *Damn!* She hurried into her nightshirt and paged Galen as instructed to let him know that she was in her room and went to bed.

Five

When Venice awoke the next morning, she realized that she hadn't heard Monique come into the room the night before. Somehow, the sunlight had found a way to shine directly on her face. She glanced at the clock and realized it was only six twenty-five. She got up, went to the bathroom, and crawled back into bed.

Monique was still fast asleep. Venice laid there for a moment, not able to recapture sleep. She was still wondering about Craig. He'd made her curious and she craved to learn more about him.

She decided to call Jarvis to get Craig off her mind. He'd be leaving for college in a few hours and she wanted to talk to him. She took the phone into the hallway, so she wouldn't wake Monique up, and sat down on the floor as the phone started ringing.

Jarvis answered in a sleepy voice, "Hello?"

"Hey, baby. Did I wake you?"

"Not really. I can't sleep anyway. I guess I'm still missing you. How's school?"

"It's okay. It helps that Galen and Sidney are here. Chanelle called me and told me she'd be here in a few days."

"That's good. You'll have your partner with you. So, what did you do last night?"

"I went to a campus block party with my roommate."

"So, how many guys tried to push up on you?"

Venice laughed. "Stop being silly. I just met a few of Galen's friends. They're nice."

"Uh-huh! Did anyone put their hands on you?"

"You know they had to in order to dance with me, Jarvis."

"I know. I'm just messing with you. I'm glad you had a good time. My plane leaves around eleven o'clock. I'll call you when I get to school so I can give you my number." There was an uncomfortable silence. "What's wrong, Niecy?"

"Jarvis, I had a weird feeling last night. I guess I've been with you so long that when I was with one of Galen's friends, I felt like I was cheating on you."

"What do you mean, *with* one of Galen's friends?"

"We just danced. He gave me a ride back to the dorm and walked me to the door."

"Venice, as much as I hate the thought of another man's hands on you, we decided to chill, remember?"

"I know, but even though we're not together, I can't help it that I still love you."

"The feelings mutual, Niecy. I'm sure I'll feel the same way if I meet somebody. Just go slow, baby. Believe me when I say the last thing I want to think about is you with some other man. I just can't handle the thought of that. I still want you, Niecy."

"I know, but...."

"Look, Venice, if you want to try and make a long distance relationship work, I'm game."

"I don't know, Jarvis. We need to really think about whether it would work. Anyway, have a safe flight and don't forget to call me."

"I will, girl. Now quit tripping. I love you."

"I love you too, baby. See you."

After they'd hung up, Venice went back inside and got back under the covers. She finally felt a little relaxed. Jarvis was always able to make her feel secure and she missed him badly. They didn't totally agree with what their parents made them do. After shedding a few tears, she eventually drifted back to sleep.

Six

After a few hours, the two women began to stir in their beds. Monique made her way to the bathroom and said, "Girl, I've got a nasty headache."

"What time did you get in last night?"

"I don't even know, but your brother's friends are crazy. They're cool though. We really kicked it last night."

They talked a little more until the telephone rang. Monique reached over and answered, "Hello?" The voice on the other end must've asked for Venice. "No, she's awake. Hold on a minute."

Monique held the telephone out to Venice. "Hello?"

"Good morning, Miss Taylor."

Her heart came to a complete stop. It was *him*. That husky, sexy-voiced Craig Bennett.

She tried to regain her senses and answered with, "Good morning. You sure are an early riser."

Craig laughed. "Always! I'm afraid that I might miss out on something."

Monique was sitting on her bed grinning and looking directly in Venice's mouth, following every word spoken. Venice turned her back to Monique as Craig admitted that he'd been hesitant to call her so soon. He told Venice that Galen had reluctantly given him the number, along with a short lecture.

He said, "I hope you don't mind that I hijacked your phone number. I meant to ask you for it last night, but I was distracted, if you know what I mean. I guess I was a little nervous."

"You didn't seem nervous to me and, no, I don't mind."

Craig asked if Venice had any plans for breakfast. Even though she was still in shock, she was able to tell him that she was available.

19

He asked how long it would take her to get dressed and they made arrangements for him to meet her in the lobby of the dormitory in an hour. Venice thanked him for the invitation and hung up the phone.

Venice couldn't move! Monique jumped up off the bed screaming, "Girl! What did he say? Was that your brother's fine friend? What are you going to wear?"

Venice made her way over to the window, still stunned. "I can't believe he's asking me out so soon. We just met."

"Damn, girl! What planet are you from? That's what people do when they're in college? They meet and then hook up. I have a lot to teach you. You've been on lock down way too long."

"I guess you're right, Monique. Craig's definitely all that and a bag of chips! I just didn't expect to meet someone the first day here. I'm still in love with Jarvis. I'm not going to rush into anything. This already feels weird. I haven't let another guy get this close to me in a long time. But it's something about Craig that makes me feel...I can't even describe it."

"Horny?"

Venice giggled. "No, Monique! You just don't understand."

"You'll be fine, Venice. Just relax."

They laughed and slapped high-fives. The phone rang again and Monique darted to answer it. "Yes, she's sitting right here. Would you like to speak with her?"

All the blood left Venice's face and she felt faint as Monique handed her the phone.

"What's up, girl?"

Venice took some air into her lungs when she realized it was Galen. Venice asked him why he'd given her number to Craig. He told her that he'd seen the way they'd looked at each other and that out of all the partners he had, Craig was the only one decent enough for her to be seen with. Somewhere in that statement was a compliment.

Venice told Galen that she was meeting Craig for breakfast in an hour and that she'd call him with all the details when she got back. Galen said okay, but stressed that she go slow. She hung up and began to get dressed.

Venice had no idea what to wear. Monique rambled through Venice's closet digging for the perfect outfit for her date and, after about five minutes, Monique pulled out this banging pantsuit. It was too dressy for Venice so she grabbed her best pair of jeans and a colorful blouse. She picked out the perfect pair of shoes to go with her selection.

Craig would be there soon and Venice didn't have much time left to shower and get dressed. After she accomplished that task, Monique helped Venice take the rollers out her hair and styled it with great detail. Venice didn't want to overdo it, so she only put on a little foundation, lipstick, and eyeliner. Just when she'd touched up her lipstick, the phone rang. He was there. It was on!

Monique gave Venice her final approval before she walked out of the room. She gave Venice a high-five and told her that she wanted to know every detail when she got back. Venice made her way down the long hallway to the elevator. She could feel her heart pounding and her knees began to get weak. She told herself to calm down and take a few deep breaths. *You can do this. What do you have to be afraid of?*

The elevator made its way downward, passing the second floor. *What will I say?* She said a short prayer as the doors opened on the first floor. As she rounded the corner and entered the lobby, there he was. *Damn! Damn! Damn!* He didn't see her coming so she was able to admire the fine specimen that he was. It was obvious that he worked out. He was wearing a nice pair of khakis with a pullover shirt that molded to his broad chest. Craig was a very handsome man with caramel colored skin, a beautiful smile, and the darkest, sexy brown eyes. That smile would make any girl's heart skip a beat. He was breathtaking and just plain fine! *My God! What am I about to get myself into?*

Just as she was approaching him, he turned and greeted her with an unexpected hug. Venice knew that she would faint for sure. His cologne put her into an instant trance, but she was able to hug him back. Venice told him that she was sorry he had to wait on her, but he quickly interrupted and told her that he didn't mind the wait. As they walked out into the courtyard, he told her that she looked very nice. Venice blushed and thanked him shyly. *My knees…please don't give out on me.*

As they walked and talked, a few people were stirring around campus. Some appeared to be coming in from all-nighters. Most were still in bed and a few were headed to church service. She wasn't sure where they were going to breakfast but assumed they were leaving campus. Once they reached the parking lot, Craig deactivated his car alarm. He was driving a beautiful black Ford Expedition with a soft tan leather interior. She wasn't able to see it that well the night before. Venice did wonder how he could afford such a nice vehicle. For now, she'd chill and get the 4-1-1 from Galen later. Craig made his way to the passenger side of the truck to open her door. *Yes! A gentleman!*

Craig wasted no time driving off the campus on their way to the mystery breakfast. He asked her, "So, have you settled into campus life yet?"

"Yes, but I'm still adjusting to noises all during the night. You can hear people talking, music playing, and doors slamming all night long. My roommate is cool though. I think we'll get along just fine. Craig, it was nice of you to call and invite me to breakfast. I was totally caught off guard."

He blushed. "Well, since I couldn't get you to hang out with me last night, I thought I'd try again while you were still delirious with sleep. I'm glad you accepted my invitation."

He turned into the parking lot of small mom & pop style cafe. People were hurrying in and out of the exit. Most of them were dressed in their Sunday best. Little girls were giggling and playing with the ribbons in their hair. Venice could smell country ham and homemade biscuits while Craig was parking the truck. A few old-timers were lingering outside the cafe sipping coffee and reading the paper.

Venice noticed a sign: "Miss Bessie's Home Cooking." With a name like that, she knew the food was going to be good. As they entered the diner, waitresses hurried past them with armloads of food and hungry guests were excited to see their meals arriving at their tables. Craig and Venice were one of three couples waiting to be seated for some delicious eating.

Craig said, " I hope you like the food here. It's like eating your mom's cooking."

He went on to say that he usually came there on Sunday mornings before church. Craig was a churchgoing man and Venice thought that was a definite plus. She asked Craig what church he attended and he explained that he still attended the church he grew up in.

Venice boldly said, "That would make you a local."

"Yeah, I am. Maybe you could go to church with me one Sunday."

"That would be nice. Thanks."

About that time, they were seated. Craig showed her the cafe specialties and told her to order whatever she wanted. The cafe did offer a grand buffet, but Venice didn't feel too hungry. She finally ordered some blueberry pancakes with sausage on the side. Craig, being a growing boy, decided to order the buffet.

He said, "Venice, they have some great omelets here. I want you to taste one in particular if you'd like to."

"I'm game. Thanks!" *That ain't all I would like to taste. You know you have some juicy looking lips.* She let out a sneaky giggle.

"What's so funny?"

"Oh, nothing. I was just thinking about something Monique said earlier."

"Are you going to let me in on it?"

"Maybe later."

Venice was happy to keep her thoughts to herself.

After the waitress took their orders, Craig asked Venice questions about her major. She explained to him she was majoring in Sports Medicine. She told him that most of the time when people watched professional sports, you never saw any female doctors; let alone African Americans.

After Craig thought about it, he agreed. "You'll probably get a job as soon as you graduate."

"I hope so. I'm planning on doing it on the professional level."

"That's all right, Taylor."

As they continued to talk, she found out that he was majoring in architecture. He told her that he'd always loved to draw and decided to follow in his father's footsteps.

About that time, the waitress brought their drinks to the table. Craig had ordered water along with a glass of orange juice. Venice had ordered water and a cup of tea. As Venice and Craig continued to talk, she couldn't help but notice the photographs on the wall of celebrities that had dined there on past occasions. There were pictures of Patti Labelle, James Ingram, and Chris Tucker, just to name a few. Miss Bessie's Diner had been in the community for thirty years. Everyone around knew and admired her for starting a business as a black woman in an era when civil rights were constantly being fought for.

Craig gave Venice the history of the magical place and the secret of its success. He seemed to be intrigued by the nostalgia and romance behind Miss Bessie's. Venice was hanging on Craig's every word as he spoke passionately about the diner.

The waitress returned to the table. "Who ordered the pancakes?"

Venice acknowledged her ordered. Then the waitress gave Craig the go ahead for the buffet table. She asked if she could get them anything else.

Venice replied, "Extra napkins, please."

The waitress softly placed napkins on the table. "Enjoy your breakfast and thanks for dining with Miss Bessie's."

Craig asked Venice if she'd like anything from the buffet table but she declined. Venice noticed several women in the diner watching him as he walked across the room. A woman would've had to be blind not to notice him. *Forget it ladies, he's with me!*

Venice felt honored to be with a man admired by so many women. When he returned to the table, he said grace and began to enjoy the feast.

Venice said, "I must say, Mr. Bennett, I thought you were going to get mobbed by all the ladies watching you cross the room."

"Where?"

"Look around. All of them."

"Are you jealous?"

"Maybe."

They both laughed and Venice shyly lowered her eyes to her plate. Craig was impressed with Venice's territorial stance. She was too good to be true. He was in love. *Yes, in love.* He knew it the moment that their eyes had met on the band field. The second he'd held her as they danced. He just knew.

They enjoyed a wonderful breakfast and nice conversation. After the waitress came to clear their dishes from the table, Venice requested another cup of tea while they continued to talk. Before they realized it, two hours had passed.

While Craig paid the tab, Venice gazed into the glass display case at the register and saw antique jewelry and old 45 rpm records of songs she hadn't heard in years. "Wow! Look at this! Look at the good condition of these records!"

She spotted "Want Ads" by the Honeycombs. "I used to dance to that song when I was little. My mom used to have it."

Craig asked the cashier if the items were for sale. She explained that they were from Miss Bessie's private collection. Craig asked her if the old gospel songs playing in the jukebox were also from her private collection.

She said, "You bet! Miss Bessie keeps these records for her customers to enjoy as they dine." She thanked them for coming and said, "Ya'll come back now, you hear?"

Customers were still pouring in as they left. "Venice, would you like a tour of the city?"

"Sure, I'd like to see more of this beautiful little country town."

Craig drove past the shopping areas, the churches, and parks. He showed Venice other nice restaurants and the movie theater. "One thing I like about this town is it still has a drive-in movie theater."

"Really! I used to love going to the drive-in."

"Good! I'm going to hold you to that."

"That would be cool! But, when we go, it's my treat. You paid for breakfast so it's only fair that I treat you to the movies."

He smiled. "We'll see. Maybe I'll cook dinner for you before we go." Venice smirked, letting him know she didn't imagine him as a chef. "Don't judge a book by its cover. I know my way around the kitchen. Momma made sure that my sister and I knew how to get down in the kitchen."

They laughed as he turned back onto the campus and drove up to her dormitory.

"Craig, thank you for breakfast, the tour, and the nice company."

"You're welcome, Venice. I couldn't ask for any better company myself."

He got out of the truck. Venice slid out the door behind him. She felt the heat of his body as he walked closely with her. He opened the door and they proceeded to the elevator. "You don't mind if I walk you to your room, do you?"

"Oh no, it's okay."

Venice felt her heart starting to pound as the elevator doors closed, leaving them alone on the elevator. Craig's gaze went from her lips to her eyes.

"Venice, I want to thank you again for hanging out with me this morning."

"No, thank you for asking."

Venice noticed he was coming closer and closer. He leaned down and kissed her with those luscious lips. He slid his arms around her waist and pulled her to him. Venice welcomed his probing tongue as well as the heat of his body. *Lord! Have mercy!*

She gave into him...easily. He felt his desire awaken instantly in response to her comfortable acceptance of his kisses.

What am I doing? Venice went into a small panic and backed into the elevator's "stop" button. Craig laughed and reached over and started the elevator again.

"Oh, I'm sorry. I'm so clumsy."

"No, you're not. I shouldn't have done that. I couldn't help myself because you have such beautiful lips."

His cologne intoxicated her and caused her senses to weaken even more. *Have I lost my mind? I have to get away from him.* She was finally able to say, "Thank you."

It was quiet as they walked down the hall to her room.

"Venice, I want to tell you again how sorry I am that I kissed you. I usually don't act like that on the first date."

"Craig, don't worry about it. It was nice."

"Thanks."

Thank God, Monique wasn't there. She invited Craig inside and asked him to have a seat. Craig accepted her offer. He looked around the room admiring the nice décor and sat in a chair near Venice's bed.

Craig could tell Venice was stunned by his forwardness in the elevator. "I see you ladies have done a good job making your room look like home away from home."

She took a bottle of water out of the refrigerator. "Would you like something to drink?"

"No, thank you. I'm still full of orange juice. But thanks for asking."

Without any warning, he stood up, approached Venice, and

stroked her cheek with his hand. "Venice, I hope I'll get to see you again. I really like you."

Venice shyly pulled away and sat down on her bed without answering.

Craig realized it was time to leave. "Well, I'd better go." She stood up to see him out. He walked over to her and put his arms around her waist, leaning down to give her an unexpected kiss on the cheek, followed by a big hug. "I'll call you later, Venice."

"Okay. Thanks again for breakfast."

After he'd closed the door behind him, Venice fell back on the bed, still smelling his cologne. *I can't believe I let him kiss me!* A single tear slid down her cheek.

Seven

Venice dialed Galen to let him know she was back. "Hello, is Galen around?" she asked after his roommate answered.

"Yeah, he's here. Hold on."

Venice played the events of the morning back in her head while she waited for Galen to come to the phone. She wondered if she should tell Galen about the kiss and decided she wouldn't dare. There was no telling what his reaction would be. After all, it was only their first date.

"How did it go?" Galen asked excitedly as soon as he picked up the phone.

Venice stuttered, "I-I had a good time. He took me on a tour of the city and we had breakfast at Miss Bessie's Diner."

"Cool! They've got some good home cooked food there. Craig behaved himself, didn't he?"

"Yes, but I need to talk to you. Could you please come over later?"

Without hesitation, he said, "I'll be right over. Peace!"

Fifteen minutes later, Galen knocked at the door, unaware that he was about to be put on the witness stand by a modern-day Perry Mason. Galen grabbed for the remote control upon entering so he could search for the game he'd been watching before he left home. Venice grabbed it from him and turned off the set. She had questions that she needed answered.

Venice started by questioning Galen about the seriousness of Craig's last relationship. Galen said he was glad that the woman in question had left because she'd tried to dominate Craig's life and bossed him around way too much.

Venice said, "I need to know if he was in love with her."

Galen felt awkward suddenly. "I guess so, but it faded away. I'm just glad she's gone. It was like Craig came back to life after she left. Why do you want to know all of this? You two just met and I know you haven't fallen for him already. Have you?"

"No! I just wanted to know what's up. I don't need any emotional drama or any old girlfriends showing up out of the blue trying to get in my face."

Galen grabbed the remote control again. "Craig's pretty cool. I hang with him more than any of the other guys."

Venice sat on the bed. "Oh! Are his parents well off? I was wondering how he was able to afford that Expedition?"

"Craig's dad died after an accident at a job site. He was an architect also. His family got a huge settlement from the accident. Craig and his sister lost their mom several years earlier to some type of illness. He never likes to talk about it, so I've never asked what happened. I guess he's still trying to cope with their deaths. It's only been a year since his dad's accident."

Venice told Galen that Craig had told her he was studying to be an architect. She then assured Galen that she wouldn't mention anything to Craig regarding their conversation. She went on to tell Galen that she did like Craig and that he had asked her out to the movies in a few days.

Galen said, "Whatever! You'll have a good time."

With that comment, Venice asked Galen if he would walk her to the library.

He said, "Let's go, girl."

Eight

A month had passed since the beginning of the semester and Venice was trying her best to study despite the loud music blasting in the dorm's hallway. Venice was starting to feel at home, although she still missed and loved Jarvis. She still kept in touch with Jarvis and Joshua and both were doing well.

She had dated Craig several times and felt much more relaxed around him. She found herself looking forward to the weekends so they could spend time together. Craig was a magnificent kisser, but they had yet to be intimate. Venice wasn't sure she'd be ready if the situation arose. She was still a little nervous about the possibility of sex with Craig and it was causing her a lot of emotional drama. Jarvis had been the only man close to her and she wasn't sure she could handle adventuring out.

Jarvis told her that he hadn't met anyone and really wasn't looking for anyone. That made Venice feel a little guilty. She still felt like she was cheating on him. But, she was also beginning to get just a *little bit* horny. It was getting hard not to think about Craig in that way and Venice was getting curious to know how good he might be in bed.

"Jarvis, I met someone."

"Who?"

"One of Galen's friends."

Jarvis let out a sigh and sarcastically said, "Oh really."

"Come on, Jarvis. We agreed."

"That doesn't mean I have to like it, Niecy."

Venice closed her eyes and tried to swallow the lump in her throat before saying, "I know, Jarvis, and it doesn't change how I feel about you."

"This is hard for me, Venice. You're going to have to give me time for this to sink in. I'll talk to you later. Okay?"

With her voice barely above a whisper, she said, "Okay, Baby. I'm getting ready to go study for an exam. I love you."

"I love you, too, and good luck on your exam. Goodbye."

The music continued to blast, making the door tremble to the beat. When Venice opened the door, the hallway was filled with zoids dancing their asses off to the latest jams. It looked like one big party. She needed a break and she wanted in. Venice saw Chanelle and Monique shakin' their butts to the rhythm, motioning for her to join them. She danced her way through the crowd of women and showed her new dorm mates what she could do. It had been a while since she'd partied and it felt good. Someone hollered out, "Party over here!" And the gang of women repeated it in unison. They were partying so hard that Venice almost didn't realize the time. She pulled her partners to the side and told them she had an exam the next day.

"Girl, I can't study and party at the same time! I'm going down to the lounge to study! If I finish early, I'll be back to hang with you freaks!" Venice shouted over the music.

Monique shouted back, "Whatever, girl! See ya!"

Venice gathered her books from the room and left for the lounge on the first floor. Her mind wandered to Craig and then to Jarvis. They hadn't had much time to talk since Jarvis was so busy with football and classes. She talked to Craig also every night. They met occasionally in the courtyard between classes on Mondays and sometimes grabbed a quick lunch but were not able to see each other much during the week. Craig was deep into his co-op studies, which required a lot of his time. He was required to spend three days a week at an architectural firm about two hours away. He stayed there during the week and came home on Fridays. He had a demanding schedule, but he promised to set aside some quality time for them soon. Venice couldn't wait!

Venice still had time to hang out with her girls though. She was getting a little curious about why she hadn't been invited over to Craig's house to meet his sister that she'd heard so much about. She figured he'd invite her over eventually. Either that or he was hiding something from her. After all, she'd been hanging with him for about a month and he'd never mentioned it.

Chanelle and Monique decided to get some air from all the steamy dancing they'd been doing. They walked across the campus, sharing their experiences during the past weeks on campus. Monique went on and on about all the guys bugging her for her phone number.

Chanelle laughed. "The only people probably calling you are some jheri-curl wearing fools. Girl, I hope you haven't already given it up to any of those no good, dope dealer wannabees."

"No, I haven't, but I bet you've given it up to that cute dude in your English class!"

Chanelle got defensive. "We're just friends. Besides, my boyfriend's going to college in Atlanta."

"You must be a fool to think he's down there being faithful. He's probably knocking boots with anything wearing a skirt. A man can't help himself. They're all dogs! All they think about is how they're going to get into the next girl's panties."

"You're crazy! My man loves me, girl!"

"Whatever, but you'll see. You better enjoy yourself while you can."

Chanelle grew frustrated. "Monique, let's go. I need to check my messages."

"Chanelle, do you think Venice and Craig have got it on yet?"

"I don't think so. She's not talking about him a lot since he's out of town so much."

"I know. She's throwing herself in the books. She says they talk just about every night on the phone, but he's real busy."

Monique smiled. "Yeah, but her ex still calls her a lot, too. I think Venice mentioned something about getting with Craig this weekend. He's pretty cool. I don't think he's trying to run any game on her."

"I agree. Besides, her brother would probably step in if he felt like dude was trying to dog her. I remember in high school one time, this guy did something to Venice and her brother stomped the hell out of that fool! She never had any problem with men after that. Guys knew neither one of her brothers played when it came to her."

Monique said, "That's deep."

The two walked back to the dorm and went to their rooms for the evening.

Venice was one of three women in the lounge trying to get their study on. It was Wednesday and she was flipping through the pages, unable to absorb what she was reading. One of the campus security guards walked through on his routine patrol. He was probably headed up to somebody's room for a quickie or to smoke a little something something with some wild girls. He was known for making those *unofficial* visits. He was cute and he knew it. It would only be a matter of time before he got busted. Some of the girls in the dorm took far too many chances. Venice folded her arms and put her head down on the table. Maybe a moment of meditation and prayer could help her get back on track. She closed her eyes and took slow, deep breaths. She'd read about this technique in last month's *Essence* magazine. "Food for the Inner Soul" was the name of the article. Well, it couldn't hurt. A few minutes later, her cell phone rang. Venice snapped out of her trance.

"Hello?"

A smooth voice responded, "What's a nice girl like you doing in a place like that?"

"Hello, Craig! Hey! How did you know where I was?"

"I know because I'm standing right behind you."

Venice turned around and in the doorway he stood. Venice hung up her phone as Craig came into the lounge.

"I called your room and Monique told me where to find you. I couldn't wait until this weekend to see you, so I got off a day early."

Venice greeted him with a warm hug. "I'm glad. I missed you, too. I'm trying to study for this exam tomorrow, but my mind's not clicking tonight."

Showing those pearly whites, he said, "I have an idea. Why don't I take you for a ride and maybe you can concentrate on your test when you get back. So, how about it?"

Venice closed her books. "Let's go! First, let me call Monique and let her know I'm leaving."

Venice called Monique from the lounge to inform her of her plans. She gathered her book bag and Craig carried it for her as they walked out into the night air.

Nine

Have you eaten?" Craig asked, opening the truck door for Venice. "No, I haven't really had much of an appetite today."

"Would you like me to cook you up a little something?"

Venice looked surprised. "So, you really do cook?"

Craig smiled. "Of course! If you like, you can study at my house while I fix dinner."

Venice felt special and couldn't hide her blush. "Are you sure? I know you're busy with classes. I don't want to be in the way."

"I'm sure."

"In that case, I accept and thanks!"

As they proceeded through town to his neighborhood, Craig said, "I'm sorry I haven't invited you over before now. We've had some remodeling going on at the house for the past few weeks and it's been a mess. We're just finally getting things back together."

Venice asked, "What kind of work did you have done?"

"Well, before my dad died, he'd drawn plans to have the kitchen remodeled and for me and Bernice to get our own bathrooms."

"That's nice. I bet it's beautiful."

"Bernice did all the decorating. I think she did a first-rate job."

Venice smiled and looked out the window of the truck admiring the modest homes along the way.

Craig's home was in an established neighborhood. All the lawns appeared professionally groomed. Craig pulled into the driveway and activated the garage door. There was another car in the garage. Venice assumed it was his sister's car.

Craig confirmed it. "Good, my sister's still here. I wanted her to meet you. She's probably getting ready to go to work. Did I tell you she was a nurse?"

Venice was a little nervous about meeting his sister. "Yeah, you mentioned it."

Craig exited the truck and before he could come around to the passenger side, Venice had already got out of the truck. Craig took her bag and put his hand at the small of her back as he escorted her toward the kitchen door. Craig unlocked the door to find his sister on the telephone. She motioned for them to come on in as she tried to take her earrings off. Craig put Venice's bag on the kitchen table and pulled a chair out for Venice to sit down.

Craig's sister finished up her phone call and put her hand out to shake Venice's hand. "Hello, Venice! I finally get a chance to meet you. I've heard nothing but nice things about you from Craig."

Craig interrupted her. "Venice, Bernice will talk your head off. Anyway, Venice, this is Bernice. Bernice, this is Venice."

"I'm sorry it took so long for him to invite you over. I told him you probably wouldn't mind the remodeling, but he insisted that we wait until it was complete."

Venice looked around. "This is beautiful! You guys have done a great job."

Bernice said, "Thank you, Venice." She put on her coat. "Well, guys, I've got to run. I have twenty minutes to get to the hospital. Venice, I'm so glad I finally got to meet you."

"Same here, Bernice."

Bernice gave Craig a hug and exited to the garage. "You have some mail on the table in the den and I'm going over J.T.'s in the morning after I get off."

Craig said, "Okay, see you tomorrow some time."

When Venice heard Bernice drive out of the garage, she realized that she was truly alone with Craig. He asked if she'd like something to drink and she quickly said that she did. Her throat felt as dry as the desert.

He handed her a bottle of Coke. "Let me help you set up your things in the den. You'll probably be more comfortable in there. We could go downstairs in the rec room, if you like."

"No, this will do just fine."

"I hope you like chicken. I have a special sauce. It's one of my specialties."

"That sounds good."

Venice felt her heart pounding as they walked into the den. She couldn't understand why she felt such an electrical charge when she came near him.

As Venice began to open her books, she couldn't help but notice the portrait over the fireplace. It was a huge family portrait, which must've been taken when Craig and his sister were extremely young. Craig resembled their mother and Bernice was the spitting image of their father.

Venice's pager vibrated and startled her. It was Galen. "What could he want?" she mumbled to herself. Venice decided not to call Galen right away. Besides, if it were an emergency, he would've put in 911. She also didn't know how her dear brother would take it if he knew she was over Craig's house.

Craig came in to check on her and saw her admiring the pictures. "Venice, I want to tell you again how sorry I am that I haven't had a chance to invite you over before now."

"Quit apologizing. I can understand that you were having some work done."

Craig smiled, discreetly admiring Venice as she continued to look at the portrait. He felt an uncontrollable urge to touch her, but decided not to. Instead, he said, "You've busted me. I see you've spotted Little Craig."

"Yes, you're so cute. It's a nice portrait. Your mom and dad were very attractive."

"Thanks." He took a sip of Coke. "I really miss them. I know you've probably been wondering about them."

"It's none of my business. I don't want to pry."

"It's okay. My mom died about seven years ago of leukemia. I told you my dad was an architect. Well, one day on a job site, he fell off the building because the builders didn't take the right safety measures. He survived the fall, but he died in the hospital a couple days later. That happened about a year ago. I don't think Bernice has gotten over it yet. She was Daddy's girl, if you know what I mean."

Craig became solemn. Venice couldn't imagine the pain he and Bernice must've felt.

She touched his arm softly and changed the subject. "Hey, why don't I give you a hand in the kitchen. I also know how to do a little something something in the kitchen."

Craig chuckled. "Well, put your money where your mouth is."

They went into the kitchen and helped each other prepare dinner. Venice made a salad while Craig cooked the main dish.

Venice said, "You and Bernice seem to be really close."

"Yeah, we've always been close. Would you like some wine to go with dinner? I put a little in the sauce for the chicken."

"I'll have just a little. You know I still have to study for my test."

Craig got two glasses out the cabinet and filled them up. He laughed and asked, "Am I contributing to the delinquency of a minor, Venice?"

She laughed also. "Not in this state. If we were back in my hometown, you could get arrested for it."

"If I ever get to come home with you, make sure you remind me."

Venice smiled and felt her body heat up again. That had a nice sound to it.

Venice took a seat at the table while Craig sat on a stool near the oven to keep an eye on the food. He decided to turn on some music and they laughed as they continued to talk.

Craig said, "While we're waiting on dinner, I'll quiz you on what you've studied so far."

Venice accepted the challenge and they began the quiz. It seemed that every question Craig dished out, she quickly threw the correct answer back at him. After finishing all the questions, Craig said, "You must've absorbed more than you thought. You got every question right, girl! You're going to ace that exam tomorrow."

Craig and Venice drank several glasses of wine by the time dinner was ready.

Venice said, "I don't think I should've had that second glass of wine."

"What do you mean second? That was your third!"

Venice giggled. "Oh, my God! No wonder I'm buzzing!"

Craig laughed. "Let's eat. Maybe that'll make you feel better."

Venice set the table while Craig took the food out the oven and placed it on the table. The aroma filled the entire room.

Venice said, "This smells great! You really do know your way around the kitchen." They sat down and began to eat. "I must say, Craig, that I'm impressed. You really do know how to scorch a mean bird."

"Thank you. I told you so!"

The telephone rang and Craig got up to look at the caller ID, but didn't answer it. Venice didn't know what to feel, other than a sting of jealously in her gut. Could it be another woman? She *hoped* it wasn't.

Craig sat back down to his dinner. "I don't want to have any interruptions tonight." He reached across the table and touched Venice's hand. "I want your undivided attention."

Venice started to shiver before shyly announcing that she'd do the dishes after dinner.

"No way! You're my guest!"

"At least let me you help clear the table."

Craig took the dishes out of Venice's hands. "I said no! Now get out of here. I have this under control."

"Okay. You can't say I didn't offer." Venice reentered the den and took a seat on the sofa. Twenty minutes hadn't passed before Craig joined her. She could hear the dishwasher running. Venice turned to him and said, "Dinner was great. Thanks for feeding me."

"You're very welcome. Would it disturb you if I put on some music?"

"No, go right ahead."

She watched him as he walked across the room to his stereo, confident and masculine. He was gorgeous and Venice felt that stirring down low. He was always able to light a fire in her just by his presence. His kisses made that fire spread throughout her entire body. She'd probably burst into flames if things went any further.

He put on some soft jazz and returned to the sofa next to her. He leaned his head back, closed his eyes, and hummed to the music. His thighs brushed against hers and she knew there wasn't a thread of resistance in her body.

Venice looked over at him. "Craig, I know you're tired. I'd better go so you can get some rest."

He raised his head and turned to Venice. "Listen, Taylor, I'm not ready for you to leave. Okay?"

Venice diverted her eyes back to her book. "Okay, but don't blame me if you can't get up in the morning."

Craig put his arm on the back of the sofa so that it rested behind her shoulders. He was staring at her, feeling the heat radiating from her body. She tried to concentrate on studying, but he started playing in her hair. Venice let out a loud sigh and, without any warning, he gently turned her face toward him and gave her a soft kiss. The kiss intensified and she closed her eyes, letting her book fall to the floor. *Oh my God!*

Craig pulled her closer to him and deepened the kiss through her parted lips. This was the kiss she'd been waiting on. She was unaware of the moan that escaped from her mouth. He leaned her back on the pillows and pressed his body against hers. She was enjoying every second of him as his kisses traveled to the cleavage of her blouse. She hadn't felt like this in a long time and her body was beginning to throb uncontrollably. His muscular body continued the rhythmic dance with hers. She inhaled his manly scent and he was so gentle with his seduction. She wrapped her starving arms around his neck, pulling him even closer. She thought to herself, *I hope he doesn't think I'm fast.*

They both seemed to be letting themselves go at that point as he parted her legs with his knee. She could feel his hot breath. Things were really heating up as she felt his hands underneath her blouse stroking her lace-covered breasts. She began to let out small whimpers, which surprised even her. She figured it must be the wine, or was it? She'd been curious about his lovemaking for the entire month they'd been dating. She could feel his arousal rubbing against her body, which made her moisten. She was yearning *badly!* Venice really liked Craig and, oddly enough, Jarvis wasn't on her mind.

Just when Venice thought it was about to happen, Craig pulled himself away from her. She looked at him, confused, as he walked across the room and sat in the recliner. He didn't say anything; he just sat there staring at her. The music continued to play softly in the background.

Venice rose up and asked, "Craig, what's wrong?"

He put his hands over his face. "Girl, let me get you out of here before I..."

"Before you what?"

Craig got up to cut the music off. "Never mind. I need to get you back to campus."

Venice walked over and touched him gently on the back. "Why are you rushing me out of here now?"

Craig backed away from her. "Venice, get your books. Let's go or you may not make it back tonight."

Venice folded her arms and pouted. "I may not want to make it back tonight, Bennett!"

He reached for her hand. "Venice, we need to talk."

She sensed that he was really serious, so she sat down to listen. She had no idea what he was about to say. She hoped that he wouldn't confess about any hidden girlfriend or something worse.

Craig stuttered, "Venice, I-I really like you. I like you a lot and before we go any further, I need to know if you're protected."

"Yes, as a matter of fact, I double protect myself. I take birth control, but I also insist on condoms."

He looked her in the eyes and said, "Venice, I know you've been wondering why I haven't made a move on you, huh?"

She looked down at her hands and replied, "Well, yeah."

"Venice, I must confess. I've wanted you since the first day I laid eyes on you."

"Really?"

"Really! You stirred feelings inside me that I've never felt before. Why do you think I didn't waste any time calling you up? Huh?"

"I thought you were just being nice, since you're friends with Galen."

"No, I wasn't about to miss the opportunity to get to know you. I guess what I'm trying to say is, I need to find out what you want. Your brother told me that you were really tight with someone back home and that you were together for a long time. I'm just not sure if you're interested in a new relationship. You have to let me know."

"I don't know what to say, Craig. Even though I've been in a long relationship with someone else, we agreed to cool it since we're separated. I've enjoyed spending time with you over the past month and I was beginning to think that you didn't want to be anything but friends. Look, Craig, I'm not going to lie to you. The guy I was with before coming to school is still very close to me and I do still have strong feelings for him. We were together for four years and we went through some serious drama that I don't care to go into right now. I'll always love him for those reasons. Maybe I'll explain it to you one day but, for now, Jarvis and I are just trying to deal with being apart. We've never been separated like this before and it's been hard. We agreed not to try and carry on a long distance relationship. It doesn't change our feelings for each other, but we had to face the fact that we're only nineteen and we have to go on living whether we're together or apart."

"Where is he?"

"He's going to Michigan State on academic and football scholarships."

"Why didn't you go with him?"

"I was supposed to, but my paperwork was lost and you know how that can be. By the time they found it, it was too late."

"Are you planning on transferring to Michigan State?"

"I don't know. It depends on how things go here at Dawson."

Craig could see Venice was carrying some emotional baggage with her, but he wouldn't pry any further. He smiled and said, "Well, Taylor, I'm impressed. You didn't have to spill your guts like that, but I really admire you for laying your cards on the table. I appreciate it."

"I just hope you're able to bear with me when it comes to my past because I went through some deep shit. Craig, I like you very much. I just want you to know that I want to have fun while I'm in college."

He saw her eyes becoming misty and wanted to hold her and comfort her. Instead he smiled and said, "Okay, Taylor. I hear you. I guess that settles it. I've ruined the mood now, huh?"

She stood close, feeling the heat of his body. "You didn't ruin the mood, Craig, but it's getting late and I really should be getting back to the dorm."

He stroked her cheek. "Can I get a rain check?"

Venice giggled. "Is that like a coochie coupon?"

She saw genuine concern in his dark sultry eyes when he said, "Look, Venice, I don't want anything to happen between us until you're sure. If you're still in love with your ex, maybe we should cool it."

"Craig, let's just see where nature takes us. Okay?"

He hugged her to his chest and answered, "That's a bet. Now let me get you out of here." Venice gathered her books. Craig pulled her against his tight chest. "Venice, I'm glad you came over tonight. I enjoyed our unexpected conversation and I want you to come back over soon. Okay?"

She wrapped her arms around him, feeling her body relax. "Sure, Mr. Bennett. I'd love to."

He gave her a seductive squeeze, lifting her off the floor. Venice giggled out loud as he put her down. He quickly took her mouth again, which lasted for quite some time. Venice could tell she aroused him instantly and knew that he wanted her just as bad as she wanted him.

They released each other, she stomped her foot, and hollered out, "Mercy!"

Craig laughed. "Girl, let me get you out of here."

Craig drove Venice to campus and told her that he'd talk to her later. "Good luck on your test."

She smiled as he ran his fingers over her soft cheeks before he cupped her face with his hands and their tongues met one last time.

Ten

Venice lay in bed, reminiscing about the night's events. She could still see Craig's sweet smile and taste the wetness his mouth left on hers. She lay there thinking about how good he'd felt against her body and how much she'd missed that feeling.

Her mind wandered to Jarvis. He was still able to say the things to her that made her fall in love with him in the beginning. He had an unbelievable spell over her and when she heard his voice, she couldn't help but want to be with him right then and there. Was she making a mistake hooking up with Craig? Was she jeopardizing her relationship with Jarvis? Only time would tell.

Venice turned over and saw that Monique had left a note that Joshua had called. It was late but she needed to talk to him. Venice dialed his number and Joshua answered, "Hello?"

"What's up, dog?"

"What's up, girl? Where have you been?"

"You're so nosey but, if you must know, I've been over Craig's house."

Joshua laughed and asked, "Well, did he hit it?"

"No, but I thought we were going to do it. He stopped and wanted to have a serious conversation."

"About what?"

"He wants to be with me and wanted to know if I used protection."

Joshua laughed. "Dang! Dude must be pretty cool to talk about that kind of stuff before trying to hit it. What did you tell him?"

Venice told Joshua everything that was said between her and Craig. Joshua admired Craig for being responsible and told Venice to go ahead and give Craig a chance. He also told her to go slow because he knew that she was still in love with Jarvis and that Jarvis was still madly in love with her.

Venice sighed. "I don't want to lose Jarvis. But, I really like Craig. He's so nice and he seems to understand what I'm going through with Jarvis. I don't want to jeopardize my relationship with Jarvis."

"If you and Jarvis are meant to be together, you'll find your way back to each other. In the meantime, girl, kick it! You're only nineteen once."

"I guess you're right. So, what's going on with you? Are you ready to come down here for homecoming and pick out some apartments?"

"Hell yeah! Cynthia's still tripping about me coming. I keep telling her that I promised you and that I'm just coming to check out some apartments."

Venice yawned. "I can't wait for you to meet him."

Joshua laughed. "Are you still going up to Jarvis' homecoming?"

"I have to. I promised him. I'm going to have to explain to Craig that it was prearranged."

"Yeah, it was prearranged before you met him. If he likes you as much as it sounds, I'm telling you now, Venice, he's not going for it. That man ain't about to let you go up there to your ex. You know once you and Jarvis get together, you're going to end up giving him some. Where does that leave Craig? You better call him and let him know you can't come."

"I'm not going to cancel. A matter of fact, I'm so horny, I can't wait to go."

"See, you're playing games already. If you want this guy, you better not go up there messing around with Jarvis, cause you know he's crazy when it comes to you."

"I just don't know what I'm going to do. I miss Jarvis. Lord! That man knows how to make me scream!"

"All right, don't say I didn't try to warn you. Have you told Craig the whole story on you and Jarvis?"

"No, but I did tell him that I have strong feelings for Jarvis for reasons I didn't want to get into right away. He suggested we might need to cool it. I just think that if I tell him, he may not want to be with me."

"So what if he finds out before you tell him? He'll really be pissed at you. I'm a man. I know. We don't like surprises."

"I asked Galen, Sidney, and Chanelle not to mention anything to Craig about the situation."

"Okay. Well, I know it's late and you have class tomorrow. I'll talk to you later. Keep your head in the books and Bryan said don't forget our tickets and hotel reservations."

"Okay, goodnight! And Josh, thanks again. Love ya!"

"Love you too, girl. Goodnight."

They hung up the phone and Venice was asleep within minutes.

Venice woke up hoping that she didn't ruin her chances of making a decent grade on her literature exam by staying out late drinking the night before. She was still tingling from the affects of being with Craig. She was also preoccupied with the conversation she'd had with Joshua. She hurriedly showered and dressed to make her way to class. Monique was still cuddled up with her teddy bears, snoring like you wouldn't believe. As Venice entered the classroom, she could see some of her classmates still going over their notes. She realized that she wasn't the only one who needed a little more time to study. Anyway, she said a small prayer while the professor passed out the test and instructed them to begin. As Venice went over the questions, she found the answers coming to her easily. Then she remembered how Craig had quizzed her the night before. It seemed that everything she'd studied was definitely on the exam. Venice breathed a sigh of relief as she finished the exam and turned it in to the professor.

"Thank you, Miss Taylor. I'll see you in class on Monday and have a nice weekend."

"You too, professor."

When Venice got outside, she felt good about her performance and decided to share her joy with Monique. When she returned to the room, Monique was finally dragging herself out of bed.

"Are you just getting in from last night?"

"No, girl. When I got in last night, you were knocked out. I had my Lit exam this morning. Remember? You couldn't hear me getting ready for class for all that snoring you were doing."

Monique couldn't help but laugh. "I'm sorry, roomie. I must've been dog-tired. So... What did you and Mr. Bennett get into last night for you to get back so late?"

"You sure are nosy! But, if you must know, he cooked dinner for me and helped me study for my exam."

She laughed. "Is that all? You mean to tell me he showed up unannounced from out of town and it wasn't a booty call?"

"I know it may be hard for you to believe it, Monique, but not every man is trying to get in your drawers. Craig's nice and he's a real gentlemen. If I'd had my way last night, it would've been a booty call! I think he's waiting on me to make the first move. I kind of like that. It lets me be in control."

Monique said, "Girl, if I were you, the next time you get a chance to be alone with him, you should seduce him!"

"Well, sister girl, you're not me! Besides, I don't want him to think I'm easy."

Monique gathered up her shower cap and said, "Whatever! I'm going to hit the showers. I've got class in thirty minutes. Are you done for the day?"

"Yes! All I had was the lit exam. Craig doesn't have class on Fridays. I might treat him to a movie or something."

Monique smiled. "Well, if I don't see you, have a good time."

"Thanks. I'll page you later to see what you're up to. I'm getting ready to go to the beauty shop. See ya!"

Venice drove to the beauty shop with Craig on her mind. She couldn't believe the conversation they'd had the night before. When she pulled into the parking lot, her beautician, Tamara, was waiting on her. Girl, I'm glad you're on time. I have a full day today. How do you want your hair?"

Venice thought for a minute. "I guess I'll just get it wrapped."

Tamara giggled. "I'll have you out of here in no time."

Galen was in class wondering why Venice hadn't returned his page. He couldn't wait to see her, but he was trying not to be upset. One thing he'd told her was that if he ever paged her, she'd better return it. He didn't care what she was doing, where she was, or who she was with. Galen felt like he wasn't asking a lot. Besides, he was responsible for her while they were away at college. His mom and dad would kill him if something happened to her. Galen knew it would be a few hours before he would be able to confront Venice, so he tried to maintain his composure and concentrate on his classes.

When Venice made it back to campus, she ran into Chanelle who was also finished with her classes for the week.

"Hey, girl!"

"Hi, Venice! Ooh! Your hair's sharp, girl. Did you just get it done?"

"Yes, I only had one class today and I'm ready for the weekend."

"What are you getting ready to do?"

"Nothing! Do you want to go watch the band practice?"

"Sure, it's not like I have anything else to do."

As they walked, Chanelle asked Venice, "Hey, where's your man?"

"I don't know. He didn't have any classes today." Venice paused a minute. "Chanelle, can I tell you something? But you can't tell anybody, and I mean *nobody*."

Chanelle said, "Girl, you know you can trust me. We go way back."

They found a spot to sit down to watch the band practice.

Venice said, "Well, you know Craig came in town last night unexpectedly and he invited me over for dinner. As a matter of fact, he *cooked* dinner for me. He also helped me study for my exam. Well, after dinner, girl, things started getting really hot! We started kissing and I thought he was going to try to hit it, but he stopped. I felt like I was ready, but I was a little nervous, too. Anyway, now I wish he would've kept going. He stopped himself and then we had a serious conversation about casual sex and protection; stuff like that. I told him I was on the pill, but insisted on condoms also."

Chanelle looked at Venice with excitement. "Girl, that's great! It's about time. I could tell he liked you. You should see how he stares at you all the time. If I were you, I wouldn't worry about anything. Take your time and don't rush things. I think it'll happen when you least expect it."

Venice stared down at the ground. "Chanelle, I'm still in love with Jarvis. Is it possible to be in love with two men at the same time? I mean, I've always been in love with Jarvis, but Craig…he's so nice and perfect and I think about him all the time. When I come near him, I feel myself getting weak in the knees and things start stirring, if you know what I mean. I'm just glad Jarvis isn't going to school close to Dawson. You know I'm supposed to go up to his homecoming. Joshua said Craig would probably be pissed off if I go visit Jarvis. Then Jarvis is going to be mad if I don't come. I don't know what to do."

Chanelle asked, "When is his homecoming?"

"Four weeks from tomorrow."

Chanelle put her arm around her girl and said, "Girl, just take a deep breath. You don't have to make any decisions right now. We've got some time. I'll help you work it out, okay?"

Venice hugged her and agreed. "Please don't say anything to Galen or Sidney."

"You don't have to worry, girl. Have you told Craig about you and Jarvis yet?"

"No, but Joshua thinks I should tell him."

"Uh-uhm, girl! If you tell him now, it'll be a cold day in hell before he'll let you anywhere near Jarvis. You know Jarvis is my boy, but he's a trip. He told you that you'd *always* be his woman and that he was coming back for you after graduation and you know he ain't playing. He's always meant what he says and proved it in the past. That's why other guys couldn't get anywhere near you when we were in high school. They were afraid of his crazy ass. Jarvis has always been obsessed with you, Venice, and you know it. You couldn't get away from him, even if you wanted to. Your daddy would probably have to shoot him or something. Venice, I bet if you don't show up for his homecoming, that fool will come down here, get your tail, and take you back up north with him. Don't get me wrong. I love Jarvis, but he's obsessed when it comes to you. You must've put some serious coochie spell on that man."

"You're silly, Chanelle. You're exaggerating a little, aren't you? Jarvis wouldn't come down here and trip like that."

"Girl, don't underestimate him. You know his dad's a pilot. He could get on a plane in a minute and be here before nightfall."

"It's not funny, but you're right. Be quiet! You're making me nervous now, Chanelle."

She snapped her fingers. "You know I'm right."

They stopped talking for a moment and swayed to the music from the band.

Eleven

Craig and his childhood friend, Skeeter, usually hung out together a couple days a week. They decided to meet in the park for a game of one on one. They'd already played a couple of games; each one claiming to have better skills than the other.

Skeeter asked, "Hey, man, what's up with you and your friend's sister?"

Craig shot a jumper over Skeeter. "Her name's Venice."

Skeeter drove the ball on Craig. "Has she broke you off any yet?"

Craig gave Skeeter a hard foul. "She's not like the kind of women you hook up with. But, I think she could be the one, man."

They stopped for a moment and Skeeter said, "What do you mean?"

"She could be the one!"

Skeeter was surprised. "For real? Say it isn't so! You mean she could be the future Mrs. Bennett and she hasn't even broke you off any yet. Damn! She must be something else."

"It's not her. I haven't made a move on her yet. You'll understand when you meet her. She's got it going on and I don't want to mess things up with her."

"I've seen her around. She's fine as hell."

"That she is! She used to run track in high school."

"You can tell by her muscular legs. Her partner is who I wanna get with."

Craig shot the ball and said, "Chanelle? Yeah, she's fine too. Venice told me Chanelle was a majorette or something in high school. But she has a man."

Skeeter asked, "Why don't you hook me up?"

"I'm not going to do that to Chanelle. You already have too many women fighting over your trifling ass now."

They laughed together and continued to play ball. Skeeter was very handsome. He was extremely muscular with skin as brown as chocolate ice cream. He had a bald head and a smile which voodoo'd the ladies every time. He also had an obnoxious quality about him, which was usually a turn off.

Back on the band field, the girls continued to enjoy the music and watch as the band director was giving the members instructions on the routine they were about to do. Venice and Chanelle decided to walk around the field and get a better seat.

The majorette coordinator ran over and asked, "Are you girls interested in going out for majorette? I have a couple of spots open."

Venice and Chanelle both answered, "Maybe next year."

The director asked, "Are you sure, because you two ladies have what I'm looking for."

Chanelle asked, "And what would that be?"

He smiled and said, "Ladies, you both have back."

They thanked him and said, "Maybe we'll see you next year."

He thanked them anyway and returned to the majorettes on the field. The flag girls were off to the side rotating their flags as the majorettes started doing stretching exercises for their funky moves. The band members went to their respective positions and waited for the band director to direct their first song. The girls found a spot on a small hill looking down on the band field to watch their formations. The band began to play a song, which sounded so good. They continued to play until the director stopped them and they practiced the song again. As the band was playing, a small crowd began to gather. This was typical because most of the time the students came to watch their friends practice the dance routines and new songs for the year. As the girls sat, several guys came over to try and get their phone numbers. Most of the time, the girls exchanged laughter with them and seemed to be having a great time. As the hours wore on, the girls realized they were hungry and decided to walk to a nearby sandwich shop.

As they stood up, getting ready to go, a truck pulled up, blowing the horn. They heard someone say, "Hey, girl, come over here!"

Venice and Chanelle turned to see who was hollering. To their surprise, the guy was motioning for them to come over. They turned back around, trying to ignore the man. He honked his horn some more, then whistled loudly. "Hey, sexy, you in the red shirt!"

Chanelle knew the guy was now talking about her.

Venice said, "Chanelle, girl, you're out here pulling."

Chanelle answered, "Sounds like a fool to me."

The guy parked his truck with the bed backed up to the practice field. He turned his music up a little loud, still trying to get their attention. The girls kept their backs to him. A few seconds later, Venice heard someone calling her, name, "Venice!"

Chanelle and Venice looked at each other in shock and as they turned in the direction of the truck, Venice saw Craig leaning out the passenger side window. The girls were only a few feet from the parking lot.

Venice said, "Come on, Chanelle."

They turned and walked toward the truck. Craig and Skeeter got out to greet them. Skeeter let the back of the truck down so that he and Craig could sit and watch the activities.

When Venice and Chanelle reached them, Venice said, "Hey, Craig."

He smiled and gave her a hug. "I've been playing a little b-ball with my boy Skeeter. Venice, Chanelle, this is Skeeter. Skeeter, this is Venice and Chanelle."

The girls said, "Hi."

Skeeter looked Venice and Chanelle up and down. "The pleasure is definitely all mine."

Craig punched him in the arm. "Quit tripping, man."

Skeeter stopped sucking on his lollipop briefly. "I'm sorry, ladies. I just haven't seen two fine women together like this in a long time."

Chanelle rolled her eyes in disbelief. She turned to watch the band, not interested in Skeeter. Craig was sitting on the back of the truck. Venice stood in front of him. He played with her belt loops pretending to hook her with his finger, pulling her between his legs. Venice started feeling the heat and her nipples hardened as he held her close.

"What are you two getting ready to do?"

"We're going to get something to eat in a minute."

He smiled at her, stood up close, and whispered in her ear, "I can't wait to see you tonight."

"Me, too."

Their eyes met as if they were reading each other's mind. He broke the trance by saying, "Let me get off you before I get my sweat all over you."

Venice leaned toward his ear. "I might like your sweat on me."

With that comment, he felt a tightening in his shorts.

"All right now. Skeeter, man, let's go. I need to take a cold shower."

Skeeter said, "Chanelle, baby, I'll get with you later, with your fine self!"

Chanelle rolled her eyes again. "I don't think so! See you later, Craig."

Craig gave Venice a quick kiss on the lips. "See you in a little bit."

Venice smiled and watched him walk to the truck, looking too damn good in his shorts and T-shirt. He had a gorgeous physique!

Chanelle said, "Girl, I think he's hooked."

Venice blushed. "We'll see."

Once they arrived at the sandwich shop, Galen walked in acting like he wanted to kill somebody. He sat down and said hello to Chanelle, then turned to Venice and angrily asked, "Why the hell didn't you return my page last night?"

"I'm sorry, Galen. I was busy studying for an exam and I forgot to call you."

"You weren't in your room. Where were you?"

At that point, Chanelle excused herself from the table to go to the restroom.

Galen asked again, "Where were you?"

"I was over at Craig's house!"

"You mean to tell me that because you were over at Craig's, you felt like you couldn't return my page?"

"I meant to call you, Galen! I just forgot! Damn!"

Galen grabbed her arm. "So why didn't you call me? You must've been letting him hit it!"

Venice pulled her arm out of his grasp and threw her cup of soda on him. "Go to hell Galen!" Venice stood up when she spotted Chanelle coming out of the restroom. "Let's go, Chanelle!"

Venice was pissed off as they exited the sandwich shop. Galen sat in the booth, soaking wet from the soda. He was still upset but realized he over did it. He knew he was going to have to eventually apologize for treating her that way. But, he wasn't going to do it right away. Right then, he had to find Craig Bennett. Galen left the sandwich shop and headed to Craig's house.

Craig was being dropped off by Skeeter just as Galen was pulling up in front of his house. Craig hollered, "Hey, Galen!"

"Hey. Can I holler at you for a second?"

Skeeter leaned out of his truck's window. "Hey, Galen." Galen nodded to Skeeter. Skeeter recognized the serious look on Galen's face. "Craig, I'll check you later."

They watched Skeeter drive off, squealing his tires down the street.

Craig asked, "What do you want to talk to me about?"

"Venice told me she was over here last night."

"Yes, I picked her up yesterday evening and made her a little dinner while she studied. Why? What's up?"

"Well, I paged her about six-thirty last night and she didn't return my page. I want to know what was going on over here that she couldn't return my page."

Craig finally understood what was going on. "Why don't you go ahead and ask me what you really want to ask me, Galen? First of all, I didn't know Venice got a page from you or anybody else for that matter. You know I wouldn't do anything to Venice that she didn't want me to. Also, whether you like it or not, I do like her a lot and I plan to keep seeing her. Venice is woman enough to know what she wants to do. She doesn't need you trying to make her feel like a child, Galen. You should know your sister better than that and I *thought* you knew me. Anyway, it's none of your damn business what Venice and I were doing. I told you that when this thing first started. Let me ask you something, Galen. What would you do if I told you I made love to your sister last night?"

Galen's blood pressure shot up. He didn't answer Craig. He just stared at the ground.

Craig then asked, "Are you mad because Venice was with me or are you mad because Venice didn't return your call?"

Galen realized Craig was right. Once again his temper was out of control. He ended up apologizing to Craig, but explained how difficult it was to picture his sister sleeping with a friend. He knew Venice was capable of making good decisions, but she was still his little sister and his responsibility. Craig told Galen to relax.

Galen said, "She'll probably never speak to me again. I kind of pissed her off earlier. I jumped on her for not returning my call and I was a little rough on her. She got so mad at me that she cussed me out and threw her soda on me."

"You're a trip, Galen. You need to go apologize to her. She was a perfect lady last night." "I will. Let me know the next time you have your card game. I've got to go find Venice and see if she'll talk to me. See ya later."

The two gave each other a handshake and Galen got in his car. Before driving off, he said, "Don't tell her I came by if you talk to her before I find her."

"No problem, man. Go handle your business."

"Cool!"

Then he drove away.

Twelve

Venice and Chanelle made it back to the dorm safely. Chanelle could see that Venice was furious. "Venice, Galen was wrong for coming at you like that. It ain't none of his business who you decide to hang with."

"I knew he was going to try that daddy shit on me. I just didn't think it was going to happen this soon."

"Girl, he'll come crawling back to you to apologize. Just wait and see."

"I don't have anything to say to that fool. I've never been so mad at him."

"Well, this is my floor. Try not to let this ruin your day, Venice. If you need me, give me a call."

"Thanks for listening, Chanelle."

Venice gave Chanelle a hug and told her that she'd talk to her later.

As the elevator arrived on Venice's floor, the doors opened and there stood Galen waiting to get on the elevator. He'd just left her room looking for her. "Hey, girl, there you are. I need to talk to you."

"Get the hell away from me, Galen! Don't you think you've talked to me enough?"

Venice pushed past him and walked down the hall to her room. Galen followed. "I'm sorry I went off on you like that, Venice. I guess I didn't expect you to really hook up with one of my boys."

He followed her into the room where she laid into him. "First of all, I told you that I forgot to return your page. It had nothing to do with the fact that I was at Craig's house. Your mind is always on sex. That's why you can't trust me. I'm not like you, Galen, and it's none of your damn business what I do with Craig. You're not my damn

55

daddy! You didn't act like this when I was with Jarvis. I like Craig and if I did give it up to him, you would be the last one to know."

Galen sat there, letting Venice vent all her anger. He realized that he deserved everything she was throwing at him. He also realized that Venice wasn't his little sister anymore. She was a young woman.

After a few minutes of shouting, Venice finally burst into tears. Galen knew it was coming. It was only a matter of when. She always cried when she was really angry. Some people took her tears for a weakness, but Galen knew this was a sign of her emptying her soul.

Galen approached his sister and gave her a brotherly hug. "Venice, I promise that I'll never doubt you again. I'll never stick my nose in where it doesn't belong. I'm just trying to look out for you. That's what brothers are supposed to do for their sisters."

Venice hugged Galen and then punched him in the stomach. She told him that she still loved him, despite his ignorance. He admitted that he'd confronted Craig and that Craig had told him to mind his own business.

Venice sat on the bed. "I'm glad Craig told you to mind your business, Galen."

"Well, he's still my boy and I'm glad you two hooked up with each other. I'll see you later, Sis."

"Thanks."

He walked toward the door. Venice gave him one last hug and told him that she loved him.

With the Galen scene behind her, Venice was unsure if she could ever face Craig again. She couldn't begin to wonder what he thought of her now that Galen had made a fool of himself. Craig probably thought she was a baby and would never want to ask her out again. If that was the case, she would just have to cross that bridge when she came to it.

She dialed up Chanelle. "Chanelle, guess who was waiting for me when I got off the elevator?"

"Who, girl?"

"Galen's sorry ass. He did exactly what you said he'd do. Crawled back and apologized like a fool. I should've made him suffer more than I did, but I accepted his apology. He told me that he confronted Craig with that bullshit! I'm so embarrassed!"

"Did he say what Craig did?"

"He said Craig spoke him out."

Chanelle asked, "Are you going to call Craig?"

"I don't know if he'll still speak to me. I'm going to apologize to him for Galen's behavior and I hope he's cool with it."

"Good luck, Venice. Let me know how things turn out."

"Thanks, Chanelle. See ya!"

It had been a couple of hours since the altercations. Venice still hadn't heard from Craig. She wondered if she should call him to see if he was upset. She couldn't help but assume the worst. She called Joshua and told him what happened. Joshua told her that he would've confronted her also and that Galen was just being a brother.

"Venice, you have to realize that you're still new to the campus and things happen to girls all the time. Galen didn't know if anything had happened to you. You scared him. If anything happens to you, he has to answer to your parents and everyone else in your family. He's not trying to keep up with you. He's just trying to protect you. Remember, he's been there for three years and he knows the campus and city better than you do. I think you owe him an apology."

Venice said, "I can't stand you. But I love your tail and I hate it when you're right. Okay, I'll apologize to him only for throwing my soda on him. What's going on with you?"

"Nothing much. I have to work tonight."

"Is Cynthia feeling any better about you coming for home-coming?"

"She's starting to."

"Do you want me to talk to her?"

Joshua said, "I don't mind. Hell, it might even help."

"I'll give her a call and let her know that I won't let you get wild when you get here."

"Thanks, I'll talk to you later. Love you."

Venice said, "Love you, too."

They hung up the phone and Venice decided to call Craig before she gave herself a nervous stomach and backed out. The telephone was ringing on the other end. She finally heard "Hello?"

"Hello, Craig. I wanted to call to apologize for Galen tripping earlier. He told me that he came by today going off on you. I wanted to tell you how sorry I am."

"Don't you worry about Galen and me. We got everything straightened out. I've already forgotten about it."

"Thanks for being so nice. I was afraid you'd be upset with me."

"Why? You didn't do anything wrong. It's over, Venice. Now forget about it. Are you still hanging out with me tonight?"

Venice was relieved. "Sure, so what is it that you have to do at church tonight?"

"Oh, just a little choir practice with the children."

"What? That's nice. I'm impressed."

"Thanks. It helps keep the kids off the streets. Choir practice won't be over before the movie starts. So, if you want to, we can do something else and go to movies later this weekend."

"It doesn't matter to me."

"Okay, then. I'll see you in a few."

Venice hung up the phone and went to take a quick shower. She was about to see another side of Craig and that excited her.

After choir practice, Venice and Craig played pool in a local hall. Craig was impressed that Venice was so good at the game. He was instantly aroused as he watched her body move around the pool table. Her movement was so erotic that Craig had to resist the urge to grab her right there in front of everyone. They spent a few hours there before going out for appetizers.

As they ate, Craig asked, "Are you going to the football game tomorrow with your girls?"

"That depends. I may get a better offer."

Craig linked his hands with hers. "I'd love to take you, but I have something to do and I won't get there until later. But, I want to take you to the party after the game. If you want to, ask your girls if they'd like to go. I can get some of my boys to go along, if it's okay with you."

"It's okay with me. I'll get with them to see if they still want to go together. We can meet you after the game, if you'd like."

"The more, the merrier. I'll find you before the game's over."

Venice asked, "But how will you find me?"

He kissed the back of her hand. "Don't you worry. I'll find you."

"Deal!"

Venice felt her body respond as she took in his manly scent. It was going to be a good weekend after all.

Thirteen

Everyone was hustling around trying to decide which party to attend. It was the third home football game of the year and a couple of frats were having parties at various locations around town. Most of the girls in the dorm were planning to go to the most popular frat party. Venice and her girls hadn't missed a home game yet. She made sure she went to see her dear brother "do his thing" on the field. Galen had been an All- American wide receiver ever since he'd been playing the game. Once he'd reached college, his skills were defined even more. Some of the coaches thought he even had a good chance of making it into the NFL.

Venice and her girls found their usual spot near the Dawson University high-stepping band so they could dance to the tunes. All of the students, especially the freshmen, made sure the football team heard their cheers and support. The band would always start up a popular song, which caused all the students to break down with the latest dances in the stands. Chanelle and Venice were well relaxed with this practice since they graduated from a black high school and Chanelle had served as a majorette in the band.

Monique asked, "What's Galen's number again, Venice?"

"This is the last time I'm going to tell you, Monique. He's number eighty-two."

Monique shouted, "There he is, girl! He knows he's wearing those pants. Look at his tight round butt! Have mercy!"

Chanelle looked at her and said, "Ghetto! Monique, Sidney will kick your ass for talking about her man like that."

Monique laughed. "Don't hate the playa. Hate the game."

Chanelle and Venice shook their heads in disgust.

After a show stopping half-time show, the game progressed on.

It wasn't long before everyone knew that their team was going to win. As the clock ticked down to zero, the stadium went wild. This win enabled the team to remain undefeated heading into homecoming. There were going to be two more away games before homecoming and if the team could keep this up, they may get into the playoffs.

As Venice and her girls exited the stadium, she heard a familiar voice from behind. "Where do you think you're going?"

Venice and her partners turned around and saw it was Craig. Venice stopped to wait for him to approach. He gave Venice and her girls a group hug. He'd become very familiar with Venice's friends after meeting them on a several occasions.

"Are you ladies ready to party?"

Monique butted in. "You better believe it. I'm ready to roll!"

Craig asked if they would mind if he talked to Venice for a minute. By that time, Monique was already working her mack on some guy holding a forty-ounce in a sack.

Chanelle said, "Take your time. We're not in any hurry."

"Thanks, Chanelle. You know you're my girl!"

Fans continued to pour out of the stadium headed to several parties. The band continued to play popular tunes as stragglers partied in the stands. Venice and Craig walked down toward the track that circled the football field.

Craig asked, "Do you think your girls will mind if a couple of my boys ride along? There's one in particular I want Chanelle to meet. I think they'll hit it off."

Venice turned to see his two friends waiting a few feet away. One was really cute and seemed to be very reserved. The other one was hollering at everyone who passed by. He was also dancing to the band's music. "Which one were you planning to hook Chanelle up with?"

"Oh, my boy Spoonie over there with the red baseball hat and jeans. You can't judge him by the way he's acting now. He's just having a good time, which is what Chanelle needs. Maybe she'll stop waiting for the phone to ring from that so-called boyfriend."

"Okay, Craig. I trust you. I hope this works because I hate to see my girl wasting away."

Craig motioned for his two friends to come over so he could

introduce them to Venice and her friends. The quiet one was Jasper Jones. He was a junior studying engineering. Spoonie's real name was Roland Daniels. Craig explained that his friends had called him Spoonie since his was six years old. When he was little, his mother said every time she caught him in the kitchen he had spoon in his hand looking for some food.

After introductions, the girls thought it was okay for them to hang out. Craig and Venice decided not to let Chanelle in on their plans. As the group left, they decided to grab a bite to eat before hitting the parties. Monique suggested "Dave's Wing Fling." They had the best hot wings in town. The group ordered their food and got to know each other better over baskets of wings. Chanelle picked up on the vibe that Spoonie was interested in her. Jasper also opened up a little and Monique was impressed with Jasper's conservative style. He appeared to be a conquest for her. Monique thought to herself, *I think I might be able to turn this shy piece out.*

After stuffing themselves, they headed over to the party, which was already bumping when they entered and everyone was deep into the music. Venice and her girls excused themselves to the ladies room on several occasions to discuss their escorts. Chanelle finally admitted that she was having a good time with Spoonie. Venice giggled and decided to admit to the setup.

"Chanelle, I'm glad you and Spoonie are getting along because I have a confession."

"What kind of confession?"

"Well, Craig thought you and Spoonie might hit it off, so he wanted you to meet. He asked me and I told him it couldn't hurt to introduce you and let nature takes its course. If it worked out, fine. If not, we tried."

Chanelle chuckled. "I can't believe you two went behind my back trying to fix me up. I'm not mad at you, but you know I have a man!"

Monique butted in. "If you've got a man, why isn't he here with you? Your so-called man is down at that fancy college sticking his rod into some tenderoni."

Venice told Monique to chill out and to quit being so ignorant and thoughtless.

"Chanelle, if you want to be faithful to your man, cool. But I don't want you to miss out on any fun while you're here. It's not going to hurt you to go out with other guys. It's up to you to determine how far you're willing to go with Spoonie or anyone else."

"I know, Venice. It's hard to be apart. You definitely know what I'm talking about."

"Don't remind me. Look, let's go party."

"Okay."

The girls found their way back out to the party. Venice and Craig danced next to Chanelle and Spoonie. Monique was grinding with some guy who still had a jheri curl. The party went on for hours before winding down and Monique was complaining that her feet were hurting. Chanelle was giggling to almost everything Spoonie said, which was a good sign.

At two-thirty, Craig asked if they were ready to go. Jasper was going to catch a ride back to campus with other friends. He thanked Craig for letting him roll with him before telling the group goodbye.

Monique said, "Jasper, next time, don't run off so fast."

He laughed and said, "All right."

As the rest of them loaded into Craig's truck, Monique moaned from exhaustion but boasted about having a good time. She said, "Craig, I'm going to pin that cute Jasper down if I ever get a chance. He seems so sweet and innocent. I like a good challenge."

Craig snickered. "You'd better watch yourself. Looks can be deceiving. You may be the one who gets pinned down."

They all laughed and agreed with Craig that she might get into a situation she couldn't get out of.

"I can handle myself and I know I can handle a sweet little thing like Jasper," Monique said defensively.

Craig said, "Okay, don't say I didn't warn you, Miss Know- It-All."

After they reached the dorm, Spoonie asked Chanelle if he could walk her to the door. Chanelle agreed and Monique jumped out and thanked Craig for letting them hang with him and his girl. Craig told Monique that it wasn't a problem and to get her butt in her room before she got into trouble.

Monique asked, "Are you coming up, Venice?"

Venice hesitated a moment. Craig smiled and said, "No, she's going home with me. Is that okay with you?"

"You know you're all right with me, Craig. Just make sure you take care of my girl. Venice, I'll see you in the morning and don't do anything that I wouldn't do."

Venice giggled. "Goodnight, Monique! Anyway, I'm not like you! You're a nymphomaniac!"

Monique let out a silly laugh and walked off toward the dorm.

Venice turned to Craig. "Do you think that's a good idea after the misunderstanding earlier today?"

Craig ran his finger down her arm. "Venice, that's behind us now. Let it go. I just want to spend some time with you."

"That's nice, but I don't have a change of clothes."

"Well, why don't you go throw a few things in a bag? I really want you with me tonight. I promise, I'll be a perfect gentleman."

"Okay, Craig. I'll be right back."

Venice noticed Chanelle and Spoonie sitting in the lounge talking when she entered the dorm. She ran down the hall to her room, gathered some personal belongings and a change of clothes.

As she entered back into the lobby, Spoonie hollered, "Tell Craig I'll catch him tomorrow!"

Venice replied, "I will. Goodnight, Spoonie. Goodnight, Chanelle."

Chanelle gave Venice the thumbs up sign behind Spoonie's back. Venice climbed back into the truck, delivered Spoonie's message, and they were on their way.

Venice said, "Chanelle and Spoonie are sitting in the lounge. Craig, I think this is the best thing that's ever happened to Chanelle. I hope it works out."

"Me, too."

The rest of the ride was quiet. Venice was beginning to feel a little nervous. She started thinking about Jarvis. She attempted to calm herself down mentally and physically.

After getting to his house, Craig asked, "Would you like something to drink?"

Venice responded, "Sure. Whatever you have handy."

"Cool. I'll pour us some wine. Why don't you toss your bag in my room."

Venice hoped the wine would calm her nerves. "Craig, is it okay if I take a shower?"

"Help yourself to whatever you need. The towels are in the linen closet. If you need anything else, just holler at me."

"Okay, but I think I can find everything."

Venice showered while Craig double-checked all the doors, cut off the lights, and set the alarm. Craig turned on the TV and began to turn down his bed. His room was very neat for a college man but, then again, it wasn't like a dorm room. His room was large enough to have a sofa, drawing table, and a desk for his computer. He had a queen-size bed with a padded cedar chest at the foot of it for additional seating. His walls were decorated with colorful African paintings and artifacts to compliment the theme. He had soft lighting that gave the room a warm and relaxing glow. Venice was impressed with his taste in artwork. Craig sipped on his drink and watched ESPN while Venice finished her shower. She found the warm water relaxing and spent quite a while under the soothing water.

Craig knocked on the door and teased her. "Hey, girl, don't use up all the hot water."

"I'll be out in a minute." Venice thought to herself, *I need to be using cold water 'cause I'm hot as hell!*

She finished her shower, powdered, and lotioned up. She decided to put on a little makeup before putting on her nightshirt and returning to the bedroom. Craig's eyes scanned her body from head to toe.

He stood up and locked eyes with her. "Make yourself comfortable. I'll be right out."

Craig went into the bathroom to take his shower. He could still smell the seductive scent of her in the air.

Venice began to wonder if that night would be the night. She hoped so. Her curiosity was starting to get the best of her. The sleeping arrangements weren't discussed and Venice didn't want Craig to think she was loose. She sat on the bed, sipping her wine and contemplating what to do.

When Craig reentered the room, he was wearing a T-shirt and shorts. He noticed Venice was acting a little nervous. "Venice, if you like, I can sleep in the guest room. I don't want you to feel uncomfortable."

What I wish you would do is hurry up and give me some loving, Venice said to herself.

Aloud she answered, "You don't have to leave your room. I appreciate your offer, but I'm okay."

"Are you sure?"

"I'm sure."

After finishing their drinks, Craig stacked pillows so that they were in a semi-reclining position. That made it easier to watch TV. As time went on, Venice started getting sleepy and instinctively laid her head across his chest. Immediately, he became aroused. Mentally, he had to talk his desire down because he didn't want to scare her away. Little did he know, she was just as aroused with their bodies pressed casually against each other. As the night wore on and nothing happened, Venice realized it would be up to her to make the first move. However, she felt that would give him the wrong impression of her. It was the first time she'd spent the night with him and she didn't want to ruin it.

All sorts of things ran through her head: *Here I am, practically naked and he hasn't even touched me. What's up? Should I just put my hands in his shorts and take it? Nah! That wouldn't be cool either. I'm just going to have to try and be a little more patient. But damn! Look at him. He is so fine and so sweet. Lord, give me strength.*

Venice decided to try and get some sleep. It was going to be hard to sleep lying next to him.

Craig lay there watching her and wondered if he should make a move. He didn't want Venice to think that all he wanted was sex, but he did want her bad. He assumed she felt his unavoidable hardness against her back. But if she did, she didn't let on.

He thought: *Lord! I don't know how much longer I can hold off not touching this woman!*

Venice definitely felt something pushing against her hips. For now, she was satisfied to know that he wanted her as much as she wanted him. Even though her heart was pounding and body was throbbing, she managed to fall asleep.

Fourteen

Being an early riser, Venice woke up first just as the sun was rising. Craig was sound asleep and had his arm securely over her waist. Venice tried to creep out of the bed without disturbing him, but it didn't work.

"Where are you going?" Craig asked.

"I was just going to the bathroom."

"Okay. Hurry back."

"Do you want anything while I'm up?"

"I want you to come back to bed. It's too early to get up."

Venice smiled. Just knowing that he wanted her beside him felt great. When she returned to bed, he massaged her back. Once again, she felt the familiar bulge against her hips.

Damn! She lay there, feeling the warmth of his body as he snuggled up to her even tighter. She couldn't understand his ability to hold out. She was about to explode. Her body was on fire and sweat started to bead on her forehead. A few minutes later, he started kissing the back of her neck sensually. Venice bit her bottom lip as his strong hands started caressing her thighs. He moved up to her breasts and reached under her shirt. She turned to him and felt him protruding even more as she wrapped her leg over his body.

He opened his eyes and said, "Venice, I'm sorry. You're about to make me do something I don't think we're ready for."

"Why don't you let me be the judge of that?"

He smiled and she gave him a seductive kiss on the lips. Pulling her closer to him, he said, "It's not our time yet, baby. As much as I want to, I don't think we should. It is the first night you've spent with me and I don't want you to feel like I took advantage of you."

Venice met his dark gaze. "Maybe I want you to take advantage of me. Plus, Craig Jr. seems to be in the mood."

Craig blushed. "What do you expect? He hasn't had anyone as sweet as you visiting before."

Venice nudged up against his neck playfully and stroked his lower body. "I'm game if you are, but I appreciate you having my best interest at hand."

"I just don't want you to have any regrets later."

"The only regret I'm having right now if that we haven't started making love."

That was all Craig could take. In a split second, he was covering her with his body and devouring her lips with his. Her nipples hardened as he stroked them with his fingers. Venice let out a loud moan as he covered the ripe peaks with his warm lips, sucking them raw. She grabbed his head and stroked his neck as he attentively concentrated on each one equally. Venice felt his impressive manhood as he ground his hips into hers. She immediately moistened and, within minutes, his fingers found the warm, wet jungle of love he'd searched for. She arched her body toward him as his fingers explored in and out of her. Venice could hardly contain the pleasure he was giving her with just his touch and wanted more.

She looked into his dark brown eyes. "I'm a little nervous."

"I'll stop if you want me to."

"I'm not that nervous."

They laughed as their lips found each other's again. Venice wrapped her arms and legs around his impressive body as their tongues tasted their new found love. Craig stopped kissing her only long enough to protect them.

"Taylor, are you sure about this?"

She pulled him down to her so that they were eye to eye. "If I get any surer, I'm going to explode right before your eyes."

She ran her hand down his heated body, took his fullness into her hands, and guided him into the space she long awaited for him to fill.

"Oh my God!" she screamed out in delight.

"Am I hurting you, Venice?"

"No! Don't stop!"

Craig was happy to oblige Venice as their bodies met in savage rhythm. There was plenty of kissing, licking, and moaning until

Craig hollered out her name in true love and ecstasy. He filled her completely and she'd never felt as reckless as she did at that moment. Matching his thrusts, arching into him, feeling his hot breath on her neck, she moaned his name long and slow. This sent him over the edge as Venice felt him moving in and out of her heat. His movement was precise and erotic as he dove deeper and harder until the tidal wave of his love exploded in her lower body.

She held on tightly and convulsed beneath his body.

He collapsed onto her chest, dripping with sweat and whispered, "You're something else, Ms. Taylor."

"I hope that's a compliment."

He ran his hand from her thigh and cupped her breast. "That's an understatement."

"In that case, you weren't so bad yourself."

He smiled and continued to stroke her nipple with his thumb. Their eyes met and Venice pulled him to her. "Kiss me, Bennett." He held her in his arms and did as he was told. They continued holding each other and eventually went back to sleep.

Venice had one final thought before falling asleep: *I'm sorry, Jarvis.*

Once they finally woke up, Craig cooked breakfast, cleaned up the kitchen, and got dressed. It was about 10:30 a.m. and Venice told Craig she needed to get back to campus. She didn't have much to say during the ride.

Craig asked, "Are you okay, Venice?"

"I'm fine."

When they arrived at her dorm, he walked her to her room and gave her a kiss on the lips. "I'll call you when I get out of church. Next Sunday, I want you to go with me. Okay?"

Venice said, "All right. See you later."

When Venice entered the room, Monique couldn't wait to tell her what she'd missed. "Girl, you missed it! That heifer down the hall in 311 had some chick's man in her room last night. His old lady found out about it and those two got in a serious fight in the hall. The chick upstairs gave that heifer a serious beatdown, then almost whipped her man's ass. Somebody finally called the floor counselor but by the time she got here, dude had left. Of course, that heifer in room 311 went to hide out in somebody else's room. She got exactly what she deserved. The counselor tried to find out what happened, but nobody told her what really went down. I'm glad she got what she deserved. That's not the first time she's been caught screwing around with somebody else's piece."

Venice replied, "I told you that's dangerous business, trying to juggle men on the same turf. You can't do that because what goes around, comes around."

Monique agreed, then went on to ask Venice how her night was. All Venice told her was that she had a good time and they just chilled.

Monique didn't believe her. "Girl, I know you're probably as raw as hell!"

"You're so vulgar! Just because I spent the night at the man's house doesn't mean we did anything."

"Why not?"

Venice wasn't about to put her business in the street, especially with Monique.

"Forget it! Have you heard from Chanelle today?"

"No, but Jarvis called for you late last night."

"He did! What did you tell him?"

"I told him you went out and that I didn't know what time you'd be in. He said he'd call you today."

"Is that all? He didn't ask you who I was with?"

"No."

"Okay. I'm going down to Chanelle's room. If he calls, tell him to call her room."

Monique was headed to the shower, but replied, "Okay."

Before Venice left the room, she decided to call Chanelle. As the phone rang, Venice reminisced about her evening.

Chanelle answered the phone, "Hello?"

"What's up, Chanelle?"

"You! What happened last night?"

"No, you tell me. I want to hear how you and Spoonie got along last night."

Chanelle told her to come on down. Once the two of them got together, they shared their adventures from the previous night.

Chanelle asked Venice, "Did you and Craig finally do it?"

Venice wasn't ready to share that with anyone yet. She was still trying to deal with it herself, so she lied. "No! We had wine, watched TV, and just hung out. What about you, Chanelle?"

"Girl, you're not going to believe me, but I spent the night with him and I let him hit it! And I mean hit it! I don't know what came over me. I've never slept with any guy on the first date before. Spoonie was a perfect gentleman. I was the one who made all the advances. I guess all that stuff Monique said got to me. He's really a nice guy. I just hope he doesn't think I'm easy."

Venice was sitting there with her mouth opened in shock. "Are you the same innocent Chanelle I grew up with?"

They both laughed.

"Venice, he kept asking me if I was sure this was what I wanted to do. I told him that if it wasn't, we wouldn't be there together."

Venice was still in shock.

"Girl, he wore me out! Jeremy was nothing like that. I couldn't help myself. I felt like a wild woman. He's a great lover!" Chanelle fell back on the bed in laughter. "I'm still tingling. I can't wait to see him again!"

"Chanelle, you guys used protection, didn't you?"

Chanelle had this weird look on her face. "Well, no. I'm on the pill so I'm okay."

"What about diseases, Chanelle?"

"I wasn't thinking about that at the time, Venice. I just made sure I was protected from getting pregnant. You don't think I've messed up, do you?"

"I hope not, but he should've known better also. You just met him and you don't know anything about him. Don't do that again if you guys decide to get together. Are you going to see him today?"

"He's picking me up this evening."

Venice said, "I hope this works out for you. Spoonie seems to be really nice. But you still have to be careful, Chanelle. Just take it slow. I know you haven't seen Jeremy in a while and everyone gets lonely."

Chanelle giggled. "Jeremy who? I know, girl and I will take it slow. Thanks for listening and I'll be more careful. I guess I was just hornier than I realized."

The two chatted a while longer before deciding to catch up later.

Fifteen

Over the next two weeks, the girls went to class, shopped at malls, and talked to their significant others on a daily basis in preparation for homecoming. Craig and Venice double dated with Spoonie and Chanelle a few times. Venice finally told Chanelle about what had happened between her and Craig the night after the game. She apologized for not telling her sooner. Chanelle was a little hurt, but understood when Venice told her that she was trying to deal with her emotions and just couldn't tell her right away. Chanelle accepted her apology.

Venice began attending church with Craig on a regular basis. She still hadn't told Joshua about the progression in her relationship with Craig. She was beginning to have feelings of guilt. She didn't expect Craig to be so wonderful and she was having unexpected thoughts about him. *I guess these are the regrets Craig was talking about. Am I falling in love with him? I couldn't be.*

Sleeping in the same bed with him was beginning to feel safe and natural. Whenever he came near or touched her, her body craved for him. They made love at every opportunity. Craig's co-op kept him out of town a lot so Venice was always ready and excited to see him on the weekends. Sometimes she found herself nervous about Jarvis and about his homecoming, which was coming up at the end of the week. Venice had to make a decision, quick. She had been hanging out with Craig for several weeks and was getting really content with their relationship.

Jarvis called to confirm her visit for the weekend. She told him she'd see him Friday afternoon. For some reason, even that felt awkward. It had been two months since they were together. Venice worried that Jarvis would figure out that she had been with someone else.

Jarvis knew her inside and out and would know something was different. Jarvis' dad setup Venice's flight for her and Jarvis planned to pick her up from the airport.

On Thursday evening, Venice phoned Craig to let him know that she wouldn't be able to see him on the weekend because she was going out of town. He didn't question her, which was a slight relief. Venice figured he was so caught up in his work that he didn't think to quiz her. Craig had a lot of projects he had to finish before Monday, but he said he would still miss her. He told her to have good time and to call him when she got back.

Venice felt guilty as she hung up the phone. She didn't exactly lie to him. She just didn't tell him any details. Her main concern was the possibility of him questioning her when she got back.

It had indeed crossed Craig's mind that Venice was probably going to visit her ex. He wondered how long it would be before he had to deal with it. He wanted a serious relationship with her but, like most men, was afraid to completely open up to her. He realized that once they started having a physical relationship, there would be no turning back. He really did want it all.

Chanelle came into the room just as Venice began packing. "I guess this means you're going, huh?"

"Don't start, Chanelle."

Chanelle sat down on the bed. "Have you told Craig where you're going?"

"I told him that I was going out of town for the weekend and that I'd see him Sunday."

"He didn't ask who you were going to visit?"

"No, but when I get back, he'll probably ask." Venice stopped packing for a moment. "What the hell am I doing, Chanelle? I've fallen in love with Craig! What am I going to do?"

"Don't ask me! I just hope you realize you're playing with fire. How are you going to be in love with two men? How did you let this happen?"

"I don't know. Just keep it to yourself. You, Joshua, and Galen are the only ones who know where I'm going to be. Galen's tripping about it, too. He told me not to put him in a situation like this again."

"I can't blame him. You're his sister and Craig's his boy."

"I didn't expect to fall for him like this. It slipped up on me. Well, I can't worry about it now. I've told Jarvis I was coming. Now, I'm packed."

Chanelle asked, "Are you going to need a ride to the airport?"

"No, I'm going to leave my car there. Pray for me, girl. I hope I know what I'm doing. Maybe this weekend can help me decide what I really want to do."

"I hope so."

The flight wasn't very long and when Venice stepped off the plane, she immediately spotted Jarvis waving. She ran over and gave him a big hug. He picked her up off the floor and gave her a kiss, which brought emotions flooding down on her. They hadn't seen each other for about two months and he really, really looked good. His smile made her melt and his touch made her weak. His faded jeans were molded to his athletic frame and women definitely noticed him.

He said, "Girl! I thought you'd never get here. You're looking as fine as ever. Turn around so I can see if you've still got that big booty."

"Jarvis! You haven't changed a bit. I can tell you're still taking care of yourself."

He flexed his muscular arms and said, "You know I have to, girl. Now let's get your bags and get out of here. I got us a room at a hotel near campus. I can't wait to get you there and do all kinds of nasty things to you."

Chills shot through Venice's body when he described what he was going to do to her.

"Niecy, I've rented a car for the weekend since I'm not going to be able to get my car up here until after Christmas."

They walked through the airport arm in arm. For the weekend, Venice was going to have to try not to think about her relationship with Craig.

Hell, men have been doing shit like this for years.

After getting her bags, they proceeded to pick up the rental car and were on their way. Jarvis took her on a brief tour of the city before arriving at the hotel.

Venice asked, "What time do you have to be at practice?"

He gave her a devilish grin. "In about two hours. That'll be plenty time for me to do what I'm going to do to you."

She closed her eyes and shivered at the thought. He was the king of foreplay.

After checking in to the room, Venice fell back onto the bed as Jarvis put her bags down. "This is a nice room. Thanks, baby."

Jarvis took his jacket off and joined her on the bed. He didn't waste any time nibbling on her earlobe. "You know, you're a sight for sore eyes."

Venice touched his face. "You are too, baby."

They gazed into each other's eyes for a moment as if they needed to recapture something lost. His lips were inches from hers when he whispered, "I love you, Venice." There was no time for a response. He leaned down and hungrily kissed the lips he thought only belonged to him.

Damn! This man knows how to make me feel good.

Venice wrapped her arms and legs around him as his tongue found its way back into her warm mouth. He kissed down her neck and continued to her breasts, even though the soft material of her blouse covered her. Taking his time, he savored on the softness of her body. She squirmed and moaned as his fingers worked her like a magician. They hadn't made love in two months and she hoped that she'd find all the answers she searched for. Jarvis started slowly unbuttoning her blouse. Venice hurriedly pulled his shirt over his head and threw it across the room. He rolled over onto his back, pulling her on top of him.

"Have you missed me, Venice?"

Planting small kisses on his neck and chest, she answered in a sultry tone, "Oh, yes."

"How much have you missed me?"

Venice looked him in his eyes, massaged his desire, and said, "This much."

He smiled as she lowered her mouth and tasted him.

"Oh! Sh-h-hit, Niecey!"

Jarvis closed his eyes and let out a loud groan as he watched himself appear and disappear. He shivered as he found himself grabbing a handful of her hair. Venice continued the sensual pleasure until he could no longer stand it. He slowly rolled over on top of her, pinning her gently into the mattress. He stared at her for a moment and she smiled into his loving eyes. It only took a couple of seconds for him to strip her remaining clothes. They began to taste each other more passionately as he flicked his tongue over her hardened nipples.

Venice was almost screaming when she said, "Come on, Jarvis! I can't wait any longer!"

Jarvis didn't let another second go by before pushing himself between her thighs. He entered her silkiness with unexpected ease. He noticed but was too caught up with pleasure to address the issue right then.

"Damn, Niecy, I missed you more than I thought I could! You feel so good!"

Venice felt the same way and tears built in her eyes as his hands explored her body. His lips found her breasts again as his hands stroked her intimate area with tenderness. He licked her up and down as she arched her back and moaned uncontrollably to his touch. His strong, muscular frame reacquainted itself with her soft, firm body.

Venice held onto him as tight as she could until all she saw were fireworks. Jarvis was the only one she'd never protected herself with, but she'd always been on the pill. They'd promised each other that if, God forbid, they ever slept with anyone else, they'd definitely use protection.

Jarvis continued to make love to her with the intensity she was accustomed to. He whispered his undying love into her ears, which caused her to tremble even more. He pushed his hips in and out of her moist body more vigorously and possessively. Venice thought her heart would burst out of her chest when his fingers delved inside to her inner core. She screamed and unintentionally scratched his back as he thrust his body even deeper. Venice admired the tattoo of her name on his bicep as he ran his tongue from her neck down to her navel. She had his name tattooed on her left shoulder blade. Her parents weren't happy with her doing it, but there was nothing they could do about it after the fact.

"Jarvis!"

"I'm here, baby. You'll never belong to anyone except me, Niecy."

She wrapped her legs around this man who was built like a black god.

"Venice! Baby!"

She clung to him tightly as his body shook with spasms and collapsed, taking her mouth and tongue into his. She shuddered hard beneath him as she moaned his name. He had released two months of frustration and loneliness on her and it was the most overwhelming feeling he had ever felt. Hot tears ran out of Venice's eyes

Jarvis looked at her and asked, "Are you okay?"

She nodded as her body shuddered again.

"You know I still love the hell out of you, don't you?" Jarvis asked lovingly.

"Yes, I know. I still feel the same way, too, baby."

He lay across her as she massaged his neck and back. She stared at the ceiling. "You're still tense, Jarvis."

Jarvis rose up on his elbow. "Have you slept with him, Niecy?"

"Huh?"

"You heard me. Have you given it up to him?"

"I don't want to talk about him right now, Jarvis."

"It's obvious. Your body wasn't tight at all."

Venice was silent for a moment. "Why would even ask me that?"

"To see if you'd tell me the truth."

"I love you, Jarvis."

"I love you, too, Niecy."

They stared at each other for a few seconds.

"Have you told him about us yet?"

"Which part?"

"You know, the main thing."

"No, why does everyone think I should tell him?"

"Who else said you should?"

"Galen did. They're friends."

Jarvis sighed. "Venice, I just think he has a right to know that we were married and that we still have strong feelings for each other."

"He knows I still have strong feelings for you. He just doesn't know we used to be married."

"Does he know about the baby?"

"No! Look, Jarvis, I don't feel like talking about that right now."

Tears were glistening in Venice's eyes as she fought to hold them back.

"Where does he stand in your life, Niecy?"

"He knows I hold him close to my heart. He's a special friend."

"I see," Jarvis stated sarcastically. "Don't you think you need to tell him the whole truth?"

"I'm not ready to share my loss with him right now. I still ache for our baby."

"I feel like I'm losing you. I can't stand the thought of you being away from me. I lost my baby and I'll be damn if I lose you, too."

Jarvis turned on his back and stared at the ceiling.

"Jarvis, don't you go get sad on me now. I'm still hurting just as much as you are. I wanted your baby so bad, but God knew best. It wasn't our time."

Jarvis asked, "So, do you still think we should've gotten a divorce?"

"If we hadn't, we would've probably ended up committing adultery against each other. You know our mothers didn't put that pressure on us for nothing. I think they were worried about it happening more than we were. We're nineteen years old and freshmen in college. I think what we did was for the best. At least for now."

He leaned over and grazed his lips against hers tenderly. "As far as I'm concerned, you're still my wife and will always be my wife. I still don't see what the big problem is. We're together right now. This proves it can work. It could've been arranged for us to at least be together on the weekends when I wasn't on the road."

"Possibly, but we didn't need to take any chances. I did meet someone and he's nice. I don't want to cause any hard feelings between us."

Jarvis stroked her thigh. "I can't help the way I feel. I still think we can make it work. We've been together too long and I'm not looking to meet anyone new. I haven't met anyone up here so far that I could get into seriously. The few I have met are 'tricks.' I think they're only interested because they heard the NFL is scouting me. I think they see dollar signs. Niecy, I hate to admit it, but I don't want to cause any problems for you. I'm not happy that you've met someone to spend time with. I just hope this doesn't backfire on me. I also hope that when we graduate, I'll be able to put that wedding ring back on your finger."

Venice looked at her hand. She was wearing it as a thumb ring. Jarvis wore his on a gold chain around his neck.

She placed her hand on his cheek. "Me, too, Sweetie. Hey, I'm hungry."

Jarvis looked at his watch. "Let's get out of here and get a bite to eat. I have to be at practice in a little while."

They took their shower together, just like old times, and headed out to get some food.

Sixteen

Jarvis took Venice on campus and introduced her to several of his new friends while they were on their way to one of the on-campus restaurants. One of the girls Jarvis had dated came over and Venice politely shook her hand. Jarvis didn't hold his tongue about introducing Venice as his girl. He'd told all the women he dated up front that he wasn't looking for a serious relationship. He made it clear that he just wanted to date casually. This made them curious to see the woman who had her name tattooed on his arm and his heart. Upon first look, the young lady rolled her eyes. She especially noticed how Jarvis couldn't keep his hands off Venice. She realized her chances of getting with him were impossible.

Jarvis knew he had to stay beware of gold-digging hoochies. Bryan told Venice that the NFL was probably going to try and draft Jarvis before he finished college, possibly in the first draft. This meant he'd probably be an instant millionaire as long as he stayed healthy and didn't get hurt. Venice never saw him as a golden opportunity. She was in love with him before he became a football star. She loved him because he was outspoken, fun, sexy, attractive, and intelligent. Jarvis knew his potential for wealth and it was hard for him to trust any one other than the women who sincerely loved him: his mother, his sister, and Venice.

After they finished their meal, Jarvis took Venice back to the hotel and told her that he'd see her after practice.

Venice said, "Hurry back and, if you're a good boy, I'll have something special for you."

Jarvis laughed. "All right, I'm going to hold you to that."

"Cool, I'm going to call Galen and give him the phone number in case he needs to contact me."

"I'll see you in a few hours. Do you want the car?"

"No! I don't know my way around and I don't want to get lost."

"Are you sure?"

"I'm sure."

Before he left, he pulled her to him. "Venice, I'm sorry that I'm so selfish when it comes to you. I hate the thought of you giving my stuff to some other man. I have to accept that for now, but I don't like it. I hope you don't have any regrets about coming up here later on."

Venice put her arms around his waist. "I'm a big girl, Jarvis. Don't worry about me. I can take care of myself." She gave him a possessive kiss. "Drive carefully."

Jarvis patted her on the butt. "See you shortly."

Venice collapsed on the bed after he left the room. "Damn!"

Venice called Galen and gave him the phone number. He asked her about Jarvis and the campus. She told him that she was having a good time.

Galen asked, "Are you up there messing around with Jarvis, girl?"

"None of your business! Don't start with me, Galen!"

"I don't even know why I asked. I know you are."

"Has Craig called you by any chance?"

"Yes, he called and asked me who you went to visit."

Venice raised up off the bed and nervously asked, "What did you tell him?"

"I told him you went to visit your ex-husband."

Venice screamed, "No you didn't, Galen!"

"Yes, I did! You should've told him the truth by now!"

Venice's voice started cracking. "Why'd you tell him anything, Galen?"

He started laughing. "I'm just playing with you, girl! Craig hasn't called me."

Venice started trembling with anger. "I can't stand your black ass!"

She slammed the phone down and burst into tears. A few minutes later, the phone rang. When she answered it, Galen said, "Dang, girl, I'm sorry. I didn't know you were going to flip out on me. But that should show you that you don't need to be sleeping around with two men. Somebody's going to get hurt. You need to make up your mind what you're going to do. I know you and Jarvis were married and all, but Jarvis isn't at Dawson. You'll probably get to see him maybe once every couple of months. At least you can see Craig almost on a daily basis. Look, I'm not telling you what to do, but I just think you need to give yourself a chance to meet other people. Just think about what I'm saying. Okay? I'm your brother and I don't want to have to get involved. I'm just afraid that if Craig finds out about you and Jarvis the wrong way, he'll go off. I couldn't blame him, but the whole situation can be avoided. You need to go ahead and tell him the truth. If he still wants to be with you, then fine. If he doesn't, then work things out with Jarvis. It's simple, Venice. This way, you don't leave anyone in the dark. You've already told Jarvis about Craig. That was a step in the right direction. Now finish it up."

Venice listened and said, "Okay, Galen, I'll talk to you later."

She hung up the phone and laid down to take a nap. She had a lot to think about and it gave her a migraine. Somehow, she was finally able to go to sleep.

Venice didn't realize how exhausted she was. She was awakened later by Jarvis' soft kisses on her face and his manly scent. She was sore and exhausted and didn't even hear him enter the room.

"Hey, baby. What time is it?"

"Midnight. I'm sorry it took me so long to get back. After practice, we had to go over some film and some more plays. By then it was nine-thirty and curfew check is at ten o'clock. We heard rumors that the coaches were going to do a double check tonight, but we didn't know what time. Well, they did check again at eleven-thirty. I'm sorry I didn't call."

"It's okay. I was asleep anyway."

Jarvis sat up on the bed. "Are you okay? You don't look like you feel well."

"I'm fine. Galen called and pissed me off, that's all."

Jarvis took off his sweats and asked, "What's wrong with him?"

"I don't want to talk about it right now. Come here."

He got underneath the covers and Venice turned to him, rubbing his face. "I love you and I've decided that I'm going to tell Craig everything about us when I get back to school. If he doesn't want to hang out with me, then it'll be his loss."

"It *will* be his loss. Look Venice, are you telling him because you're ready to tell him or because you're listening to everyone else?"

"I need to do this. I don't want him to find out from someone else. That'll only make things worst."

"Okay, Venice. You do what you feel like you need to do. Now, where's my surprise?"

She whispered into his ear. "Take your clothes off."

He smiled and knew exactly what she was about to do. She gave him one of her famous full body massages like she used to give him every night after football practice. Afterwards, feeling relaxed from her touch, Jarvis couldn't help but make love to her once again. Venice enjoyed every inch of him and as he worked her over so completely, she felt like she would pass out. He made her body throb from head to toe. It was going to be a long night. This had to be true love.

She snuggled up to him the rest of the night, feeling like she wanted to stay. But she realized it would be short-lived. She fantasized about the many nights she'd fallen asleep just like that when they were married. Venice was very excited about the homecoming activities in the morning and could barely wait.

Have I made a mistake? But how in the hell could I make a long distance relationship work? But, I love the hell out of this man and what about Craig?"

These thoughts fought in her mind for hours and after her mind was totally exhausted, she fell asleep.

The night was short. Jarvis woke Venice up so they could attend the parade. After they arrived on campus, he found some of his teammates and introduced Venice. They attended just about every activity taking place. Venice bought a lot of souvenirs to take back to her friends. They spent the entire day enjoying each other's company. The game was going to start in a few hours and Venice and Jarvis felt like they should head back to the hotel for a nap. They'd sampled a lot of food and were both stuffed.

Jarvis' parents were also in town and Venice was going to be riding to the game with them. They'd be going out afterwards and Jarvis wanted Venice to meet him in the tunnel of the stadium after the game.

Venice sat with Jarvis' parents to help cheer him on. Portia, his sister, didn't get to come, but Jarvis promised her that she'd get to come next year. Jarvis' dad was also a former college running back and he constantly gave Jarvis advice on his game. His parents were excited to see Venice there to support their son. They knew in their hearts that Venice and Jarvis couldn't stand to be apart from each other. They loved Venice like their own daughter. They knew she was good for him and the decision to have them divorce was hard on everyone, but necessary.

As expected, it was going to be a victory party. Jarvis had an exceptionally good game. He rushed for over a hundred yards and Venice could tell the fans of the college had welcomed him with open arms. They were chanting his name and Venice could hear women sitting around her discussing how they wanted to hook up with him. Venice had no idea it was like that. She felt a little jealous and threatened.

After the horn sounded the end of the game and the players congratulated each other on the field, Venice made her way down to the fence surrounding the field. She waited to see if Jarvis still wanted her to meet him in the tunnel. There were a large number of other women hanging around. Venice hoped they were waiting for their significant others and not Jarvis. As the players ran toward the tunnel, Venice searched for Jarvis in the crowd. She finally saw him over on the sideline talking to reporters. He spotted her and waved his helmet up in the air. Once he'd completed his interview, he walked over and some of the women started calling his name trying to get him to talk to them. Jarvis paused for a moment to thank them for congratulating him, but didn't stop to talk to them. He continued toward Venice and his parents. When he got to Venice, he climbed up on the bench and kissed her. "Well, how did I do?"

"You were great!"

Mr. Anderson said, "Son, you did it! You see what I told you worked."

"Yes, sir. Thanks, Pops."

Mrs. Anderson said, "Baby, we're going back to the hotel for a while. We'll see you shortly. Venice, are you riding back with us?"

"Yes, Ma'am."

As they started to walk away, Venice asked Jarvis if he wanted her to wait for him.

"No, go ahead. It's going to be a while before I get through in the locker room."

"Okay, I'll see you, baby."

"Hey! Give me some more of those luscious lips before you leave."

Venice smiled, leaned down, and gave him a lingering kiss.

The crowd of women stared and one of them said, "Who the hell is she?"

Mr. Anderson heard the remark as he walked passed them and replied, "She's just my son's wife."

All of the women looked stunned and their mouths fell open in shock. Jarvis and Venice never knew that conversation took place. His parents were very protective of their relationship. They knew there would be gold-digging women after their son and wanted to make sure he didn't stray. After loving on Jarvis, Venice ran to catch up with the Andersons and head to the hotel.

Back at the hotel, Venice couldn't decide which outfit to wear to the party. She finally decided on a black catsuit. The outfit showed every curve she possessed and she knew it. Jarvis had dropped his clothes off at the hotel earlier and was going to be wearing black jeans, an off-white pullover shirt, and a leather jacket.

Venice was stepping out of the shower when he entered the room, singing. He grabbed her, threw her on the bed, and started kissing and tickling her.

Venice squirmed with laughter. "Stop, Jarvis!"

He started trying to pull off her towel. "Uh-uh. What do you have under this towel, girl? Let me see."

Venice playfully tried to keep the towel on. "Stop Jarvis! I'm sore!"

He kept tickling her until he'd finally won and threw the towel across the room. He quickly tossed his clothes on the floor and started kissing up and down her wet body.

Dizzy and breathless, Venice said, "We're going to be late."

"I don't care."

Taking deep breaths, Venice closed her eyes and grabbed Jarvis' head as she enjoyed the warmth of his lips sliding down her body.

He stopped just above her sweetness and planted small sensual kisses on her hot skin. She missed the old feeling and moaned to his touch.

She felt his hot breath on her neck as he whispered to her, "Niecy...Baby...I...."

She pulled him to her, looked him in the eyes, and said, "I know, baby. I love you, too."

She held on to him tightly as he loved her like he'd never loved her before. This went on until neither of them could take any more.

Venice finally hollered out, "Oh Jarvis! Baby! Oh my God!"

Jarvis pounded his fist on the pillows a couple of times as he exploded inside her body and groaned, "Damn!"

He kissed her softly on the cheek and laid down next to her, breathless. She ran her fingers through the silky hair covering his chest and said, "I hate you, Jarvis Tyler Anderson! I'm so-o-o sore."

"Come here so I can kiss it and make it better."

They both laughed and Venice said, "Seriously, baby. No matter how we end up, I want you to know that I'll always love you."

Jarvis smiled and pulled her up on his chest. She couldn't help but reminisce about how he'd just served her up with his good loving. He'd worked Venice's body over until she was delirious and weak.

"Venice, this feels too damn good. I don't know if I'm going to let you back on that plane tomorrow." She smiled and kissed him on the chest and lips. He seductively ran his hands down to the arch in her back. "Do you still want to go out? We don't have to, if you don't want to. We could stay here and do this the rest of the night."

"No way! I need to get out of here. You're trying to kill me. I don't know if I'm going to be able to walk after what you just did to me. I need some Epsom salt."

"I wasn't by myself, girl! You almost made me pull a muscle."

They laughed together as Venice got up and headed for a soothing bath. He joined her and they talked and lathered each other's bodies. He held onto her tightly and then splashed water playfully. Finally, they got dressed and headed out to the party.

The party was wonderful and Venice was having the time of her life. She danced with Jarvis and some of his friends. She held onto

Jarvis and didn't want to let him go. He felt the same way. Some of the women Jarvis had dated stared enviously. His mind and eyes were obviously only for Venice.

Once the party ended, they drove back to the hotel. They both knew it would probably be the last time they'd be together for a while. It all depended on how things worked out for them at school. It was a happy and sad occasion. Needless to say, this night would probably be the most intense of all.

Jarvis started touching and kissing on Venice before she could open the hotel door. They'd stopped and picked up some snacks and drinks to nibble on. Venice giggled as he playfully chased her around the room. They ended up on the bed, out of breath, and decided to eat their food.

Jarvis turned on the radio. "Venice, this weekend has been the bomb. I think I'm going to hold you hostage."

"I wish I could stay, too, baby. I've really enjoyed being with you this weekend. It feels like old times."

They both looked at each other in silence for a moment.

Venice said, "I'm going to hit the showers. I'll be back in a few."

Jarvis blocked her path, bringing his lips within inches of hers and embracing her. "I want you back, Niecy."

"You haven't lost me, baby."

She leaned into him and ran her tongue across his lips, then gave him a slow, erotic kiss. Heat immediately consumed both of their bodies. Venice could see that he was clearly aroused. He sensed the desire in her also. She finally pulled away and said, "Hold that thought, baby. I'll be right out."

Venice entered the bathroom for her shower.

There was a knock at the door and when Jarvis answered it, his dad asked if he could come in. Jarvis invited him in and went to tell Venice so she wouldn't come out undressed.

"Son, I apologize for barging in, but I want to let you know that I'm proud of you. You're doing wonderful here and I believe the only thing missing in your life is that young lady in there."

Jarvis sat in the chair next to his dad and said, "Thanks, Pops."

Jarvis had confided in his father, who knew the entire story surrounding Craig.

"So what are you going to do about her?"

"I don't know, Pops. I'm working on it. There's only so much I can do since we're so far apart.

"Is she serious about the guy?"

"I don't know. I hope not. I don't want to lose her."

"Well, she's a good girl and I don't want to see you lose her either. You two were made for each other. Have faith and everything will work out. Fight for her, but don't push her. I think what your mom and her mom did hurt the situation. Distance is only a number and if you two love each other like I know you do, nothing or nobody can come between you."

"That's past tense now, Pops."

"It'll work out, Son."

Venice returned to the room wearing a gorgeous royal blue nightgown ensemble.

Mr. Anderson stood up, gave her a hug and kiss, and said, "Hey, sweetie, it's so good to see you. Now, let me get out of your way."

Venice said, "Don't run off, Pops. Stay a while."

He laughed. "I don't think so. I'm going to see if the missus wants to go downstairs to the lounge."

Jarvis took a sip of his soda and said, "All right, Pops. I'll see you in the morning."

By the time Jarvis closed the door behind his father and turned around, Venice had taken off her robe to reveal the lacy little piece of material underneath. She turned around to reveal the thong back. Venice hadn't surprised him with a sexy nightgown in a long time and Jarvis was caught completely off guard. When he saw her, he spit his drink across the room.

As he coughed to catch his breath, Venice walked over to pat him on the back. "Are you okay?"

Jarvis sat down in the chair, still coughing, and nodded that he was. When he was finally able to catch his breath, he admired her lingerie and put his arm around her. "What are you trying to do to me? You're going to make me hurt myself in here tonight."

Venice massaged his neck and whispered in his ear, "I'm majoring in Sports Medicine, remember? You're in good hands."

She straddled his lap and as he pulled her closer, Venice felt him come to life. He continued to admire her athletic, feminine features.

She placed her arms around his neck. "Jarvis, I don't want this to end."

He ran his hands up her thigh. "It doesn't have to, baby. I'm waiting on you."

She smiled and kissed him. "Let's talk about it later. Okay?"

He agreed and got up to put the food away. After he finished his shower, he came to her with an urgency. She took a deep breath and moaned as he gently entered her mind, body, and soul.

"I love you so much."

"I-I love you, too, baby."

Venice was at his mercy as he loved her as hard as he could. She clenched her teeth in ecstasy as Jarvis plunged deeply into her body.

"Venice, you belong to me and don't you ever forget it!"

With passion on her face and in her voice, she whispered, "Always, baby. Always."

An hour or so later, they finally settled into the bed. The scent of their lovemaking covered their bodies as they held each other the rest of the night. Neither of them actually went to sleep. They just laid there, in thought, regretting her departure the next day and neither was looking forward to it.

Seventeen

The morning came around quickly and, after breakfast, Venice was on her way back to the airport. Venice knew it was going to be a sad goodbye as they sat in the terminal waiting for her flight to board. She laid her head on his shoulder and held his hand as they waited. His parents were nearby having a cup of coffee, also waiting for the flight. Jarvis told her that he wanted her to come back in two weeks. Venice looked into his sad eyes and told him that she would try, but she couldn't promise him anything.

It wasn't long before the stewardess called for boarding. Jarvis' mom and dad came over and hugged them goodbye. They told Jarvis to stay in the books and he told them he would call them later. They went ahead and boarded their plane, telling Venice they hoped to see her soon. She agreed and told them to have a safe flight.

After their plane taxied the runway, Jarvis grabbed Venice's hand and walked her over to her gate. He said, "Venice, this weekend was one of the best times I've ever had. I'm going to miss you, girl. I don't want to put any pressure on you because I know you're going back to Dawson to spill your guts to dude. I just want you to know that I'm here for you. Okay?"

Venice had tears running down her face as she laid against his heaving chest. Jarvis wiped away her tears and cupped her face and kissed her gently on the lips. Venice hugged him tightly as she kissed him back, not wanting to let him go.

She finally said, "I'd better go."

"Are you going to be all right?"

"I have to, Baby. Take care of yourself."

He smiled, hugged her again, and gave her one last passionate kiss. He said, "I'll see you soon, sweetheart."

"Okay."

Jarvis watched as Niecy walked down the long hallway to the plane.

No man ever could ever take your place, Jarvis.

He stayed until her plane took off and disappeared into the clouds. He then turned and walked away.

No woman could ever take your place, Niecy.

Back at Dawson, Venice decided that she didn't want to lie to Craig anymore as she made her way back to campus in her car.

When she entered the room, Monique could see that Venice was preoccupied. "I can tell by the hickey on your neck that you had a good time."

"Huh? Oh, yeah, it was nice."

Monique sensed Venice wasn't in a talking mood so she left her alone. Venice called Galen to let him know that she was back. From there, she immediately called Craig and told him that she needed to talk to him right away. She needed to get everything off her chest immediately.

Venice felt a calm come over her as she drove to Craig's house. When she pulled into his driveway, he was waiting for her on the porch.

When she approached him on the steps, he smiled and gave her a hug. "Did you have a good trip?"

"Craig, I need to talk to you."

He looked at her seriously. "Okay. Let's go inside."

He followed her into the den and they sat down in silence for a moment. Finally, Venice said, "Look, Craig. This is hard for me, but I feel like I need to tell you something about me."

"Are you okay?"

"Yes…but…Craig, I've been struggling with some emotions these past few weeks. I've mentioned the person in my past to you before and I remember telling you that I'd always love him. Well, I feel like I owe you an explanation. When we were together our junior year, I got pregnant. Our parents didn't want us bringing an illegitimate child into the world, so they approved for us to get married."

Craig was shocked. *Married!*

She went on to say, "It wasn't a big deal for us because we were in love and had been together for a couple of years. Anyway, we got married and when I was about four months pregnant, I lost my baby. It almost killed me and Jarvis took it really hard. Well, we stayed married, even though we lost our baby. But, it wasn't until this past spring that it was decided by our parents to go ahead and get a divorce. We were leaving for college and our parents thought it would be for the best. Jarvis received some scholarships up north. I had a scholarship there also, but the university messed up my paperwork so I ended up here at Dawson. So you see, before I was eighteen, I was a wife and almost a mother. That's why I told you I'd always love him, no matter what."

Feeling a little relieved, Craig reached over to wipe away her tears.

Venice continued, "Before I came to Dawson, I promised him that I'd visit him during his homecoming. That's where I was this weekend."

"Venice, why didn't you tell me this before you left?"

"I don't know. I didn't want you to be upset with me."

"Do you think telling me now makes it better?"

"I don't know what to think, Craig. You have every right to be upset and I'm sorry I didn't tell you the truth sooner."

"Venice, did you sleep with him?"

Venice looked into his saddened brown eyes. "I'm so sorry, Craig. I didn't mean to hurt you."

"So, I guess that's where the mark on your neck came from?"

"I found myself falling in love with you and I didn't know how to handle it. I haven't loved anyone outside of Jarvis before. This is new territory for me. Jarvis said I should tell you the truth about us. I just hope that you can forgive me."

Craig was looking at the floor, visibly hurt and pissed off. He angrily asked, "Why couldn't you just talk to me, Venice? We've been able to talk about everything else. Did you tell him how you felt about me?"

"No."

"Why not?"

"I don't know. I guess I was afraid I'd lose him. I've never had to deal with anything like this before."

"So he does know I exist?"

"Yes, I told him about you weeks ago."

"And he's cool about it?"

"Not really. He knows we decided to chill on our relationship. He said I should tell you everything before you found out."

The fury finally came. "When did he give you the expert advice? When he was screwing you? Why are you even telling me this? Why are you even here? It's obvious you went where you wanted to be. Venice, you have a goddamn husband!"

"Ex-husband! Craig, I didn't want you to find out the wrong way."

Craig looked at her, crazed. "Who else knows?"

"Just my family and Chanelle."

He asked solemnly, "Are you going to see him again?"

"I can't answer that right now. This entire situation is complicated because I'm in love with you, too. I hope you'll bear with me until I can sort this out."

"It would've been nice to hear you tell me that you loved me under different circumstances. It really doesn't matter now."

"I'm sorry."

"So am I, Venice."

Craig stood up and walked over to the window. He dropped his head and said, "Venice, I don't know what I wanna do right now. I think you need to leave. I need some time to think."

She went over to him and put her hand on his arm. "Craig, I'm really sorry. I didn't mean to hurt you. I do love you."

She closed the door behind her and left the house. Craig watched her from the window as she got into her car and drove away. He wanted to hold her and tell her that no matter what, he still loved her. He just couldn't. A man's got his pride. Anyway, she was only a woman. Unfortunately, he loved this one.

Eighteen

Craig was having a hard time dealing with the situation with Venice. Skeeter came over a few weeks later to hang out and watch TV. Craig had already told him what went down with Venice and Skeeter could tell that Craig was still down in the dumps.

"Man, you're still trippin' over girl? You need to move on, dog. Ain't no way I would let some chick mess with my head like that."

"She's not just 'some chick' okay?"

Skeeter took a sip of his drink. "Man, she's got your nose wide open. There's too many women around here for you to be worrying about her. If I were you, I'd just let it go. It's obvious that she's not ready for you."

"I don't know about that. I love this one. I just wasn't expecting her to get with her old man like that. I knew she wasn't over him, but I didn't expect this."

"What's up with them?"

"They used to be married."

Skeeter sat up and hollered, "Married!"

Craig got up and poured him some juice. "Yeah, married. She got pregnant in high school, but ended up losing the baby. They stayed married up until last spring before leaving for college."

"Damn! She's kind of hot, isn't she?"

"Uh-uh, man, she's just been in some unusual situations. She can't help it that she still has feelings for dude. They've been together for about four years."

Skeeter asked, "So where do you fit into all that?"

"She said they decided to chill since they were going to be so far apart. I just don't know if I can handle her hooking up with him whenever she feels like it."

"Well, if you want to still be with her, you need to put some loving on her so good, it'll make her forget about him. The rod is a powerful tool. You just need to make sure you use it the right way."

"It's not about the sex, Skeeter. I'm digging her just as hard without the sex. If I lose her, I'll probably lose my damn mind."

"Maybe she is 'the one.' Especially if you're jones'n that bad for her."

"I guess. I haven't talked to her in weeks. I don't even know if she'll speak to me again after the things I said."

"Well, you'll never know if you don't go see the girl. Look, believe it or not, I like her. I think she's good for you. I've never seen you this messed up over a chick before so she must be the one."

Craig didn't respond. He just stared at the TV watching the game.

Since two weeks had passed, Venice was facing the fact that Craig didn't want to continue a relationship with her. He hadn't called or come by since they'd had their talk. Venice threw herself into her classes. Jarvis called to check on her, but she really didn't feel like discussing it with him. Galen called to tell Venice that she did the right thing.

"Don't stress out over this, girl. Let the chips fall where they may. If he wants to be with you, he'll call. I saw him the other day. He asked how you were. I just told him that I hadn't had a chance to talk to you and I didn't want to get involved."

"I think I did the wrong thing by telling him, Galen."

"No, you didn't. He had a right to know. You may not believe it right now but eventually, you will. You and Jarvis shared an unusual situation."

"Whatever! Look, I need to get out of here. I'm going for a walk."

"All right, give me a holler if you need me."

Venice agreed and hung up the phone. She grabbed her coat and left the room. As she got onto the elevator, her heart begin to ache and tears started rolling down her face. Even though she still loved Jarvis, she didn't want to lose her relationship with Craig. She loved him, too. When she reached the lobby, she walked toward the front door, but stopped for a moment to button her jacket. When she did that, she felt someone embrace her from behind. It startled her when she turned to find Craig standing there.

He smiled, took the tissue from her hand, and wiped her tears. "I hope those tears are for me. Where are you headed? I was just trying to call you."

Venice was speechless. He reached for her hand. "Come with me, Taylor."

Craig led her out the door. Venice shyly followed as the cold air hit her face. Craig didn't say anything else. He just led her to the parking lot.

When they reached his truck, he turned to face her. "Venice, I'm mad as hell at you. But, it's not all your fault."

Venice dropped her head. "Yes, it is."

He held her in the cold air for a moment and then opened the door for her to get in. Once they got inside, he said, "Venice, everything happens for a reason. All I want is for us to be happy. I don't know where to go from here, but I'm willing to deal with it for now." He paused for a moment, then looked down at his hands and continued, "Look I'm sorry you lost your baby. That had to have been terrible for both of you."

"Thanks. It was terrible."

He turned her to face him and gave her a gentle kiss on the cheek. Venice was still too shaken to respond. He asked if she wanted to go for a ride and talk. She nodded in agreement and he started up the truck and pulled out the parking lot.

Craig drove to the city park where he found a spot by the lake.

He turned off the truck and said, "Venice, I've had two long weeks to think about what happened between us. I'm still pissed that you lied to me. But, I admire you for coming to me when you got back. It hurt, but at least I know the deal. So, where do we go from here? Huh?"

"I don't know. I guess it depends on what you're willing to deal with. I honestly can't tell you that I won't see him again. I thought when I got here and met new people, things would be different. But, after being away from him so long, seeing him again sort of rekindled things.

"So, do you still love me?"

"Yes, Craig, I do. But knowing the situation I've put you in, I couldn't blame you if you wanted to date other women. I don't know where this is going to lead us. I want to be with you and I also want to be able to maintain a relationship with Jarvis. If you don't want to be with me, I'll understand."

"Venice LaShawn Taylor, the last thing I ever wanted to do was to share someone I love with another man. That's not my style. I do believe you when you say that you love me and I can understand why you still have feelings for him. And no, I don't want to see any other women. I wish you felt the same way. I don't want you to think I'm less of a man if I decide to walk away. I also don't want you to think I'm a punk if I decide to stick around. You're asking a hell of a lot from me. I can't promise you anything. I just have to take it one day at a time."

Venice said, "I understand and I'm sorry."

They sat there in silence for a moment, watching the ducks in the pond.

"Are you hungry, Venice?"

"Not really."

"I think I could eat a bite or two. Do you want to hang out for a while?"

Venice smiled. "Sure."

He started the truck and headed to one of the fast food restaurants in the area. Venice was glad they were able to talk about it. At least it was a start.

Three days passed and it was time for Homecoming Week at Dawson. Venice decided that she was going to try and have a great time with Craig and their friends. Craig invited Venice to spend the week at his house. Bernice was going to Vegas on vacation with her fiancee, J.T. They never liked to be in town when all the festivities were going on so they always headed to Vegas.

That allowed Craig to have the house to himself for parties or whatever. Venice was a little reluctant. She knew that Jarvis would be looking for her. She also knew he would page her if he couldn't catch her in her room. It would be hard for her to return his call from Craig's house. It would also be disrespectful to try. She was just going to have to call him first.

Jarvis was a late night caller. That's when they held most of their conversations. Venice knew that Jarvis would be pissed if he found out how close she'd become to Craig. He'd also be upset to know she was spending the week at his house. Venice decided she couldn't worry about it. She loved him but he wasn't able to be with her and besides, she did enjoy Craig's company.

Each night, there was going to be something going on. There would be a Greek step-show, a fashion show, or some type of concert or party. Venice wanted to see everything if her body would hold up. Joshua and Bryan wouldn't be arriving until later in the week. On Monday evening, Craig told Venice to go on over whenever she got out of class. He'd given her a key to the house the day before because he'd be out of town on his work-study job and wouldn't get in until late. He'd have campus classes the rest of the week so he could enjoy the homecoming events and Venice's company.

As Venice arrived at the Bennett home, she settled in with her bags. She paged Craig to let him know that she was at his house and asked if he wanted her to start dinner. He told her to help herself to whatever she wanted.

He explained, "I'll be at the house around six o'clock"

"I'll see you then."

Venice had retired to Craig's bedroom to watch TV when his phone rang. As she sat there, his answering machine picked up. Venice felt like she was invading his privacy but she also felt a need to hear who was calling.

The answering machine finally picked up and a woman's voice said, "Hey, baby! It's been a long time since I heard that sweet voice of yours. I know you know who this is. I'm coming down for home-coming this weekend and I thought maybe we could get together. Anyway, call me when you get in at 555-2323. Hope to hear from you soon, baby. Bye."

Venice was shocked and felt like the drama was going to be her payback. Could she be someone from Craig's past or present?

Realizing that she was alone in the house, Venice hollered, "I can't believe this shit! Who in the hell is this? I guess it's true when they say 'What goes around, comes around.'"

Venice was suddenly feeling depressed. She wondered how she was going to be able to play off hearing the message once Craig got home. She was just going to have to act as if she hadn't been in his room, so she got her suitcase out of the bedroom and put it in the den. She returned to the kitchen to finish up dinner.

It wasn't long before she heard the garage door open and Craig entered the kitchen. He greeted her with a kiss on the cheek and bragged about dinner smelling so good.

He said, "Do you mind if I take a shower before dinner? I want to get out of these clothes."

Venice told him that it was fine and he went into the bedroom. Venice was curious to know if Craig was checking his messages. If so, would he fess up? This was going to be a test. Venice set the table for dinner. In a few minutes, Craig came back into the kitchen. He hadn't showered yet but he had this confused look on his face.

Venice asked, "What's wrong?"

"Nothing's wrong. I had a message from my old girl on the answering machine. She's coming to town for homecoming and for some reason, she thinks we can hook up."

"Oh really?"

"Venice, Miranda is in the past," Craig stated reassuringly. "She's not the nicest person and she can't show up thinking she's going to get with me. You don't have to worry about that."

Venice responded with, "After what I did to you, I couldn't really blame you if you wanted to."

Craig jumped up from his seat, pulled her to him, and said, "Look, Venice, I thought we said we'd let that go. I don't want to hear anything else about that. Okay? I'm not a revengeful person and I wouldn't dare do anything like that just to get back at you. Do you hear me?"

"Whatever you say. I just don't want to be mixed up in any drama this week, that's all."

Craig pulled Venice closer to him and told her not to worry. He gave her a kiss on the forehead and said he was going to hit the showers.

Venice felt a little better, but she remembered what Galen had told her about this chick. He said she was a control freak. Venice decided to stay calm and occupy her mind with homecoming. Craig got out of the shower and told Venice he was going to call Miranda back and let her know that he already had plans. He called the number back as Venice sat at the kitchen table. Venice asked if he would like some privacy and he told her she didn't have to leave the room.

The woman on the other line answered the telephone. Craig told her that he'd received her message. He went on to tell her that it was nice she was going to get to come for homecoming. However, he already had plans with someone else and wouldn't be able to hook up with her. From the look on his face, Miranda didn't take the news too well.

Craig said, "Why are you tripping like that? I thought you would've matured a little by now. I guess I was wrong."

Venice could tell Craig was beginning to get pissed off.

"Well, Miranda, I see we still can't be cordial with each other, even after all this time, but I'm not surprised." Craig paused, then continued, "Miranda, I don't want to argue with you anymore. This just proves that we were never meant to be and the best thing we ever did was calling it quits. Look, I hope you have a great time for homecoming."

After that statement, Craig held the telephone down and shook his head. He put it back up to his ear and said, "Well, she hung up. Now maybe she's finally gotten the message." He hung up the phone. "Miranda is crazy. She's spoiled and she's selfish. Venice, I don't want to talk about her anymore. Let's eat."

Venice and Craig sat down and forgot all about the previous scene. Actually, they went on as if the telephone call never happened. Venice felt slightly better and less threatened by Miranda. Craig was apparently no longer under Miranda's control.

After dinner was over and the kitchen was clean, Craig asked Venice what was on the homecoming agenda for the night.

Venice said, "I think tonight is the frat and sorority auction."

"Want to go watch it, Venice?"

"Not particularly. Those auctions are okay but I heard they get wild after a while. Some of the boyfriends and girlfriends just can't handle their significant others going out with other people. But, if you want to go, we can check it out."

"No, we don't have to. I'd rather wait for the concert tomorrow night."

"That's fine with me. By the way, I've already bought the tickets to the show. It's my treat!"

"Now, why'd you do that? I wanted to treat you to the show."

"Well, next time it's your treat."

They continued to talk as they watched TV. Craig asked Venice if she played backgammon. She told him she was an average player, so they went down into the rec room and played a few games. It was beginning to get late and they both had classes the next morning so they decided to call it a night. Venice showered, then went to bed. Craig told her goodnight. He was going to be up a while studying. He went downstairs so he wouldn't disturb her. Venice turned in for the night and fell asleep before her head hit the pillow.

As morning came, Venice realized that Craig had been up all night working on some drawings. Or, was he avoiding her. Venice wondered if Craig still wasn't ready to get with her; especially after she had been with Jarvis.

It was seven a.m. and Venice's first class was at eight. She told Craig good morning and hurried into the shower. Craig had one class, which wasn't until one o'clock.

As Venice dressed, she told him to try and get some rest before his class. She gave him a kiss and told him she would see him around four o'clock. Venice wanted to go to her room to call Galen, but she didn't have time.

Craig said, "I'm going to lie down for a few hours before class. I'll see you this evening."

Once Venice left, Craig said, "Damn, I've got to get over this Jarvis situation."

Venice's classes that day seemed short. Everyone, even the professors, were caught up in the homecoming spirit. The campus was decorated throughout with the school colors. Everybody was buzzing about the concert that night featuring Tamia, Levert, and the O'Jays. It was a cool day and the game Saturday night would probably be very cold. Venice had to decide what she was going to wear. Chanelle had left a message on her answering machine about going shopping. Venice called her back and told her to meet her in the lobby at two o'clock so they could go to the mall. When Chanelle entered the lobby, she had a funny look on her face.

Venice asked, "What's wrong with you, Chanelle?"

"Let's go. I'm kind of tired so I want to get back and take a nap before the show."

Venice noticed Chanelle was a little short with her. When they got in Venice's car, she asked again, "Chanelle, what's wrong? Is everything okay?"

Chanelle put her hand on Venice's hand to prevent her from starting the car. "Venice, I'm late for my period."

Venice didn't know what to say as Chanelle burst into tears. "I can't eat, I can't sleep, and when Jeremy called me today, I almost started crying."

Venice tried to remain calm. "Have you thought about buying a home pregnancy test?"

"I'm too scared! In a way, I want to know and in a way, I don't want to know. Venice, what am I going to do!"

"Does Spoonie know?"

"No way!"

"Don't worry, Chanelle. Everything's going to work out. I really believe you're fine, but you can't get yourself upset like this. You're throwing your body chemistry off."

Chanelle agreed and the two left for the mall. When they got there, they got their minds off the problem and ended up having fun picking out homecoming outfits. Venice told Chanelle she wanted something new to wear to the concert also, but couldn't decide if she wanted a skirt or pants.

Chanelle thought it would be nice to wear a long skirt outfit for the concert and then get a pants outfit for the game. Venice was feeling the suggestion and picked out a straight skirt with a sheer overlay. It was a beautiful red with a short jacket. Venice already had shoes to match the outfit so that would save her a little money.

Chanelle picked out a short set with a double-breasted jacket. It was gray with the white pin stripes. Chanelle's muscular legs would definitely compliment the outfit with gray pantyhose and shoes.

The two friends continued through the mall before deciding to stop for a snack. They both ordered pizza and Coke.

Once they sat down, Venice said, "Chanelle, no matter how this turns out, don't look down on yourself. Accidents happen and I know you didn't mean for it to go down like this."

"I know. I'm just going to have to pray about it and leave it in the hands of the Lord. I'll tell you this. If I'm able to get out of this crisis, I won't ever take that kind of chance again. Oh, Venice! Jarvis called me last night."

"What did he want?"

"You."

"What did he say?"

"He said he feels like he's losing you and he doesn't know how to deal with it. He asked me if you were serious about Craig."

"What did you tell him?"

"I told him that I didn't want to get in the middle of this, but that I do know that you love him and miss him."

Venice grew sad. "What did he say?"

"He said that he didn't know what he would do if he lost you. He realizes you like Craig, but doesn't know how serious it is."

"I really need to see him, Chanelle. He's my heart and I love him so much. I don't want to lose him either. I can't help it that Craig is so nice. This whole situation is a trip, but I can't see Jarvis like I want to. He said he understood."

Chanelle said, "Venice, he probably said he understood, but his heart doesn't. I don't want to see any of you hurt, but this love triangle is eventually going to fall apart. I hate to see who's left standing. Craig must be hitting it correctly, because I've never seen you confused about Jarvis before."

"Chanelle, it's not about the sex. Craig's just wonderful."

They held each other's hand for a moment, then decided it was time to go.

Nineteen

It was concert night. Venice and Craig arrived early enough to get great seats. Craig knew Tamia was going to be looking good and Venice knew that Levert was going to have it going on also.

The concert lasted about three hours and then sadly it was over. A lot of the concertgoers were headed to after parties, but Venice and Craig decided to go out for drinks and then head back home since it was a school night.

They went to a local restaurant and ordered appetizers and drinks. Galen and Sidney came in later. Craig invited them to join their table. After eating and sharing many laughs together, Galen and Sidney had to leave so that he could make curfew. Venice and Craig also decided it was time to go.

They arrived back at the house at about eleven-thirty. Craig, once again, told Venice he had a few more drawings to work on before morning. She solemnly told him goodnight and went into the bathroom to get ready for bed. Craig lit candles around the room so that he didn't have to turn on bright lights that might disturb her sleep. His drawing table had a small lamp on it so he wouldn't have to strain his eyes. He had another drawing table downstairs, but preferred to stay close to her.

When Venice reentered the room after taking her shower and saw the candles, she thought they gave the room a nice relaxing mood and the aroma was breathtaking. Craig had put on some soft jazz, which he liked to work by.

Venice expressed how much she liked the candles. "I love the candles. Just make sure you don't fall asleep before blowing them out."

"You're right, or it'll really be hot up in here."

They both laughed and Venice retired to bed, leaving Craig up to work.

"Is the music too loud?"

"No, it's just right. Thanks for asking."

It wasn't long before Venice drifted off to sleep.

It was about one forty-five when Venice woke for no apparent reason. She opened her eyes to discover Craig on the computer with his back to her. She eased out of the bed and slowly crept toward him. Craig didn't realize she was there until she draped her arms around his neck and kissed it. He stopped working and pulled her around in front of him.

Venice straddled his lap and asked, "What are you doing up?"

Craig wrapped his strong arms around her body and gave her a kiss on the neck. She began massaging his shoulders and said, "It's late. Don't you think you need to get some sleep? I miss you."

Craig looked into her desire-filled eyes, then traced his finger up her thigh. He laid his head against her chest and let out a deep breath. Venice could tell he was tired so she continued to gently massage his neck and shoulders as she felt his hands roam over her soft body. The heat she felt was so intense, she started to perspire. She looked into his eyes and, without saying a word, he started unsnapping her shirt. Once he opened her shirt and revealed the picturesque body he'd missed, he kissed her, then hungrily took her nipple into his mouth. Venice closed her eyes and shivered to the dance of his tongue around her swollen nubs. Venice tightened her grip as he ran his hands and mouth over her entire body. Getting up from the chair, he carried her over to the bed and laid down upon her. They looked into each other's eyes for a moment.

Craig said, "Taylor, you feel wonderful, baby. I've missed you."

"I've missed you missing me."

"I'm leaving it in the past, Taylor."

Venice saw the desire in his eyes and knew in her heart, this man loved her.

With her arms around his neck, she licked his earlobe and whispered, "Come on, baby."

"Hold that thought."

Reaching into his nightstand, he pulled out a foil package to protect her. He crawled back over to her and once again ran his tongue over her entire body. Venice felt extremely relaxed. She arched her back when Craig's tongue played with her navel. Finally, he pushed her thighs apart with his knee and positioned himself above her. His dark gaze met hers again as he covered her lips with his. She began to breathe heavier and felt her heart pounding in her chest as Craig slowly began to push himself deep into her.

It had been a long awaited pleasure, so he made sure he took it slow as he entered into her moist body. She wrapped her legs around his tight physique as he began to push his body in and out of hers. Venice moaned even louder as his breathing got heavier. The dark, curly hair on his chest was no match for Venice's tongue as she licked at his nipples. He sucked in air when the warm tip of her tongue met his chest.

Craig rolled over and positioned her above him as he moved his hands underneath her, stroking her softly and intimately. His strong hands pulled her even tighter to him as his fingers danced in and out of her love. When Venice sat on top of him, their gazes locked on each other momentarily.

"Taylor, I-I want...I need you so bad."

"Sh-h-h, just make love to me, baby."

Craig rolled her over on her back and kissed her with his probing tongue; tasting, exploring. Venice met his thrusts. They became more intense each time he pushed in and out of her trembling body. Craig gripped her hips tightly and began to call out her name. First in whispers, then in screams.

"Venice...Baby! Oh! Venice!"

Craig buried his face into her neck as he shuddered to a halt inside her warm thighs. Salty tears ran down her cheeks as he stroked them away while kissing her on the neck, ears, and lastly, her soft lips.

Venice thought that Craig was definitely all that. He made love to her so powerfully, yet tenderly, which made her body feel like it was on fire. She pulled him tightly to her and buried her face into his warm neck. She could still smell the masculine scent he'd showered with earlier mixed with the scent of their love and it was heavenly. Venice woke up a couple of hours later and laid there watching Craig sleep. She realized that she'd almost lost him after her rendezvous with Jarvis. She was still unsure about which one of them she really wanted to be with. She realized many men wouldn't want a woman who'd slept with another man. Especially, if they weren't seeing anyone else on the side. For a moment, she wondered what Jarvis might be doing.

Venice was awakened by Craig stroking her lower back in the morning. She was lying on her stomach, but she soon turned to face him.

He gave her a morning breath kiss. "Good morning."

"Good morning to you, Bennett."

"Nice tattoo."

Venice really didn't know how to respond, except to say, "Thanks. Looks like we're going to be late for class."

Craig remained motionless. "I can't believe you have his name tattooed on your body. You must…really…never mind."

Craig got up out the bed and went into the bathroom to shower. Venice could see that the tattoo had shaken him up a little bit. She waited for him to come out and said, "Craig…I don't want to have to keep on explaining my relationship with Jarvis to you. I told you what was up and I still want to be with you."

Craig looked at her without emotion. "We really need to get to class."

She showered and got dressed, but before they left the house, he pulled her close and said, "I'm sorry I was trippin' earlier. That tattoo just caught me off guard. I didn't see it the last time we were together. I'm sorry."

"You don't have to apologize. I should've told you about the tattoo. I forget it's there."

"Forget it, Venice. Just don't take too long getting back over here this evening."

"Why? You gonna have something for me?"

He smiled as he pulled her to his body and whispered in her ear, "I love you, Venice LaShawn Taylor."

Venice blushed. "I love you too, Bennett. I'll see you later."

Before letting her go, he gave her a kiss, licking her bottom lip before his tongue dove in. Venice felt lightheaded as he finally took his lips off hers. She had to steady herself for a moment before realizing that he'd actually taken her breath away.

"Are you all right, Venice?"

"Of course not! You just took my breath away...in more ways than one."

"You took my breath away the moment I laid eyes on you."

Their embraced lingered in silence as they stared into each other's eyes. Craig felt himself growing as his body pressed firmly against hers.

Finally, he said, "We'd better go before we start something we'll have to finish and we really don't need to miss class."

"I know you'll give me a rain check."

"Unlimited supply, Taylor. Unlimited."

It was hard to release her embrace, but somehow she managed. They left off in separate cars to class...late.

As Venice drove to campus, she called Chanelle on her cell phone. After two rings, Chanelle answered, "Hello."

"Hey, girl, how are you feeling?"

"I'm okay. My first class isn't until nine-thirty. What time is it now?"

Venice glanced at her watch. "It's about seven-fifty."

Chanelle asked, "Aren't you going to be late for your class?"

"Yeah, girl, but I don't care!"

"So I guess you had a good night."

"Yes, ma'am! I can hardly walk."

"Dang! My man Jarvis has some serious competition."

"Don't say that, Chanelle."

"Why not? It's true. You don't know which one you want."

"Girl, you know I'm in love with Jarvis. But, Craig takes my breath away. I love him, but it's a different love. It's hard to describe."

"I feel you, girlfriend, and I'm happy for you. I think you two look great together, but be careful. I hope everything works out for you guys. If not, that's cool also because you know Jarvis is my boy."

They talked a few more minutes, then Venice told Chanelle to meet her in the campus courtyard for lunch. Chanelle agreed and they hung up.

Venice finally made it to class and eased into her seat. Luckily, the professor was writing on the board when she came in. This professor was famous for embarrassing students entering class late. By the clock on the wall, Venice was approximately ten minutes late. The professor gave his students fifteen minutes flextime before they were counted absent. One of her classmates, Tim, slid his notes over so Venice could copy what she'd missed. The rest of class went on without any problem. Her mind couldn't help but backtrack to the previous erotic night. She didn't want to tell Chanelle, but she really did have stronger feelings for Craig than she let on. She couldn't get him off her mind and when the professor finally called on her, she was lost in her daydream. After a nudge from Tim, Venice snapped back to reality and luckily answered the question correctly. At the end of class, the professor announced that even though it was homecoming week, the campus didn't shut down. They would be having a quiz during the next class on the previous three chapters covered. The class let out a disappointing moan.

Venice told Tim, "I'm glad he gave us a warning. The last thing I wanted to do this week was get caught by a pop quiz."

"Me, too. You better be glad he didn't see you come in late. I'm going to the library to study later. You wanna meet me?"

"What time?"

"About three."

"I'll try but if I'm not there by three-thirty, I probably won't make it. I'm going to the ball tonight. Are you going?"

"If you'll be there, I'll be there. Hope to see you in the library, but I'll definitely see you in class."

Tim winked at her and walked off.

When Venice reached her last class, she sat next to Tim as always. They were in the same major, Sports Medicine.

Venice asked, "So have you made up your mind about the ball?"

"I might go. Are you asking me to go with you?"

"Not this time. I'm hanging with my girls tonight."

"How are you going to get away from Mr. Perfect that I see you around campus with?"

"Ha, ha. You're funny. He understands that I want to hang out with my girls for a while during homecoming."

"Sure he does. I bet he already has you on lockdown. Especially if you've broken him off a little something, something."

They laughed together and Venice punched him lightly on the arm. "You sure are silly!"

About that time, the professor began calling the roll.

With classes over for the day, Venice headed back to her room to get the itinerary together with her girls. Monique was in the room with several bags of new clothing on her bed. As Venice put her book bag down, Monique came into the room modeling a "sharp" evening dress with a back so low, Venice was surprised you couldn't see the crack of her ass.

"Damn, Monique, that's a sharp dress! Where did you find it?"

"If I tell you, I'll have to kill you. I don't tell my secrets."

Venice giggled. "What Cake Daddy bought it for you?"

"You think you know me! Anyway, I can't reveal my sources!"

"That color really looks good on you, Monique. You go, girl!"

The dress was a beautiful silver, slinky dress, which revealed just enough and left the rest to the imagination. The dress was made for Monique's tall figure.

Later that evening, Craig called Venice from the lobby of the dorm. She met him downstairs and they sat on one of the sofas to talk.

"Venice, I know I asked you to come back over this evening. I forgot you wanted to go to the ball with your girls."

Venice smiled and put her hand on his thigh. "Baby, you made me forget everything after that loving you put on me."

Craig blushed. "You haven't seen anything yet. I've been holding back."

Venice closed her eyes and said, "My God! What are you trying to do to me?"

"You'll find out. Anyway, have a good time with your partners. I hope you have fun. The frat ball is usually the best one out of all the others. Am I going to see you tonight?"

"I'm not sure yet. It depends on who's driving and how tired I am. I know I have a ten o'clock class tomorrow. I'll give you a call when I find out what I'm going to do. Is that cool with you?"

Craig gave Venice a playful shove. "You know that's cool with me. I'm having some of the guys over for a card party tonight, but I still want to see you. Galen said he might try to sneak out after curfew so he can play. I know Spoonie and Skeeter will be there. Anyway, make sure you ladies take pictures so I can see how nice you look in your dresses."

Venice agreed and told Craig to have fun playing cards. Then she said, "Well, I'd better go so I can stop by and see if Chanelle is still going."

"Why wouldn't she go? Is she okay? I haven't talked to Spoonie lately. How are they doing?"

Venice rose from the sofa. "She likes him. They seem to be getting along fine."

"That's good. I thought they'd hit if off. Well, I'm out! Be careful tonight and make sure you have a designated driver. If you need a ride, give me a call and I'll come get you."

Venice walked him to the door. "Drive carefully and I'll talk to you later."

"You call me when you know what you're going to do? I really do want to see you tonight."

"Me, too. I'll work it out."

"That's a bet."

After giving Craig a kiss, Venice watched him walk out to the parking lot. So did a group of women walking toward the dorm. Venice smiled with pride.

After the elevator doors opened, she made her way down to Chanelle's room. As she knocked, Chanelle's neighbor came out of her room and looked her up and down.

Venice asked, "Do you have a problem?"

The girl laughed and said, "No!"

"Well you need to keep your eyes to yourself."

The girl walked off. "You can't tell me what to do and you better watch your man."

Venice was fuming as Chanelle opened the door and let her in. Chanelle looked flushed and saddened.

Venice asked, "Girl, who is that fool across the hall? I started to smack that heifer silly. I thought you were going to meet me in the courtyard."

Chanelle was only half-listening. "What did she do?"

"She was just staring at me and walked off, telling me to watch my man."

Chanelle laid on the bed. "What did she mean by that?"

Venice angrily said, "Chanelle, I don't know. She must want him! I've never noticed her before."

"Don't worry about that fool. You know Craig ain't fooling around."

Venice sat on the bed beside her. "Whatever! He's a man and you know how they act when women throw tail at them."

"Venice, don't you let that skank start putting suspicion and doubt in your head. Craig doesn't seem to me like he would even touch anything looking like her."

Venice asked, "Where's your roommate?"

"I guess she's still in class. She sure is weird. I try to make conversation with her, but she just talks when she has to. She usually just sits around staring."

"Seems to me like your girl's got issues. Now, get up off that bed and show me what you're wearing tonight!"

Chanelle rolled over and said, "Venice, I don't feel like going."

Venice pulled Chanelle up off the bed. "Oh, no you don't! You're not going to lay around in this room tonight. You know we all planned to go together tonight and you can't say you don't have anything to wear. So get up off your booty and you'd better be ready by seven o'clock."

"Okay, okay, but I still haven't come on yet and Spoonie can tell something's wrong. I've been avoiding him a little."

"Don't do the man like that! You need to try to act normal or tell the man what's wrong. Chanelle, you know I feel your pain. Remember, I've been through this before myself. It's scary but just hang in there."

The two friends hugged.

"Thanks for the support, Venice. I'll try to pep up and I will be ready by seven."

"You'd better be," Venice said teasingly.

Venice left to head back to her room. She stood in the hallway for a moment and thought about the loss of her baby. She said a short prayer for her friend and walked to the elevator.

It was about six o'clock when the telephone rang. Venice answered the phone and was delighted that it was her mother.

"Hello, baby!"

"Hi, Momma! How are you?"

"Oh, I guess I'm okay. My arthritis has been acting up a bit, but I rubbed some of my special ointment on and I feel much better."

Venice asked about her father and Bryan and his family. Her mother told her all was well. She did mention that her dad finally got up on Sundays and went to church with her. It had been years since her father attended church. Venice never asked why. It was a subject nobody touched. Her mom went on to tell her that Crimson had spent the previous weekend with them because Bryan and Sinclair had some high society dinner to attend.

Venice asked, "Did Crimson act like she had some home training?"

"You know, she doesn't act like that until Bryan and Sinclair come around. So how are your classes coming along? Are you getting enough to eat?"

"Yes, Momma. I'm having a good time. My classes are good and I'm getting plenty to eat."

"Galen told me you've been dating a friend of his."

Damn traitor!

Venice almost swallowed her tongue. "Yes, Momma. His name is Craig Bennett."

"Do you like him?"

Venice was totally unprepared for the question. "Yes, he's very nice. He's a junior studying architecture."

Her mother continued the cross examination. "I was wondering why you haven't mentioned him to me?"

"I didn't do it on purpose, Momma. We haven't been seeing each other long."

"Mmmm. Well, all I'm going to say is remember what I told you. Don't be down there acting like you don't have any sense and you know what I mean."

Venice recognized her mother's way of beating around the bush with sex talk.

"Don't bring any more babies to this house before you're married. You hear me? Venice, I don't mean to upset you, but it really hurt your father and I when you got pregnant so young. We tried our best to raise you kids up in the church as best we could. We wanted you to learn right from wrong, but some times I feel like we should've done more. I should've known you were having sex with Jarvis when you two stopped arguing with each other all the time. You couldn't stand to be in the same room with him one minute, then before we could turn around, ya'll were going out. We've been friends with his parents for a long time, so when that happened, none of us were prepared for it. Anyway, that's water under the bridge now. At least Sinclair tried by getting you on birth control. I still can't believe you didn't come to me though. Anyway, Jarvis is still your husband in the eyes of God. I'm just sorry we had to do the right thing legally and have ya'll get a divorce. It was for the best, Venice, and I pray every night that you two remarry after graduation. I know there's true love between you and there's nothing stronger than true love. But if you like this young man, I can live with that, too."

"I hear you, Momma."

"So, have you heard from Jarvis?"

"We keep in touch."

"Well, tell him hello the next time you talk to him. I'm going to let you go. Tell your brother to call home some time. I know he ain't playing football twenty-four hours a day and ya'll better be going to church down there. Tell him his picture was in the paper the other week. I added it to his scrapbook."

"Okay, Momma."

Venice told her mother that she would deliver the message and that she would talk to her the coming weekend.

Twenty

Venice got up from a quick nap and started to get ready for the ball. Monique had already finished her shower, so Venice gathered up her towel and robe and entered the bathroom. As the warm water hit her body, she thought of her night with Craig and the upcoming party. Venice was using a fragrant body wash to give her skin a smooth texture. She wanted to make sure she had it "going on."

Once everyone was dressed, they loaded up into Monique's car and headed to the convention hall. Frat brothers were giving each lady a beautiful yellow rose as they entered. Venice caught the eye of several men. Her black dress showed elegance and style and she wore it well. Monique, however, was the show stopper. Her opened back dress was as sexy as she was and she utilized her "Miss Thang" stroll as she navigated the room. As usual, Monique spent the majority of the night on the dance floor while Chanelle and Venice found themselves being picked up by a couple of seniors. Chanelle wasn't really in the mood. She was preoccupied on her situation.

Spoonie walked in and approached their table. He pushed his way through, grabbed Chanelle by the arm, and whispered into her ear.

The seniors didn't like this and said, "Hey, man, these ladies are with us."

Venice and Chanelle looked at them with disbelief. Venice said, "No, we're not! We were just talking."

Then one of the guys said, "Freshmen! Man, let's go! They ain't nothing but some little rudy poots anyway."

Spoonie ignored them and Chanelle got up from her chair to follow Spoonie over to the side.

Spoonie came dressed for the occasion. He had on a very nice suit with a collar less shirt. As he and Chanelle talked, Venice noticed Chanelle getting agitated. She wondered if she should step in. When she was about to, a young man asked her to dance. She accepted his offer but kept her eye on Chanelle and Spoonie who were now sitting down at the table. The young man Venice was dancing with was trying to have a conversation with her, but she wasn't paying much attention to what he was saying. At the end of the song, she thanked him and he tried to get her telephone number. Venice told him that he was nice, but she was already involved with someone. The young man told her that if she every got tired of her man to look him up.

Venice giggled and thanked him for the dance again.

When Venice returned to the table, Chanelle was crying.

Venice said, "Spoonie, give me and Chanelle a minute, okay?"

Spoonie was obviously disgusted as he got up. "I'm going to get something to eat. Be right back."

Venice sat down and asked Chanelle, "Girl, did you tell the man what's up?"

"Venice, I just can't. I'm scared."

"I know you're scared, but you don't need to keep this from him. He has a right to know why you're tripping."

"I'm going to tell him, but I want you to be there. Okay?"

"I'll be with you. Now let's get Spoonie and go sit down somewhere a little quieter and talk."

The two women located Spoonie talking to Monique. They went out into the hallway and found a window seat.

Spoonie said, "Okay, now will somebody tell me what's up?"

Chanelle said, "Spoonie, I'm sorry for the way I've been acting, but I've been under a lot of stress lately with my classes and other stuff."

"We've all been under stress before but, Chanelle, you've been really tripping for a while now."

Venice could tell that Chanelle was still beating around the bush, but Spoonie wasn't going to be satisfied until he had answers. Chanelle looked at Venice as if to give her the "go ahead" to take over the conversation.

Venice said, "Spoonie, it's not Chanelle's fault for the way she's been acting. She's been upset lately because..."

Then Chanelle blurted out, "Spoonie, my period's late."

Spoonie's head dropped at that point. "How late?"

Chanelle dropped her head into her hands and cried. "Five weeks."

Spoonie put his arm around her and pulled her over onto his shoulder to comfort her. "Chanelle, don't cry. Everything's going to be all right. Have you taken one of those tests or seen a doctor?"

Chanelle couldn't respond so Venice said, "No, she's too afraid. I told her that she should tell you what's going on, but I understand how she feels."

Spoonie said, "Chanelle, baby, you should've told me. I'm not going to let you go through this all by yourself. Remember, I was also there."

Chanelle was beginning to slightly calm down. Spoonie wiped her tears with some tissue and looked at Venice. "Look, I'm going to take Chanelle with me so we can figure out what to do. Chanelle, do you want to go somewhere so we can talk?"

"Yes, I don't feel like being here right now. Venice, I'm sorry I got you into this, but thanks for being there, girl."

"You know you're my girl."

Venice and Chanelle hugged and Spoonie gave Venice his pager number so she could check on Chanelle later.

Venice told her, "Homegirl, don't you worry about a thing. You're going to be all right." Chanelle smiled and reached out for Spoonie's hand as he led her out the door. Venice felt a lot of pressure rise off her shoulders. She said a little prayer for Chanelle, tucked the pager number into her purse, and went back into the dance.

It was about 1:30 a.m. and Venice was buzzing from all the punch she'd consumed. She realized that she had a 10 a.m. class later that day. Monique was still "kicking it" on the dance floor. Venice danced a few more times, then decided to sit down because she was starting to buzz a little. Just as she sat down, someone put their hands over her eyes from behind.

"Guess who?" the voice said.

Venice wasn't quite sure who it was. She could tell it was a man trying to disguise his voice. Venice pulled the hands off her eyes and turned to find Tim.

He shouted, "Hey! What's up, dogg?"

Venice jumped up and gave him a big hug. "Nothing much. How long have you been here?"

"About a hour. Where have you been?"

"Oh, I've been walking around and I've been on the dance floor also, but I'm getting a little tired now."

"Don't even try it. Don't think you're going to get out of dancing with me! You need to lay off that punch though. You know it's spiked with vodka. That's a "flyy" dress you're wearing. You mean your old man let you out looking that sexy? He's a fool!"

Venice laughed and grabbed him by the arm. "You're so silly! Anyway, I can wear what I want. Craig isn't the boss of me."

Tim led her to the dance floor and said, "There's no way I would've turned my woman loose in a den of wolves looking that damn good!"

Venice yanked his arm and began to slow dance with him. "Mind your business! Damn, I'm buzzing!"

Anyone could tell that Tim had a thing for Venice. He was, however, merely a good friend to her. Since they shared classes, they spent a lot of time studying together and working on class projects. Occasionally, they went out for lunch or dinner. Craig was cool with their relationship, but he also could tell Tim had a crush on Venice. Venice really did enjoy Tim's company. He was funny, nice, and kind of cute. But, her heart and mind were far from looking at him in any way besides friendship. Besides, Tim had a girlfriend. A crazy one at that.

When they finished their dance, Venice went over to tell Monique that she was ready to go. Monique wasn't ready. Venice let her know that Chanelle had left with Spoonie and then issued directions. "Monique, don't wander off with any strangers. You make sure you get someone you know to walk you to the car and don't drive if you've had too much to drink, okay? I know I've had too much."

Monique answered with, "Okay, Momma!

"I'm not playing, Monique!"

Monique pouted. "I'm sorry, Venice. I'm just messing with you. I'll be careful and you watch that closet freak you're leaving with. He ain't fooling nobody. You know he wants to get in your drawers."

Venice snickered. "You are so silly. I'll page you when I get to the room. Don't forget you have classes today. See ya."

As Tim escorted Venice into the parking lot to his car, he told her that he was glad he'd run into her.

Venice said, "Where is your crazy girlfriend anyway?"

"She said she had a test tomorrow and was going to stay in and study. That was cool with me. It gave me a chance to get out. But, I didn't expect you to arrive without your man."

Tim drove out the parking lot and made his way toward the interstate.

Venice answered him. "I told you earlier today that this was girls night out. Anyway, Craig's having a card party at his house."

"No wonder. His major is tough. It helps to relax and take the stress off. Playing cards is fun. He's going to be banking big dollars in a few years."

"I guess."

Tim adjusted his CD player and Venice started singing out loud to the music.

He could see that she'd had a little too much to drink, but she had a nice voice. She decided to page Spoonie. It was only a couple of minutes later when her cell phone rang.

"Hello?"

"Venice, Chanelle feels a lot better now. Thanks."

"Good! Tim is giving me a ride back to campus because Monique wasn't ready to go. u take care of my girl."

"Don't worry. I will. She wants to talk to you. She's right here. Hold on."

Spoonie handed the telephone to Chanelle.

"Hello?"

"Girl, are you okay? Where are you?"

"I'm fine. Just a little tired. We're over Spoonie's uncle's house. I decided that I'm going to at least take a home pregnancy test in the morning. Spoonie bought it on our way over here. I'm not going to my first class tomorrow. I did stop by my room to get some clothes for the night. I also decided that I'm going to tell Jeremy that I think we need to call it quits for now. I just can't handle a long distance relationship right now."

"Well, whatever you decide to do, I'm with you, girl. You make sure you get in touch with me later."

"Okay, and Venice, say a little prayer for me tonight."

"I've already taken care of that. Get you some rest. See you."

As soon as she hung up the phone, it rang again.

Craig was on the other line. "Where are you?"

"Can't you say hello first? Well, if you must know, I'm in the company of a very handsome young man."

Craig's voice was filled with curiosity. "Who?"

Venice and Tim both fell out laughing. "I'm with my other man."

"Quit playing, Venice. Who's with you?"

"Tim is giving me a ride back to the dorm because my "freak-a-zoid" roommate wasn't ready to go."

"Let me holler at Tim for a second."

"Why?"

Craig said sternly, "Give the man the phone, Venice!"

Venice giggled and gave Tim the phone. He looked surprised. "What's up Craig?"

The conversation went on and on with Tim describing that Venice was buzzing.

Venice stared at him and hollered out, " I'm not drunk!"

Tim said, "Man, she's messed up!"

There was a pause in their conversation, then Tim said, "All right, peace!"

Tim laughed and handed the phone back to Venice.

"Hello?"

"What time is your first class?"

"Ten o'clock. Why?"

"Because I told Tim to bring your drunk tail over here. That's why."

Venice had this "No you didn't" look on her face, but could not help but blush. "Well, I guess that's that, huh?"

Craig didn't appreciate her sarcastic tone. "Venice, I'm going to look over your sarcasm because I know it's the liquor talking. I'll see you in a minute."

Venice hung up the phone and leered at Tim. "Can you believe that shit? I mean Craig's my boo, but damn!"

"You know you like that shit, Venice. That man didn't mean anything by it. He's just looking out for your ass. You women always make a big deal out of nothing."

"You just drive. Hell, when did you get your Ph.D. in relationships?"

Tim laughed as he turned onto Craig's street. When he pulled into the driveway, they could see Craig sitting on the steps sipping on a soda. It was about two-fifteen.

Craig came out to the car to greet them. Tim got out the car, shook Craig's hand, and dropped the hint that Venice was trippin' about the way he handled her.

Venice laughed at Tim. "Thanks for the ride. How much do I owe you?"

She gave him a hug and kiss.

Tim said, "Go on somewhere, girl! I'll see you in class and you better not skip it."

Craig was standing there looking at Venice. She was obviously drunk.

She said her good-byes to Tim again, then walked over to Craig and put her arms around him. "Hey, baby! You sure are looking fine as hell!"

He softly said, "Go on inside, Venice."

She giggled. "You hurry up and get your butt in here. I've got something for you."

Venice left them standing in the driveway and she entered the house. Craig shook his head and Tim burst out laughing.

Craig grinned. "Man, that ain't funny. She's trippin'."

Tim continued to laugh. "I know you're going to have fun tonight."

"Go 'head on with that, man. I'm not messing with her tonight."

Tim got into the car and said, "Yeah, right! You know drunk sex is the bomb. The freak comes out in them."

Craig waved him off and chuckled. "Whatever. Thanks again for driving her over."

Venice came out of the bathroom and sat on the bed and kicked her shoes off as Craig entered the house. She turned over and laid down on the bed.

Craig sat down next to her and angrily said, "Venice, have you lost your mind? You better not ever drink like that when you're out again! The next thing you know, somebody's going to try and push up on you or something and make me have to hurt them."

He turned her over to face him and addressed her sternly. "Don't do it again!"

Venice gazed up at him. "Okay. I'm sorry, baby. Just make the room stop spinning."

"Your butt's going to be sick as hell in the morning. That's what you get."

Venice was buzzing so much all she could do was mumble.

Craig calmed slightly and looked her up and down. "You look really nice in your dress."

"Thanks."

He leaned over and began to unzip it for her. Venice rose up and straddled his lap. He held her there and they just stared at each other. She put her arms around his neck and gave him a soft kiss. He rubbed her hips, pulling her closer to him, kissing her on the neck and chest.

She moaned and said, "M-m-m-m, that feels so good."

He finished unzipping her dress and said, "Venice, you'd better get some sleep. You're going to be hung over in the morning."

She ran her hand up his thigh. "Sleep is the last thing I'm thinking about right now."

"Venice, you're gonna make yourself sick if you keep on."

"Damn, Craig! What's up? Do you want to do this or what?"

"Venice, chill, okay?"

Venice got off of his lap and hollered, "You make me sick!"

He jokingly said, "Alcoholic!"

Venice pointed her finger at him. "I hate you."

He laughed at her and said, "I love you, too."

He knew that she was drunk so he did his best to overlook it. At that point, Venice jumped up and ran into the bathroom and threw up. Craig sat there for a minute laughing, then he went in to help her out. After she finished getting sick, he helped her shower and then put her into bed. Venice fell asleep almost instantly. Craig hung her dress up, got into bed, and held onto her the rest of the night

Twenty-One

On Friday morning, Craig quickly got up and headed for the shower when the alarm went off. Venice felt like she'd just gone to sleep and was still out of it.

Craig said, "Come on, Venice. Get up. It's eight o'clock and you have a ten o'clock class."

Venice grumbled. "I'm not going!"

She pulled the covers over her head but Craig pulled them right back off. "Oh, yes you are! You're not going to skip class today. Now get up!"

Venice had never been a morning person, so she stumbled her way into the bathroom feeling extremely sick.

Craig teased her. "I thought you could hang with the big dogs. I guess this means you're not going to party tonight."

Venice shouted back, "Leave me alone!"

Craig laughed and said, "I told you, you shouldn't have been drinking."

By the time Venice exited the bathroom, Craig was already dressed. She started putting on her clothes and lashed out at him. "I can't stand you."

Craig just laughed and replied, "Don't get mad at me. It's not my fault. You shouldn't have been drinking."

Venice licked her tongue out at him and put on a pair of jeans, a large sweater, and her Nikes. She topped everything off with a Dawson University baseball hat.

"Let's go!" Venice told Craig in a grumpy tone.

Craig laughed because Venice would undoubtedly be sick all day. As they walked to the garage, he said, "If you can't hang…"

Venice gave him another nasty look, pulled the cap down on

her head, and put on her sunglasses. They climbed into the truck and headed for campus.

After they got there and got out of the truck, Craig asked, "Girl, are you going to make it?"

"Just give me a second. I'll be okay."

About that time, Venice ran toward some bushes and threw up again. Craig laughed and got some paper towels out of his truck so that she could wipe her face.

He asked her again, "Are you sure you're going to be okay?"

Venice was still throwing up and when it seemed like it was over, he said, "That's it, Venice. Let me take you to your room so you can go lie down."

"Hold up a minute. I'll be fine. I have to go to this class."

"You can't sit in class like this."

"I need to at least stay for roll call. I'll get to lie down when I get out. I'll catch up with you later."

Craig laughed and asked, "Are you sure? You look terrible."

"Quit laughing. I'll make it. Just walk me to my room so I can get my bag."

He walked her to the room and waited while she gathered her books. Venice almost toppled to the floor. Craig caught her before she fell and said, "Okay, Venice, that's it. Get in the bed and you better not get up until I come back. Understand?"

"Yeah," she replied reluctantly, collapsing on her comforter.

Craig pushed a garbage can over to her bed, in case she felt sick again. He closed the curtains and left quietly.

When the campus clock chimed two o'clock, Venice woke up, not remembering how she got to her room. She had to lay there for a while before it came back to her. She hadn't heard from Chanelle and was a little worried. She'd promised that she was going to contact Venice after she took the home test. After going to the bathroom, the room began to spin again. She checked her answering machine. Most of the messages were for Monique. Venice decided to call Chanelle's room, but there was no answer.

"Now where in the world could she be?"

About then, her pager went off. It was an unknown telephone number. Venice called the number back.

"Hello?"

"Hey, Venice," Chanelle responded from the other end.

"What took you so long to get in touch with me? You said you were going to page me after you took the test."

"Well, after I took the test, it was neither positive or negative. So, Spoonie's uncle has a friend who works at a medical lab. We went down there so I could take a blood test."

"Great! So what happened?"

"I'm not pregnant!"

"Thank God! Are they sure?"

"They're sure. The technician told me to go to the doctor for a checkup since I'm regular every month."

"I'm happy for you, girl. Did Spoonie go with you?"

"Yes, he stayed right with me. I also called Jeremy and told him that we need to chill. I feel so much better now."

"So are you and Spoonie all right?"

"Venice, he's the best thing that's ever happened to me. I was surprised about how compassionate he was. He never acted as if he wanted to run from this. He also apologized to me for being so careless. He told me that he wanted to continue to see me. I enjoy his company very much and I want to be with him. I think that if things would've turned out differently, he still would be there for me."

"Girlfriend, I'm so happy for you. You take care of yourself because you have some needed rest to catch up on. Tell Spoonie hello for me."

"Are you going to any of the parties tonight?"

"Hell no! I'm still sick from last night. Craig was pissed because I drank too much. I couldn't even make it to class, I'm so hung over. I'm waiting on him to come back and pick me up to go back over to his house. I'm sick as a dog!"

"I hope you feel better. I'm going to let you go. Take care."

"You, too. I'll talk to you later."

Venice hung up and fell onto her bed. She looked around the room and could see that Monique did make it back last night. It was strange to see her dress thrown on the floor. She was a neat person and it was unusual to see her treat her clothes that way. Venice figured that she must've been too drunk to hang it up. Venice turned over and drifted back off to sleep.

Galen was at football practice wondering why he hadn't talked to his sister or seen her in a few days. He realized that she was in good hands, but needed confirmation for himself. It would be around five o'clock before he would have the opportunity to call her. That was when the football team went on their dinner break so he'd have to wait. As the team continued to scrimmage, you could hear the band's music in the air. It wasn't long before the coach blew his whistle to let the players know it was dinner time.

Galen was one of the first players to make it to the locker room. He dialed Venice's number. As he waited, he finally heard a sleepy voice say, "Hello?"

"Hey, girl, you napping?"

"Yeah, Galen. What's up?"

"Can't you call a brotha sometime? You seem to be hanging with Craig so much, you've put me down."

"There you go assuming. For your information, I went to the frat party last night with Chanelle and Monique. So... I didn't get in until about two-fifteen. Didn't you go over to Craig's for the card party?"

"Nah... I couldn't make it this time. Did you take care of the anniversary flowers?"

"Yes, I called Sinclair the other day and she's going to get some red and white roses and you owe me half. I had to give that skank my credit card number before she'd do it. I can't wait to tell Bryan!"

"Don't go starting nothing between them. I'll talk to Sinclair. She responds better to me. Look, call me sometime, page me, or something. I almost forgot you were going to school here. Anyway, Sidney wants to borrow some type of suit for an interview. I'm going to feed my face and I'll talk to you later. Peace out!"

Venice hung up the phone. Somehow, she'd been able to hide her sickness from Galen but she still had a major headache. She turned over and went back to sleep.

Venice woke up after hearing movement in the room. She opened her eyes and saw Monique sitting on the bed. Venice sat up and turned on the light. "Monique, are you okay?"

Monique was crying. Venice slowly got out of bed and sat next to her. "What's wrong, Monique?"

Monique refused to answer. She just hugged Venice and started sobbing hysterically. Venice was getting nervous so she let
Monique get her cry on. After a few minutes, Venice tried again.

She calmly asked, "Monique, what's wrong?"

Monique got up, grabbed a Kleenex from the dresser, and sat
back down. "Venice, last night after the party, I gave these two
friends a ride back to campus. Before we got back, they wanted to
get something to eat. One of them suggested that we go eat in one
of their rooms. I agreed since I went in on the food. But when we
got to the room, they started messing with me. You know I'd had a
little to drink so I wasn't thinking clearly."

Venice was starting to get pissed because she sensed something
bad had happened.

Monique went on to say, "Anyway, one of them started kissing
on me and rubbing up against me. They pushed me down on the
bed and before I knew it, they'd taken my underwear off and were-
were…"

Monique burst out sobbing again.

Venice asked, "Monique, what did they do to you?"

"They raped me, Venice…both of them. They made me do
things to them and they said if I didn't, they were going to get some
more guys to come join in."

Venice's hangover seemed to disappear instantly after hearing
this. She was shocked and angry. She jumped up and said, "Son of
a bitch! They raped you! Oh, hell no! I'm calling the police and
campus security!"

Monique jumped up to stop her. "No! It's my fault. I was drinking when I wasn't supposed to and I went up to their room on my
own."

"I don't give a damn! They made you do something you didn't
want to do!" "Venice, it's my word against theirs. Leave it alone
please. I'll know next time. I was stupid."

Venice hugged her and said, "You weren't stupid, Monique. You
were too trusting. I'm here for you. You let me know what you want
to do and I'll stick by you. Okay? You make sure you point them out
to me the next time you see them. You hear me?"

Monique agreed and laid her head on Venice's shoulder. Venice
patted her back and was finally able to get her to sleep.

Twenty-Two

Venice was still upset, but decided to try and find the suit Sidney wanted. She couldn't help but feel sick to her stomach over what happened to Monique. Her headache was coming back, but she felt like she should do something. Whoever did that to her should have to pay.

Monique woke up and Venice asked, "Hey, girl, are you okay?"

"I'll be fine."

"I wonder if it's going to be cold at the parade?"

"Everyone I talked to said it's usually cold in the morning and gets hotter as the day goes on."

Venice pulled out a beautiful black suit.

Monique asked, "Are you wearing that tomorrow?"

"No, Sidney wants to borrow it for an interview."

Monique came over to inspect the suit. "That's a nice suit. Too bad we're not the same size."

The two laughed and then the telephone rang.

Venice was glad to see Monique laughing but she knew she was still hurting inside. Monique answered it and realized it was Craig calling for Venice.

Venice told him she'd see him later and hung up the phone.

"Monique, I'm going over to Craig's. Are you going to be all right?"

"I'll be fine. You go ahead."

"Are you sure, because I don't mind staying here with you."

"Thanks, but I'll be fine. I need some time to think anyway."

Venice went over and put her arm around Monique's shoulder. "If you need me or want to talk, you know where to find me. I don't care what time. Pick up the phone and call."

"I will. Thanks, Venice."

"You're welcome."

"What did you do to that man? He can't stand for you to be out of his sight one minute. He must be addicted to the coochie."

Venice giggled. "Monique, don't make me laugh. My head still hurts. You're so nasty. But for real, girl, are you sure you don't want me to stay?"

"I'm sure. But thanks for offering. So I guess this means you'll be going to the parade with your piece instead of me?"

"If you want me to go with you, I'll come back early in the morning. I can tell Craig to just meet me there."

"No, don't do that. I'll find you guys. Okay?"

"Okay. Peace out!"

Venice went to take her shower so that she could meet Craig.

On the drive over to Craig's, Venice couldn't help but think about what happened to Monique. She'd heard about girls getting date raped, but never thought it would happen to anyone close to her. She found herself getting angry all over again. She wished Monique would do something about it. It would only be a matter of time before they did it to someone else.

When Venice pulled into Craig's driveway, she spotted an unfamiliar car parked in front of the house with D.C. license plates. Since Craig had given her a key to the house, she used it to enter the house through the open garage. When she walked in, she could hear voices coming from the den.

As she walked through the kitchen, she heard him say, "What do you mean, whose child have I been molesting? You're crazy and you need to mind your business and stop listening to all those chickenhead friends of yours."

Venice knew her presence was not known, but was she right to ease drop? She didn't care. She was trying to find out who Craig was arguing with. Could it be? No! Maybe!

A voice then said, "I've barely been gone six months and you've set up house with a baby. Where is she?"

Craig's voice was noticeably tense. "I told you that is none your business. What do you want, Miranda? Why are you here?"

Damn it! It was her!

The female voice said, "You know what I want. I thought

maybe I could stay here with you for old times' sake. I know Bernice goes out of town every year at this time, so what do you say?"

"Miranda, you must be out of your damn mind! Do you remember that you walked out on me? A person only does that to me one time. Now I've moved on. We weren't meant to be together anyway. We have nothing in common and I don't like your attitude. You're selfish and deceitful."

Venice felt weird so she went back out the door and decided to go around to the front door and ring the doorbell. Craig came to door and opened it. He must've been highly agitated because he turned to go back into the den without even saying hello. Venice walked inside and followed behind him. When she entered the room, she saw this preppie looking woman wearing a lavender linen pantsuit. Her nails and hair were professionally done and she had her nose in the air.

She stood up and walked toward Venice, putting her hand out to shake Venice's. "So you must be Craig's little friend. Now, don't you look sweet."

"Have we met?"

Craig grumbled and said, "Venice, this is Miranda. Miranda, Venice."

Venice, not wanting to show she didn't like the meeting, sat her bag down and extended her hand to Miranda's. "Nice to meet you."

"Yes, me and Craig go a ways back. Don't we, baby?"

Miranda eyed Craig like he was her favorite dessert.

Craig said, "Miranda, I'm not your baby and it's time for you to leave."

Venice was getting angry. "Are you visiting for homecoming, Miranda?"

"As a matter of fact, I am."

"Well, I hope you enjoy your visit. Craig, I'm going to start dinner. Miranda, it was nice meeting you."

Miranda reached for her Coach purse and walked toward the front door. "Likewise! Craig, baby, we'll talk later."

Venice was in the kitchen, but she could still hear the conversation.

"Miranda, we don't have anything else to talk about. I wish

you'd go on with your life. I don't want any drama this weekend so don't start any shit! Do you hear me?"

Miranda smiled as she walked to her car. "You know I wouldn't do anything like that."

Craig mumbled, "Like hell you wouldn't."

Miranda got in her car and drove off. Thank goodness she was gone.

Venice was setting the table when Craig entered the kitchen. She didn't want to talk about what had just happened. She was still too sick to her stomach and upset about Monique to worry about it. She was silent and avoided eye contact with Craig. Craig probably assumed that she wanted to question him, but she wasn't up to it. She just wanted to lie down. Venice was content with the way Craig handled the situation, but nevertheless upset that Miranda had the nerve to come over there.

Venice finally said, "Craig, I still don't feel well. I'm going to lie down."

"Are you all right?"

"Not really." Venice paused and then blurted it out. "Look, Craig. Monique told me she was raped last night."

"What? Where? By who?"

"She said she gave these two so-called friends a ride. They stopped to get something to eat and they invited her up to their room to eat. That's when it happened. They told her that if she didn't do what they wanted, they were going to run a train on her."

"Did she report it?"

"No, I tried to get her to, but she said it'll be her word against theirs. Plus, she went to their room willingly. Craig, it's all my fault. I shouldn't have left her last night."

"It's not your fault and it's not her fault either. I don't care! She still needs to report it! I'll talk to her tomorrow. I'm gonna make her show me who they are."

"She's really upset. I offered to stay with her tonight, but she said she wanted to be alone."

Craig shook his head and hissed under his breath. "I'll take care of their asses."

Venice went into the room, changed, and crawled into bed.

Craig was beginning to feel even more serious about their relationship and he didn't want anything to mess that up. He cleaned the kitchen and put away the food. As Venice lay in the other room, she still felt a little uneasy by Miranda's presence. By the time he came into his room, she was in bed. Craig came in and asked if she needed anything. Venice told him that she was fine, then apologized for being drunk the night before. Craig told her it was in the past and he hadn't given it another thought.

It was about nine o'clock and Venice was trying to study a little. Friday was the big pep rally day. Venice's last class ended at twelve o'clock and the pep rally was going to be at noon. Craig's classes were going to be lab, so he could basically set his own hours as long as he finished his projects.

Craig asked, "Are you going to the pep rally with your partners?"

"I don't know yet. I think Chanelle is meeting Spoonie. Why?"

"I just asked. If you want to, I can meet you."

"I'll try to find you, if I can."

The mood was still out of sync. Miranda's presence definitely had an effect on Venice's attitude. This was the first time since Venice met Craig that she'd felt jealous. After what she did with Jarvis, she knew she didn't have a right to be upset, but she was. Her feelings for him had grown stronger over the past weeks. She was also still worried about Monique.

Craig still could tell the air was thick so he asked Venice if she felt well enough to ride to the store with him. He hoped this would be an opportunity for them to talk.

Venice said, "I'll do anything to keep from looking at this book."

They pulled out onto the street headed to the area supermarket. When they finally reached the store, Venice told him that she'd wait in the truck. He was only in the store for a few minutes. As he got in the truck, he handed her the sack. He told her to go ahead and look in the sack. Venice reluctantly peeked in the sack and was elated that he'd bought her favorite: peach cobbler pie and ice cream. She realized that it was some type of peace offering.

She looked at him as he pulled out of the parking lot and said, "Thanks."

There was more silence on the ride home. Craig finally said,

"Venice, I'm sorry about today. I don't like what's going on between us."

"Me either, Craig. I thought I could handle coming face to face with her, but I was wrong."

"Venice, I don't want Miranda."

"You did once, so why not again?"

Craig slightly chuckled. "Because I'm with the woman I want."

Venice blushed. "Thanks, baby. I'm sorry. I'm still sick and I'm worried about Monique."

He smiled and said, "I know."

As Craig pulled into the driveway and activated the garage door, he told Venice that he wouldn't string her along for the hell of it. "Momma taught me to respect women. I wouldn't dog you out so will you please cheer up?"

They sat in the truck as the door lowered. She turned to him and said, "I'll try."

He smiled and said, "Cool. Do you want to try and eat some ice cream?"

"I'll pass, thanks."

They made their way back to the bedroom. Craig said he was going to study a while. About an hour later, he crawled back into bed next to her with his pie and ice cream. Venice was staring at him as he ate it. He looked at her and said, "You want a taste?"

"Maybe a little."

He scooped up some ice cream and pie and she took a bite, seductively. Craig almost dropped the spoon and said, "Don't do that."

"Don't do what?"

He laughed. "You know what you're doing."

He got up to return his bowl to the kitchen and when he came back, Venice was sitting up in the bed smiling.

He said, "You're silly."

He got into bed and she scooted over close to him. He started scanning the channels with the remote while she decided to let her hands wander a little. He looked down at her and closed his eyes to enjoy the massage. Venice looked up at him, then crawled on top of his body and kissed his neck and chest. He wrapped his arms around her and pulled her to him. He sat up and pulled her nightie over her head. He smiled, then kissed her greedily. She opened a foil package and prepared him for her, then eased himself inside her warm body. Craig was taken with her forwardness and laid back to allow Venice to have her way with him. She kissed him provocatively as he held her body tightly against his.

She continued to pleasure him and he moaned as Venice whispered, "Oh, Craig."

This enflamed his body and he kissed her harder on the mouth, tasting her.

"Damn, Taylor!"

Venice began to move her body over his with deep affection and, within minutes, she collapsed on his chest. He smiled up at her and held her securely in his arms as she laid on his chest breathing heavily. A few minutes later, her pager went off. After picking it up, she saw it was Jarvis. Without saying a word, she laid it back on the nightstand. Venice didn't want to move and Craig wasn't about to let her. He didn't need to confirm it for himself. He knew it could only be Jarvis paging her that time of night. Craig didn't let it bother him though, because at that moment, she was in his bed, making love to him. She held onto him the rest of the night. As expected, it flashed through her mind that Jarvis was going to be pissed off when she talked to him. She decided to worry about that tomorrow.

Twenty-Three

It was Friday and the weekend, baby! Venice was extremely excited to have her first college homecoming. She received a call from Joshua when he got in. He'd told Venice that he would page her when he got up on the campus. Venice couldn't wait to see her best friend and finally introduce him to Craig. Galen was supposed to pick Joshua up, so there no telling where they were. Venice figured she would wait a while before she paged them. In the mean time, she was going to hang out with her girls.

This year was going to be a little different. Bryan was also bringing some of his partners to homecoming. Thank God Sinclair wasn't coming! Venice was a little disappointed that she wouldn't get to see Crimson though. Regardless, she was still planning on having a great time. The band was tuning up for the huge pep rally planned in the student center courtyard. Many students were already there to claim their spots for the rally.

As Venice walked up the steps into the courtyard, she heard Monique call out to her.

"Woo, woo, woo, woo!"

"Girl, you sure are crazy. How are you doing?"

"I'll make it."

"If you see them, you point them out to me. Okay?"

"Venice, leave it alone. Please?"

"I can't, Monique. How long have you been here?"

"I just got here and I saved your spot. Where's Chanelle?"

"She said she was coming with Mr. Spoonie."

"All right now. They sure have gotten close over the past few weeks."

"He's a nice guy. He'll be good for Chanelle."

"So where is your friend Joshua?"

"He's around here somewhere with Galen."

About then, the girls heard the drums of the band echoing in the air. This always meant the band was on their way. The court-yard was full of students and their families, alumni, and visitors in town for the game. The majorettes appeared first as they rounded the corner. Venice thought the guys standing next to them were going to pass out. All you could hear was, "Lord, have mercy! Look at the legs on that one!"

Monique and Venice were standing upon an upper platform, which gave them a great view of the courtyard. The crowd was going wild, dancing to the beat of the band. After a short speech, the student body president introduced the starting lineup on the football team, Galen included. The cheerleaders led a cheer. The band went directly into another popular dance number. The majorettes showed their skills by dancing and kicking with the abil-ity to still hold a perfect smile. Venice and Monique, along with hundreds of others, were really enjoying the pumped up pep rally.

It wasn't long before Venice felt someone's arms embrace her from behind. It sort of startled her but when she turned, she saw it was her boo and some of his friends. Craig hugged and kissed her neck, then said, "Monique, let me holler at you for a second."

Monique followed Craig off to the side and asked, "What's up?"

"Venice told me what happened to you and I'm sorry. But, Monique, you need to report it."

She folded her arms and said, "Craig, leave it alone. It was my fault."

"You better show them to me!"

"Okay!"

About that time, two guys pushed through the crowd past her. She heard one of them say, "Hey Monique, baby. Girl, you sure know how to party."

Monique scooted away from the guy, then another one looked her up and down and said, "Just like candy."

They burst out laughing as they continued to walk through the crowd.

Craig asked, "Is that them?"

"Yeah."

"Cool. Don't worry, Monique. They won't bother you or any-body else again."

"I hope not."

"Tell my girl I'll catch up with her later. I see some old friends I want to holler at."

"Okay."

Monique went back and joined Venice. She said, "Craig said he'll catch up with you later."

"Where did he go?"

"He saw some old friends or something."

Venice smiled and said, "Okay."

"Venice, I noticed that you don't try to keep up with Craig. Why is that?" "Why should I? I mean a man's going to do what he wants to do regardless. That's added stress I don't need. I don't have time to try and track a man down."

"As fine as Craig is, I would be worried as hell to let him out of my sight. I see girls all the time trying to push up on him. He's friendly with them, but they try to take his friendliness for flirting."

"If Craig's going to hook up with somebody, I can't stop him. It's all about how far he's willing to go. Don't get me wrong. I don't want to think about him messing around. But if he does, I'd rather he told me than find out from someone else. I told him a long time ago that if he wanted to date other women, he could. Especially since I still visit Jarvis some times. He didn't want to and now that I've gotten closer to him, I don't want him to either."

Monique smiled and said, "Girl, that was deep as hell! You need to teach that shit in the lounge at night or something. These foolish girls I hang with are always paging their men and tracking the hell out of them."

"They just don't know, that's partly what makes them cheat. No man wants to feel like he's on lockdown or constantly under surveillance. If you give them their space, they ain't going no where. But, if you crowd their asses, they can't wait to get away from you. I've always given my men their space. Hell, I had them tracking me down and I was being a good girl."

They laughed together and Monique saw that Venice really did have her head on straight. But, she still was torn between two won-derful men.

"Girl, Jarvis paged me about two this morning, but I couldn't call him back, if you know what I mean. Craig knew it was him, but he didn't say anything. I know Jarvis is going to be tripping when I finally talk to him."

"I figured he would page you. He called the room first. I just told him you were out."

Venice grew silent and admired the females on the homecoming court in their matching outfits who really looked nice. Venice and Monique agreed that it seemed like the person who spends the most money campaigning usually ends up winning homecoming queen.

When the pep rally was over, Venice and Monique started walking toward their dorm. Craig had disappeared into the crowd. Venice figured he'd eventually catch up with her sooner or later. As they walked and talked, they saw alumni, old and young, wearing homecoming, frat and sorority T-shirts, representing.

Venice said, "I'm thinking about pledging next year. What about you?"

"I don't know, girl. If one of those skanks put her hands on me, I might have to give her a beatdown."

The two gave each other a high-five and laughed loudly as they entered their dorm lobby.

When they walked in, there stood Galen and Joshua talking to some girls.

Monique hollered out, "Ooooh! I'm telling Sidney!"

He turned and said, "Girl, go on somewhere!"

Venice went over and gave Joshua a big hug, which they held for quite some time.

He said, "Niecy, you're looking good! Galen has been taking me everywhere. There's so many fine women up here, I'm going to lose my mind."

"Slow down, Joshua. I want you to meet my roommate." Venice introduced them and then asked, "What are you guys getting ready to do?"

"We came over to get you and your girls. Where's dude?"

"I was with him for a minute in the courtyard until he saw some of his friends and disappeared. I guess he'll page me or something when he gets a chance."

Joshua looked at Venice and said, "Don't trip Venice. It's homecoming."

"Whatever! Do ya'll want to get something to eat?"

"I do, but I don't know about Galen."

"Let me go up to the room for a minute and I'll be back down."

Joshua went back to staring at all the women. "I'll be right here when you get back."

Venice laughed and said, "Don't get into anything."

He grinned devilishly. "I'll try."

People were everywhere. Venice and Monique waited for the elevator, but it was taking too long so Venice decided to take the stairs.

"Monique, I'm going to take the stairs and stop by Chanelle's room to see if she wants to hang with us. I'll be up shortly. Okay?"

"See ya! Wouldn't want to be ya!"

Venice knocked on Chanelle's door, but didn't get an answer. She must've still been hanging out with Spoonie. Venice took the stairs to her floor and when she entered the room, Monique was on the phone.

"Here she is now. Do you want to holler at her?"

"Is that Bryan?"

Monique said, "It's your rod!"

Venice took the phone, "Hello?"

"What are you doing?"

"Getting ready to go get something to eat with Joshua. Do you want to come?"

"Sure! Are you meeting him somewhere?"

"He's waiting for us in the lobby with Galen."

"I'm on my way. Hey! Are you going out tonight?"

"I'm not sure. Are you?"

"Some of my partners want to go to some party."

Venice told Craig to go ahead and hang with his boys if he wanted to. She told him that she was going to stay in that night.

Craig asked, "Are you sure?"

"Yes, Craig. Now I'll see you in a minute. Look, would it be okay if Joshua hangs with you tonight. I know Bryan and his boys are going to end up no telling where. Joshua would have more fun with you and your friends."

"Sure, Venice, but if you want to get together, I can tell them I already have plans."

"No, I want you to take Joshua out. You've been hanging with me all week."

"Okay. I'll see you in a minute."

As she hung up, the phone rang again and Venice answered, "Hello?"

It was Jarvis. He angrily asked, "Oh, you can't answer my pages now?"

Venice was speechless for a moment, but she was finally able to say, "I'm sorry, Jarvis. It was late."

"I don't give a damn what time it was. It never stopped you from calling me back before. Where were you?"

Venice became agitated. "Don't ask me something you don't want to know the answer to."

"It doesn't matter anyway. I know where you were and what you were doing. I'm tired of this shit, Venice!"

"Jarvis, don't do this right now! You know how I feel about you. That's all that matters."

"The hell it does! The first chance I get, I'm coming down there and getting this settled for once and for all."

Monique could see that Venice was getting upset. "Don't come down here starting anything, Jarvis!"

"See ya!"

He slammed the phone down in her ear. Venice just stood there and quietly hung up the phone.

Monique asked, "Are you okay?"

"I'm fine. Thanks for asking. Let's go. I'm going to leave Chanelle a message on her phone so she'll know where we are."

Monique said, "Joshua sure is cute!"

Venice solemnly said, "Everybody's cute to you, Monique."

They left the room to meet the guys downstairs.

After meeting back up in the lobby, Craig leaned over to Monique and said, "Those guys won't be bothering you or any other girl any more."

"How do you know?"

"I just know. Now forget about it."

Monique did feel reassured and decided not to inquire any further. Craig didn't notice Venice's mood was off, but Joshua picked up on it the moment she walked back into the lobby. He decided to be nosey later.

Moments after slamming the phone down, Jarvis stormed out of his room. He had to get it out of his system. As much as he loved Venice, she was driving him completely out of his mind. He was dying a slow death knowing another man was putting his hands and everything else on *his* woman.

When he pushed the door of his dorm open, he nearly knocked Lydia to the ground. Luckily, she was able to step aside at the right moment. Lydia was an attractive, dark chocolate sista with long, shapely legs. Her southern accent stood out among the majority of the students, as well as the microbraids that hung midway her back.

"Oh! I'm sorry, Lydia. Are you okay?"

"I think so. Where are you going in such a hurry?"

Lydia shared a class with him and she was about the only female on campus who didn't seem to be chasing him. They had spent some time together studying and working on class projects, but that was as far as it went.

"I needed to get some air. Where are you headed?"

"I was coming to see if you wanted to catch a movie or something."

"I don't know, Lydia. I wouldn't be much company right now. I've got a lot on my mind."

She put her hands on her hips and asked, "Who is she and what did she do?"

Shoving his hands in his pockets, he answered, "It's personal."

Locking arms with him, she said, "In that case you could use some cheering up, so let's go and I won't take no for an answer."

"Okay! Okay! You win this time."

They went to the movies, but Jarvis could not forget the heated argument he'd had earlier with Venice.

Back on campus, he walked Lydia to her room.

"You want to come in, Jarvis?"

"Nah, I don't think so. I'd better be getting back. Thanks for inviting me to the movies."

Lydia walked right up to him and pressed her body into his and said, "I won't bite."

She took him by the hand and led him into her room.

An hour later, Jarvis was sitting on the edge of the bed with his hands over his face. "Lydia...this should've never happened. I was angry and hurting and I let things go too far."

Pulling the sheets over her naked body, she said, "I'm not sorry. I like you, Jarvis, and I would like to get to know you even better."

He stood up and started getting dressed. Rubbing his hand over his short, wavy hair, he softly said, "I'm in love with someone else, Lydia. I don't want to hurt you, but this could never happen again."

"If she really loved you, she wouldn't have hurt you like this."

Jarvis came over, sat on her bed, and kissed her on the cheek. "You're a good friend, Lydia, and I want to keep it that way. Just friends. Okay?"

"What's so special about her? You have her name tattooed on your arm and still she hurts you."

"We've been together for almost four years and we have a unique past. That's all I can tell you because it's personal. I hope you can respect that, Lydia. You're a beautiful, desirable woman and I hope you can understand."

Hugging him, she said, "She's a lucky woman."

"I'm a lucky man. Thanks for being there for me. I want to apologize for what happened."

"No harm done. Jarvis, I just wish things could be different, but I admire the love you have for her. I hope she knows it."

"Believe it or not, she does. I'd better go. I'll see you in class."

"Take care, Jarvis."

After lunch, the guys dropped the girls back off at the dorm. Venice was exhausted and wanted a nap. Before she went upstairs, Joshua asked her to come talk with him. They walked around outside and Joshua said, "So what did Jarvis say to you that has you so shook up?"

"You know me too well, Joshua." She paused for a moment as they sat on a bench. "Jarvis is pissed off because I didn't return his two a.m. page the other night. Hell, I was with Craig! Now he's threatening to come down here and settle things. I just don't know if he's serious or not."

"Niecy, don't worry about Jarvis. He's just going through Venice rehab and he can't handle it. Give him a few days to cool off. He won't come down here, so quit stressing over it. Okay?"

Venice felt slightly reassured and embraced him. "Thanks, Josh."

He walked her back to her room and they went their separate ways. She was glad he'd hit it off with Craig. They should have a lot of fun that night. Venice called Bryan and talked to him for a while, then fell asleep. Monique went walking around with their friends from across the hall.

Venice woke up to an empty room. She looked at her watch and saw that it was about six o'clock. She decided to get the clothes out that she was wearing to the parade in the morning. Chanelle phoned to say that she was back over at Spoonie's uncle's house. He was having a homecoming cookout and she called to invite Monique and Venice.

"Hey, girl! What are you doing?"

"Trying to pick out something to wear in the a.m."

"Where's Joshua?"

"He's somewhere with Galen and Craig. They're supposed to be going to some party tonight."

"Are you going to come over?"

"I don't have anything else to do. I'll see you in a little bit."

Chanelle seemed happy that her buddy was coming over.

Venice socialized a while with Chanelle and her new friends. Monique never showed up at the cookout. Venice guessed she found something better to do. Once eleven-thirty rolled around, Venice told Chanelle that she was heading back to the room. Chanelle walked her to the car and thanked her for hanging out with them. Venice told Chanelle that Spoonie's uncle was really nice.

"Chanelle, tell Spoonie's uncle thanks for inviting me."

"You bet, girl. I'll see you later. Bye."

When she got back to the dorm, Monique had a roomful of zoids playing spades and drinking liquor.

Monique hollered, "Hey, roomy! You want in?"

"Yeah, I'll take next game."

Tara from across the hall asked, "Do you want to partner up?"

"Yeah, give me a glass of that. What are ya'll drinking?"

Monique said, "It's the bomb, dogg!"

Venice took a sip and said, "Damn, ya'll are a bunch of winos."

Venice went ahead and joined in playing cards with her friends. It wasn't long before all of them were feeling real good.

Monique asked, "So Venice, where's your rod tonight?"

"He took Joshua to some party. Why?"

Monique said, "It's just odd for you to be hanging with us."

"Hell! Ya'll act like I'm whipped or something."

Monique threw her card on the table and said, "Well, aren't you. I mean you've got the best of both worlds. You're getting sexed on a regular basis here and got another brotha tapping that ass out of town. Venice, you're a freak!"

They all laughed and Tara said, "She's right, Venice." Tara went over and picked up the prom picture of Venice and Jarvis. "And both of the brothas are fine as hell! I would be satisfied with either of one of them and this hoe's got both of them. Damn! Life ain't fair!"

Venice was buzzing. "Ya'll are crazy."

Monique said, "Hoe, you know you love that shit. Who wouldn't? I'm having a hard enough time trying to hang with the one man I kind of like."

Tara said, "Monique, your problem is that you give it up on the first date."

They all laughed again and Monique said, "Don't hate the playa! Hate the game!"

The women played cards and got their drink on the rest of the night.

Twenty-Four

It was game day and Venice still hadn't heard from Jarvis. She thought for sure he would've called by then. So much for thinking, but she still loved him anyway.

The parade was huge and colorful. Venice knew Crimson would've enjoyed it. She vowed that the following year, Crimson was definitely coming. The bands battled each other for trophies and several frats and sorors competed in the annual step show. Venice, Monique, and the girls walked around looking at items in different vendor booths. It looked like a flea market with T-shirts over here and African artifacts over there.

Good cooking filled the air. Everyone was excited and fired up for the big game. Venice and Monique bought several pieces of jewelry for the game. They walked around for a while longer talking to different guys; regulars and alumni. Venice even met an alumni who played pro ball with Bryan. She told him where Bryan was staying and exchanged hotel information for her to pass on to her dear brother. Craig and Joshua were nowhere to be found and she hadn't heard from them yet.

Later, Venice met Bryan in the hotel lobby and gave him the tickets and his ex-teammate's phone number. He was wearing his fraternity T-shirt and hat.

When he saw her, he gave her a big hug. "Thanks, baby girl, for getting the tickets for me. Hey! You look like your hips have spread a little. What are you doing down here?"

"You are so silly! I'm the same size I was when I left home. You're just trying to make me paranoid."

"I'm just teasing you. What are you getting ready to do?"

"Nothing much. I came to see if Joshua wants to hang out.

Have you seen him today?"

"Not this morning, but I heard him coming in around three a.m. I think they had a good time. Why?"

"I asked Craig to take Joshua out with him last night. Some friend of his was having a private party. I guess that means he had a good time."

"Girl, let them have their fun. You need to have your fun, too. I'll go check on him. I have his ticket anyway."

"Give it here. I'll go check on him. I'll see you later."

"Look Venice, here's you some extra cash. I gave Galen some last night. It's just a little something so you can enjoy the weekend."

"Thanks, B. I really appreciate it."

Venice gave him a hug and told him that she would call him later.

When she got back upstairs, she knocked on Joshua's door. After a few minutes, the door opened and he softly said, "Hey, Niecy, what's up?"

"Look at your drunk ass! What did ya'll do last night?"

Joshua slowly walked back over to the bed and fell across it. "Quit talking so loud! Damn!"

Venice hit him and said, "Joshua! Get up! I thought you were going to hang with me today. You look like shit!"

"Leave me alone, Momma! Damn!"

Venice picked up his clothes off the floor. "What did ya'll do last night?"

"Girl, mind your business. Your boy's cool! I had a ball!"

"You need a shower. It's funky in here."

Joshua slowly sat up. "Niecy, girl, what would I do without you."

"I thought you were going to go look at the apartment with me."

"I am. Now get out of here so I can get my shower."

"I'm not leaving, I'm waiting right here. You don't have nothing I ain't seen before."

As Joshua entered the bathroom, he asked, "What time are you picking me up for the game?"

"Around five-thirty. That gives us three and a half hours to hang out."

"It's not going to take that long, is it? I want to lay back down before the game." "Nobody told you to drink like a fish last night."

"Okay, girl. I'll be out in a second."

Venice went over to him and gave him a hug and kiss. "I'm glad you had fun."

He smiled and popped her with a towel as she ran across the room. She looked down at the floor and said, "Jarvis is still pissed at me."

"He'll get over it. I told you that he's just blowing off steam."

Venice sat down on the bed and said, "All because I didn't return his two a.m. page. Hell! I was over at Craig's house and I wasn't about to disrespect him like that."

"I understand, but you know how Jarvis is, Venice. He's having a hard time dealing with this relationship you're involved in. He'll come around. Give him some more time to cool off."

"Do you think he's messing around with somebody up there?"

"I don't know. The way he's acting toward you, it doesn't seem like it. But, we as men feel like we can do things that women can't do. I know it's an ignorant statement, but that's how we think. This is hard for Jarvis to picture you moaning and groaning with another nigga."

Venice smiled. "You're crazy! It would be hard for me to think of him with some chick, too, even though I'm kicking it with Craig. This is extremely hard, Joshua."

"I realize that. Now let me get my shower and we'll talk some more."

They went and looked at the apartment and put their deposit down. Venice knew Joshua was still hung over so she took him back to the hotel so he could get some sleep before the game. After she dropped him off, she opened her purse and realized Bryan had paid her fifty dollars for the tickets and an extra hundred and fifty dollars for a gift. Bryan always had a giving heart. He was very successful in the NFL and as a sports agent and he had no problem sharing it with his family and friends.

The cash was right on time. Venice headed for the mall to get her nails done. It was about two-thirty and she still hadn't heard from Craig since the day before. However, she was not about to call. Venice got her nails done and decided to look for something

new to wear when she went out that night. Her cell phone rang and
it was *him*.

He asked, "Hello, Venice. Are you busy?"

Sarcastically, she said, "Sort of. What's up?"

Craig told her that they had partied a little too much and he
was just waking up. He went on to tell her that he was sick with a
hangover and needed her to pick up a few things, if she didn't
mind. He gave her a list of items.

Venice said, "I'll be by there when I finish up my errands."

Little did she know, Craig had a major surprise in store for her
later. When she looked at her list, she realized it was some type of
home remedy for hangovers. She picked up the items and was on
her way to his house. He let her in and he was walking around in
slow motion just like Joshua. Seeing him in pajama pants and bare-
chested caused a stirring in her stomach.

You're mad at him, Venice. Quit drooling.

He sat down at the kitchen table with his head down on the
table and asked her if she would mind mixing up the items for him.
Venice chastised him as she mixed up the remedy.

"Craig, you know you shouldn't have been mixing liquors.
That'll mess your stomach up every time. Joshua is in the same
shape you are, but I made him go look for an apartment anyway."

"Did ya'll get it?"

Look at those sexy eyes. Damn!

"Huh? Oh,... yeah."

"I don't know what I was thinking. Joshua is crazy. That boy
was trippin' last night."

Venice handed him the glass and he finished it off. Venice
could tell he was suffering so she proceeded to help him back to his
room so he could lie down. The warmth of his body near hers had
her on the edge of cracking. She wanted to feel his arms around her.

"Venice, do you mind hanging around for awhile. I need to
make sure that I don't oversleep for the game."

"No, I don't mind."

"Thanks, baby."

When he said that, her eyes couldn't help staring at his luscious
lips.

"See you in a little bit."

"Okay."

Venice spent the next hour or so in the den reading and listening to music. She called Joshua to check on his progress. He was coming along slowly, but progressing. Venice said, "Joshua I'm going to kick your butt! Craig is just as sick as you are."

"Go on with that, girl! Don't be over there trying to trip on him. You should've been out partying yourself last night."

"For your information, I was. Anyway, go take a Tylenol or something. You better be ready when I come to pick you up."

"You better not be late. Bye, girl."

They hung up and Venice continued to read her book.

After a few minutes, she decided to take a shower to relax her nerves. After her shower, she put on her robe and read a little more. Craig eventually woke up and joined her in the den. When he stood in the doorway, she tried not to stare at his unbelievable body. It was calling her. Jarvis had a well-sculptured body, but Craig was cut also. He confessed to Venice that he had to help the band and needed to be early. She barely heard a word he said because his eyes were doing a number on her and she knew it.

Venice asked, "What are you doing to help the band?"

"I just help them set up for the homecoming show every year. No big deal."

"That's nice. How's your hangover?"

"It's almost gone. I'm going to fix me one more of those drinks and I should be straight. Venice, come over here for a second."

Venice got up out of the chair and walked to him. "What?"

She could feel his warm breath on her lashes and the chills shot through her like an electric charge. He pulled she closer and said, "You're something else, you know that? I really appreciate you helping me out."

"I didn't mind."

She tried not to make eye contact, but couldn't help herself.

As she leaned against the wall, he played with the belt on her robe, leaned his body against hers, and started kissing the curve of her neck. Venice closed her eyes as warm lips explored the area.

"Damn! You smell good!"

"Thanks. I thought you were sick."

"I'm okay now."

Her lids closed tighter as she felt strong hands caressing her warm skin. She could also feel he was aroused as he continued to run his hands over her body. The kiss came to her without speaking another word. Her legs became wobbly and her breathing erratic.

"Come with me, Taylor."

"What are you doing?"

"I can show you better than I can tell you."

He pulled her onto the bed with him, gently stroking her cheek with the back of his hand while drowning himself in her desirable eyes.

"I thought you had a hangover?"

Craig answered softly, "It's gone" as he kissed her gently biting her lip. He reached for her robe and tossed it to the floor.

She was still trying to play hard with him, but she couldn't resist lacing her fingers around his neck.

Good Lawd!

He began to run his hands up and down her body in a slow rhythmic motion. Without breaking his gaze, he whispered, "You feel so good, Venice."

She felt like she was going to scream as he dipped and kissed her tenderly while probing her mouth with his tongue. Within a few seconds, Venice noticed something was a little different. He was a little more aggressive than usual. He was working on her weakest hot spots and he knew it. She was breathing heavily and felt a throbbing sensation in her lower body. Venice was getting very excited and found herself raking her nails up and down his back. Craig continued to pleasure her by kissing downward toward her stomach and nipples, taking his time with each one. Her body was burning as she felt his tongue play with her navel.

She let out a loud whimper when he came up and kissed her on the ears and whispered, "I want you."

He moved to kiss her harder on the mouth as he took his time tasting her. Craig gently worked his way downward once again to her stomach. She took a deep breath when she closed her eyes to enjoy the sensation she was feeling. Then, without any warning, she felt Craig's warm lips *there*. Startled and in shock, she hollered out his name as he used his tongue skillfully in her most intimate area. He held onto her with a strong grip as if he thought she would try to get away. She didn't know how to respond or feel. She felt out of control and at his mercy.

Craig was very comfortable as he slowly worked his magic on her. She was still a little nervous and tried to wiggle away. He held onto her in a way where she could not move out of position. She eventually had to give in to her emotions and let her body and mind enjoy the wonderful torture he was giving her. Venice had felt this once in the past but she never remembered it feeling like this. Venice felt like he was going to devour her entire body. The experience happened a few years ago with someone very special to her, but this was absolutely better than anything she could ever remember. She moaned out loud and long, as he continued to kiss her with tenderness. At one point, she felt as if he were making love to her with his tongue. Venice was mesmerized and in a daze. She occasionally let out a soft moan and Craig seemed to be very attentive to what she was experiencing. He made her feel out of control and she began to scream out uncontrollably. She grabbed his head and tried to get him to stop, but she really didn't want him to stop.

"Stop...Craig, please! Oh! Baby! Don't stop! Don't stop! Craig!"

She was confused and out of her mind as she felt her body shiver. Finally, he did stop and after applying protection, slid himself into her hot, moist body. She was still moaning when he entered her and thrust his hips for what seemed like an eternity. Venice felt like her body was on fire and she was overcome with emotion as she moved with him. Toward the end of their passion-filled journey, Craig moaned long and hard, then laid across her dripping with perspiration and the scent of her fragrance. Venice struggled to regain her composure, but she was still stunned and breathless.

Craig let out a loud sigh as he played in her hair, not losing eye contact. "Sweetheart, I know you were mad at me. I'm sorry I didn't call you. Will you forgive me?"

"Apology accepted."

He wrapped her up in his arms and he began to feel a little guilty as he pulled up the comforter.

"Baby, I'm sorry I lost control with you. I hope I wasn't too forward. I'm crazy about you and I don't want you to think it's purely physical."

"Losing control isn't always a bad thing. I'm crazy about you, too."

Feeling more secure, Craig turned her over and gave her a massage, which should've been against the law. He still wondered in the back of his mind whether she thought about Jarvis when she made love to him. Seeing that tattoo always reminded him that Jarvis very much a part of her life.

Venice needed to wind down and Craig's massage was the perfect remedy. She felt like bouncing off the walls as his hands worked every muscle that she owned. Venice knew she had someone special and she didn't want to lose him. The massage lasted another fifteen minutes when he said, "Venice, come shower with me."

Venice wondered what else he was going to do to surprise her. He helped her off the bed and they proceeded to the bathroom. Craig stepped in first and reached for her hand as she followed. The water ran over their bodies and he rubbed suds over her back continuing his massage. Venice turned and returned the sensuous favor. She closed her eyes and lost herself in the moment until he pulled her to him.

"Craig, we can't do that in here without…"

"I know. I came prepared."

She leaned up and kissed him hungrily. "Let's get ready to rumble!"

Craig couldn't help but take her on another erotic journey. What he did to her in the shower would make her look at showers differently for the rest of her life.

Some time later, Venice laid across the bed watching TV as Craig cleaned up the bathroom. She decided to give Chanelle a call. When she answered the phone, Venice could tell something was wrong.

"Hey, homegirl, what's up? Is everything okay?"

"Venice! You're not going to believe what happened to me."

"What happened?"

"I was taking my shower a few minutes ago and my roommate asked if it was okay if she used the bathroom. She said she had to go pretty bad. So I told her cool, come on in. Well, girl, the next thing I knew, that heifer was coming into the shower with me, butt naked." Venice hollered out, "You're lying, Chanelle!"

"No, I'm not! Venice, I freaked out and pushed the shit out of her. She fell back on the floor and I grabbed my robe and got the hell out of there. I went up to your room and called the dorm director. She met me in the hallway and went back to my room so I could get some clothes and to take care of the situation."

Venice was stunned. "I knew something was wrong with that girl. She just stared at us a little too much. That's why I didn't like hanging in your room a lot. So, what did the director say?"

"She asked my roommate why she did it and told her that she would have to be removed from my room. She said she was going to have to report the incident and call her parents. I just want the bitch out of there. Girl, my heart is still beating fast. It's a wonder she hadn't tried to do something to me while I was sleep."

Venice laughed and asked, "When is she moving out?"

"As we speak."

"Well, are you okay?"

"I'm fine now, but I wish I would've had some clothes on. I would've beat the shit out of her. I didn't give her any indication that I was that way. I was just nice to the girl."

"Have you told Spoonie?"

"Yes, I called him before I called you. The director is going to let me know when she's completely out. I hope it won't take long. I'm crashing in your room until she's gone."

"Damn, Chanelle, you're pulling the chicks now. You go, girl!"

Chanelle laughed and said, "It's funny now, but it wasn't funny then. You should've seen me getting the hell out of there. I was soaking wet and was slipping all over the hallway running."

"The good thing is you've got a room to yourself."

"You better know it, girl! So, what are you guys up to?"

"I can't tell you right now, but I can tell you that my baby just put something on me that I haven't felt in a long time. I'm still tripping."

"Where is he?"

"In the bathroom right now. If I tell you, you better not tell this to a soul. Not even Spoonie."

"Okay! Okay!"

"Honey, he took me to another level."

"What?"

Venice took a deep breath and said, "Girl, he went down on me and, honey, let me tell you. I'm still freaking out!"

"Hello! I told you if you'd ever have it done, you'd be turned out. It's the bomb! Wait a minute. What do you mean in a long time?"

"Michael. Remember?"

"Oh! I forgot all about him!"

"I also forgot who I was talking to. You know all about it."

"What can I say? That was one of Jeremy's best qualities and he could work it. I don't know if Spoonie's into it though. I guess time will tell. Anyway, I'm happy for you. I'd better get off your phone so the director can call me. Monique left after I got here. She said she would be back in a little while."

"Okay, I'll see you later. Watch your back, Chanelle!"

"Funny, Venice. Talk to you later."

Venice hung up the phone and laid back on the bed, shocked about what happened to Chanelle.

Craig reentered the room smelling wonderful. He laid down across Venice's back and said, "I have a big surprise for you later."

"What is it?"

"If I tell you, it won't be a surprise. What time is it?"

Venice gave him the time and sat up on the bed. Craig sat up behind her and hung a small gold heart-shaped necklace around her neck.

Venice asked, "What is this for? Is this my surprise?"

He proudly stated, "I wanted you to know that you really do have my heart and no, it's not the surprise."

Venice went over to the mirror to admire the necklace. It was beautiful! She came back over to him and wrapped her arms around his neck. "Thank you, baby! I'll never take it off."

She nuzzled her face against his neck as she hugged and kissed him there and on him lips. His glorious scent was hypnotic as well as erotic. They held each other tenderly in silence and then got dressed.

Twenty-Five

The game finally started with several ceremonial introductions, including the homecoming court. The senior players were introduced as they ran out onto the field. There was a slight chill in the air. Hopefully, it wouldn't get too cold.

At last, it was the kick off and the crowd went wild. Dawson U scored a touchdown on their first possession. Students were partying hard in the stands and Venice, Joshua, and Monique were right with them. The band played all new songs and they were getting down in the bandstand. It was a fun time for Venice and her friends. The game continued and you could see several of the Greek sororities and fraternities doing their traditional steps.

Monique and Venice snickered as they spotted many people wearing outfits they shouldn't have on.

Monique said, "No Miss Thang didn't try to squeeze into that dress. Look at all those rolls."

Venice hit her on the leg and said, "Girl, you're crazy, but you're so right."

Joshua asked, "Hey, did ya'll hear about those two guys that got beat up after the pep rally?"

Venice and Monique answered, "No, what happened?"

"I don't know. I overheard some people talking about it. They said about four guys jumped them and it had something to do with some girl who had a train run on her or something."

Venice and Monique looked at each other in shock. Venice grabbed her hand and gave it a squeeze. They both knew then that Craig may have had something to do with it, but they didn't share their suspicions. It was over.

It wasn't long before it was half-time. Venice still hadn't seen

Craig and wondered where he could be. *He had to be there some-where.*

She wasn't going to say anything to him about what Joshua told them because she knew in her heart he was involved. Venice continued to wait for Craig to page her when he finished helping with the band. The visiting band put on a great performance, dancing to most of the recent hits. The majorettes were poised and also danced a great routine. But now, it was Dawson U's turn. The fans were on their feet as the drum major did one of the incredible back bends to make his hat touch the ground. Then, it was on! The band continued to play and dance throughout their routine.

Next, the announcer said, "Ladies and Gentlemen, please bring your attention to the field where we have four of Dawson's own. They call themselves 'Passion' with the lead being sung by Junior Architectural Major, Craig Bennett."

Monique screamed, "Venice! It's Craig! Why didn't you tell us he was singing?"

Venice's heart was pounding when she answered, "I didn't know myself! I'm just as surprised as you are."

Joshua was eating a sandwich and said, "I knew about it."

Venice hit him. "Why didn't you tell me?"

He looked at her and replied, "Cause the man told me not to tell you."

The band began to play a medley of famous love songs.

Craig started out by saying, "I'd like to dedicate this song to a very special lady who's wearing my heart around her neck and to all the other beautiful ladies here tonight."

The crowd went wild and Monique hollered, "Please tell me he's talking about you! What does he mean, wearing his heart around your neck?"

Venice showed Monique and Joshua the necklace. "He gave it to me this afternoon."

"Go on with your bad self, girl."

Joshua said, "That was a true playa's move."

Venice gave him one of her looks as she stood, stunned. Craig and his group hit all the notes as the band accompanied them. He had a beautiful voice and his group blended right in with him. The crowd went wild at the end of their performance. Venice was unaware of the tears, which streamed down her cheeks. She couldn't believe what she'd just witnessed and she couldn't wait to see him. This must've been her surprise.

Craig, how could I not love you.

Once the half-time show was over, the stands emptied with fans heading for the concession stands. Monique was hungry so they joined the hundreds of others headed for some grub. Venice could wait no longer. She paged Craig and it wasn't long before her phone rang.

"Hello?"

The voice on the other end was laughing. "Hey, baby! So, what did you think?"

"I'm speechless! Why didn't you tell me?"

"I wanted it to be a surprise."

"You have a beautiful voice. I'm really impressed. Where are you?"

Distracted, he hollered at someone passing. "Thanks, man! Sorry, baby. What did you say?"

"Where are you?"

"I'm over by the T-shirt stand, the one with the red and white awning. Where are you?"

"I'm to the right of you at the concession stand with Monique and Joshua."

"Stay put. I'll be right over."

Venice hung up the phone and chills shot through her body.

Several guys were passing Venice, admiring her. A couple of them stopped to ask if she wanted some company. Venice told them no thanks as she scanned the crowd for Craig. Joshua walked up and put his arm around her shoulder, acting like he was her man. He then said, "Venice, look at you. My baby's all grown up."

"You're silly. Are you having fun?"

"Hell yeah!" Joshua paused. "Have you heard from Jarvis yet?"

Venice replied solemnly, "Nope."

"So, what's up?"

"What do you mean. What's up?"

"Never mind."

Venice turned and said, "I told you he's not speaking to me right now. I guess he's still pissed off about me not returning his page."

"I didn't mean to upset you."

"I know. I'm okay."

They left the conversation at that.

I hope you're having a good game, Jarvis. Please don't be mad?

Monique was talking to some guys over to the side when Venice's phone rang.

Chanelle asked, "Venice, where are you?"

"I'm over by the concession stand with Joshua and Monique waiting on Craig."

"V, I almost had a heart attack when they announced his name. You're wearing a heart or something around your neck, aren't you?"

Venice laughed. "Yes! I'm still in shock, too. I had no idea they were going to sing."

"Call me when the game's over."

"Okay. Talk to you later."

They hung up the phone and Monique bought Venice a hot dog. They decided to hang out in the crowd for the rest of the game. They saw several friends from the dorm and chatted briefly. Then she saw Bryan and his friends. Of course they were acting "buck wild." Bryan was enjoying himself so much with his partners: Gator, Tate, and Derrick. It would've been a different story if Sinclair had come.

Bryan loudly walked over to her and said, "What's up, baby girl?"

He picked her up and gave her a big hug. He finally put her down so she could introduce him to Monique. Bryan gave Joshua a high-five, then introduced his partners to Monique. Venice already knew them. They continued to talk and watch the game. Bryan was really wild! Galen was playing exceptionally well. Bryan said he heard some NFL scouts were in the crowd. Hopefully, Galen would get drafted when he graduated. Venice said her prayers for Jarvis also.

Venice couldn't wait for Bryan to meet Craig.

What's taking him so long?

Finally, she felt arms around her waist and a kiss on the back of the neck. This was Craig's signature approach. Bryan looked at him like he wanted to kick his ass. He and his friends had been drinking and tailgating all day, so he was trippin' a little.

Venice saw Bryan coming over and said, "Bryan, this is Craig. Craig, this is my big brother, Bryan."

Bryan put his hand out to shake it and said, "Man, when I saw you grab my sister like that, I started to jack your ass. Brothas have been rolling up on her all night."

Craig shook his hand and said, "Nice to meet you, Bryan. Venice, has somebody been messing with you?"

"No! Don't pay Bryan any attention. Any guy talking to me raises his protective radar."

Bryan went on to introduce Craig to his partners, then pulled him to the side.

Venice saw this and said, "Bryan! Don't start!"

"Girl, I got this! Chill!"

"Craig, do you like my sister?"

"Yeah! I like her."

"So that was my sister you were singing about, right?"

"Of course."

He told Bryan to look at the necklace Venice was wearing, if he wanted to verify it. He explained that he'd given it to her earlier in the day. It was a gold heart locket.

"All I'm going to say is, I trust my sister's judgment and don't play with her. You catch my drift?"

Craig understood the big brother concern and responded with, "No problem, Bryan. I love Venice. I'm not going to do anything to disrespect her."

They shook hands again and went back to join the others.

The game was nearing the final minutes and Dawson U was clearly winning the game. Many people had already started leaving the stadium to get ready for the after parties. Craig joined some of his friends a little away from Venice and her group.

Bryan turned to Venice and said, "He seems to be all right. Do you like him?"

Venice put her arms around her brother's waist and looked him in the eye. "Yes, I do. He's told me on several occasions that he loves me."

Bryan gave her his undivided attention. "Oh really? What have you told him?"

Smiling, she said, "I love him, too."

"What about Jarvis? I know you've still got it bad for him. Right?"

"Always."

"Didn't you go see him the other week?"

"Yes and we had a great time."

"Did you sleep with him when you were up there?"

Venice looked at him and grinned. "Lord have mercy!"

He said, "I knew it! Hell, you can't help yourself, can you? Venice, you ain't never gonna get that man out of your system. You need to quit trying to fight it and face the fact." Venice held onto his arm. "Face what fact?"

"That he's the one for you and he always will be."

"It's not the sex, Bryan. You know that. Jarvis and I fit. But Craig, he also fits in a different way."

Venice had always been able to tell Bryan "anything." He was the one she had all her sex talks with. It was odd that Bryan never felt uncomfortable talking female stuff with her either. He kept the lines of communication open with her so he'd always know what she was getting into.

"Maybe you're right, Bryan, but I can't worry about that while I'm here. I'm with Craig at this moment and he's sweet and he's so fine!"

"You say that, but I know you and I know Jarvis. This is just a temporary fix for you so be careful, little sister. That's all I'm going to say. You know Jarvis has always been a fool for you? Craig seems smooth enough to shake you and Jarvis' happiness up a little. Watch yourself, all right?"

"I will."

"Just remember to keep protecting yourself if you're going to be messing around with both of them. Okay?"

"Okay, Bryan."

"Venice, I don't want to see you get mixed up in anything you can't get out of and you know what I mean. I'd hate to have to get involved if one of them decides to snap or something. But, we'll talk about it later. Okay?"

Venice agreed and they ended their conversation. They went on to talk about something else. Craig had noticed the deep conversation between brother and sister so he kept his distance a little longer.

The game finally ended and the crowd began to pour out of the stadium. Galen came over to the fence to talk to them for a moment. Bryan and Joshua were congratulating Galen on his good game. Craig was now back over with them and he held Venice's hand and asked her if she was ready to go.

"Let me tell Bryan goodbye."

Venice went over to her big brother and hugged him and told him she would call him tomorrow. As she hugged him, she whispered in his ear, "Thanks."

Bryan gave her a kiss on the cheek and told her goodbye. Venice gave Galen a high-five and walked off with Craig and Joshua.

Venice let Craig choose which party to attend. Monique called to find out where they were going. Venice called Chanelle and Spoonie and told them where to meet them. The site would be at the convention center, not far from the campus. The party was being sponsored by one of the fraternities. When they got there, the parking lot was full of cars. Many others were also just arriving. It was about eleven-thirty and Venice was ready to get her dance on. She knew she was looking good and she had her man on her arm. Nothing could ruin her night.

As Venice exited the dance floor and thanked another guy for asking her to dance, she spotted Miranda talking to Craig. She wasn't just talking though. She had her arms around his waist and was pressing her body against him. She was tiptoeing, trying to whisper in his ear. Craig was trying to get her arms from around his waist. They didn't see Venice, but she knew Miranda must've realized she was in the room.

Venice stood back to see how Craig was going to handle the situation. Miranda was clearly getting agitated as Craig kept trying to walk off from her. She grabbed his arm and used subjective motions with her hands, seemingly arguing with him. Craig grabbed her forearm and put his finger up to her face in anger. Venice was unsure if she should go over, then decided to do just that. Besides, Craig was with her.

Venice walked up and said, "Hello, Miranda. What's going on?"

Miranda looked at Venice with disgust. "This doesn't concern you, little girl! You need to mind your damn business!"

Venice pushed Craig aside and got in her face. "He is my business! You need to take your ass on somewhere and get on with your life."

Miranda tried to put her finger in Venice's face. That's when Craig pulled Venice back and said, "Miranda, what is it that you don't understand? I can't figure out why you can't get this through your head!"

As they walked off, they heard Miranda say, "It ain't over, bitch!"

Venice turned to respond, but caught herself. Craig pulled her through the crowd and out the room. Venice was steaming. She paced back and forth in a six-foot area of the hallway.

She wasn't saying a word until she erupted with, "Craig, what the hell is wrong with that fool? How could you have ever been with someone like that?"

Craig couldn't answer her right away because he was wondering the same thing. He was also trying to go back in his mind to figure out the point when Miranda turned sour. When he was with her, she didn't seem so bitter. Or rather, he didn't notice.

"Venice, let's go for a walk."

Craig knew Venice needed to cool off. He'd never seen her so pissed off. However, the way Venice went off on Miranda told him that she could definitely take care of herself.

Joshua came out and asked if everything was okay. Craig told him everything was cool. They exited the building to walk around the hotel's garden. Craig found a bench in the garden near a water fountain. They sat down and he put his arm around Venice's shoulder.

"Venice, I'm so sorry about everything. I had no idea Miranda would come here and try to cause problems. I want you to know that, regardless of what you may hear, you're the one I want to be with. I see now, Miranda has a lot of hate in her and I'm not sure how far she'll try to go. She still has some friends on campus who may try to start something with you. If that happens, you make sure you let me know."

"If any of her skank friends start anything with me, I'm going to put them in their place."

Craig smiled, still amazed by Venice's temper.

Venice asked, "What are you smiling at?"

"You. I'm surprised. You're dangerous, girl."

She tried to keep from laughing. "Stop trying to make me laugh. I'm still mad."

They both burst into laugher.

"You were wild. That messed my head up when you pushed me out of the way."

"It was a reaction. I didn't even think about it. That chick knows how to yank my chain."

"I'll take care of this. I promise." Craig gazed lovingly at Venice and said, "You owe me a dance, Venice. Let's go."

Venice cooled off as they went back inside. When they reached the dance floor, Miranda was over to the side looking like she was mad at the world. She watched Craig and Venice dance and realized she was out of luck with Craig. She felt a little satisfied that she was able to cause a little turmoil.

Miranda told her partners, "Look, I'm out of here!"

The night was coming to an end and the crowd started to diminish. Chanelle and Spoonie came over to say their good-byes for the evening.

Chanelle said, "Girl, I saw you over here handling Craig's old girl. Is everything all right?"

"Yes, everything's under control. I'll tell you about it tomorrow. See you guys later and drive carefully."

Craig told them goodbye and asked Venice if she was ready to go. She was but they waited for Joshua to finish talking to some girl. When Joshua joined them, Craig asked him if he wanted to crash at his house. He thanked him but told him to drop him off at the hotel. Joshua knew Craig and Venice needed some privacy. They walked together out into the parking lot.

Joshua said, "Thanks for letting me hang out with ya'll. I had a really good time and I got some numbers, dog!"

Venice said, "I don't know why. You know Cynthia's got you on lockdown."

Craig laughed and said, "Don't mind her, man. Handle your business."

It was about three a.m. when they dropped Joshua off at the hotel. As he got out of the truck, he gave Venice a big hug and kiss and said, "Hey man, you make sure you take care of my girl."

"Don't worry, I will. See you in the morning."

Once they drove off, Craig said, "You two are really tight. It's hard to believe that you never hooked up with him."

"That would be like messing around with my brother. Joshua's my blood, that's all."

Craig headed for the interstate, then told Venice he wanted to stop and get something to snack on. He called an all-night diner and ordered some hot wings. He knew there was something to drink at the house so that area was covered. On the way to the house, she fell asleep. Craig, for some reason, enjoyed watching her sleep. He pulled up to the diner's drive-up window and picked up the order.

The waitress that gave it to him said, "If you didn't have that girl in the car with you, I'd let you take me home with you!"

She was about fifty years old and let out a loud laugh. Craig thanked her, laughed also, and pulled off. The smell of the hot wings woke Venice up.

Craig asked, "How was your nap?"

"Short."

"We're almost home. I practically got picked up by someone."

"Who?"

"That old lady at the diner."

Venice snickered and said, "I must say, Bennett. You're quit the ladies man."

Back at the house, Venice kicked off her pumps. "I'll take a couple of those hot wings."

She proceeded to walk toward the bedroom, taking off her jacket and unzipping her skirt as she walked away. Craig stopped for a moment to admire the sexiness in her movements. After she was out of his sight, Craig shook his head and mumbled, "Damn!"

He heard the shower turn on as he poured their drinks and without another thought, Craig put the bottle down and walked toward the bedroom. Venice was letting hot steamy water run down her back, massaging her tired muscles. She couldn't help but think about Jarvis. She hated it when he was angry with her. She told herself that she would call him as soon as she could to straighten things out. With closed eyes, she let the warm water splash in her face and over her soft cinnamon skin. About that time, Craig entered the shower.

"What are you doing in here?"

"Relax. Trust me."

Smiling, he took some gel in his hands and began to lather and massage her body. He started with her shoulders and back and went on from there. The touch of his strong hands against her skin was electrifying. She also took some gel into her hands and lathered his chest and arms.

They continued to lather each other and Craig said, "You don't realize what you do to me? I'm starting to get used to this."

Venice smiled back and asked, "What do I do to you?"

"Everything."

He found her lips and once again tasted the sweetness her mouth gave him. She blushed, then held his hand in hers and massaged his hands and fingers. In its own way, what she was doing was very erotic.

When she finished, he gave her another kiss, deepening it. "Thanks. That was nice."

"You're welcome."

He grabbed a towel and stepped out of the shower. A few moments later, she also exited the shower and joined him in the bedroom. Venice fell across the bed.

She said, "I'm so tired! It's been a long day."

Craig, dressed in shorts and a T-shirt, replied, "Come here."

She crawled up to him and straddled him. "What's up?"

He looked at her seriously. "You."

Needless to say, they planned to spend another night of heat and fire. He took his time with her as he caressed her body. He whispered in her ears as he kissed her body gently. He knew he had her right where he wanted her, begging and moaning.

Venice was nearing the point of hyperventilating when Craig kissed her and whispered, "How does that feel, baby?"

Breathless, she said, "M-m-m-m, nice."

Craig began to give Venice what she was waiting for. She gripped the sheets as he flicked his tongue on her body. Then it only took one thrust of his hips and Venice's breath left her body. His rhythm was quick and exact. He knew her spot. This went on for quite some time until Venice screamed out in Spanish. Craig looked down at her in shock as she continued to whisper to him in Spanish. Venice had never done this with anyone unless they were hitting it correctly. This excited him even more as his body trembled and his love flowed.

Exhausted, he stared down at her with a strange look on his face. Breathless, she slowly opened her eyes and said, "Stop looking at me like that."

"Where did that come from?"

"You know where it came from. You know what you were doing to me."

"I was hoping for a response, but I never expected that. I almost lost my damn mind, girl. You made me wanna tear up something."

Venice smiled. "It feels like you did. I thought I was going to have a heart attack. You're trying to get me addicted to you."

He played in her hair and asked, "And what would be so wrong with that?"

"I'm scared," Venice readily admitted.

"Of what?"

"This. Us."

"It's because of him. Isn't it?"

Venice was silent for a moment.

"Craig…it's so complicated."

"Because you're making it complicated. You know how I feel about you. Maybe if I spoke Spanish, I'd know what you were saying."

Venice grinned and asked, "Do you want to know what I said?"

He kissed her cheek. "Yes."

She put her arm around him and said seductively, "I said you feel so-o-o good! I want you so much! Then I said some curse words and finally I said that I love you."

Craig blushed. "I wish I could've heard it in English."

She brushed her lips against his and said, "The night is young."

He smiled and they continued to kiss deeply and meaningfully. She laid in his arms for the rest of the night. Craig was finally content that he knew Venice loved him, but Jarvis still lurked in the shadows.

Twenty-Six

Craig craved Venice all the time. She was smart and fine. He had no idea that he would end up turned out over her. He'd dated women before, but none like her. He couldn't put his finger on it, but it was definitely different. Craig found himself staring at her all the time, trying to figure it out. He could see why her ex was so possessive and dreaded losing her. Venice had an air about her. She didn't take any shit off anybody and she and was very, very, independent. Some men would've thought that she was too independent. Craig had never dated anyone who didn't constantly call or try to keep up with him. Venice was one of a kind and he wanted her all to himself.

It was about four-thirty when Craig was awakened by Venice's voice. As his mind adjusted, he laid there listening.

"Please don't. Please! I won't say anything! Stop! Please!"

Craig rose up to listen closer. Venice began to whine in her sleep and appeared on the brink of screaming out.

"Venice! Venice! Wake up! What are you dreaming about?" Craig asked, shaking her awake.

Venice began to come out of it, but she didn't seem to recognize him. She screamed out and started pushing him away. He grabbed her arms and shook her again.

"Venice! It's me, Craig! Venice! Wake up!!"

It took a few seconds, but she finally woke up completely and hugged him tightly. She began breathing very hard.

He hugged her. "Calm down. What's wrong? What were you dreaming about?"

"I don't remember. I just remember being scared. I just want to go back to sleep."

Craig was a little puzzled, but decided to momentarily leave it alone. He pulled the covers over them and Venice immediately went back to sleep. Craig, however, couldn't go to sleep. Venice's actions had caught him off guard. She hadn't even recognized him at first. Even though it would be difficult, he decided to wait until morning to pursue the issue.

Venice woke up Sunday morning feeling exhausted. Craig was still asleep and she wanted to just lie there and watch him sleep. He was so sweet and sensitive, which was very special to her. How could she be so lucky to find someone to help fill the void of missing Jarvis so much? Venice knew her mother would love to meet him and she was anxious to take him home to meet her family. Thanksgiving was coming up and it would be the perfect time. Bryan had already given his okay. The final call would be up to her daddy, the other man in her life. She didn't know how Jarvis would take the news.

Craig began to stir out of his sleep. He opened his eyes slightly to find Venice staring at him. "Good morning."

"Good morning."

He pulled her over to him so they'd be lying face to face with his arm around her waist. "Venice, is everything all right with you?"

"Why do you ask?"

"You don't remember what happened last night?"

Venice assumed that he was talking about their passionate session and blushed. "I could never forget that, Craig."

"Not that, Venice. You don't remember screaming out in your sleep and fighting with me?"

She looked confused and said, "Fighting with you?"

"Venice, you were talking in your sleep. Something about please don't."

The blood left Venice's face. "It must've been a bad dream. I don't want to talk about it anymore, okay?"

Craig wasn't satisfied with her answer. "Has someone been bothering you, Venice?"

"No, Craig. It was just a bad dream."

"Whatever you say. But I need to tell you that I find myself getting spoiled waking up next to you. It's been a while since I've been with someone seriously like this, but I'm starting to like it. We haven't actually talked about where we want our relationship to go, so I'm opening the door for you to express yourself, if you'd like to."

Venice smiled and replied, "Baby, you know I enjoy your company, but you also know I have issues. The main issue being Jarvis. I'm in love with him, but I'm also in love with you. I'm dealing with a lot of stress because I let this happen and I don't want to hurt either of you. Can't we just take it one day at a time?"

"Venice, I know what I want. I want you. I know you're trying not to cause anyone pain, but in this situation, someone *is* going to get hurt. I hate the thought of you with him, but I'm sure he feels the same way. They say it's better to have loved and lost than not to have loved at all. That's the only thing that keeps me going, besides knowing that you love me back."

"That was beautiful, Craig."

"Thanks."

Craig then took his pillow and hit Venice with it playfully. She grabbed her pillow and fought back. He chased her through the house and cornered her in the den. Venice tried to fight her way out, but wasn't so lucky. He grabbed her around the waist and they plummeted onto the sofa. Both of them laughed and struggled for breath. They took a moment out to rest. Then he started tickling her. He held her down with his body, pulling her arms above her head so that he could tickle her underarms.

Venice screamed and laughed at the same time. "Stop! I'm going to get you back!"

"Whimp!"

He gazed at her lovingly and Venice knew in her heart that he wanted to get intimate again. Instead, he helped her up and asked, "Are you hungry?"

Venice pressed her body against his and ran her hands up his muscular chest and around his neck. Gazing into his chocolate chip eyes, she said, "They said there's nothing like breakfast in bed."

She backed him into the bedroom and they crawled back under the covers. Smiling, he asked, "What are you doing?"

Venice giggled. "If you don't know, then I'll have to show you."

Moments later, with their sweat drenched bodies intertwined, Venice said, "That's the best breakfast I've every had."

"Me, too. I would love seconds, but we'd better get over to the hotel to see your brother off."

"Okay, but dinner's on me."

"Have it your way. I'll pick up the whipped cream."

Laughing, they got dressed.

They all met in the lobby and Bryan once again gave Venice money. She told him that she was fine, but he insisted. He asked for her bank account number so he could send her money that way. She thanked him and gave him a goodbye hug and kiss.

Joshua and Craig were having a chat over to the side until it was time to go. Joshua came over to Venice. "Girl, you take care of yourself. I had a great time. Craig is cool, so try not to mess it up. Okay?"

Venice had tears in her eyes. "Okay. I'm going to miss you, Josh. Thanks for coming."

"You know you're my boo. You just start finding us some furniture for our apartment."

"I will, Joshua. You guys have a safe trip and call me when you get back."

They agreed and finally pulled off from the hotel.

She knew this was the end of her wonderful week with Craig. She'd be returning to the campus and he'd be starting his co-op training again on Tuesday. They knew they wouldn't get to see each other often, but Venice was hoping to see Craig as much as time would allow. She again contemplated inviting him home for Thanksgiving.

As Venice packed her belongings and helped him clean up the house, she asked, "Craig, if you don't have any plans for Thanksgiving, I'd like to invite you to go home with me to meet my family."

Craig stopped making the bed and answered, "I'd like that. Thanks for inviting me. Look, Venice, you don't have to go back to campus today. Why don't you stay?"

"Thanks, baby, but I've been here all week. Plus, we both need to get some sleep for our classes in the morning. If I stay, I probably won't let you get any sleep."

"I'm not going to get any sleep anyway because my bed will be empty and cold."

"Craig, I'll be back next weekend. I really need to spend some time in my room before my dad pays me a visit."

He reluctantly accepted her argument so she took her suitcase out into the garage to put it in his truck. Craig followed behind her and locked up the house so he could drive her back to campus. When they reached the dorm, Craig walked Venice to the room only to find Monique MIA.

After he sat her bags down, he hugged her. "I'm going to miss waking up next to you." "Me, too."

Craig stared at her for a moment and then took Venice's face in his hands and kissed her ever so tenderly. Exiting the room, he asked if she wanted to catch a movie. She walked him to the elevator and agreed on the spot to hook up with him later.

Before she could get back in the door, the phone was ringing. She grabbed for it. "Hello?"

"Hey, Niecy."

Venice sat down on the bed, exhaled, and said, "Hi, Jarvis."

"Look, Venice, I know I may have over reacted a little the other day."

"What do you mean, a little?"

"Sweetheart, I don't want to argue. I'm trying to apologize to you. This is hard for me because I feel like I had every right to be pissed off at you. Maybe I handled it wrong, but I meant every word I said. I don't like what's going on and I don't know how much longer I can deal with it. I want to be with you so bad and I hope you still want to be with me."

"My feelings for you are the same, but I like Craig's company and he's nice. I enjoy his company and you can't expect me to sit in my room and not socialize."

"I didn't say I expect you to do that, Niecy. I do expect you not to give up *my* stuff to the first brotha who smiled at you."

"What do you want me to do, Jarvis? Huh? Let me ask you something. Are you still a Michigan virgin? Well, are you?"

He calmly responded, "Are you asking me if I've been with anybody?"

"You know that's what I mean!"

"Once, but I also take a lot of cold showers because it's *you* that I want."

Venice selfishly became sick to her stomach, realizing that he'd sleep with someone else. She could now relate to how Jarvis was feeling.

"Are you seeing anyone now, Jarvis?"

"No, I want you and only you. How many times do I have to tell you?"

"What do you expect me to do, Jarvis?"

"Just pull up, Niecy. I've been trying to reach you all week so I know you've been with him. I don't want you giving it up to him anymore."

"Jarvis..."

"If I can, you can."

"Jarvis, I'll be up to visit you soon so we can talk."

"That will be nice. I need to see you."

"I'll call you back a little later, all right?"

He was silent on the other end and finally said, "Okay."

She hung up the phone, unpacked, and settled back into her room.

Hours later, Venice decided to go for a walk and found a bench overlooking the courtyard. Her cell phone rang and when he answered it was Joshua.

"Hey, Josh, what's up?"

"You tell me. I just got through talking to your boy."

"What did he say?"

"He's worried about ya'll. So...what happened?"

Venice closed the book that she was reading. "We talked about our situation. He said he wasn't sharing me."

Joshua chuckled. "Yeah, he gave me an uncensored version. So, what's up? What are you going to do?"

"I'm not going to do anything right now."

"I told you he wasn't going to deal with this situation long. You knew that."

"Well, why was he acting cool about it in the beginning?"

"That was for your sake! Look, Niecy, you know Jarvis is emotional when it comes to you. Do what you have to do. It'll work out."

"All right, Joshua. I know you're tired from the trip. Get some rest and I'll talk to you later. Thanks for coming."

"You bet. Take care."

Venice got back into the groove of dorm life. Staying with Craig those few days spoiled her. Monique seemed happy to have her back in the dorm. It was Monday morning, time to get to class. The alarm clock went off, awaking both women to early morning grumbling.

Monique said, "Venice, what time will you be through with classes today?"

Venice pulled the covers over her head. "Not until eleven. Why?"

"I wanted to know if you felt like going shopping. There's a new store that opened up in the outlet mall, and I want to check it out. Are you game?"

Venice thought for a moment as she got out of bed, gathering her belongings to go take a shower. "I guess so. Do you want to meet in the courtyard?"

"Cool! I'll pick you up after class."

Venice went into the bathroom to get ready for class.

The day went on as usual. When her classes ended, Venice walked to the courtyard and waited for Monique to pick her up. Some Greeks were practicing their steps loudly nearby in preparation for an upcoming step show. Someone came up behind her and put their hands over her eyes. She reached up and pulled them down and turned to see Galen and Sidney.

"What's up, baby girl?"

"Hey, Galen. Hey, Sidney."

Sidney asked, "Venice, what ya doing?"

"Waiting on Monique to pick me up. What are you guys up to?"

Galen replied, "Not much. We're headed to the house for a minute. I have practice later on."

Sidney sat down beside Venice. "Girl, his tail is coming over to get some leftovers with his greedy butt."

"You know I'm a growing boy. Anyway, somebody's got to eat it."

Venice glanced at Sidney and asked, "What kind of leftovers?"

Sidney pulled out her sunglasses. The sun was kicking. "I still have a tray of luncheon meat, Buffalo wings, and cheese and crackers. My girls went in and bought the food for us to nibble on. Do you want to come by and get some? You know you're welcome."

"No, not today. Maybe tomorrow."

"So…how are you and Craig doing? I heard my baby sister was about to kick some ass at the party the other night."

Sidney punched Galen's arm and asked, "Venice, is it true? Chanelle told me Craig's ex had her hands all over him and then she put her finger in your face."

"It's true, but I handled it."

Sidney gave Venice a high-five. "You go, girl!"

"Venice, I don't think Momma and Daddy would like for you to get kicked out of school for fighting. You'd better be careful."

"It's over, Galen."

"Okay." Galen looked at his watch. "Let's go, Sid. I want to get a nap in before practice. See you, Venice, and tell Craig hello."

"I will. See you later."

Once again, Venice sat there alone waiting for Monique to arrive. She positioned her sunglasses on her face, crossed her legs, and read her book. Craig kissed Venice on the neck after sneaking up behind her.

He climbed over the bench and said, "What are you reading?

"Biology. I'm waiting on Monique. Where are you headed?"

"I wanted to see you before I head down the road for the week."

"Well, you see me. Now what?"

Craig looked over Venice's shoulder and saw some of Miranda's friends staring at them. Craig pulled Venice to him and planted a long, wet kiss on her. He jumped down off the bench, pulled Venice along with him, and said, "Come on. Let's go."

As they walked past the women, Craig stopped and said, "Hey, Andrea. Where have you been hiding?"

"I've been around. How's Miranda?"

"I wouldn't know. Venice, this is Andrea and Trish and this is my sweetheart, Venice."

Both parties went through the formalities.

Craig asked Andrea if he could talk to her for a second. She got up off the bench and walked over to the side with him. Craig put his arm around her shoulder and said, "Andrea, I don't know what kind of games Miranda has put you and your posse up to, but if I hear anything about you guys picking with Venice, you're not going to like me very much. So my advice to you and your crew is to back off. Miranda had her chance and she screwed that up. Do you understand where I'm coming from?"

Andrea said, "I hear you."

Craig said, "No, I asked you if you understand where I'm coming from?"

She rolled her eyes and replied, "Yes, Craig."

"Cool."

As they rejoined the others, he said, "Ladies, have a nice afternoon!"

He put his arms around Venice's waist as they headed toward the parking lot. As they walked, some girls passed them and said, "Hey, Craig!!"

"Hello, ladies!"

Venice said, "It seems you're a wanted man."

He grinned. "Just being friendly. Baby, you have nothing to worry about."

When they reached his truck, she saw that he had his luggage inside. "Let me give you a ride back to the dorm." She didn't respond. "Venice, is everything okay?"

"Couldn't be better, except for the fact that I'm not going to see you for a few days."

"Don't remind me."

As he drove across campus, he rubbed her thigh. "I should kidnap you and take you with me."

"Believe me, it wouldn't be against my will. Maybe one week I can go with you."

His dark brown eyes penetrated hers. "That would be real nice."

Once they reached her dorm, he walked her to the room. Venice put her arm around his neck and gave him a slow, passionate kiss. The heat rose in her body. "I'm really going to miss your luscious lips."

"I'm going to miss more than that from you, baby."

He ran his thumb along her bottom lip, gazing into her saddened eyes.

"Well, let me get out of here. The sooner I leave, the sooner I'll get back to you."

As he got up, Venice stood in front of him, resting her head against his chest. He ran his hand up and down her back to soothe her. "I'll be back before you know it."

Venice hugged him tightly and solemnly said, "Call me when you get in."

Craig pulled her closer to his broad chest, pressing her firmly against him. "You bet. I'll call you the moment I get to my room."

He stared at her for a moment, then lowered his mouth onto her quivering lips. That was when the tears began to run down her soft cheeks. He finally raised his lips from hers and wiped her tears away with his hand. Venice opened the door for him and watched him walk down the hall to the elevator. She closed the door and thought what a long week it was going to be. She hoped hanging out with Chanelle and Monique would help pass the time.

Twenty-Seven

Tuesday, Craig finally got the call he'd been waiting on. He was in his office when the secretary told him that he had a call from Bryan Taylor. He closed the office door and picked up the phone. "Hello, Bryan. How are you?"

"I'm fine. What's up? Is Venice okay?"

"She's fine. Chanelle thought I should talk to you regarding a dream Venice had one night last week."

Bryan was instantly concerned. "What happened?"

Craig explained that he wasn't sure if it was a dream or if something had really happened to Venice. He told Bryan that Venice cried out hysterically in her sleep.

"Bryan, she was saying don't hurt me. Let me go. The rest was mumbling. When I woke her up, she was crying and she didn't know why. When I asked her about it, she said she couldn't remember the dream. I know you and Venice are very close. That's when I asked Chanelle. I didn't want to worry Galen. Chanelle said I had better talk to you about."

Bryan took a deep breath. "I knew this would eventually come up, but I didn't expect to have to deal with this so soon. What I'm about to tell you is something Venice wouldn't want her friends to know. Anyway, a couple of years ago, there was this guy at her school she was friends with. They did a lot of studying together. He'd come over to her house and she'd been to his house also. Well, one day, she went over to his house and the guy snapped or something and pulled a knife on her with the intention of raping her. It just so happened, Jarvis stopped by to talk to her since he knew she was over at his house studying. When Jarvis got there, he heard Venice begging and crying. He kicked the door in and beat the guy up pretty bad, putting him in the hospital. The police came and arrested the guy.

Afterwards, several other girls came forward and said the guy had actually raped them. The police arrested him on about three counts of rape and assault. Venice was a little traumatized from the incident for a while. We believe she sometimes has flashbacks when she's under stress. Now you understand why we're extra protective of her and why Jarvis is so close to her. Venice was bonded to Jarvis. That incident sealed it even more. I was out of town when it happened and I felt so helpless. When I came home, Gator and Tate were talking about having the guy taken out. It was a bad situation for all of us. Let me know if it happens again. She may need to speak to her counselors again. I appreciate you looking out for her and getting in touch with me."

Craig said, "Thanks for filling me in. Hopefully, it was just a bad night. Thanks for calling me back."

"Anytime. Let me give you my pager and home numbers."

They exchanged numbers and ended their conversation. Craig felt relieved since he knew what probably caused the dream. He'd have take special precautions with Venice's feelings.

It was "hump day" and Thanksgiving was approaching. Venice hadn't asked Craig if he'd made a decision about Thanksgiving. Monique was going home but Chanelle couldn't because she was still pledging a sorority. They kept the girls pretty much isolated from the rest of the college population during pledging. When Venice did see her, all she could do was make eye contact. But, one night, Chanelle snuck out of the dorm by lying down in the back seat of Venice's car so she could meet with Spoonie. It was a daring move, but a necessary one. She'd been on line for four weeks and her patience was growing thin. The caper went off without a hitch.

Venice decided to skip her classes on Friday and drive up to surprise Craig at his job on Thursday afternoon. Hopefully he wouldn't be too busy to spend the evening with her. It would also afford her the opportunity to see where he was co-oping. Venice couldn't wait for classes to come to an end. Galen called her and he got another cussing from his sister for running his mouth to their mother. Galen apologized and told Venice that he thought she'd already mentioned Craig to their mother. Venice told Galen her plans for surprising Craig.

She asked him, "Do you think you can keep that bit of info to yourself?"

"Forget you! Call me when you get there and you better not start skipping classes for a booty call."

"Goodbye, Galen!"

Venice slammed the receiver down.

Venice told Monique where she was going and to let Chanelle know also.

"Monique, page me if you need me. I'm going to have my cell phone while I'm driving and I'll call you when I get there. If my mom calls, take a message, then page me so I can return the call. The same goes for Jarvis."

As Monique stood in the door of their room to see her off, a dorm mate came running by, telling them that a girl on the floor above them was having a baby in her room. Monique looked at Venice in shock. They heard sirens, which must've been the paramedics arriving. You could sense panic and fear in the air. Venice felt sick to her stomach at that very moment. She said a silent prayer hoping student and baby were okay.

Monique said, "I'll get the details and page you later. Have fun!"

"Thanks."

Venice knew she had a two and a half hour drive ahead of her. She put in her favorite CD and, for some reason, she couldn't get the news of the baby out of her head. Venice felt sad for the girl and her parents, but mostly for the innocent little baby. Venice knew she had to shake this vibe that had consumed her. She took the CD out as she drove down the interstate and popped in some gospel music. Venice had a pleasant voice and sang along with the CD. It wasn't long after that she began to feel better. Venice looked at her watch and before she realized it, she had already been driving an hour. She was little a hungry, so she opened a pack of peanut butter crackers and guzzled down a coke that she'd packed for the road. Her cell phone rang and she answered, "Hello?"

"How are you, Niecy?"

"Not good."

"What have you been up to, baby?"

"Trying to reach you."

"Look, I'm sorry, okay?"

Venice said, "Okay."

"I love you, girl. That's why I freaked out about you. I don't want another man to know just how special you are."

"I'm glad you called. I missed talking to you."

"Niecy, I'm trying to handle this thing you've got going the best I can, but it's hard. So you might have to listen to me blow off steam some time."

Venice asked, "Do you love me?"

"What do you mean? Hell yeah! You know that!"

"Then that's all I need to know. Because, you know I love you, no matter what."

He paused for a moment and said, "I still don't like it that he's putting his damn hands on you."

"Jarvis!"

He laughed, then seriously said, "I mean that shit! I'll holler at you later, Niecy. I love you. Peace out!"

"Goodbye, J. I love you, too."

She hung up and felt guilt in the pit of her stomach.

Venice finally made it to the city where Craig was employed. She knew the name and address of the company, but no idea how to get there. She pulled into a service station and asked the attendant for directions. She got lost for about fifteen minutes, but finally found her way back on track.

The building where he worked was eight stories high and looked like a glass cube. Venice pulled into the parking lot about dusk. She took a deep breath, got out, and walked inside the lobby. She went to the ladies room to make sure she was still looking fresh and cute in her long green straight skirt with a slit up the back. Her ivory silk blouse was low-cut and showed off the voluptuous assets men adored.

Venice made sure her makeup was flawless by freshening her lipstick and combing her hair. Craig's company was on the fourth floor and when she entered the elevator, several people followed.

One gentleman stood behind her and whispered, "You sure are wearing that skirt."

Venice ignored this comment and was elated when the elevator doors opened. When she walked into the reception area, a young man told her that Craig's office was the third door on the left. The excitement was mounting when she reached his door and opened it. Once she did, Craig was leaning against his desk and a tall, leggy female was wiping his necktie with a paper towel.

They were both laughing and she seemed to be standing a little too close for Venice.

Craig spotted Venice and jumped up. "Hey, Venice! What are you doing here?"

The woman leered at Venice with a smirk on her face and tossed the paper towel in the trash. The skirt of her Donna Karan suit was just as short as the jacket. She was attractive, a little too attractive to be working so closely with Craig.

Venice stated sarcastically, "I'm sorry to barge in. Did I interrupt something?"

"No, baby! Come on in. Valerie, this is my girlfriend Venice."

The woman came over and extended her hand to greet Venice. "Nice to meet you, Venice. Let me get out of your way so you two can talk. I'll have those specs for you tomorrow, Craig."

"Thanks, Valerie. Have a good evening."

After she closed his door, Venice said, "Nice woman. What does she do around here?"

"She's my boss."

"Some boss. She looked like she was standing between your legs to me."

Craig saw where the conversation was headed and said, "Don't go there, Venice. What brings you all this way?"

Venice was still shaken up from witnessing Craig's boss being so chummy. "I missed you and wanted to surprise you."

Craig took her by the hands and they sat down on a sofa in his office. "This is a nice surprise. I'm glad to see you."

He gave her a kiss and Venice pulled away. "Nice office for a co-oping student. What other kind of perks is your boss giving you?"

Craig stood up and said, "Okay, Venice. I'm not screwing my boss. She's fine for her age, but I don't do stuff like that. Why are you acting like this?"

Venice walked over to look out his window. "Because!"

Craig put his hands up in surrender. "Look, it's late. I'm tired and hungry and my girl's in town. Please don't pick a fight with me. I'm too tired. Let's get out of here and grab something to eat. Is that cool?"

Venice agreed and they left Craig's office.

Venice trailed him to his hotel four blocks away. Craig let her walk ahead of him into the hotel so he could admire the view from behind. Luckily, they were in the elevator alone as they headed to Craig's room on the sixth floor.

Craig said, "Deja vu! This situation seems familiar. You look beautiful, baby."

He wrapped his arms around her waist from behind and kissed the curve of her neck. Craig opened the door to his room and put her bag near the closet. She kicked off her shoes and asked to use the phone to call Monique and Galen to let them know she'd arrived safely. Craig motioned to the phone as he removed his shirt and tie. He had decided to grab a quick shower.

Venice asked, "Are we going out to eat or ordering in?"

"Whatever you want to do. Check out the hotel menu and decide."

Venice thumbed through the menu while Craig started up the shower. She called Galen, got his answering machine, and left him a message before doing the same with Monique. She lay back on the pillows and rewinded the events that had just played out in front of her eyes. Venice didn't care what Craig said. His boss was being a little too friendly with him.

Venice could hear Craig singing in the shower. The steam was coming from under the bathroom door. He did like his showers hot. Minutes later, he came out of the bathroom wearing nothing but a towel. His body was dripping with water and he never looked sexier. The silky hair on his chest was as soft as hair on a newborn baby's head. He ignored Venice gawking at him as he searched for his lotion.

Damn she's beautiful!

Breaking the silence, he asked, "Have you decided what you want to do?"

"Let's go out."

"Fine with me."

"Do you need any help with that lotion?"

Craig approached her on the bed, crawled up next to her, and cuddled. He put his wet arms around her.

Venice hollered, "You're wet!"

Venice screamed as he held her down and began to tickle her. She struggled to get away, but was unsuccessful. When he stopped tickling her, she was soaked from head to toe. He rolled off her and started caressing her body gently. Venice felt the heat of his touch through her blouse.

"I'm glad you surprised me."

Craig's face was inches from hers and Venice could smell the sweetness of his breath. The intoxicating scent of the soap he had used made her lightheaded. He had her beneath him as his lips made the journey from her neck, down to the roundness of her breasts. Venice could no longer be mad at Craig for being too close with boss. It was only a matter of seconds before her blouse, skirt, and everything else was on the floor. They made love from the bed to the floor to the chair to the shower. They were exhausted and almost completely forgot about dinner. After showering, they dressed and headed out for a night on the town.

It was a cool, breezy night. Venice had on a pair of jeans with a red button down sweater. Craig wore a long sleeved, white cotton shirt with his jeans, which fit his thighs and butt with perfection. One of his baseball caps topped off the ensemble.

The riverfront downtown was bustling with activity and people. The aroma of various delicious foods filled the air and made their stomachs growl. The wonderful smell of pastries accompanying the delicious aroma of coffee filled the air as they passed one cafe. They walked hand in hand until they came upon an Italian restaurant.

Craig asked, "So, what do you have a taste for?"

"You."

Craig blushed and smiled and planted a big kiss on Venice's cheek. "I'll feed you when we get back to the room."

They walked around the corner and there it stood: "The Seafood Shack."

Craig said, "I've never eaten here, but I heard the food is good."

They entered the doors to the sound of New Orleans jazz music. The waitress seated them and gave them menus. As they gazed over the menus, Venice decided to run her foot up his leg under the table.

Craig blurted out, "Don't start something you can't finish."

Venice giggled. "I know what I want. I'd like the sampler platter with crabcakes, crab legs, fried shrimp, and fish."

"I'll just get a salad."

Venice looked at him in disbelief. "I know you're kidding."

Craig chuckled. "I just wanted to see what you would say. No, I'm going to get the shrimp scampi and the lobster tail."

They burst out in laughter. The waitress brought their drinks and took their orders. While they waited, Craig took Venice's hand into his. "You've become a little wild woman, Taylor."

"What do you mean?"

Craig leaned toward her and said, "It's getting to the point where I'm having a hard time keeping up with you. You're wearing me out. I'm beginning to think I'm out of shape. I thought I was going to have a heart attack back in the room."

"Baby, you're nowhere close to being out of shape. I'm not wild, but if I am, you bring it out in me."

"Venice, if I had it my way, I'd take you into the restroom and go for it."

Venice stood up and said, "Okay, let's go."

Craig leaned back in his chair in shock. "For real???"

Venice sat back down. "Gotcha!"

Craig shook his head and blushed. Their food arrived with steam rising from their meals. Craig fed Venice some lobster tail dipped in warm butter. In turn, Venice popped some of her crabcakes into his mouth. They ate until they both were stuffed.

After Craig paid the bill, they decided to walk around a bit to look at the different shop and vendors. They came across a laser tag amusement center and decided to play. After a few games, Craig wanted to take Venice on a sky lift. She was reluctant since she had a fear of heights. Craig finally convinced Venice and she held on tight as the lift took them high above the city lights. She eventually relaxed as she snuggled in his arms. Craig teased her by saying he was going to rock the seat.

Venice screamed out, "Craig, don't do that!"

He leaned over and nuzzled his face against her hair. "You know I wouldn't do that to you, baby."

Venice enjoyed Craig's fiery kiss in the cool night air and buried her face in his neck until the lift brought them back down. Craig asked if she cared to go up again. Feeling a little more relaxed, Venice agreed and they went for another ride. This time, they couldn't keep their hands or lips from each other's body. Venice was really enjoying her evening and didn't want it to end.

They finally made it back to the hotel and headed to the lounge. It was a quaint piano bar with soft, dim lighting. They sat in a corner booth and ordered drinks. Venice had to get a soda because of her age.

Craig put his arm around Venice's shoulder and asked, "What's happening on campus?"

"Nothing much. Classes and test. Classes and test."

There was a moment of silence while they listened to the piano player. Then Venice asked, "Craig, do you have any plans for Thanksgiving?"

He took a sip of his drink and replied, "I haven't thought about it much. Bernice usually works on Thanksgiving morning and sometimes we go by my aunt's for dinner. Why do you ask?"

"I wanted to invite you home with me for Thanksgiving."

Craig smiled and said, "Thanks, Venice. What do your folks think about it?"

"I've already talked to Momma. She said it was fine with her. So, what do you think?"

"It's okay with me, but let me get with Bernice and make sure it's cool with her. Now, come on and dance with me."

They danced to soft, piano melodies for a while. They were laughing and dancing and having a great time.

Craig ordered a bottle of tequila to take back to the room and said, "It's getting late. We'd better go. I've got to get up early for work."

As they reached the elevator, Venice put her arms around Craig's waist. "Do you really have to go to work?"

Craig replied as the doors closed on the elevator. "Yeah, I guess."

Venice sighed. "If you've got to go, then you've got to go."

When they got to the room, Craig called his boss and told her that he wouldn't be in the next morning. He explained that all his projects were caught up and he would see her next Tuesday. Fortunately, she approved his request.

Venice was delighted. As she undressed, she was already slightly buzzing from the tequila. Craig closed his eyes and let out a huge sigh. Venice climbed on top of him and ran her hands over his chest. She touched him intimately and immediately felt him come to life beneath her. She brought her lips to his as she slowly undressed him. He cupped her face in his hands so he could deepen his kiss. Their tongues danced magically together before briefly coming up for air. Their eye contact was undeniable of their wishes.

Venice was still a little sore from their earlier encounter, so she rested her hands against his chest. He gently guided her over his desire and braced her hips to meet each one of his thrusts. There was no denying the love and hunger they felt for each other as they shuddered with satisfaction. Venice felt shivers of heat shoot through her body everywhere he touched her. He covered her hardened nipples with his mouth, using his tongue to torment her further.

"Taylor...I-I love you."

Venice stiffened as she reached a peak of pleasure only one other man was able to take her to.

"Craig! Oh my God!"

Ripples of heat, fire, and electricity consumed them both as their bodies went up in flames. Venice seductively wiped the sweat from his brow and upper lip while staring into his dark, satisfied eyes. She lay down across his chest and listened to their hearts make the attempt to slow down.

She squirmed slightly. "Don't move. I want to stay inside you as long as possible. I'm afraid if I let you go, you won't come back."

Rising up on her elbow, Venice searched his eyes and could tell that his comment was serious.

"Craig, I'm not going anywhere."

Craig pulled Venice tighter to his chest and they fell asleep.

The next morning started earlier than expected. Venice's pager went off. When she checked to see who was paging her at 8 a.m., it was Galen. Venice jumped up because she sensed something was wrong. Afraid to call Galen back, she woke Craig up and asked him to call for her.

Craig groggily said, "Hey, Galen, Venice got your page. She wanted me to call. Is everything all right?"

"Well, we don't know yet. Daddy collapsed late last night and he's in the hospital. They're running tests on him to see what caused it."

Craig asked, "Do you want me to tell her?"

Venice was pacing the floor, extremely worried.

"Yes, thanks man. You can explain it to her. Tell her Bryan said not to worry and that it's probably nothing. He'll keep us posted."

"We'll be back in town in a little while. You don't have a game this week, do you?"

"No, we're off this week. Call when you get in and take care of my sister."

"You know I will."

Craig hung up the phone and asked Venice to come sit down so that he could explain everything to her. Venice began to cry and Craig got her a glass of water.

"Do you want to call Bryan?"

Venice was taking a sip of water and nodded that she did. She gave Craig her address book with Bryan's number. Craig called and luckily, Bryan answered the phone.

"Hello?"

"Bryan, this is Craig. Galen called and told us what happened. Venice is here with me in Johnsonville. She's upset and wants to talk to you."

Craig handed Venice the phone. "Bryan, what's going on?"

Bryan explained that their father had taken ill, but it didn't seem to be serious. He told her that there was no need for her and Galen to miss school to come home. His words calmed her, but didn't reassure her that her father would be fine. Venice told Bryan that she would head back to campus that afternoon and to call as soon as there was an update. Bryan asked her to put Craig back on the phone. Bryan asked Craig if Venice had her car in Johnsonville. Once he told him that she did, he asked Craig not to let her drive. Craig told Bryan that he'd take Venice back to campus and make sure her car made it back also. Bryan thanked him and said he'd call them later with any update.

During the ride back to campus, Craig hugged her tightly and said, "Don't worry, Venice. Everything's going to be okay."

The rest of the ride home was quiet.

The next couple of days were tense. Venice went to her classes but was unable to concentrate. By the time the afternoon set in, Galen met her after class and told her that their father was going to be fine. He would be coming home in about three days.

Venice was relieved and felt like she could get her life back on track. She did want to go home the weekend. She just had to see her father. Galen had a game so he couldn't go. She had no problem driving home alone, but Craig insisted on driving her. She welcomed the company and his support. They would leave Friday evening and arrive around midnight. The days leading up to the weekend flew by. It had been almost three months since she'd been home. It was going to be good to see her family, especially Crimson. Since they were going to be arriving in the middle of the night, Venice and Craig were going to stay at Bryan's.

Bryan and Sinclair had a very nice home. Crimson had her own room upstairs along with an adjoining "play room" where all her toys and dolls were kept. Sinclair didn't want her bedroom to be cluttered with that kind of stuff. The master bedroom was down the hall from Crimson's. It had a large four-poster bed, a beautiful marble fireplace, and a sitting area. That was Venice's favorite room in the entire house. There were two guest bedrooms on the hall. On the main floor, they also had a living room and formal dining room with a beautiful cherry table, which seated ten. They used this room often for dinner parties.

Bryan's office was off the kitchen. That way, he didn't have far to go for the occasional sandwich. Sinclair really did have a good eye for decorating. Venice had to give her that. Their kitchen was huge and Sinclair loved to cook. She specifically wanted a restaurant-style oven, which was very expensive. Price was not an option since Bryan loved to eat.

Bryan's office was fully furnished with office equipment including a computer, fax, printer, etc. Another favorite room of Venice's was the downstairs recreation room off the three-car garage. It had a fully stocked bar, big screen TV, and pool table. There was also a small bedroom with bath in the basement. Sometimes, when Bryan had the fellows over to watch sports, this is where they hung out.

It was about eleven-thirty when Venice called Bryan. They were about thirty minutes away from home. Bryan was still up and told them to pull around back so he could let them into the garage. Once they arrived, Bryan greeted them and gave them the option of staying upstairs or downstairs. They decided to hang out downstairs.

As they settled into the room, Bryan asked if they were hungry because there was still some dinner in the fridge. Venice wasn't hungry. She was tired, but wanted to go up and see Crimson. Venice promised not to wake her.

While Venice went upstairs, Craig and Bryan talked as they watched some film on a player Bryan was scouting. Bryan asked Craig if he would like something to drink. Craig accepted a beer and they drank together. Venice came back downstairs after giving Crimson a kiss. She told Bryan and Craig goodnight and turned in.

Bryan and Craig talked for about another hour. Then Bryan said, "Man, I know you're tired. I'm going to let you turn in. If you need anything, help yourself. There's some soda or whatever behind the bar in the fridge. If you want snacks, look in the cabinets. I'll see you guys in the morning. Is Venice all right?"

"She's all right," Craig responded. "Just tired."

"Thanks for taking care of her for me."

"No problem."

After Bryan went upstairs, Craig entered the bedroom. Venice already had on her nightclothes. Craig changed and crawled under the covers. Craig couldn't help but to caress Venice's face as she slept soundly. He pulled her close to his body.

She opened her eyes, put her arms around his neck, kissed him, and said, "Thank you."

She turned over and pulled his arm around her waist so they could fall off to sleep.

The next day brought about what Venice thought was thunder. It turned out to be the bucking and jumping of her eight-year-old niece at eight o'clock on a Saturday morning. Sinclair had already left for the flower shop. Venice eased out of bed to let Craig get some well-deserved rest.

Venice put on her robe and went upstairs to see her adorable niece. When she walked into the kitchen, Bryan was cooking breakfast and Crimson was dancing around the table. When she turned to see Venice, she ran and jumped up into her arms, wrapping her long legs around Venice's body, almost knocking her down.

"Hey ,Auntie! What took you so long to come see me?"

"Girl, you've grown and it feels like you've gotten heavier. Did you get the package I sent you?"

"I sure did and I love all the neat stuff. Are you going to take me somewhere today?"

Venice got Crimson to unclamp her legs so she could sit down at the table. "We'll see. I brought a friend home with me. His name's Craig."

Crimson looked funny and said, "Where is he?"

"He's asleep, so don't be so loud. Your jumping around is what woke me up."

"Momma said you and your boyfriend were coming to visit. Is he your boyfriend?"

"I guess so, nosy."

"I thought Jarvis was your boyfriend?"

Venice was surprised for a moment. "Who are you? Oprah Winfrey?"

Crimson thought for a moment and then said, "I don't like boys because they stink."

Bryan laughed. "We'll see what you think in a few years."

Venice went over to Bryan. "Can I help with anything?"

"No thanks. I have everything under control." Bryan glanced over at Crimson. "My baby girl called you out, didn't she?"

"She's nosy like her Mammy. I'm going to go lie back down for a while. I'm still a little tired from the drive. Have you heard from Momma?"

"No, but Jarvis called. I told him you were still asleep."

Venice swallowed hard. "Thanks, B."

"Have you talked to him lately?"

"I talked to him the other day."

"What's up?"

Venice poured a glass of orange juice. "We're all right."

Bryan left the conversation alone after that.

Venice told Crimson, "I'll see you in a little while. I'm still tired."

Crimson grinned. "I'll be waiting for you."

Venice made her way back downstairs and eased back into the bed. Craig was still asleep. Venice always loved to watch him sleep. She stroked his face and snuggled up to him. His body felt so warm against hers and Venice was feeling a little horny. It had been days since they'd done it. She wanted to release some stress and needed some tenderness. She began to kiss his neck and chest, which instantly aroused him. She ran her hand over his chest and caressed him.

Craig woke up and remembered where they were. "Venice, what are you doing?"

"I'm trying to seduce you."

"Your family's right upstairs."

"They're not coming down here."

Venice continued to caress his body. Craig laughed and tried to move her hands away. He was a little nervous about the close quarters. "Come on, Venice. I don't think this is a good idea."

Venice asked, "What's wrong? Are you scared?"

"I think it turns you on to know your brother is right upstairs."

Venice snickered. "My brother knows what's up. Why do you think he let us sleep down here together?"

Venice became more aggressive. She straddled him and ran her tongue over his nipples and neck. He tried to resist her, but was close to giving in.

"Venice!"

"What?"

She reached under the covers and took him in her hands. Craig flipped Venice over on her back and said, "Stop! This isn't cool, okay?"

Venice stared up at him with disappointment. "Whatever!"

She kicked the covers back, got up, and went into the bathroom to shower. When he heard the shower come on, Craig went over and knocked on the bathroom door.

"Yes?" Venice asked from the opposite side.

"Can I come in?"

"It's open."

Craig entered and pulled back the shower curtain. "I'm sorry. I'm just uncomfortable trying that here. Surely you understand where I'm coming from."

Venice didn't respond right away. She finally turned to him and said, "You're not nervous about being in here."

"Are you mad?"

"No, just disappointed."

Craig took in her nakedness and his body stirred. Seeing suds on her cinnamon skin made his throat dry and body hot. He said, "I'll see what I can do for you later."

Venice smiled and pointed her finger at him. "I'm going to hold you to that. Now get out of here."

Before closing the curtain, Craig reached in and splashed some water in Venice's face. She threw some back at him as he ran out the room. Venice finished her shower and got dressed. Craig also showered and dressed, then they went upstairs for breakfast. When they finished breakfast, they headed over to her parents' house. As they drove away, her pager went off. It was Jarvis. Venice didn't say anything so Craig knew it must be him. Venice didn't call him back on her cell phone. She decided to wait until she got to her house.

Venice's mother met them at the door and welcomed her baby girl home. Venice introduced Craig and then went inside to find her father sitting in his favorite recliner in the den. She gave him a big hug and kiss. "How are you feeling, Daddy?"

"I'm fine, baby. What are you doing, leaving school to come all the way here?"

"I wanted to make sure you were okay. You had me worried."

"Oh, baby, I'm all right. Who is this fine young man with you?"

Venice motioned for Craig to come over. "Daddy, this is Craig Bennett."

Mr. Taylor put his hand out to shake Craig's hand. Craig said, "Nice to me you, sir. I hope you're feeling better."

"Have a seat Craig and, yes, I'm feeling much better. I understand you're a friend of Galen's?"

Craig sat down while Mrs. Taylor brought them some iced tea. "Yes, sir. I've known Galen for three years now."

Mrs. Taylor took her seat in the recliner next to the man of the house. "We're so happy to finally meet you, Craig."

"Me, too."

Moments later, Venice asked, "Do you have any errands that we can run for you, Momma?"

"I do need a prescription filled and I think we're out of milk. You know that niece of yours really can drink some milk."

Mrs. Taylor searched the room for her purse. When Venice realized what she was doing, she said, "Momma, I think I saw your purse in the hallway."

"I think you're right. Let me go get the prescription for you."

After they left the room, Mr. Taylor asked, "Son, did Venice tell you that I used to be a policeman?"

"Yes, sir, she did. How many years did you serve?"

"I was an officer for twenty-one years and loved every minute of it. The only thing I hated was being away from the family so much. Fortunately, they turned out fine."

Craig laughed and said, "I bet you've seen some wild things, Mr. Taylor."

"Son, I have to admit that I've seen some things that would make the average man cry. But you have to have an iron stomach and be able to put your emotions aside. Especially when you come home to your family. It makes you appreciate life a whole lot more. I miss it sometimes. On the other hand, I'm glad I don't have to do that anymore. Cops have a stressful job, with all the decision making in tense situations."

The men continued to talk while Venice went up into her room to return Jarvis' page.

"Hello?"

"Hey, J. What's up?"

"When did you get in?"

"Late last night. I wanted to come home and see how Daddy was doing."

"So how's he doing?"

"He seems fine. How are you, Mr. Anderson?"

"Besides missing you, I'm doing okay. Did Galen come with you?"

"No, Craig came with me."

For a moment, Venice thought Jarvis had hung up because she couldn't even hear him breathing.

"I see. Well, I'd better let you get back to Pops. I hadn't talked to you in a few days, so I was checking in on you."

"Jarvis?"

"Yes?"

"I miss you."

He replied sarcastically, "Yeah, I bet."

Venice burst into tears. The situation was beginning to take its toll.

"Niecy, please don't cry. You know I can't stand for you to cry. I didn't mean to upset you. I know you're worried about your dad. I'm sorry."

Venice continued to sniff and wipe her tears in an attempt to get a hold of herself, but she couldn't stop them.

"Niecy, do you hear me? Please stop crying."

"I'm-I'm sorry Jarvis. I didn't mean to do that."

"You don't have to apologize to me. It's my fault."

"I do miss you, Jarvis."

"I believe you, baby. Look, go take care of your dad and call me when you get back to school. Okay?"

"Okay and thanks for calling."

"Hey! We *are* going to make it, Niecy. You'll see. I love you."

"I love you, too."

When Venice hung up, she sat there for a moment trying to put herself back together. Hearing Jarvis' voice always did things to her that no other man had been able to do. Until then. Venice grabbed her purse and headed back downstairs.

Craig stood up when he saw Venice and her mom.

"Craig you don't have to go if you don't want to. You can stay here and watch the game with Daddy."

"Are you sure?"

"Yes, I'm sure. I'll swing by and pick up Crimson so she can go with me."

Mr. Taylor said, "Craig, I'd love the company."

Craig agreed since he really did want to see the game. Mrs. Taylor walked Venice out on the porch. "Venice, Craig seems to be a nice young man."

"He is, Momma."

"Jarvis called me last week."

"What did he want?"

"Nothing. He was just calling to say hello."

Venice stared out into the yard for a moment, feeling it coming.

"Venice, you know that boy's still in love with you."

"I know, Momma. I still love him, too."

"So, what's going on with you and Craig?"

"Momma, leave it alone. Okay?"

"Watch your tone with me, girl."

"I'm sorry. I don't feel up to talking about it right now."

Her mom accepted her plea and told Venice to be careful as she walked toward Craig's truck.

Twenty-Eight

With Venice out of town, Monique was enjoying having the room to herself once again. Chanelle came down to the room a few times to hide out from her sorors. She hoped they would cross over that weekend. Monique heard a knock at the door. When she opened it, Chanelle rushed in.

"Girl, hurry up and close the door!"

"Chill, Chanelle! Those hoes better not come up to my room starting no shit."

"You're crazy, Monique. That's a trip about that girl having that baby in the room. Have you heard any news?"

"I heard from a girl on that floor that the baby's doing fine. It's a little girl. The chick that had the baby was able to hide the pregnancy. She was a P.E. major and wore sweats all the time. She was pregnant when she got here. She never told anybody that they know of. I would've been scared to death."

"Me, too. Have you heard from Venice?"

"She left a message that she arrived safely. I expect her to call today to say how her dad is doing. You know Craig drove her?"

Chanelle lay on Venice's bed and said, "For real! I thought he might be too busy."

Monique went over to the mirror to smooth her fresh hairstyle. "I guess not. I think Mr. Craig has his nose wide open for Miss Thang. She must've really put something on that man and I ain't talking about voodoo."

"Yeah, Monique, but he's not totally in the driver's seat. Jarvis still has his name written all over Venice."

"I know that's right! Every time he calls, she's shook up when she gets off the phone. Sometimes, I catch her crying. I can't imagine what she's going through."

"Monique, between you and me, Venice and Jarvis used to be married."

Monique turned away from the mirror and glared at Chanelle. "Married! What happened? Does Craig know?"

"Yes, Craig knows. I don't want to completely tell her business, but I will say it wasn't their choice to separate. I also know they're still very much in love. That's why you see her crying so much. She's in love with both of them and she's torn."

Monique sat on her bed in bewilderment. "No wonder. Venice must be going through hell."

"Don't say anything to her or anyone else. Be patient with her if she seems short with you."

"No problem. Thanks for telling me."

Chanelle changed the subject. "I'm so tired of all this pledging crap! Those fools are making me hate their asses. One of them thought she was going to kick my tail the other day, but my line sisters and I stood up to her."

Monique asked, "If I decide to pledge, are you going to hook a sista up?"

"Hell no! I'm going let your tail suffer just like I have."

"That's low down, Chanelle. I ought to open this door and call some of those fools and let them know where you're hiding out."

Chanelle laughed and asked, "You wouldn't do a sista like that, would you?"

"Hell yeah!"

They laughed together and continued to chat a while longer.

Crimson came running downstairs with her jacket, jumping the last three steps and startling Venice. Venice thought Crimson had fallen and knocked herself senseless.

Sinclair said, "Child, you're going to kill yourself one of these days." Sinclair helped her with her jacket. "You'd better behave yourself. Remember your aunt has a license to spank."

Crimson gave Sinclair a hug, promised she would behave, and

ran out the door. Sinclair left and told Venice to make sure that she locked up. Before she left, she called Bryan on his cell and told him she had Crimson and that Sinclair was headed back to the shop. Venice set the alarm, locked up the house, and was off to the grocery store.

Hours later, Venice came back with the items that her mother requested. Since she'd been gone, her mother had cooked pork chops, sweet potatoes, turnip greens, and hot water cornbread. The smell hit her as they walked up on the porch. Crimson ran through the door and jumped in her granddaddy's lap.

Mr. Taylor said, "Hey, shorty! Where did you come from?"

Craig entered the room from the kitchen to continue to watch TV and started tickling Crimson.

Craig said, "Galen called and said his game will be on TV tonight."

Crimson tried to tickle Craig.

Venice was walking toward the kitchen and said, "I know. Bryan told me. He's having some friends over to watch the game."

Mr. Taylor said, "I know that ain't nobody but Tate and Gator. It'll be fun. Those guys are crazy. They played in the NFL with Bryan."

Venice returned to the kitchen to have dinner with her Mother.

"Venice, I'm glad you came to see your daddy. He was so happy to see you. He and Craig seem to get along fine. I'm really happy that you found someone to spend time with."

Venice took in a mouthful of greens. "Thanks, Momma."

Mrs. Taylor got up to add some more food to her plate, then boldly said, "But he's no Jarvis, huh?"

Venice didn't even blink or respond. She just continued to eat. They shared the quality time together without interruptions. Craig was nice enough to wait on her father and Crimson while Venice talked with her mother.

When he came into the kitchen for refills, Mrs. Taylor said, "Craig, make yourself at home. I have plenty of food so eat up."

Craig thanked her as he refilled the cups and got the pepper for Venice's dad. They finished their dinner and dessert.

Venice and Craig cleaned up the kitchen while Crimson went out back to play on the swing set. Bryan had purchased it so that

Crimson would have somewhere to play over her grandparents' house. It wasn't long before Mr. Taylor had unzipped his pants and was snoring in his recliner. Venice's mother decided to take a little nap also. She reclined in her chair and joined in with the snoring. Venice and Craig decided to play a pick up game of basketball. Crimson eventually grew bored and played with them. Venice and Crimson were on the same team but they lost anyway. After Craig's victory, Venice and Craig sat out in the swing while Crimson swung from the tree limbs. Craig drifted off to sleep.

Venice went over to play with Crimson and they went down to the creek in back. Venice took Crimson's shoes and socks off so she could wade in the water. She did the same.

"So, muskrat, how's school?"

"It's okay, but there's this nasty little boy who keeps on pulling my hair."

Venice kicked some water toward her. "You tell that knuckle-head that if he pulls your hair again, he's going to start to turn into a donkey."

Crimson laughed. "Okay, thanks Auntie. Where's Craig?"

"He's asleep."

Crimson said, "We ought to find a frog and put it in his shirt."

"Crimson! That wouldn't be very nice. But... let's see if we can find one."

They giggled together and looked for a frog. Finally, Venice found one and gave it to Crimson. As they went back up to the swing where Craig was sleeping, they found it difficult not to laugh. Craig was really getting his sleep on when Crimson gently laid the frog on his stomach. They stood there snickering as the frog just sat there.

A few minutes later, the frog began to reposition himself. Craig woke up, saw the frog, jumped up, and hollered. He chased Venice and Crimson around the yard and it wasn't hard for him to catch them. He caught Crimson first, held her down, and tickled her silly.

Venice was trying to get her shoes back on when he caught up with her. He sat on her and tickled her until she was almost in tears. Crimson tried to help Venice out by jumping on Craig's back. Instead, he held them both down.

They finally screamed, "We give up!"

He let them up and told Venice, "That was cold blooded, girl. I'll get you back later."

Venice just laughed. "I'm really scared."

It was getting close to game time so they went back inside. Venice's dad was awake, but her mother was still asleep.

Venice hugged her dad and said, "We're getting ready to head back over to Bryan's, daddy. I don't want to wake Momma up. Tell her that I'll call her later or see her tomorrow for church. Can I get you anything before we go?"

Mr. Taylor said, "No, baby. Your Momma and I are just fine. Make sure you call when you get there so I'll know you made it safely."

"We will."

He got up to see them out. Crimson was holding her granddaddy around his waist as they walked. "I love you, Granddaddy. Tell Grandmomma I love her, too. Okay?"

"Okay, shorty. Here's a dollar for your piggy bank."

"Thank you, Granddaddy!"

Craig thanked Mr. Taylor again for his hospitality, shook hands, and went to buckle Crimson in the truck.

Venice said, "Daddy, are you sure you're feeling okay? I can stay over here tonight, if you want me to."

"I'm fine. Go on and enjoy yourself. I'll see you tomorrow, and Venice?"

"Yes, sir?"

"I like him. I like him very much."

"I love you, Daddy. Tell Momma also."

Venice made him go inside the house before they drove off and before they'd made it two streets away, Crimson was sound asleep.

Craig said, "I had a good time and your mom can really cook. I really miss that mother's touch. Bernice can cook okay, but it's not like Momma's was."

"I don't think any daughter can cook just like her mom. I don't care how many times I've tried; I just can't get my dressing like my mom's. I don't expect anyone to ever figure that one out."

Craig laughed and made his way around town until they made it back to Bryan's neighborhood.

When they arrived, Craig pulled into the garage as instructed by Bryan. He was home and so was Sinclair. Craig carried the sleeping Crimson into the house because she was too heavy for Venice. Bryan met them in the den and took her upstairs. He told them that his friends should be over shortly and to help themselves to the snacks and drinks.

Venice said, "I'm going to take a shower and if those fools get here before I get out of the shower, don't pay them any attention. They don't have any sense. I'm going to call Daddy and let him know we made it."

Craig jokingly asked, "Can I come?"

"Sure."

He laughed, sat down, and started scanning the channels. Bryan came back down and joined him on the sofa and they popped opened their beers.

Bryan asked, "Where's Venice?"

"Taking a shower."

Bryan held his beer up and said, "Let the games begin."

Venice laid out her clothes, which consisted of a T-shirt and some jeans. She remembered she had forgotten to call Monique. She laid across the bed to call her and as the phone rang, her mind wandered back to the poor girl who had that baby in the dorm. "Hello?"

Venice said, "Hey, Miss Thang! Do you miss me?"

"It's about time your tail called me. Chanelle has been down here asking if I'd heard from you. How's your Dad?"

"He's doing really good. He doesn't even look like he's been sick."

"Is Craig holding up all right?"

"He's doing fine. He's sitting in the other room with my brother waiting on the game. My niece put a frog on him today. It was hilarious. We're going to church with my mom in the morning. Tell Chanelle to hang in there. Hopefully she'll cross tomorrow."

"I hope so. I'm tired of her sneaking around. Oh! The girl who had the baby is okay and so is the baby. It was a little girl. They said she'd kept it hidden from her roommate and her parents."

Venice said, "That's so sad. I hope whatever issues she has will get worked out. What else has been going on?"

"Well, we went to this house party last night and some fool pulled out a gun. You know we started stampeding. I knocked a few people down myself trying to get out."

"Who did you go with?"

"This guy I met the other day."

Venice said, "Monique, you'd better quit hooking up with those street thugs. Next thing you know, you're gonna catch a bullet or something."

Monique laughed and said, "You're a party pooper, Venice, but I hear you. I'll be more careful. Thanks."

Venice yawned and said, "Well, chick, I'm getting ready to hit the showers before Bryan's buddies get over here to watch the game. You'd better behave yourself."

Monique answered, "You know me."

"That's why I said it. Don't be down there tripping. Do you hear me?"

"Yes, Momma, and next time, take me home with you."

"If you weren't going home for Thanksgiving, I would have invited you."

"I know, girl. Anyway... Next time. I'll let you go. Tell everyone hello and I'll see you when you get back."

Venice said, "Peace out!!"

Venice took her shower and changed into her jeans. She could hear that Bryan's friends had arrived.

When she entered the room, Gator said, "There's my girl!"

He came over and gave her a big hug, picking her up off her feet. Craig was watching out of the corner of his eyes while he took a sip of beer.

Venice said, "Hey, Gator. You can put me down now."

As he put her down, he asked, "Oh, what's wrong? You're too big for me to pick up since you're a college woman now?"

"I guess so."

"I bet if your boy wasn't sitting over there, you wouldn't care."

Bryan and his other friend, Tate, laughed and looked at Craig.

Tate also came and gave Venice a hug and kiss. "Nice to see you, Venice."

Bryan laughed and said, "Craig, you're going to let them kiss on your woman like that?"

Gator asked, "What happened to Jarvis, Venice? Ya'll was kicking it big time."

The room grew silent for a moment before Bryan said, "Damn, Gator!"

"What? I just asked what happened between them."

Craig was cool, but watched Venice squirm in her seat.

She said, "Chill, Gator."

Gator went over to Craig at the bar and said, "I didn't mean any harm. It's just that we didn't expect to *ever* see Venice with anybody except for Jarvis. I was beginning to think that fool had some type of voodoo spell on her. I should've kicked his little ass when I found out he was hitting it. "

Venice screamed, "Gator!"

Craig didn't appreciate Venice's private life being exposed, but wanted to avoid drama in her brother's house so he said, "No offense taken. Thanks."

Venice put her hands over her face in disgust and listened as they continued to discuss her business in front of Craig.

Gator said, "Craig, you have to excuse us. We've been around Venice since she was Crimson's age."

Bryan grabbed some peanuts and said, "He's right, man. You might as well get used to it. It's our job to screen Venice's friends. Jarvis caught hell for a long time, but he's cool now."

Venice hollered, "Hey! Nobody's going to check anybody out tonight."

Tate opened his beer and said, "Be quiet, girl, and let grown men handle their business."

Venice jumped up in disgust. "I don't believe this. Bryan, you need to get your boys."

Bryan got up to adjust the lights. "Sit down, girl, and don't tell me to get them. I've never been able to control them anyway. You know how this works."

Gator said, "Craig, don't get us wrong. When you look at it, Venice, being the only girl besides Crimson and my two babies, has about five daddies. We've always been like that with her. My girls are gonna catch the same hell when they get old enough."

Craig said, "I understand. I'm glad Venice has people looking out for her. I'm looking out for her also."

Venice was sitting on the sofa listening to them discuss her like she wasn't even in the room.

Tate said, "We're always going to be in Venice's corner. It never hurts to have reinforcements."

Venice stood up and said, "I don't believe you guys. Stop!"

Bryan hugged Venice around her neck. "Hush, girl! We have to get that business out of the way. Okay, Venice?"

The guys all laughed.

Craig joined in and said, "I was kind of expecting this from you, Bryan, being on your turf. But, I didn't expect you to have a posse."

Venice didn't find their little game funny anymore. She figured she had out grown all of that when she left high school. Bryan and his friends always tried to intimidate the guys she dated. Craig saw that Venice was a little upset, but he knew she was fighting a losing battle with them. He probably would've done the same if he had been much older than Bernice.

Venice got up and stormed up the stairs. Bryan asked, "Where are you going?"

She didn't answer him. She just continued up the stairs, pissed off.

Bryan laughed and turned to Craig. "Man, she's pissed! But, she'll be all right."

Tate added, "She should be used to it by now."

Craig smiled. "I'll go check on her."

When Craig got upstairs, Venice was in the kitchen slamming things around and fixing a sandwich. She leered at him and asked, "Do you want one?"

"No thanks. Are you okay?"

"I'm fine. They're a trip! I'm starting to get sick of their intimidation games. They practically had me in tears on prom night and thought it was funny. Jarvis quit paying any attention and started retaliating against them. They started respecting Jarvis more, so they eased up on him. After that, they started looking out for him. Through it all, I knew they really liked him. That's why they did it. I'm sorry they treated you like that."

"Venice, they didn't mean anything by it."

Venice took a Coke out the fridge, slammed the door, and said, "They knew what they were doing. They were testing you to see how you would handle yourself."

Craig handed her a paper towel. "How do you think I did?"

"Fine and I'm glad you didn't let those fools rattle you. I think you surprised them. I've dated some guys who never took me out after my brothers and his silly friends got a hold on them. I really love those guys, but sometimes they can go too far. You wouldn't believe what they gave me for graduation."

Craig sat down and asked, "What?"

"Well, Bryan bought my car for me, Tate paid for my senior trip to the Bahamas and Gator, bless his heart, bought me some mutual funds and told me not to touch them except for an emergency."

Craig said, "I wish I had friends in high places. That was cool."

"I guess. I still hate it when they do what they do."

Craig laughed and said, "Come on back down and watch the game with us."

"I might come back in a while. I'm going up to look in on Crimson and holler at Sinclair."

Craig got up from the table, gave her a hug, and told her that he'd see her downstairs. Venice sat in the kitchen and finished her sandwich. She could hear that the game had started. The fellows were hollering on every play.

Venice finished eating and went upstairs. Sinclair was on the phone with some friends. Venice knocked on her door and heard her say, "Come in."

Sinclair told the person on the phone to hold on. Venice stuck her head in and said, "I'm sorry. I just came up to look in on Crimson."

"No problem. I'll see you in the morning and, Venice; it's good to see you. Goodnight."

Venice told her goodnight and closed the door. Venice made her way down the hall to Crimson's room. She eased in and saw that her room was as neat as a pin. Sinclair had Crimson's Sunday dress laid out. It was red trimmed in white satin. Crimson had kicked the covers off, so Venice covered her back up and gave her a kiss.

When Venice came back downstairs, she went into Bryan's office to use his phone. Even though Jarvis had a game that night, she wanted to leave a message on his voice mail.

"Hey, baby. It's me. I'm sorry about freaking out earlier. I'm glad you called me. I hope you had a good game tonight. I'm heading back to school tomorrow and I'll call when I get in." She paused for a moment and then added, "Jarvis...Baby...I *do* love you. Goodnight."

Venice made her way back downstairs to the noise. The game was in full swing and Galen was playing a good game. She wished Joshua would've been able to come by, but he had to go out of town for some type of training class. Sadly, he wouldn't be back until the middle of the week. Venice would just have to catch up with him the next time.

Venice found her a seat next to Craig.

Gator asked, "You cool, baby girl?"

Venice pulled a blanket over her and said, "I'm all right."

Craig leaned over and whispered, "Are you sure?"

"Yes, I'm used to them."

They continued to watch the game and Galen made two touchdowns. Bryan called their dad to see if he was watching the game and to make sure that he was fine. They talked for a few minutes before hanging up.

After a while, Venice fell asleep leaning against Craig's chest.

Bryan laughed and said, "Craig, you might need to wake Venice up and tell her to go to bed."

Craig chuckled and said, "All right."

Craig woke Venice up and helped her up from the sofa. He started to walk her to the bedroom. When she looked around, Bryan and his friends all had smirks on their faces.

Gator said, "Oh, hell no! I know Bryan ain't letting ya'll sleep in the same room."

Tate said, "Bryan must really like you, Craig, cause ain't no way in hell I would let you in there!"

Venice went around the room and gave all of them a hug and kiss. "Cut it out!" As she walked away, she said, "I love you guys! Goodnight!" Then she gave all of them the middle finger salute.

They burst out laughing as Craig closed the door behind them. Venice lay across the bed. Craig covered her body with his and asked if she needed any help undressing.

Smiling naughtily, she answered, "Don't start anything unless you're willing to finish it."

They could hear Tate holler out, "Craig, you've been in there long enough!"

Craig ignored the remark, stroked Venice's face, and brought his lips to hers. Venice welcomed his mouth, pulling him tighter to her. He dipped his head and kissed the curve of her neck down to her nipples, which were protruding through her T-shirt. He couldn't help but play in the auburn highlights of her soft hair.

Finally, he sat up on the bed and smiled. "You're killing me, girl. I want you so bad. Get some sleep. We have a long trip ahead of us tomorrow. I'll be back in a little while."

"I'll try to wait up for you."

"Okay."

Craig kissed her on the cheek and closed the door behind him as he left the room.

After the game was over and everyone was gone to their prospective places for the night, Craig returned to the room and loved Venice as hard as he could without waking up the house. Tears were shed, love was confessed, and guilt set in. He wanted this woman in his life, but was she willing to commit?

Twenty-Nine

Sunday morning, they hurriedly dressed and went on their way to church. It had that down home appeal where everybody knew each other. The service was going along great. The Taylor family took up a full pew. Little did the Taylors know, Venice and Craig had a surprise in store for the entire family. When it came to the part in the program for the song of preparation before the sermon, the music started to play and Craig got up from the pew and stood next to the pianist. Everyone in the Taylor family was stunned, except for Venice. Her dad was at church for the first time in a long time. Sometimes it takes something like a near death experience to wake people up. What happened to her dad scared him. More so than when he was a policeman. At least then he could control the situation a little bit. Venice had asked Craig if he would sing her dad's favorite song if she were able to work it out with the choir director. It was an old spiritual that her dad had always loved since he was a young man. Needless to say, Craig did the song justice. His high tenor voice brought the congregation to their feet, shouting joy and praise. Venice found herself a little overcome by the message in the song. Mr. Taylor was visibly grateful for the gift from his daughter and her new love. It was a good service.

After returning to the Taylors for dinner, the men gathered in the den to watch football. Mrs. Taylor had completed dinner except for the cornbread. Once it was ready, the family sat down and had dinner. Venice and Craig had to leave. They wanted to get back to campus before ten o'clock at the latest. Venice knew Craig was still tired from the football party the night before. She offered to drive back to give him an opportunity to catch up on his sleep. He accepted her offer without argument. It was going to be a lengthy drive, so they didn't waste any time with dinner and then said their good-byes. Craig thanked the family for their hospitality and told them that he hoped to see them again soon. As Venice and Craig pulled out, the Taylors stood in the driveway and waved goodbye until they were out of sight.

Before they could the reach the interstate, Craig was fast asleep. Venice decided to put in some music to help with the drive. She wanted something with a fast tempo because she was little tired herself. After about four hours, she stopped to stretch her legs and to gas up. Craig went on a bathroom break. The last two hours or so went by pretty fast. It wasn't long before they were back on campus. Venice did about eighty miles an hour all the way back.

When they reached the dorm, she put the truck in park, leaned back, and let out a sigh. "Finally."

Craig got Venice's bag and walked her to the room. As they walked, she thanked him again for taking her to see her father. When they walked in the room, Monique was lying in the bed watching TV.

She rose up and said, "Welcome back, roomy! Hey, Craig."

"Hello, Monique."

Craig put Venice's bags down next to the bed and told them he was going to head on to the house.

Venice said, "Make sure you call when you get home so I'll know you made it."

They exchanged many hugs and kisses and he headed home.

Monique said, "Girl, your other man has already called to see if you were back. He really has it bad for you."

Venice sat on the bed and reached for the phone. "We go a ways back, Monique."

Monique started painting her toenails, then asked, "What about Craig?"

Venice dialed Jarvis and responded, "I love him also, Monique."

The phone rung on the other end and Jarvis' answering service picked up.

"Hey, Jarvis, I'm sorry I missed your call. I'm just letting you know that I'm back at school. Call me when you get this message. Bye."

Venice hung up and said, "Monique, I'm tired. We'll talk about this some other time. Cool?"

"Cool. I know you're tired."

Venice called her parents to let them know she made it back, then called it an evening.

When Craig got home, Bernice was there. She welcomed him back with a hug and asked, "Did you have a good time?"

"It was really nice. You'd like Venice's family and her dad is doing much better now. I think she's convinced since she's seen him for herself."

"That's good. I'm glad you took her. I can understand how she felt. Oh! I almost forgot. Make sure you check your messages. Your phone has been ringing off the wall."

Craig sifted through the mail, then went into his room and threw his bags on the floor. He plopped down on the bed and pushed the button to check his messages. He went through his messages until he came to a message from one of the fraternities on campus. They were calling Craig to let him know that he'd been selected for their fall line. He was somewhat surprised because he had heard they were not going to have a line. The big brothers left instructions for him to meet with them that night in a designated point. He was happy with the news, but also saddened since that meant he wouldn't be able to go home with Venice for Thanksgiving. Craig picked up the phone to call Venice with the news. He knew she wouldn't be happy. He'd never mentioned to her that he'd interviewed to pledge. He wasn't sure how Venice would take the news.

"Hello?"

"Hey, sexy. I called to let you know I made it in."

"I'm glad."

"Venice, I know I didn't tell you before, but I interviewed to pledge Tau Nu Fraternity and when I got in tonight, there was a message calling me on line tonight."

"Tonight! I didn't even know you were interested in fraternities."

"I know and I'm sorry to spring this on you, but I'm not going to get to go home with you for Thanksgiving."

Venice was noticeably upset. "I wished you would've told me Craig. Look, go do what you need to do. I'm tired and I'm going to bed. Good luck with your pledging."

Before he could say another word, she hung up the phone.

Craig didn't want to go on line while Venice was upset with him. He had to talk to her.

Monique knew Venice was pissed, so she said, "Girl, don't unpack tonight. You can do that tomorrow. Do you want to go get something to eat?"

"Thanks, but I'm not hungry."

"Well, if I were you, I'd take a shower and crash."

"I think that's what I'm going to do. That was Craig calling to tell me that he pledged Tau Nu Fraternity and they're pulling the line tonight. He didn't even tell me that he was considering pledging. Well, that ends him going home with me for Thanksgiving."

"Don't sweat it, girl. I'm surprised he hasn't pledged before now. You might be pledging one day yourself. I'll make sure you don't get lonely over the next few weeks. We're gonna party! You've been hanging with Craig so much, I don't get to kick it with you."

"I know, Monique. We're gonna hang, okay?"

"Deal. Now go get yourself chilled out and I'm glad your dad's feeling better."

"Thanks."

Venice entered the bathroom, turned the shower on, and just let it run over her tired body for what seemed like eternity. Afterwards, she went back into the room, crawled under her covers, and fell asleep within ten minutes. Monique smiled and continued to change stations looking for something to watch.

A few hours later, Venice was awakened by a soft, yet strong touch. She opened her eyes to find Craig sitting on her bed.

"What are you doing here? Where's Monique?"

"She let me in and gave us some privacy. I needed to see you before I do this."

Venice rose up and sarcastically said, "How thoughtful."

"Baby, don't be mad. It's going to be hard enough not seeing you for the next few weeks. Do you still love me?"

Venice pulled the covers back, sat next to him, and laid her head against his chest. "Yes, I still love you. I just don't like you right now."

Craig slid his arm around her waist and pulled her into his lap. Venice put her arms around his neck and looked into the eyes she would undoubtedly miss. She licked her lips as he pulled her to him, taking her sweet lips to his.

Venice moaned as he ran his hands over her soft, firm thighs. Knowing they could not be this way for several weeks, Venice undressed and welcomed him into her bed. Craig ran his finger down the front of her chest. Her nipples responded immediately to his touch. He raised her shirt over her head and stared at her remarkable body. She took his hand, placed it against her breasts, and kissed him slowly.

Craig kissed Venice senseless, taking her breath away as usual. He eagerly removed his clothes and kissed her body from top to bottom.

She said, "Craig, you're beautiful baby."

"You're the one who's gorgeous and I love you so much. I'd never hurt you."

"Just love me, Craig."

She arched her fragrant and tender body into his as their bodies ignited into a fiery passion. Venice wrapped her legs around his waist to give him the best access to her loving. His muscular frame entered her body continuously, savoring every moan and whimper she released. He lost control of his senses as their tongues shared the sweet nectar of their mouths. Craig tried to get as deep as he could, leaving her in tears, sore and exhausted. She didn't want to release her grip from his body, but it was time for him to go.

After a quick shower, Craig took Venice into his arms once more and kissed her thoroughly and completely. Finally, as he was leaving the room, he said, "I love you, Taylor, and I'll see you in a few weeks."

Venice's throat ached, but she was able to say, "I love you, too. Be careful."

The next day when Venice got out of class, she met Galen in the student lounge and caught him up on the activities of the weekend. She also informed Galen that Craig was now on the Tau Nu pledge line.

Galen said, "It'll be a while before you two get to hook up again. They probably won't come off line until a couple of weeks before Christmas. Are you going be able to hold out that long? Or are you going to fly back up north to Jarvis for some candy?"

"Forget you, Galen! Why do you always have to piss me off?"

Venice told Galen she was getting ready to head on to the room.

"Tell Sidney hello and that Momma sent her something. You need to come by my room and get it at some point."

"What did she send Sidney?"

"None of your business! But if you must know, she sent her a chess pie. Momma said she knows you're always over at Sidney's eating her out of house and home. So, she sent her a pie."

"Ain't that nothing. Well, see ya! I'll be by to get it later."

Little did Galen know that their mom had sent Sidney some gift certificates for the grocery store also. Galen could really eat!

Thirty

A few weeks had passed and Venice still had not had a chance to talk to Craig or Chanelle. She passed the time away talking to Joshua and Jarvis and hanging with Monique. The Tau Nu pledges were being kept at some secret location. One good thing about the girls is they got to stay in their dorm rooms. They just couldn't socialize with any outsiders unless they crept around.

Chanelle had to sneak on occasion to see Spoonie or come down to their room. It had been awhile since she was able to do either. There were a lot of snitches that would've loved to see a pledge get busted by their big sisters or big brothers.

Venice couldn't understand why Craig hadn't tried to call or see her. She was feeling really neglected. Jarvis called and asked her to fly up for a visit. Venice was seriously thinking about doing it. She told him she'd let him know before the weekend.

Venice said to herself, "What the hell? Craig's in seclusion anyway."

Well, she did it. She left on a Friday and returned on a Sunday. Once again, she spent another unbelievable weekend with Jarvis. The distance had really put a strain on their relationship and Venice felt like she needed to see him to make amends. After all, if he really wanted to, he could've called the whole thing quits. She was glad he hadn't given up on them. Venice knew she was taking a chance, but she was lonely. This time when she left, she didn't tell anyone except Joshua. Galen was out of town playing football and Monique was never in the room. No one else would ever know she was gone; not even Chanelle.

The leaves were almost off all the trees and everywhere you looked, the look of winter was fast approaching. It was a few days before Thanksgiving. Venice called home a little more than she did prior to her father's illness. She wanted to make sure he'd made a complete recovery. The semester was going to be drawing to a close before Christmas. Venice was happy about this since Craig's co-op study would finally be over. Hopefully he would be crossing over into Tau Nu fraternity also. The driving back and forth was starting to take its toll, but the co-op was considered a necessary investment for his resume and future. It was an experience every college student needed before heading off into the work force.

Joshua called Venice almost every other day. Venice called him the other days and he was still great on giving her advice. Sometimes she liked it and sometimes she didn't. She really respected him though. She also talked to Jarvis very late every night after football practice. He knew he would be seeing his girl Christmas break and he couldn't wait.

Bernice was marking the calendar each week doing the countdown until her July wedding to J.T. She had a lot to do and not a lot of time to do it. She said it was hard to do without a mom to turn to for guidance. But, she was determined to do the best that she could under the circumstances. They were in the den watching a little TV together for the first time in long time. Bernice had cut her hours back from the hospital because she was starting to get burned out. This allowed her to spend a little more time around the house to make wedding plans and also help Craig take care of some of the business regarding the house.

Bernice asked Craig if he was sure he'd be able to handle running the house alone. He told her he was practically running it already. She knew he'd still be there and Bernice would still have that security blanket. Craig always knew he could do it. He didn't want Bernice to worry about him. Bernice's original plan was to get married after Craig graduated. However, he seemed to have become more responsible earlier than she expected. Bernice was very proud of him. He stepped right into their daddy's shoes without missing a beat.

Since Craig was on line, Venice called Bernice to see if she wanted to go home with her for Thanksgiving.

"Have you decided if you're going home with me for Thanksgiving?"

Bernice responded, "Venice, I think I will. J.T. has to work so it'll do me some good to get away. When do you want to leave?"

"How about noon on Wednesday?"

"That's fine with me. I'll pick you up at noon. By the way, have you seen or talked to Craig?"

"He left a message on my answering machine. I think they allow them to talk to their families. This way, I know he's okay. You know those frats can get out of control sometimes."

Venice said, "Yeah, I heard. I hope he's doing all right. I miss him. Bryan says I need to be patient. He's in the same frat."

"Pledging is not all that bad. I pledged when I was in college and you'll probably pledge, too."

"Maybe. If you talk to Craig, tell him I miss him and…"

"Yes, Venice?"

"Tell him I love him also."

Bernice smiled and said, "I will. Take care."

Venice and Bernice were preparing to go over the rivers and through the woods. She was kind of excited because she was getting a well-deserved break from work and was anxious to meet the Taylors.

Thanksgiving morning, Bernice and Sinclair helped Mrs. Taylor cook dinner. Venice's drunken Uncle Walter showed up as loud as ever and smelling like day-old liquor. He sometimes came by on Sundays, but since this was the holidays, he just couldn't pass up the opportunity to make an appearance. He tried to hug and kiss on Bernice, but Bryan was able to rescue her.

Uncle Walter was Venice's dad's older brother. He used to sell cars but when the dealership closed down, he really went to the dogs. Crimson was happy once again to have her auntie back home. Venice couldn't help but spoil her. She told Bryan they needed to hurry up and have another baby because Crimson was going to be an awful brat if they didn't.

After Thanksgiving blessings were said, the family sat down and had a wonderful dinner. After dessert was served, Bernice and Sinclair disappeared in the Lexus that Bryan had given her for Christmas the previous year. Mrs. Taylor took a plate to the elderly Mrs. Montgomery across the street. Everyone else had dozed off after stuffing themselves with Thanksgiving goodies. Venice and Bryan were the only ones left.

"Venice, let's go out on the porch. How are you and Craig doing?"

Venice shoved her hands in her coat pockets. "I wouldn't know. I haven't talked to him in weeks. He's on line with your frat."

"For real! That's all right. What's wrong? You missing your baby?"

Venice nudged him and said, "It's not funny, Bryan. All that frat stuff is so secretive. He could at least try to call me."

"It's best that he doesn't. Girl, stop whining. This is when you find out what your man is really made of."

"I don't care."

"You'll see when you pledge. Chanelle is on line, too, isn't she?"

"Yeah, she should be coming off soon. It'll probably be another three weeks before I see Craig."

"Hang in there, girl. You'll be okay."

There was a silence as they watched cars go up and down the street.

Venice confessed, "Bryan, I've been going up to visit Jarvis."

"I know. Do you still feel the same about him?"

"Yes. When I'm with him, I start tingling. I don't know what to do. He knows me, Bryan. He knows what makes me tick. I feel great when I'm with him. Then, when I'm away from him, the spell subsides but I still miss him. When I'm with Craig, my heart speeds up. I can't sleep when I'm away from him. I want to be with him as much as possible and I'm in love with him, too. I need help."

Bryan put his hands over his face and said, "You've got yourself in a tough situation. I don't know what to tell you. I do know you need to get it together. Neither one of them is going to put up with this much longer."

Venice silently nodded in agreement. "I really didn't expect this to happen, Bryan."

"I know you didn't. Is Jarvis coming home for Christmas?"

Venice sat back in the swing and said, "It depends on whether or not they go to the playoffs."

Bryan made the swing move and said, "Well, hopefully he'll get to come home. Make sure you guys talk. Ya'll need help from a higher power."

Venice stared out into the yard and said, "Maybe we do."

Back on campus, the pledges of Tau Nu were busy serving the

homeless at the shelter. Craig couldn't help but think of Venice. When he and the other pledges got a chance to relax, they shared what they were missing out on with each other. One of the things Craig missed most was the smell of Venice's perfume and the softness of her body. Like all the other guys, Craig wondered what his lady was doing to occupy her time. Their time online would make or break relationships.

When the pledges finished with the last soup kitchen, the big brothers decided to take them back to their secret house and surprise them with their own Thanksgiving dinner. The pledges were able to relax a little. Craig ate his meal, then took a moment to get in a little studying before turning in for the night. As he drifted off to sleep, he said to himself, "Goodnight, Venice."

Thirty-One

Saturday morning, Venice and Bernice made their way back to town. Before leaving, Bernice thanked the Taylors for their hospitality. She wanted to go by and tell Sinclair goodbye. They really got along very well together. Venice couldn't imagine what those two had in common. Whatever it was, it left Sinclair in a good mood.

Bryan gave Venice a sealed box to give to Craig when he crossed over. He said, "Give this to Craig when his line crosses and do not open the box, Venice!"

Bernice told Bryan and Sinclair, "You two are going to have to come for a visit when you get a chance. I really would enjoy having you down. I'll call you with my work schedule and maybe we can set up something."

They assured her they would visit soon. After Venice promised Bryan she wouldn't open Craig's box, they shared hugs and kisses and then they were on their way.

During the ride back, Bernice said, "Venice, I make it a point not to get to involved in Craig's business. But, I know something went down with you guys a few weeks ago. I'm glad that whatever it was, you were able to work it out. He really cares a lot about you and I know you care for him. I guess what I'm trying to say is if you ever want to talk, I'm here. I feel like I could be objective, even though Craig's my brother."

"Thanks Bernice. I really appreciate you offering. Craig didn't tell you what happened?"

"No, and I didn't ask. I just noticed he was hanging around the house a lot and I didn't see you come over for a while. Venice, I respect his privacy and he respects mine. We get along just fine keeping it that way."

"I understand, Bernice. I really didn't mean to hurt Craig. I just have some things I'm trying to deal with."

"I'm sure things will get back on track for you guys after this pledging is over."

"I hope so."

When they made it back into town, Venice realized she was going to be alone once she reached the dorm. Bernice asked her to stay the rest of the weekend at the house.

Venice thought for a moment, then told her she would. "Thanks for the invite, Bernice. It'll be kind of spooky in the dorm by myself."

"Why don't you take your bags into Craig's room. Hopefully, he'll call today and you'll get to talk to him."

Bernice and Venice settled in after their long trip. Mrs. Taylor had sent plenty of food back with them. They chatted for a while and then turned in for the night. It was about 2 a.m. when the phone rang. Venice was so tired that she didn't even hear it. There was a knock at the bedroom door, which woke Venice out of her sleep.

Bernice peeked in and said, "Venice, Craig's on the phone."

Venice jumped out of bed to get the phone as Bernice closed the door. In a sleepy voice, Venice said "Hello?"

The tired sounding voice on the other end said, "Hey, baby! What are you doing over there?"

"Missing you. Are you okay?"

"As well as can be expected. I can't talk long. Bernice told me she had a good time with your family."

"I think she did. She and Sinclair hit if off real good. How much longer are you going to be on line?"

"I don't know. I hope not long. I've lost five pounds from all that jogging and I'm not eating as much."

Venice paused for a moment before saying, "Be careful. Okay?"

"Always."

"Bryan sent you something in a box. He said you can't open it until you cross over."

"That's nice. Well, sweetheart, I'd better get off this phone. I miss you and keep my bed warm for me and make sure you have a black dress ready for the crossing over ball."

Venice couldn't mask her emotions any longer. "Craig, I need to see you."

"What?"

"I need to see you."

"Venice, you know I can't."

"Why not? Chanelle is always sneaking around so why can't you?"

"It's different."

"How?"

"You don't understand, Venice."

"Forget it, Craig!"

"Venice...I love you."

It was quiet for a minute and then Venice said, "Love you, too." Before she hung up the phone, she noticed Craig's hesitation.

"Venice?"

"Yeah."

"I'll try."

"Thanks."

Venice was content and had no problem falling back to sleep.

Two nights later, they met at his house. He told his frats he had to take care of some family business. They knew Craig's family situation and allowed him two hours to take care of it. Venice made sure they used up an hour and forty-five minutes of the time. She really needed this and so did he. It was hard for him to leave her nakedness in his bed and sneak away like a thief-in-the-night. Before he left, Venice thanked him over and over for taking the risk.

A few more weeks to go.

Chanelle and her line crossed over. There was soror frenzy going on in the dorms. The pledges' doors were decorated in the sorority colors and the pledges were showered with gifts. Venice had already picked out a special sweatshirt and umbrella for her girl. Monique and Venice shared in Chanelle's joy. Spoonie bought her the sorority's leather jacket. It was very expensive and Venice knew this meant a lot to Chanelle. Venice and Monique hung out in Chanelle's room while fellow pledges and big sistas came by to offer congratulations. Needless to say, the girls didn't get much sleep in the dorm that night.

The next morning, all the new pledges were decked out in sorority attire. Chanelle's sorority was not the only one that crossed over. It would still probably be another week before Craig would be finished. It had been two more weeks since Venice had some loving from Craig. She was starting to get really grouchy and her partners knew why.

Monique said, "Dang, I'll be glad when your boy gets off line. I don't know how much more I'll be able to take of your attitude."

"Forget you, Monique!"

Venice rumbled through her closet looking for something to wear to class the next day. The telephone rang. Monique answered and told Venice it was for her. It was Tim on the phone. He was in the lobby and wanted Venice to come down.

When she got off the elevator, the lobby was full of people going in and out. Venice gave Tim a friendly hug, sat down, and let out a big sigh. Tim came by to see his girlfriend but she wasn't in her room so he called Venice down to pass the time away. After several minutes of small talk, she excused herself. Tim told her to hang in there and he would see her in class.

Venice got on the elevator and headed back to the room. Once there, Monique told her that she'd heard some pervert went into the dorm next to their building and exposed himself to a girl coming out the showers.

Venice asked, "How did he get in?"

"I heard someone had propped the door open with something. Anybody can walk in when they do that."

"Did he do anything to her?"

"No, just scared her. She screamed and the fool took off running. Security is telling all the women to be careful. I'm glad we have private showers."

Venice said, "You and me both."

Yet another week went by. Everyone was coming up on mid-term exams. Venice told Monique as they were studying in their room, "Girl, believe it or not, with Craig on line, I've been knocking out my exams. I hope he's doing well on his."

Monique said, "He's probably as dumb as a door knob. You know he's got all that build up. You now it affects their brain." They laughed together and Monique added, "Venice, when Craig does come off line and ya'll hook up for the first time, you know it's going to be on. You'd better be careful. Craig just might put something in your oven."

"You're crazy! We make sure we take precautions."

Monique was washing her face and asked, "Are you going to try to be a sweetheart for the frat?"

"I don't think so."

"They're pretty cool. I might try. Do you mind?"

"Knock yourself out."

Thirty-Two

It was two weeks until Christmas break and yet another week was coming to a close. Craig still hadn't crossed over so Venice had been going to church with her girls. She missed going with Craig. The last time she'd heard his sweet voice was at her momma's church weeks ago. She was hoping he'd cross that weekend so they could get together. Venice would just have to wait and see.

Jarvis was still calling and telling her all kinds of things. He talked phone sex to her a lot and he was good at it; too good. Venice always hung up hot and bothered. Jarvis took advantage of the fact that Craig was on line. That's why he did it. He just hoped he was the one who got to put out her fire first.

Venice and Monique were just getting back in from the laundry. They threw their baskets on the floor and began the task of folding. Monique checked the answering machine for messages. The messages started replaying. Venice continued to put her clothes away when there was a knock at the door.

When she opened it, there stood a dorm mate, Tara, from across the hall. She asked, "What are ya'll up to?"

Monique said, "Nothing much. Just trying to get these dang clothes folded. I'm failing my Calculus class. So what else is new?"

"Bored. That's why I came over here. Hey, did ya'll hear about the Tau Nu big brothers getting hoes for the pledges?"

Venice looked up and said, "What!"

Monique asked, "What are you talking about?"

Tara went on to say, "I heard that the big brothers like to make sure none of the pledges are virgins so, before they cross them, they hook them up with hoes and have one big freak fest. Ain't that nothing! These crazy men around here will do anything."

Venice jumped up off the bed and left the room, slamming the door. Monique and their friend were startled and jumped when the door slammed.

Tara asked, "What the hell is wrong with Venice?"

"Her man is on the Tau Nu line."

Tara threw her hand over her mouth. "Dang! I didn't know I was cracking on her man. Let me get out of here before I put my foot in my mouth again. I'll check ya'll out later."

"All right! Don't worry about Venice. She'll be straight. Craig wouldn't do anything like that. Let me go check on her. I'll see you later."

They left the room together and Monique went down the hall to look for Venice.

Monique figured the only place Venice would run to was Chanelle's room. As she got on the elevator, she mumbled to herself, "I hope C wouldn't do that to Venice."

When Monique got to Chanelle's room, Venice was sitting on the bed talking to Chanelle and asking, "Chanelle, have you heard anything about the pledges having to screw before they cross?"

"I heard some of the frats do that. I don't believe Craig would follow those fools."

Monique said, "Me either."

Venice said, "It would be a chance for him to get back at me for what I did."

Monique asked, "What did you do to him?"

Everyone in the room became quiet. Chanelle gave Monique a look to let it go.

Venice then said, "If he did do it, I don't think I could blame him."

Monique asked again, "What did you do to him?"

Venice said, "Mind your business, Monique! Damn!"

Chanelle said, "Monique, chill, okay?"

"Chanelle, I'll talk to you later."

Venice got up from the bed and thanked her for listening, then left.

Monique said, "I'll be up later."

She thought she was going to get the 411 from Chanelle, but she was wrong. Chanelle never told Venice's business or betrayed their friendship. Monique was out of luck.

Venice got on the elevator and made her way back up to the room. When she opened the door, the phone was ringing. She answered it and heard a voice say, "Hey, girl! What's up?"

It was Jarvis.

Venice said, "Not much. What are you up to?"

"Exams and more exams and missing you."

Then he started talking nasty to her. He knew the things he whispered to her always got her blood boiling.

"Jarvis, you're so nasty."

"You like it."

"Are you coming home for Christmas?"

"Looks like it and I can't wait to see you."

They talked a while longer and Venice told him good luck on the rest of his exams. He wished her the same and told her that he loved her.

Venice responded, "I love you, Jarvis."

The noise level in the hallway increased as the night wore on. Monique found out from Chanelle that a party was being held in the gym sponsored by the student government association.

Monique said, "Come on, Venice, go with me. You need to get out of here."

"I may come over there later. I'm gonna try to call Joshua."

Monique put on her jeans, a sweater, and some boots. She put on some makeup and styled her hair. She opened the door and went across the hall to see if Tara and her roommate were going. They were already set to go. Monique came back over to the room and let Venice know they were leaving.

Venice sat up on the bed and turned off the TV. She put in one of her favorite CDs and laid back down trying to mellow out. She heard a commotion outside the room and she opened the door to see what was up. Another sorority was crossing their pledges. Venice slammed the door because this only reminded her of what her she was dealing with. The phone rang and it was Bryan.

"Hey, girl! What's up?

"Not much. Just sitting here debating if I'm going to this party."

"Is something on your mind?"

"No, I just wanted to talk to you. I haven't heard from you in a while. Jarvis called me a little while ago."

"How's he doing?"

"He's doing fine. Exams just like me."

"Uh-huh…ya'll still kicking it?"

"When we get a chance."

"It not fair to string Craig along. You need to tell him the truth."

"I care for him, Bryan. I love him, too."

"Has his line crossed yet?"

"No."

Venice explained the rumors to Bryan about the required sex.

Bryan replied, "It'll be fine and don't pay any attention to the rumors. Okay?"

"I'll try. I'll call you in a few days. Love you."

"Venice, it'll work out."

"I hope so. Tell everybody hello and I'll talk to you later. Bye."

Venice got her pager, got dressed, and decided to go to the party. She joined her partners and seemed to be having a good time. It wasn't long before Tim spotted her. He joined them and seemed to pick up on the fact that Venice wasn't herself. A slow song began to play and Tim held Venice differently that night. She also laid upon his shoulder differently. Tim rubbed her back and pulled her closer. Venice didn't even notice the difference. All she could think about was how much she missed Craig and how she couldn't hurt him.

After the song was over, Tim pulled her by the hand and they found a seat. Tim said, "What's up with you tonight?"

"Don't ask. I want to just chill."

Tim moved his seat closer. "Fine with me."

Venice looked at Tim and said, "You'd better scoot your seat back over there before your crazy girlfriend catches you."

"She doesn't own me."

About that time, Tim's girlfriend came from out of nowhere and kicked the bottom of Venice's chair. "Bitch, I told you to…"

Those were the last words she got out of her mouth. Venice jumped up and grabbed her by the throat. Tim also jumped up and tried to break the two women up. Neither of them were hitting each other. Just holding on. Venice somehow got the other girl down and was squeezing her neck.

Venice angrily said, "I'm sick of your silly ass!"

Spoonie ran over to get Venice off the girl. Venice had a lot of anger and was, unfortunately, releasing it on Tim's girl. The crowd in the gym ran over to see what was happening. Spoonie and Tim got the two separated and out of the building before security could intervene.

Spoonie, Monique, and Chanelle got Venice outside. Spoonie said, "Damn, Venice! What are you trying to do, kill her!"

"Forget ya'll! I'm sick of her!"

Venice started walking alone back toward the dorm. Spoonie told Monique and Chanelle that he'd walk with her and make sure she made it back to the room okay. As they walked, Venice didn't say a word.

Spoonie said, "If you're not going to talk, then listen. Chanelle told me that you had some stuff on your mind tonight. Craig's my boy and I have all the confidence in the world that he's being cool. You should know Craig better than that by now. But maybe I was wrong about you. You need to quit letting these chickenhead girls around here fill your head with all that trash. I'm not taking up for the frats because some do some messed up shit."

They reached the fountain in front of her dorm where Spoonie told her to sit down. She sat down and Spoonie said, "I know it's been a long, hard five weeks not seeing him, Venice. But you're gonna have to trust him."

Solemnly, she asked, "Spoonie, I snapped, didn't I?"

"I was shocked to see you jump on that girl like that. You could get kicked out of school for stuff like that. Don't do that again! It's not worth it. I know you were defending yourself, but be careful."

"Craig hates me, doesn't he?"

"Why would you say that?"

"You know...because of my past and my ex-husband."

"Look, that's none of my business. But I do know that man loves the hell out of you in spite of your past."

"I don't want to hurt him, Spoonie."

"He knows you love him and he knows you're torn."

"It's not fair for me to do him like this."

"He's aware of the risks."

"I really love him."

"I know...let's go."

Venice hugged him and said, "Thanks, Spoonie."

"You're welcome. Now come on so I can make sure you get to your room."

They walked into the dorm and up to her floor. As they walked down the hall, some of the girls looked at Venice strangely. Most of the girls knew Spoonie was Chanelle's man. Venice figured they assumed she was gonna try to disrespect her best friend and hook up with him.

She invited him into the room and Spoonie said, "Remember what I said. Don't listen to these fools around here. They'll probably have some rumors out on you and me before I leave the dorm."

Venice walked over to Spoonie, gave him and hug and a kiss, and said, "Thanks for giving me a shoulder to cry on."

"No problem. That's what I'm here for. Now...let me get out of here. I'll see you later."

Thirty-Three

Saturday morning came in with a bang. Monique and Venice were sound asleep when they heard from outside, "Good morning, beautiful ladies of Edwards Hall! Coming to you from the men of Tau Nu Fraternity Inc.!"

When Monique rose to look out the window, she could she Craig's line outside giving the morning wake up call. Venice turned over and looked at the clock and saw it was 6:30 a.m.

Monique said, "I wish I had some hot water to throw out there on those fools. Don't they know it's Saturday?"

Venice got out of bed and walked over to look out. She saw Craig in the middle of the line. They had their sweatsuits on and the hoods over their heads.

Venice opened the window and hollered out, "Take that noise away from here!" She angrily closed the window and crawled back into bed. Craig smiled because he knew that fiery voice anywhere.

Within a few seconds, they jogged away singing some type of frat song.

Venice said, "Fools!" Then jumped up and went into the bathroom. When she came out, she crawled back into bed and went back to sleep.

A few hours later, the two got up and discussed their plans for the day. Monique had a hair appointment and Venice was going to spend the day with Sidney. As they dressed, Monique said, "Venice, I'm going to get a "B" in Calculus."

"How did you manage that?"

"I broke the professor off a little something something."

"Tell me you didn't!"

"Don't holler, Venice. Damn!"

"So what if he doesn't give you the grade?"

Monique went over to her closet and pulled out a videotape. She had two tapes: one setting up their rendezvous and the other recording their rendezvous.

Monique said, "He doesn't know I have insurance."

"Girl, you're crazy. You'd better watch yourself."

They dressed and went their separate ways.

When Venice arrived at Sidney's house, she spotted Galen's car. She knocked on the door and he let her in. He was on his way out to meet some of the fellas for a game of basketball. He kissed Venice on the cheek on the way out while eating some type of sandwich.

Venice closed the door as she came inside. "Sidney!"

From the back room, Sidney answered, "Hey, girl! Come on back!"

Venice put her purse down on the chair and found Sidney in the bedroom making the bed

Venice sat down in the chair and said, "I guess you're changing the sheets, huh!"

"Don't go there!"

Venice went over to put on some of Sidney's perfume. "I don't see what you see in my triflin' brother. He could've stayed here and helped you."

"No! I wanted him to go on. He's really different with me. You guys don't see it. Most of the time, he does the housework around here."

"Are we talking about the same person?"

Sidney laughed. "Yes, I'm talking about Galen. He's very sensitive and sweet."

Venice burst out laughing and continued to smell Sidney's different perfumes and lotions. Sidney moaned and grabbed her head.

Venice turned around and said, "Sidney, are you okay?"

Sidney sat down on the bed and said, "I'm okay. I just got a little dizzy."

"Are you sure? You're sweating."

Venice made Sidney lay down on the bed while she went to get her some water. When she came back into the room, she asked, "Do you want me to page Galen?"

"No, I'll be fine. Just give me a minute."

Venice sat on the bed next to her and said, "I think I need to get you to a doctor, Sidney."

Sidney sat up in the bed and replied, "There's no need, Venice. I'm fine. I'm just a little pregnant."

"You're lying!"

"In a way, I wish I was."

"Does Galen know?"

"Yes, he's known for a few weeks now."

"How far along are you?"

Sidney sat the glass of water down on the nightstand and said, "About ten weeks. Don't say anything to Galen. I think he wants to break the news to you and your family himself."

Venice laid back on the bed and said, "So what are you guys going to do?"

"I'm not sure how long I'll be able to hide it."

"I'm happy for you guys. I'm going to be an Auntie again. I hope it's a boy!"

"So do I. Galen said it didn't matter to him."

They continued to talk about the blessed news. Venice decided Sidney should take it easy so she left to go by Craig's church. As she walked across the parking lot, she could still hear his voice and realized how much she missed him. No matter what was happening between her and Jarvis, she still cared for Craig.

As usual, the Sunday services got off to a great start. They went through the regulars: announcements, collections, etc. The choir sang several songs throughout the morning. Venice could see Craig sitting in the back row. They had a large choir membership, estimated to be about a hundred members. Before the minister began his sermon, the choir stood up for the song of preparation. Craig stepped out to the microphone and began the song. Venice's heart felt like it was going to pound out of her chest. The congregation was on their feet. When he reached the second verse, he spotted Venice in the crowd. He smiled and never skipped a beat. Several members of the church had the spirit take over them. It was a very moving scene. When church finally let out, they waited outside hoping for a chance to talk to Craig. They greeted several members they'd met since coming there.

Finally, Craig exited the church talking to some other church members. Venice looked behind him to see if he had his frat brother escort. Luckily, he didn't.

Chanelle ran up to him and hugged him. "Man, you tore that song up! You really have some pipes on you, boy! That was beautiful!"

Craig was staring at Venice as he threw his choir robe over his shoulder. He smiled and hugged Chanelle, not breaking his gaze from Venice.

"How are you, Ms. Taylor?"

Before she could reply, he pulled her to him and gave her an unexpected kiss, right there in front of everyone.

Venice was a little surprised and embarrassed. "I missed you, too."

Craig partially released his hold on her and said, "You two will be happy to know that we crossed over about three o'clock this morning."

Chanelle shouted, "That's great!"

Venice stood back and asked, "Why didn't you call me?"

"Baby, it was too late. I didn't want to wake you. I've been up almost twenty- four hours and I'm dead on my feet. Please just be happy it's over. Okay?"

Venice opened the door to his truck for him so he could put his robe inside.

"You're right. I'm sorry. I am glad it's over. Five weeks was a long time, if you know what I mean."

Chanelle walked off to talk to some of the church members to give them some privacy.

Craig said, "Was Bernice inside?"

"No, I don't think so."

Staring at her with his seductive eyes, he asked, "Do you mind driving me home? I feel like I might fall asleep at the wheel."

"I don't mind. Let me ask Chanelle if she would drive my car back to campus."

Chanelle had no problem with it so they went their separate ways. She barely got out of the parking lot before Craig was snoring. When they reached the house, she woke him up and let him know they were home. Venice took off her jacket and before she had a chance, Craig was behind her unzipping her skirt. He turned her around and started unbuttoning her blouse. Flames immediately ran from her toes to her head as her breath left her body. She stood there as he undressed her slowly and erotically. After removing her blouse, he gently kissed her for several minutes on her shoulders, face, and neck. Immediately, she felt his desire come to life.

"Venice, I want you so bad. If you only knew how much I missed you."

Her body went limp as his hands explored her body, feeling her hardened nipples against his palm. They stared at each other, realizing how long it had been since they had touched each other.

Venice finally said, "Craig, I-I..."

"Sh-h-h-"

He lowered his face to her nipples and took them into his mouth. Venice arched her back and moaned as his tongue traced the tips, slightly biting them. He lowered her on the bed and pressed his body firmly against hers. Normally, he would've taken his time preparing her for his loving, but not this time. Within seconds, he stripped their clothes, protected himself, and pushed deep into her aching body.

Venice closed her eyes and held her breath as the slow rhythmic motion of his hips pleasured her. She'd almost forgotten how good he felt inside her body, but her memory quickly came back. He took her swollen nipples once again into his mouth and sucked them until she screamed aloud. He stared at her as he took her with great hunger and demand. He wanted to see her facial expressions as he loved her.

He whispered, "Open your eyes, baby."

Venice's lashes fluttered for a moment, then clearly showed him she was in ecstasy. She moaned slowly and provocatively as he stared deeply into her dark brown eyes. He prodded his tongue deep into her mouth as he kissed her hard on her soft lips. He nibbled his way down to her navel, stopping just above her moistness. Venice was now shivering as she screamed with pleasure. This excited him even more and he reminded her again to look at him. Once again, she tried to look at him and hold her composure at the same time, but she was unsuccessful. He felt unbelievably huge inside her body or maybe it had just been so long since they were last together.

They made love for what seemed like hours and there were plenty of moans and screams. She pulled him tighter to her as she ran her tongue along his lips. He buried his face into the curve of her neck as his love exploded.

"Venice! I love you!"

Wiping the moisture from his brow, she cupped his face in her hands and said, "I love you, too, Bennett."

Obviously, they had some catching up to do. But, first, they needed a nap to recover from their unforgettable reunion.

Hours later, hunger drove them to the kitchen. Dressed in his shirt, Venice asked, "Are you hungry?"

"For you."

"Be serious, Craig."

"I am, baby."

"Craig!"

"Okay, okay! No, I'm not really hungry. I just want something to drink."

He washed his hands and got a bottle of water out the refrigerator and sat down at the bar. He watched her as she washed up a few dishes. His shirt was covering the best parts of her, but what skin showed caused his body to stir. He left the room for a moment and when he returned, he came up behind her and put his arms around her waist and pressed his body against her, caressing her breasts. Venice felt his hardness as he nipped at her shoulders and neck. Inhaling his manly scent, she closed her eyes to savor his touch and his mouth.

Craig turned her around to face him, then picked her up and sat her on the counter. As he stood in front of her, he begin to kiss her even harder on the mouth. He positioned himself between her legs and surprised her by sliding into her. She lost all concept of time as he grabbed her hips, pulling her closer to meet his thrusts. She wrapped her legs around his body as he continued to push deeper into her inviting heat. He slowly licked and kissed her sore nipples until she could stand it any longer.

"I love you, Venice. I always have and I always will."

"Oh, Craig!"

She held onto his neck as dishes and cups started falling to floor. They both screamed as they finished breathless, delirious, and exhausted. He didn't want to move and neither did she.

Holding onto each other for dear life, he said, "Now see what you made me do."

"Uh-huh! You broke those dishes! I'm telling Bernice!"

They burst into laughter as he helped her aching body down from the counter. Venice looked at him in amazement and asked, "What happened to you over the last five weeks?"

"Nothing. I just missed my baby."

Embracing her, he kissed her forehead and said, "I want you to stay the night. Okay?"

"Okay."

She limped back into the bedroom and fell across the bed as he finished cleaning up the kitchen. Venice smiled and said under her breath, "Craig's got a little freak in him."

They made love all during the night. There were more screams, moans, and a lot of whispers of love into each other's ears. Craig loved hearing her profess her love to him. She hadn't done it often, but he knew she was finally letting a little of her guard down.

Out of breath and dripping with sweat, he whispered, "I'll never let you go, Venice. If he wants you, he'll have to take you and it ain't gonna be easy."

Exhausted and weak, Venice responded with a tender kiss. He pulled her securely into his arms and all she could do was nestle her face into his neck. She needed time to recover and to think.

Craig, Jarvis, Jarvis, Craig. This shit was going to make her have a nervous breakdown.

Her body was sore and her mind had shut down. She couldn't think about it any more. It was a happy crossing over night.

Thirty-Four

Christmas was fast approaching. Galen still had not told Venice about his upcoming fatherhood so she asked Sidney if she minded if she brought it up to her dear brother. First, Venice confided in Bryan to see if he knew. He didn't, but told her that Galen better hurry up and let their parents know. They couldn't understand why he was reluctant. Bryan was not surprised about the situation. He figured they would end up together anyway. Bryan still had hopes that Galen would make it to the pros. If not, he still would be okay. They both still had their senior year ahead of them.

Venice picked an afternoon after mid-term exams were over. Most students were packing to depart home for the holidays. Venice called Galen and asked him to go Christmas shopping with her. They walked through the mall looking in the different windows.

He then asked, "What's Craig up to?"

"He's still taking exams, but he'll be finished tomorrow."

Galen stopped to look at some jewelry and said, "My last test is tomorrow also. So what are you planning on getting him?"

"I want to get him a gold bracelet but I don't see one I like."

"Does he have a nice watch?"

"I haven't noticed. What are you getting Sidney?"

Galen hesitated and turned around, watching the shoppers going by.

"I don't know. This year is going to be a little different."

Feeling he was about to spill his guts, she said, "Different how?"

They walked past a few more stores and he said, "Let's go to the food court. I want to get something to drink."

Galen bought two sodas and they sat down at a nearby table. He took a sip of his soda and said, "Venice, I've been wanting to tell you something for a few weeks, but for some reason, I couldn't."

"What is it?"

He continued to drink his soda, leaned back in the chair, and said, "Well...I'm going to be a daddy."

Venice had to act surprised since she already knew about it. "Daddy!"

Galen started laughing. "Yeah, Sidney's almost three months pregnant."

Venice hit him in the arm and asked, "Why are you just now telling me? How's Sidney handling it? What are ya'll going to do?"

Galen straightened his baseball cap. "Well...we got married last weekend."

Venice was shocked because this part she didn't know.

"Married!"

"Yeah, we wanted to surprise you guys. I told Momma and Daddy last weekend. They handled it better than I thought they would."

"I'm surprised. They freaked out when I got pregnant. I think Bryan freaked out worst than Momma and Daddy, but I don't know why."

"You know Bryan thinks you're above all that."

Venice sipped her drink and said, "That's crazy! Accidents do happen." Venice hugged her brother. "Well, congratulations, bro. When are you going home for Christmas?"

"Next Monday. Sidney's coming with me."

"That's good! I'm going to have my Christmas with Craig and his sister this weekend. Then I'm leaving Tuesday."

"Come on. Let's finish shopping."

The weekend after exams approached quickly. Most students had already left for the holidays. Venice spent her last few hours in the dorm packing her clothes for the next three weeks. Venice made sure she had Craig's gift in her purse. Tonight would be the night she would give it to him.

When she arrived at his house, it was fully decorated with Christmas lights and all the trimmings. It was one of the brightest and prettiest homes on the street. Bernice had put the Christmas tree up the day after Thanksgiving. She made sure she took a vacation during Christmas time so she could spend some time with her brother and family. That time of the year could be very depressing for people who had lost loved ones. Craig and Bernice had lost both parents so they comforted each other during Christmas. Bernice let her in and Christmas music by Luther Vandross was blasting. Venice could smell a pine scent from the decorations of the mantle and the awesome smell of cookies baking.

Bernice whispered, "So...what did you end up getting my little brother for Christmas?"

"Where is he?"

"Don't worry. He took the dog for a walk."

Venice pulled the small box out of her bag and told her about the watch. Bernice told her that Craig would really love it. She said he needed a new watch.

Then she started singing, "I know what he got you!"

"You do! Can you give me a hint?"

Bernice smiled and stirred the cookie batter. "Sorry, no can do. He made me promise."

"That's not fair!"

"Sorry for you, darling."

"Traitor."

Venice continued into Craig's room to put her bags down. On the way back into the kitchen, she stopped to admire the beautifully decorated tree. Bernice explained to Venice that her mother had started collecting ornaments when they were babies.

"Some of these decorations are even older than I am. We put them on the tree every year."

"That's really nice."

Bernice was quiet for a few seconds, then hollered, "I have some hot buttered rum, if you would like some."

"I think I will."

About that time, Venice's pager went off. She looked at the number and noticed it was Jarvis. She didn't like to call him from Craig's house, so she went out on the front porch and called him on her cell phone.   "Hello?"

"You page?"

"Yeah. What are you doing?"

"Not much. What's up?"

"When are you going home?"

"In a couple of days. When are you coming in?"

"I'll be home tomorrow. Make sure you holler at me when you get in. I need to talk to you about some stuff."

Venice saw Craig coming down the street and said, "Okay. I'll talk to you later."

"All right. I love you."

"I love you too, Jarvis."

She hung up the phone and turned to find Bernice standing in the door. Venice looked surprised and said, "Bernice…"

"Venice, I didn't mean to ease drop on your conversation. Craig really likes you and so do I."

Venice explained, "I don't want to hurt him, Bernice. I love him."

They sat down on the porch and Bernice said, "I believe you, but I know something has been going on between you two. It's none of my business. My concern is my brother's feelings."

"Did Craig tell you anything about my past?"

"No, he didn't and I didn't ask."

"Well, I think you have a right to know because it's kind of complicated."

Venice went on to explain the entire story to Bernice. She told her about the unexpected pregnancy and all about her relationship with Jarvis, the marriage, the assault, everything. When she was finished, Bernice told her how sorry she was for what she had been through. Bernice also told her that she understood how she was torn between her past and her present. She offered to help her in any way she could. Venice thanked her and gave her a hug. They got up and went into the house for some hot buttered rum. A few minutes later, Venice asked if Craig had named the puppy she had given him for crossing his fraternity.

"Yes, he calls him Bear."

"That's a good name. I'm going back out on the porch to see if he's made it down the street yet. Don't forget to call me if you need some help."

Bernice said, "I will and Venice, whatever you decide, don't beat yourself up about it. Now go on and relax yourself."

It was a cold evening so Venice put on her coat and gloves and sat in the porch swing drinking her hot rum waiting on Craig and Bear. He didn't see her on the porch until he was about to come up the steps and asked, "When did you get here?"

Venice giggled and said, "I've only been here a little while. Here's something hot to warm you up."

"I'd rather have you."

Craig joined her in the swing with his rum. Bear was trying to jump up into the swing, but Craig wouldn't let him.

"Let's go in, Venice. It's cold out here."

She agreed and they went into the bedroom to put their coats up. While they were in the room, he pushed her down on the bed and asked, "Where's my gift, Taylor?"

Bear was barking and trying to jump up on the bed with them. Venice was laughing and screaming as he tickled her.

"Stop! I can't breathe!"

Craig held her arms over her head and tickled her even more.

"Where's my gift, Venice?"

"I don't know! Please stop!"

Kissing her neck, he said, "Pretty please?"

Out of breath, she answered, "Pretty please with sugar on top."

He lowered his head to her mouth and tasted the sweet rum with his tongue. Her arms encircled his neck as his hands roamed over her hot body. Touching her intimately, a moan escaped her lips and he jumped up to lock his door. She sat up on the bed and watched as he removed his clothes to reveal his beautifully sculptured body.

"Craig?"

"Yes?"

"I'm aching."

"Where?"

"Everywhere."

"I have just the medicine for you."

"I knew you would. I'll try not to scream too loudly."

"I can't promise the same thing."

"Craig, don't embarrass me around Bernice."

Smiling devilish, he answered, "Trust me."

Blushing, she threw her clothes on the floor next to his and allowed him to cure her ache.

After Bernice went upstairs, Craig asked, "You feel up to a bubble bath?"

"For real?"

"I don't joke about my bubble baths."

Venice blushed and agreed. Craig filled the tub with plenty of bubbles and she couldn't wait to ease into the warm bubbles. As she stepped in, he went around the room and lit candles. She closed her eyes, laid her head back, and let out a deep breath. Craig eventually slid into the hot water next to her and pulled her over in front of him. He turned on the jets, which whirled the water and bubbles around them magically. She laid back against his chest as he gently massaged her body with bath gel and brought it to a lather. Venice gently caressed and enjoyed the massage he was giving her.

Craig asked, "What are you so tense about?"

"I didn't realize I was."

Venice turned to face him and said, "Craig, I'm sorry for causing so you so much stress." "Leave it alone, baby. I don't want to talk about that tonight. Okay?"

Venice nodded and laid back against Craig's chest once again. Little did Venice know, Craig often wondered if she thought about Jarvis when she was with him. Craig decided not to worry about it and just enjoy her company.

It was going to be a long, hard three weeks. Venice was a little uncertain what the future held for them. She knew Jarvis was going to be home for Christmas. Maybe that would give her the opportunity to finally make a decision. It was about midnight when Craig told her that he wanted to go ahead and give her his gift. She sat up in bed and watched as he reached into his desk and pulled out a small box. Craig had lit the twenty something candles in the room, giving the room a romantic glow. He gave her the box, which she opened it with curiosity. It revealed a beautiful pair of gold and diamond earrings inside. Her mouth fell open and she began to cry. Craig said, "Don't start that. It's just earrings."

Craig took the earrings out and put them on her. She never expected diamonds, maybe a bracelet or something, but not something so special.

Venice said through tears, "Craig, they're beautiful! You should-n't have! They're too much!"

"No, they're not. I thought they'd look nice on your sexy ears and I wanted you to have them."

Venice crawled into his lap, put her arms around his neck, and gave him a very passionate kiss. She fumbled with her hands in her lap and said, "I don't deserve them."

He sternly responded, "Chill with that!"

Venice eased out of the bed to retrieve Craig's gift from her travel bag. She handed it to him and he opened it up to reveal the beautiful gold watch she'd picked out earlier.

"Dang! This is what's too much! Thanks, baby!" He leaned over and kissed her through the salty tears streaked down her cheeks. As he wiped them away, he said, "Don't ever think you don't deserve the best, Taylor."

"I'll try, Bennett."

They finally thanked each other properly and, sure enough, Craig couldn't keep his word. Neither could Venice. It was going to be embarrassing to face Bernice, knowing she probably heard all the moans of pleasure coming from his bedroom. Sleep over took them hours later as they held each other into the night.

Thirty-Five

Later the next evening, Craig invited some of the guys over for a card game. Venice decided she would chill out in his room and catch up on her reading. She was excited about their Christmas Party taking place the next night. Craig told her it was a tradition carried down from their parents.

Venice helped Craig make snacks for the card game. The menu consisted of nachos and cheese, Buffalo wings, peanuts, and chicken salad sandwiches. The first to arrive was Spoonie, who gave Venice a big hug and kiss. He joined them in the kitchen, telling them that he'd spoken to Chanelle twice a day since she went home for the holidays. To make himself useful, he answered the door when Skeeter arrived. Craig went in to greet him and reintroduced him to Venice.

Skeeter stood there looking Venice up and down like she was a plate of food. Venice felt a little uncomfortable when he did this and Craig noticed it.

He pushed Skeeter and said, "Man, stop that and go on downstairs and set up the table." Skeeter laughed, still looking at Venice, and said, "You don't have to push, but you're a lucky man!"

Spoonie heard Skeeter and really didn't care for his attitude either, but tolerated him. Craig had told Spoonie that he grew up with Skeeter. They were like night and day. Finally the last of the card players arrived: J.T. Bernice had to work and this gave him a good opportunity to get in on the card game. They played with nothing higher than a dollar, which kept the game pretty even. As they began, Venice set the snacks up on the table in the rec room on the bar and went back upstairs.

After she left the room, Skeeter said, "Craig, I know you're tearing that ass up. She is too fine! Don't let me catch you snoozing."

"Shut up, Skeeter, and play your hand."

Skeeter said, "Nah, man. Is it as sweet as it looks?"

Craig sternly said, "I said, shut up!"

Skeeter laughed. "Punk."

Spoonie looked at Skeeter and just shook his head. He couldn't understand how Craig was still friends with him.

While the card game was taking place, Venice decided to go upstairs and work out a little in the spare bedroom. Bear hopped on the bed and laid down while she jogged on the treadmill. Venice had really spoiled him since she 'd been there, but Craig was trying to make him a vicious guard dog. She turned up the music, an upbeat tempo, to help her keep the rhythm going. After running for about fifteen minutes, she worked out on the weights. She ended up spending about an hour working out. Her shirt was sweaty down the front and her legs were sore along with some other body parts. She hadn't worked out in a few weeks, but she wanted to get back into the routine.

She completed her workout and grabbed the towel to wipe her face as she headed back downstairs. She ran right into Skeeter at the bottom of the stairs. He looked her up and down and said, "What have you been doing with sweat all over you like that?"

He lifted his hand as if he were going to touch the front of her shirt. Venice pushed past him and said, "Working out."

Skeeter headed toward the kitchen, shook his head, and said, "That's a damn shame!" Venice and Bear proceeded to the bedroom where she made sure she closed the door. She didn't like Skeeter very much. He made her uncomfortable.

Once Skeeter returned to the rec room with more snacks, Craig asked, "Did you find everything all right?"

"What I did find was your old lady. She's a fine piece of ass!"

Craig looked at him and angrily said, "Watch your damn mouth, Skeeter!"

"My bad! I'm sorry, bro."

Spoonie looked up at Craig, knowing his patience had worn thin. J.T. just sat there staring at his cards.

When Craig threw his cards in, he decided to go check on Venice. "I'm out! I'll be back."

Skeeter hollered out, "If you need any help, give me a holler!"

Craig ignored him, ran up the stairs, and entered the bedroom. Venice jumped up off the bed in surprise. When she saw it was Craig, she relaxed.

"What are you jumping for?"

"What are you're talking about?"

Craig came over and sat down next to her. "What's wrong with you? You're acting strange."

Venice stood up and grabbed her cosmetic bag and towel. "I don't know what you're talking about."

Craig grabbed her by the arm and said, "Venice!"

"It's just that your friend, Skeeter, makes me a little uncomfortable."

Gritting his teeth, he asked, "What did he do?"

Venice tried to keep Craig calm by answering, "Nothing! He just stares at me like he has x-ray vision or something. He makes me feel naked, the perverted way he looks at me."

"I'll talk to him."

"No, Craig! Leave it alone! That'll only make it worse. I'll just ignore him."

"Hell with that! I've been knowing that fool all my life and when he gets out of line, I'm going to get him straight!"

The last thing she wanted to do was come between Craig and his friends. He walked out of the room and hollered for Skeeter to come upstairs. Venice was embarrassed and went into the kitchen to get a soda. A few minutes later, they walked into the kitchen.

Skeeter said, "What's up, partner?"

"Venice told me that you've been giving her some looks that make her kind of uncomfortable. I want it to stop. Now! I also want you to stop with the comments. You got it!" Skeeter turned to Venice and said, "I'm sorry. Venice, I didn't mean any harm. You're just so fine I couldn't help but to check you out. That's just how I am. I didn't mean to make you feel uncomfortable."

Venice didn't respond. She just drank her soda and looked the other way.

Craig said, "That's cool, Skeeter, but just chill. Okay? I don't want her feeling like that around you or any of my friends."

"I'm sorry, Venice."

Venice turned to look at him and said, "Okay."

Skeeter said, "Now that we got that taken care of, let me get back to kicking your butt."

"Okay, I'll be down in a minute."

"See ya, Venice."

"See ya."

Craig pulled her against his body firmly and said, "Venice, don't you ever try to keep anything like that from me again. You hear me?"

"Okay. I'm sorry."

He gave her a quick peck on the lips, then jokingly told her that she was funky and needed to take a shower. She threw her towel at him as he ran out of the kitchen and back downstairs to the card game.

Venice took her shower and called Chanelle to tell her what went on. She also mentioned that her sweetie was also playing cards. Venice told her she'd be home Tuesday evening and about the diamond earrings. They talked more about their plans for the three-week vacation. Chanelle was happy because they could hang out together.

Chanelle said, "I saw your other man yesterday. We talked for a minute and all he could talk about was you. Girl, that fool loves your tail. He said he can't wait until you get home."

"Damn! Chanelle, what am I going to do? I mean, Jarvis is the only man I've every loved until now. Craig is so irresistible! I love both of them, but I don't deserve to be with either one of them."

"Yes, you do. It'll work out."

"I hope you're right. I'll see you in a few days."

Venice decided to light all the candles, put on the headphones, and listen to some music as she laid in bed. The music put her into a deep, relaxing sleep. She was awakened later when Craig took the headphones off her ears. She opened her eyes slightly, turned over, and went back to sleep.

Craig blew out the candles and left the room again. Venice didn't notice the time, but it must've been at least midnight. Little did she know, everyone had already left. Craig didn't want to play cards long because he knew he had errands to run for the party the next day. Venice didn't even realize that Craig had slid back into bed until she felt his arm around her waist as he snuggled up to her. He buried his face into her neck and within minutes he was snoring.

* * * * *

It was six o'clock when the first guest arrived. Craig and Spoonie were already dressed and had the music playing in the rec room. Venice took her time getting dressed. She had on this beautiful, red velvet dress that Craig had not seen. It was form-fitting and showed every curve she that had. The back of the dress was open with about five wide straps going across the back attached with rhinestone buttons. She had on red suede pumps to match. Her hair was blown straight and hung loosely around her face. Bernice was going to wear a straight, black velvet, quarter-length dress. The top part was black satin. She had her hair up in a French roll, with cascading curls dangling in front of her eye.

Venice put the finishing touches on her makeup. Craig entered the room and his breath caught in his throat. "When did you get that dress?"

"Today. What's wrong with it?"

Craig shook his head. "Nothing's wrong with it. It's just...sexy."

His dark gaze fell upon hers and they read each other's mind.

"Bennett!"

Craig laughed, looking her up and down. "I thought I knew every curve your body had. I was wrong."

"You're crazy."

"Crazy about you."

Their eyes met each other lovingly.

"Venice, look in that drawer and see if any CDs are in there, please."

She opened the drawer, moved some things around, and came across a snapshot. Venice pulled the picture out and saw that it was a picture of Craig, Joshua, and a group of guys at a party. Her back was to him as she studied the picture. Craig wasn't paying attention since he was looking for CDs on the other side of the room. Her eyes widened when she noticed Craig sitting in a chair with what looked like a large-breasted stripper straddling his lap. On the picture, Craig had his tongue out pretending he was going to lick the woman's breast. The woman had her arms around his neck and she was half-naked. Venice looked at the other guys in the picture and was angry to see Joshua also enjoying it. She didn't recognize the other faces.

Since Joshua was in the picture, she knew it was taken during home-coming week. When she finally came to her senses, she turned and asked, "What is this?"

When Craig saw what she had, he dropped his head for a moment and said, "It's nothing. That was the party I took Joshua to. We were just messing around."

Venice waved the picture in his face angrily and said, "This doesn't look like nothing to me!"

She threw the picture at him and left the room, slamming the door behind her and rushed upstairs past Bernice who was coming down the stairs at that same moment. She stopped as Craig came out of the room to follow Venice.

Bernice stopped him, made him go back inside his room, and asked, "What have you done now, little brother?"

Craig sat down on the bed and replied, "Venice found this picture of us at Skeeter's friend's party messing around."

Bernice took the picture out his hand to look at it. "My dear brother. First of all, why would you want something like that sitting on your lap? Secondly, why would you let somebody take of picture of you? And lastly, since they took the picture and you know you're in a relationship, why would you keep the picture where Venice might find it?" Bernice shook her head at Craig's stupidity and said, "That girl is pissed and I don't blame her! Those women are nasty! You didn't...?"

"No! I was just messing around for the camera."

Bernice gave the picture back to him and said, "I don't know how you're going to get out of this one. If I found a picture of J.T. like this, I'd go off too! You need to go find Venice and talk to her."

Craig sat on the bed a while longer after Bernice went to join their guests. He had to figure out what he was going to do to make it up to her. He checked the kitchen, the front porch, garage, and several other rooms, but couldn't find her. He went downstairs and asked Spoonie if he'd seen her.

He replied, "No. What's up?"

"She found that picture from that party with the stripper on my lap."

Spoonie kind of laughed and said, "Oh man! Is she pissed??"

"You should've seen her face. She went off, then threw the picture at me before she left the room."

"Do you want me to talk to her?"

Craig surveyed the room and responded, "No, but thanks. I've got to fix this on my own. I don't know where she went."

Venice had gone up to the attic to see about Bear. She was hurt, but she now knew how Craig must've felt when she told him about her rendezvous with Jarvis. It must've hurt a lot worse than what she was feeling. Venice was beginning to think she might've overreacted. She decided to go on down to the party and be sociable for Bernice's sake.

When Venice finally made her way downstairs, there were about fifteen to twenty-five people already there. Half of them were men and some had brought dates. But when Venice entered in that red dress, all eyes were on her. Jealously immediately settled in the pit of Craig's stomach when he saw how the men were drooling over her.

Before Venice could take three steps into the room, someone asked her to dance. The song was slow and Craig couldn't pour drinks for trying to watch where the man's hands were. Once the song was over, she made her way over to Bernice.

Bernice whispered, "Are you okay?"

"No, but I will be."

"Venice, I know how you feel. I talked to Craig and told him how insensitive that picture was. I don't want to get in the middle of this with you guys but, if you want to talk, let me know. I know you're crazy about him and I know he's crazy about you. So, don't let it ruin what you two have together."

"Thanks, Bernice."

One of Bernice's friends came over for Bernice to introduce him to Venice. He was the one she'd just finished dancing with. Bernice made the introduction, then walked off to speak with other guests.

The handsome young man smiled and asked, "So...Venice...are you having a good time? Can I get you something to drink?"

Venice looked into his hungry eyes and said, "Yes, I'll take a glass of soda."

"I'll be right back."

As he walked off, he looked her up and down as if she were good enough to eat.

Craig, still watching from across the room, yelled out, "Spoonie! Man, look how dude's checking her out."

"Chill, Craig."

When the young man arrived at the bar, he said, "I'll take a scotch and water and a glass of soda."

Spoonie poured the drinks as Craig folded him arms across his chest angrily, watching the guy grope Venice with his eyes.

"Thanks, man! Hey, do you guys believe in love at first sight?"

Spoonie responded, "For some people."

"Exactly! I think I just found my future wife."

Craig unfolded his arms and started toward the guy. Spoonie discreetly grabbed his arm. He looked up at Craig and slowly walked away.

Craig said, "I'm going over to talk to her."

"Wait! Let her cool off a little longer, man."

The young man, Victor, brought Venice the soda and he continued to talk to her occasionally, touching her on the back or arm. Craig walked off furiously and asked Bernice who he was. Bernice told Craig that he was one of J.T.'s friends from work.

Bernice asked, "Why do you want to know?"

"Because he can't seem to keep his hands to himself."

Bernice gazed through the crowd and saw that Venice was talking to him. Bernice turned to Craig and said, "You better not start nothing up in here. She's not doing anything but talking to him. She can't help it that she's noticeable in that dress. It's killing you, ain't it baby?"

Craig just stood there staring with a crazed look in his eyes.

"Why don't you go over and ask her to dance? She's probably waiting on you to ask her. I'm sure she's cooled down now."

"I will in a minute."

Craig went back over to the bar. As he made his way through the crowd, their eyes met for a brief moment. Venice turned away and Victor asked her for another dance.

Craig started to get more restless. He needed to talk to Venice and he wanted to talk to her right then. When the dance was over, Craig went over and interrupted their conversation. He took Venice's hand into his and asked if she could help him in the kitchen for a moment. Venice excused herself from Victor and Craig led her through the crowd. Craig followed her upstairs, admiring her beautiful body as her hips swayed when she walked. Desire and anger rose in his body simultaneously.

Why did she let him touch her like that!

Once in the kitchen, Craig asked, "Venice, what is it going to take to make you believe the picture is innocent? I didn't do anything with that woman. What is it going to take for me to make it up to you? We were just messing around at that party. If I had done anything wrong, don't you think Joshua would've told you?"

Venice stood there leaning against the counter with her arms folded, listening to his explanation but staring at the floor. Craig went on to say how much he loved her and wouldn't hurt her. Venice turned away and checked on the chicken wings in the oven. Seeing her bend over at the stove hit him like a brick wall. He had to touch her and let her know she was the only one for him.

When he tried to put his arms around her waist, she stepped back, threw her arms upward, and said, "Craig, don't!"

She started arranging the chicken wings on the tray. Craig slammed his cup down on the counter and said angrily, "Oh! I can't touch you now? It looks like you're letting whoever your new friend is touch you, but I can't. You're going off on me about a damn picture! That doesn't make any sense!" Then out of nowhere, he hollered, "At least I didn't sleep around behind your back."

Venice turned and leered at him. "Thanks for throwing that back in my face, Craig." Venice was hurt by his words, even though they were true. She walked around the table to leave the room. Craig met her at the table and blocked her exit.

He held her firmly against his chest and said, "We're not through talking, Venice."

"Stop, Craig! Let me go!"

When he grabbed her, he hurt her arm and it made her even angrier. Craig saw that she grabbed her arm in pain. Venice knew Craig was just as upset as she was and she just wanted to leave the room.

He turned her lose and said, "Venice, I'm sorry. I didn't mean to… hurt you."

He reached out to rub her arm and she stepped back and went around the table, walking away from him.

About that time, Victor, hearing what seemed liked arguing, entered the kitchen and asked, "Is everything all right in here?"

Craig turned and approached him, saying, "Look, man! What's going on in here is between me and my lady. It doesn't concern you, so you need to mind your damn business and get the hell out of my kitchen!"

Venice ran over and stood between the two to hold Craig back. She had never seen him like this and was afraid he would finally lose his temper. With her backside pressed against Craig's front, she said, "Victor, everything's fine. This is Bernice's brother, Craig, my man. You can go back downstairs. I'm okay."

Victor stared at Craig. "Are you sure?"

Craig gritted his teeth and said, "She's sure!"

Venice told him again to go downstairs. Craig, feeling the warmth of her body, turned her to face him and angrily said, "What are you doing, Venice? You're making me go crazy!"

"I didn't do anything wrong, baby. I'm just being sociable."

Craig tilted her chin up so he could look into her eyes. His heart melted when he saw tears filling them. Holding her securely he said, "Look, sweetheart. For the last time, I said I was sorry. What do you want me to do? That picture doesn't change how I feel about you or how you make me feel. I wouldn't risk losing you for anything or anybody."

They didn't move a muscle when Bernice entered to get the tray of wings. She looked at them and asked, "Is everything all right in here?" Still in each other's arms, they both nodded their heads. Bernice finally left the room and said, "Okay. Thanks for the wings, Venice."

Craig ran his hand across her cheek and said, "I'm sorry about what I said. I didn't mean to hurt you or throw that back in your face. I was angry and I wasn't thinking straight."

She wanted to, but she couldn't let herself give in so easily. Craig was desperately trying to get her to forgive him. He leaned down and tried to kiss her, but she pushed him off and said, "Stop!"

She grabbed a pack of cups and some napkins and went back downstairs.

Damn!

Craig dropped his head, wondering why he'd pushed too fast. He grabbed another bag of ice and went back downstairs to help Spoonie. When he got back to the bar, Spoonie asked, "How did it go?"

"I almost had her. I apologized the best I know how and I guess you know that fool she was talking to came upstairs and tried to get in our business. I had to let him know that Venice belonged to me. I told him to get the hell out of my kitchen, but he acted like he wanted to do something."

Spoonie said, "Man, I'm not trying to defend dude, but it ain't his fault. He didn't know Venice was your lady. It's not like you and Venice have said two words to each other since the party started. I think every man in this room wanted to get with her. You've got to admit it, man. She's wearing that damn dress."

"Don't remind me."

Spoonie was right. Several of the women gave Venice envious looks. She was getting just a little too much attention from the fellows. All the men in the room constantly stared at her everywhere she went. They were asking who she was and if she was with anyone. J.T. tried to explain to several of his friends that Venice was "hands off." Some showed they were disappointed. A few others acted like it didn't matter to them. Craig decided to try and ask Venice for a dance and, thankfully, she accepted. Craig's embrace was secure and hot. She didn't want to let him know she was on fire, but he knew. He always knew.

"What's on your mind, Venice?"

"I don't feel like talking right now."

She didn't want to make eye contact, so she kept her eyes closed as they danced. There was a nice song playing, which was very appropriate for their situation. The lyrics had to do with making up and trying to get things back the way they were. Venice was unsure if he'd requested the song. But, as the song played, he softly sung in her ear. Craig's voice was somewhat similar to the artist's voice and her body instantly turned to jelly. Feeling his strong arms around her and the love in his voice stripped her anger away.

She laid her head against his chest and whispered, "I'm sorry."

He smiled and planted a sultry kiss on her lips, bringing out all the passion and heat he carried for her. It didn't matter that the room was full of people. As far as they were concerned, they were the only ones there. She let out a soft moan and he knew she desired him as much as he desired her. He ran his hands over the soft velvet fabric of her dress, molding his hands to every curve of her body.

He kissed the curve of her neck and said, "I'm sorry, baby. I love you."

With their foreheads pressed together, she smiled and said, "Let's go."

"Wait! There's something I want to do first."

Pulling her by the hand, he sat her down in a nearby chair and told her not to move and disappeared in the crowd. A few minutes later she heard, "I'd like to do this one for the love in my life. Ms. Venice Taylor, the lady in red."

Venice was surprised, speechless, and a little embarrassed. All eyes were on her as Craig began to sing to her. Craig stared directly at her and she could tell he was sincere and singing directly from his heart. Venice stared back at him as tears ran down her cheeks. She raised up and put her hands over her mouth. Some of the men in the room looked at Craig with envy, but did give him props on what he'd done for his lady. When he ended the song, everyone in the room gave him a standing ovation. Venice put her arms around his neck and they gave each other a long, sensual kiss.

She whispered, "Thank you, baby!"

"You're welcome!"

"I'll be right back." He went over to Bernice, gave her a kiss on the cheek, and said, "We're going upstairs for a while to talk. We'll be back later to help clean up."

"Don't worry about it. We've got it covered. Get out of here."

Craig went back over, took Venice's hand, and they disappeared upstairs.

When they made it upstairs, Venice could hardly wait to feel Craig consume her body. She realized she'd overreacted and had to make it up to him. He pulled her into his arms as they entered his room and immediately covered her mouth with his. She didn't hesitate to part her lips for him to taste all her wants. Her body quivered as his hands glided up her thigh and under the hem of her dress. Her knees buckled as she felt his hand reach into her satin panties. Her breath left her body as he stroked her intimately.

"Venice, I want you so much."

He cupped her hips and laid her upon his soft mattress. They feasted upon each other as their bodies ignited. He pulled away for a moment to catch his breath and Venice searched his dark eyes for the reason he loved her so much. How could he, knowing she belonged to someone else.

He leaned down and whispered, "Let me help you out of that dress."

Seconds later, they got reacquainted with each other's body. The heat their skin generated was more than they could handle. His warm lips on her body made her moan to every searing kiss.

"Venice, I'm sorry I brought up Jarvis."

"Baby, I can't blame you. I was upset with you about a picture when I've actually..."

"Stop! I don't want to talk about it anymore. Let's take a bath."

He started to devour her mouth harder and she began to shudder as his hands kneaded her entire body. He moved between her legs and wasted no time pushing himself inside her as the bubbles and steam danced around them. He began to make love to her and she closed her eyes breathing deeply. Craig gently stroked her hair and ran his tongue up and down her body. He continued to push himself into her even harder as he kept her body pinned against the tub. He called out her name and groaned uncontrollably as he moved in and out of her trembling heat. Venice moaned, "Oh God! Oh God! Baby! Oh God!"

Craig finally called out to her as he climaxed for what seemed like hours. Venice didn't feel her own body jerking as she released. Craig held his grip on her so tight, he left marks on her body, which would probably be bruises in the morning. Craig slowly planted butterfly kisses over her neck, shoulders, and face. She held onto him securely, looking into his eyes. Then she gave him a soul-stirring, foot-stomping, smack your Momma kiss. They started laughing as Craig, still somewhat paralyzed and exhausted, laid back in the bubbles.

"Venice, I'll always be here for you, no matter what."

"Thanks Craig. That means a lot to me."

They enjoyed the massage of the warm water for about twenty more minutes in silence. They just looked at each other and smiled. Finally, he shut off the jets and let out the water. He waded around the tub to blow out the candles while Venice splashed the water playfully at him. She grabbed a towel and got out of the tub and said, "Do you want to go back downstairs?"

"No, do you?"

"I'd rather stay here with you."

He also got out of the tub and grabbed a towel and wrapped it around his well-toned body. They went back into the bedroom and fell across the bed. Craig said, "Man, I'm tired!"

"You should be…you tried to kill me."

"I think you're confused, Taylor. You tried to kill me."

Venice asked, "Where's Bear?"

Craig turned over on his back and said, "Bear's in his room. Come here."

He pulled Venice on top of his body, which was still wet from the bath. He wrapped his arms around her body and closed his eyes.

Venice laid there looking at him seriously and asked, "Did you mean it when you said you'd always be there for me?"

Craig traced his fingers along her thigh. "I meant it, Venice. I know you've got a lot on your mind and I know you're torn. I don't want to make it any harder for you. I'm not going to lie to you. I think about losing you all the time. I feel like I'm on death row, not knowing if you're going to pull the switch."

"I'm sorry. If you want to stop seeing me, I'll understand."

Craig looked at her in disgust and said, "You'll be the first to know."

After talking a little while longer, they fell asleep.

The party was still going strong and they didn't even know it.

J.T.'s friend, Victor, was still looking for Venice and J.T. told him to give it up. A couple hours passed and Craig woke up and found Venice asleep across his chest. He turned her over on her back and unwrapped the towel from her body.

Venice woke up and asked, "What are you doing?"

"Sh-h-h-h-h."

He positioned himself on top of her and started kissing his way slowly down her body, stopping at certain desirable areas. He then found his way down to the place she loved for him to be. It was there he controlled her mind, body, and soul. She could never handle her emotions when he made love to her this way. She wiggled as his tongue danced against her body. Venice couldn't hold her composure any longer and she moaned out loud and long. It was obvious she didn't care who heard her either. She arched her back as he reached up and caressed her nipples. Venice thought she would die when Craig whispered, "You taste so good, baby."

After applying a condom, he slid inside her. She screamed, "Oh, baby!"

He stopped what he was doing, looked Venice in her eyes and said firmly, "Don't you ever let another man put his hands on you like that again. Do you hear me?"

Venice, still breathless, responded, "I'm sorry."

He knew he wasn't the only one "whipped." He also wanted Venice to know he was not going to just let her walk back into Jarvis' arms without a fight. She stroked his head, neck, and back gently with her hands as he finished loving her. Craig was drained and in love. He shifted his weight from her sore body and once again drifted into a satisfied sleep. Venice, however, couldn't sleep. This had been an unusual day for her. What could possibly happen next?

Thirty-Six

The alarm clock went off at six forty-five. Craig eased out of bed and took his shower before waking Venice. She was sore from the intense night she'd shared with him and it was difficult to move. Craig had to help her with her pantyhose and skirt. Her legs felt like she had run a marathon and loss.

"See what you did to me."

Smiling proudly he said, "And to think, I held back. Don't worry, baby. I'll give you a rub down when we get back."

"Promise?"

"Promise."

Once service was over, they took Spoonie to the airport to catch his plane home. Then they drove back to the house the long way and neither mentioned the events of the previous night. Craig wanted to forget about the bad part and hoped Venice would also. Venice called her mother and father and told them she'd be home Tuesday evening. Her mother told her to be careful and to call before she left.

Venice had a few bruises on her back and she couldn't wait for her massage. Craig's touch was sensual and hot. Halfway through the massage, the purpose was defeated by another heated and passionate rendezvous.

"Craig, you're going to send me home limping."

"I'm sorry, baby. I promise I'll fix you up before you go home. Tonight, I'll bathe you in Epsom salts, then pray I can keep my hands to myself."

She ran her tongue across his lips and pecked him slowly and erotically on his lips and said, "Thanks."

"Venice, you keep that up and you'll be going home limping."

259

That laughed and held each other tightly, absorbing the warmth of their bodies.

They were relaxing in the rec room when the telephone rang. Bryan was calling to verify when Venice was leaving. Craig gave her the phone and she informed him of his itinerary. Afterwards, he told her he thought it might be best if she flew home instead of drove. He was concerned for her driving alone during the holidays. She insisted she'd be fine, but Bryan argued the point until Venice got defensive. She felt he was babying her again. He told her under no circumstances was she to drive and that he was going to get her plane ticket. She flat out refused and slammed the phone down.

Craig was confused and wondering what was going on. "What's wrong, Taylor?" Without answering him, she disappeared upstairs.

The phone rang again. Craig answered it in a puzzled state. "Hello?"

"Hey, Craig. Where's Venice?"

"She just went upstairs. What's wrong?"

"Nothing except for her acting childish?"

"Can I help?"

Bryan went on to explain what he'd discussed with Venice. Craig, not wanting to get in the middle of it, said, "Let me talk to her. I'll get back with you."

Craig hung up and went upstairs to find her. He looked around the house for a while, then he heard Bear barking. She was sitting out on the porch in the swing with Bear in her lap. Craig sat down next to her and said, "Bryan called you back." She didn't acknowledge him. She kept on swinging. Craig explained, "Baby, Bryan's only trying to look out for you."

"My brothers have been trying to look out for me all my life. The only reason I continue to let them get away with it is..." She hesitated for a moment. "Something almost happened to me a couple of years back."

Craig listened, not to give away the fact that he already knew what had happened. Venice stared out into the yard and went on to tell him the horrible details Bryan had already told him. Craig put his arm around her shoulder and wiped away the tears.

She said, "That's why my brothers are so overly protective of me. They think I'm still traumatized by it. I've gotten past it now. I did have a hard time trusting men after that, but I'm trying to be more independent. I'm trying to take care of myself."

"Venice, brothers have been protecting their sisters for generations. It's our job. Even though Bernice is older than me, that didn't stop me from jumping a guy almost twice my age and size when he called her a hoe. I got my ass kicked but I defended my sister. You need to let your brothers protect you as long as they can. Good brothers don't come along often. I hate that happened to you, Venice. Be thankful it wasn't much worse and that you have good friends and brothers to look out for you. I care about you, too. Let your brothers do their job. Now...you might want to call Bryan back so you can talk about it. Look, Venice, tell Bryan if he wants me to and you don't mind, I'll drive you home. Okay?"

Venice had tears in her eyes and nodded her head in agreement. "Okay, thanks."

Venice got up from the swing and went back inside to call Bryan. Venice had no idea of the drama waiting for her. Jarvis was already home for the Christmas holidays and anxiously waiting for her to arrive.

Tuesday morning, Craig loaded the suitcases in Venice's car about nine. She said her good-byes to J.T. and Bernice. Venice felt a little sad to be leaving the Bennett household. She knew that when she came back, she would have to spend more time in her dorm room. Luckily, her grades hadn't suffered from her spending so much time with Craig. The second semester classes were going to be a little more demanding, but Venice was ready.

They'd been on the road for about three hours and Venice was able to get a little sleep as Craig drove. He played some of his favorite CDs to pass the time away. Venice woke up and told Craig she'd drive the last three hours if he wanted her to. He told her he'd let her know if he got tired. They stopped for gas and lunch halfway through the trip. The weather was very cold and there was a sever weather warning for snow moving in. Venice insisted on driving the remainder of the trip so Craig could catch a nap. Before he knew it, they were in her hometown. Craig woke up, looked at his watch, and realized she must've been rolling. She cut their trip by a good thirty minutes. He stretched and asked, "How fast were you driving?"

"You don't want to know. I wanted to get here before it started snowing."

She made her way through town and pulled into the driveway at the back of her house. They both got out and stretched from being in the car so long.

Venice said, "I'm so tired."

About that time, Crimson ran out of the house. She jumped up in Craig's arms, hugging him. He said, "Hey, squirt!"

She jumped down, ran around the car, and jumped up on Venice, nearly knocking her down.

"Hey, Auntie! What did you bring me?"

Bryan came out and hollered, "Crimson! Get your little tail back in this house! You don't have on a coat! Hey, Craig. Hey, Venice."

Venice was trying to walk with Crimson still in her arms and said, "Hey, Bryan."

She hurried to get Crimson in the house. When she entered the house, she could smell the aroma of some good home cooking. Her mother met her at the door and gave her a big hug and kiss. "How's my baby? I'm glad you finally got here. Some snowy weather might be moving in. Dinner's almost ready and I know you're hungry. Where's Craig?"

"Outside with Bryan. We heard about the snow on the radio. Where are Galen and Sidney?"

Her mother was taking something out of the oven. "They've gone shopping or something."

Venice took her jacket off and hung it in the hallway. "Where's Daddy?"

"He's playing cards with some of his friends. He'll be home soon."

Craig and Bryan entered with the luggage. Venice's mom greeted Craig. "Thanks for bringing our baby home."

"I didn't mind, Mrs. Taylor. It was my pleasure."

"Okay! Dinner will be ready in about thirty minutes."

Bryan said, "Ma, I have to make a run. Craig, you can ride if you want to."

"Thanks, Bryan. I believe I will."

Before leaving, Craig gave Venice a small peck on the lips.

A little while later, Venice covered a sleeping Crimson up on the sofa and said, "Momma, I'm going up to take a bath. Crimson is asleep on the sofa."

Her mom told her to go ahead. She was going into the den to sit down anyway. Venice climbed the stairs, still a little sore from the past fiery nights with Craig. She put her bags in her room and started running the bath water. She laid out the clothes she was changing into and finally eased into the hot, sudsy water. As she laid there, she realized this would possibly be her last few nights with Craig before he returned to Dawson. She closed her eyes and laid back to soothe her sore muscles. A few minutes later, she heard Bryan's voice coming from downstairs. She knew they were back and Bryan was growling that he was ready to eat.

She heard her mother say, "Ya'll go ahead and fix your plate. Venice, dinner's ready!" Venice hollered back, "I'll be down in a minute!"

Venice closed her eyes and laid her head back on the tub. A few seconds later she was startled by familiar hands stroking her shoulders. Venice was surprised to turn and see Craig grinning.

"What are you doing in here? My mom's going to kill you!"

Craig squatted down and put his hand over in the hot water to caress her thigh. "I don't think so. She's downstairs setting the table. I could probably get some and be back downstairs before anybody missed me."

"You don't know my mom! Hand me the towel, please."

"Why are you trying to cover yourself? You don't have anything I haven't already seen." She stepped out of the tub, wrapped her body in the towel, and let the water out. She went to the door and peeped out to see if anyone was in the hall. She ran across the hall to her room.

She told Craig through the crack in her door, "Go back downstairs before somebody comes looking for you."

He tried to push her door open and said, "Not before I get a kiss."

Venice held the door open and laughed. "No, Craig. Now go on."

"Not until I get some sugar."

Venice's mother hollered again, "Venice, Craig, dinner's ready!!"

In unison, they replied, "Okay!"

Venice laughingly whispered, "Quit playing, Craig."

He finally pushed his way into her room and closed the door behind him, locking it. Venice backed up and said, "You're crazy!"

Craig masked a devilish grin as he stalked toward her. "Come here, Venice."

She backed up and tumbled onto her bed. Craig immediately crawled on top of her and covered her lips with his. He prodded her mouth with his tongue and was instantly drugged by her taste. He ran his hand up her thighs and under her towel. She arched her body into him and nuzzled her face into his neck. All this was going on while her family was downstairs. She could feel that he was aroused as she brushed her naked body against him. He lowered his gaze and proudly admired her beauty.

"Lord have mercy, girl."

"We have to stop, Craig."

He kissed her again and moaned, "Uh-uh."

Breathless, she said, "Craig, baby, you…damn…my God!"

He finally stopped, then wrapped her back up in the towel and said, "Now see what you did to me."

Sitting upon the bed, he covered his face as he tried to talk his desire down. He laughed, saying, "It's not funny, Venice."

"You brought it upon yourself. Sorry for you, baby."

"I'll get you back later, so rest up."

With that statement, he closed the door behind him, leaving her alone. Venice fell back on the bed tingling from head to toe.

About fifteen minutes later, Venice joined her family downstairs for dinner. When she entered the room, she was shocked to see Joshua and Jarvis sitting at the table with her family having dinner. She stopped in her tracks, stunned.

Joshua jumped up and said, "Hey! There's my girl!"

He came over and gave her a big hug and kiss.

Venice whispered, "I'm going to kill you."

"It wasn't my idea."

She went around the table to greet her other man.

"Hi, Jarvis."

He stood up and unexpectedly gave her a hug and kiss right on the lips.

"Hello, Niecy."

She quickly glanced over at Craig, who was ignoring them, and said, "Has everyone been introduced?"

Bryan said, "Yeah, girl! Everybody knows everybody."

Bryan then gave her an *I bet you didn't expect to have to deal with this now* look.

Her mother noticed the tension and said, "Venice, sit down and eat."

"Yes Ma'am."

She sat down next to her mother and they talked about the upcoming Christmas holiday. She looked over at Jarvis, who winked at her and she knew he was going to be cool. Especially with the awkward situation facing them.

The Taylor house was beautifully decorated with lights and a huge Christmas tree in the living room with lots of presents under the tree. The stairs had garland and red bows going all the way up the stairwell. It was beautiful and good to be home. It wasn't long after they began eating when Sidney and Galen returned. While Galen was saying hello to Craig, Venice went upstairs with Sidney.

Venice asked, "Sidney, can you believe both of them are sitting downstairs in my momma's kitchen?"

"I figured they would be heading over here. We ran into them at the mall. Your man was asking Galen when you were coming in. Venice, you knew it was eventually going to happen. What are you going to do?"

"I have no idea. Craig is going to be here until Saturday. Jarvis will be here for three weeks. I'm glad he didn't show out in front of Craig."

Sidney crawled up on the bed and said, "Well, you've got your hands full. I wouldn't want to be in your shoes for nothing. I don't know how you're going to get out of this. You better get on back down there before they kill each other. Good luck."

Venice slowly got up and said, "You're no help."

"Sorry for you, sis. Tell your mom that I'll get something to eat when I wake up."

"Okay, do you want me to get you something to drink?"

"No thanks."

After dinner, Bryan invited Joshua and Jarvis to come play ball with them at Gator's house. Venice peeped out to see that Craig seemed to have no problem being in the same company with Jarvis. She hoped Bryan and Galen would make sure everything remained cool.

The evening went on without any problems. Mr. Taylor finally came home for dinner. Bryan had called Gator to confirm they had enough people for the pick-up basketball game. Venice thought Craig would be too tired to play, but the mention of basketball brought instant energy to him. He went upstairs to change.

Venice met him in the hall and asked, "Are you cool with this? I didn't know Jarvis was coming over."

Craig smiled and said, "I'm cool, baby. Don't get stressed out over this. As long as he's cool, I'll be cool. I'll see you later."

After the men left for Gator's house, Venice decided to go visit Chanelle to bring her up to speed on the current events that had her head spinning. She was still stunned from the boldness of Jarvis kissing her in front of Craig. She always knew he went after what he wanted and she also knew she wouldn't be any exception.

Once the two got together, they caught up on all the activities from the past hours and days. Chanelle was laughing and told her, "Girl! This is it! You know Craig is not going to let you out of his sight. Jarvis is going to try to get you to ditch Craig so he can hook up with you. This is going to be buck wild. What are you going to do?"

"I have no idea. You should've seen me, girl. When I walked into the kitchen and saw them sitting there, I froze. Then Jarvis stood up and kissed me on the mouth right in front of Craig. You know that's his way of staking his claim. He always does that when some man is giving me too much attention."

"What did Craig do?"

"I don't know. I stopped breathing for a moment and just sat down next to Momma and started eating."

They laughed together for a few hours. Then, Venice asked Chanelle if she would go with her to take Crimson to the movies. Chanelle was happy to get out of the house with her best friend. They went to eat after the movies and did a little shopping to help pass the time away. After a few hours, Venice wondered how the guys were getting along. She hadn't heard from any of them, so it must be going smooth.

Venice was feeling a little tired, so she dropped Chanelle off at home and told her that she'd see her later.

Crimson was talking a mile a minute, telling Venice all about what Santa Claus was bringing her. Venice listened to her attentively and told her she had better be good so she would get what she asked for. Once back at the Taylor home, the guys were still gone. When she got inside, she called Sinclair to see if it was okay if Crimson spent the night. Sinclair told her it was okay with her and to let Bryan know. When she hung up the phone, her mother was coming back in the door from visiting her neighbor across the street. Venice explained to her that she was going to keep Crimson with her since it was late. Venice gave her dad a kiss and went upstairs to put Crimson to bed.

Later, Venice went and had a woman-to-woman talk with Sidney. She wanted to know when Sidney knew Galen was the one for her. Sidney explained that at first, Galen was just the average immature freshman but over the course of a summer, he'd started to grow on her.

"Look, Venice, knowing if Craig or Jarvis is the right one is not something you try to figure out. It's a feeling different from any other feeling you've ever felt. You'll know when the time is right. Quit stressing about it and just let nature take its course. It's obvious they're both crazy about you. I see it as a win-win situation, either way it goes."

"I guess you're right, Sidney. I just hope neither of them says the wrong thing. I would hate for them to get into fight over me."

Venice looked at her watch and said, "Well...there's no telling what time they'll get back from Gator's house. I'm going downstairs to watch TV with Daddy. Do you want me to get you anything?"

"If you don't mind, fix me a ham sandwich."

Venice got up and said, "I'll be back in a second."

Sidney laid back on the pillows, wishing her new sister-in-law luck. She was going to need it.

Thirty-Seven

Gator had a small indoor court at his huge mansion on the outskirts of town. He had done very well playing in the NFL and provided well for his wife and two small children. Venice was their baby-sitter before she went off to college. The fellows had played several games before they decided to sit down and relax. They talked about their NFL days and then they started teasing Galen about becoming a husband and Daddy.

Gator, being who he was, slipped and said, "I don't know what you're laughing at, Jarvis. You were just in Galen's shoes a few months ago."

As soon as he said it, everyone realized he shouldn't have brought it up. He forgot Craig was dating Venice now. Bryan said, "Damn, Gator!"

"What?"

It was silent for a moment, then Jarvis said, "You're right and if I had it my way, we we'd still be married."

Galen glanced over at Craig, who didn't show any expression as he listened to Jarvis.

Gator then asked, "Do you want her back?"

Bryan and Galen in unison said, "Gator!"

Bryan stood up and said, "Ya'll going to play ball or sit around and gossip like some old ladies?"

Gator said, "No, let the man answer."

Jarvis said, "Hell yeah, I want Venice back because I still love her and as far as I'm concerned, she's still *my* wife." Jarvis got up and said, "Craig, I'm just expressing the way I feel."

Craig responded, "I understand."

Gator was impressed with Jarvis' honesty. So was everyone else.

They played a few more games, then Bryan looked at his watch and said, "We'd better get back to the house. I left Crimson over there and I know Sinclair is going to trip since I haven't called."

Gator guffawed. "That's right. I forgot Sinclair has you on a curfew."

Bryan got up and threw a towel at Gator. "Forget you, man! I'm the boss in my house!"

"Yeah right. Hey, thanks for the game. If ya'll aren't doing anything tomorrow, come back so we can get a rematch."

When they got in the car, Bryan called Sinclair and told her that he'd be home shortly. Sinclair told him that Venice had already put Crimson to bed. Bryan talked a minute or two longer and hung up. It was quiet in the car and once he got back to the Taylor home, everybody said their goodnights.

Galen asked Joshua and Jarvis if they wanted to come in and get something to drink. They agreed and followed him into the house. Everyone was in the den watching TV and Venice was still asleep on the sofa. Mrs. Taylor gathered her things and told them she'd see them in the morning. She came over and woke Venice so Galen and the guys could sit down.

Galen said, "I'm going to run up and check on Sidney and take a shower."

Craig didn't want to sit down since he was sweaty.

Mrs. Taylor said, "Craig, baby, you can go take your shower in the bathroom down the hall."

He thanked her and she told Venice to go get him some towels.

Venice sluggishly said, "Yes, Ma'am."

When she walked past Joshua, he put his arm around her neck and said, "Wake up, girl!"

She pushed away from him and said, "Stop, Josh!"

Joshua acted like he was going to chase her. Craig had already walked down the hallway to his room. When Venice passed Jarvis, he pinned her against the wall outside the den, touched her intimately, and whispered, "Give me some sugar, Niecy."

"Jarvis, stop and move!"

"Oh, you're gonna treat me like that since your little boyfriend is here. That's cool. I'll take care of you later."

Mr. Taylor yelled, "Jarvis!"

"I'm cool, Pops. I'm just playing with her."

Venice finally pushed past him, still feeling the heat from his touch on her lower body. Once he returned to the den, Mr. Taylor searched the room for Craig, then said, "Jarvis, don't you start no shit!"

"Pops, you know me."

"You're right. I know you. I mean what I said!"

"Okay. I'll be cool."

"You'd better. Craig's a nice kid, whether you want to believe it or not."

Craig waited on an exhausted Venice down the hall at the linen closet. She handed him the towels and said, "If you need anything else, I'll be in the den."

"Thanks, baby. I'll see you in a little bit."

"Okay."

She just walked back down the hall dragging her feet in sleepiness. When Venice got back to the den, her father was getting up to go to bed. He said, "Baby, I'll see you in the morning." He gave her a kiss and said, "All right, fellows, ya'll better behave yourself in here. Don't make me have to put a cap in ya'll asses. Jarvis, remember what I said and Joshua, keep an eye on him."

"All right Pops. I'll make sure everyone stays cool."

"Thanks. Tell Galen to make sure he turns the TV off when ya'll are done."

Venice laid back down on the sofa and pulled the blanket over her. A few moments later, Galen came back down and told Venice to go to bed.

"Leave me alone, Galen."

Jarvis walked across the room and moved Venice's feet so he could sit down next to her. He ran his hand under the blanket and over her hips. She squirmed and said, "Jarvis."

He withdrew his hand and asked, "What? Are you nervous? You normally like me touching you. You don't have to say anything. Pops threatened me so I have to be a good boy."

"Baby, I'm just tired. Okay?"

He leaned down and whispered in her ear, "I want you, Niecy."

"Chill, okay?"

"For now."

Before pulling away from her, he gave her a full kiss on the lips, lingering to taste her. Joshua looked over at them and said, "Hey, I'm going to tell you two right now, I'm not breaking up any fights up in here tonight. Ya'll better stop over there."

Galen responded with, "Me either. I'm gonna let those fools fight it out. I don't even see what they see in her anyway."

Jarvis and Joshua were laughing as Venice tried to recover from the intoxicating effect his kiss left on her. She started feeling a familiar throbbing in her middle and her skin began to burn. Craig walked back in wearing a T-shirt and a pair of sweats. He sat down in Mr. Taylor's recliner and watched as Joshua and Galen play against each other. He glanced over at Venice and smiled. He could see Jarvis was sitting close but he had to expect that between them.

She said, "I'm going to bed. I'll see you guys tomorrow."

She leaned over and gave Jarvis a kiss on his luscious, awaiting lips. She then got up and gave Joshua a hug. Lastly, she walked over to Craig and gave him a similar lingering kiss goodnight. Jarvis' blood boiled in his veins and he didn't like it one bit. Venice belonged to him and there was no way he could sit there and stay cool.

Get your damn hands off my woman!

Venice looked back at him and smiled before leaving the room. Jarvis was unsure if he'd said that out loud or in his mind. Either way, he meant it.

It was about eleven o'clock when Galen put the game on pause and built a fire in the fireplace. While Galen was busy with the wood, Craig went over and started playing Joshua on the video game. Venice went on up to her room and eased into her bed, being careful not to wake Crimson. She laid in bed with her heart pounding, knowing the two loves of her life were downstairs together. What are the odds?

Thirty-Eight

Christmas was approaching fast and Craig would be leaving soon. The next morning, the household was bustling. Crimson got up early and wanted Venice to get up. She told her to let her sleep and pulled the covers over her head. Crimson hopped out of bed and ran downstairs for breakfast. Crimson ran into the den and found all the guys still asleep.

Mrs. Taylor said, "Sh-h-h, Crimson. Come out of there and let those boys sleep." Mrs. Taylor closed the door to the den and brought Crimson into the kitchen so she could fix her some breakfast. Venice had no desire to get up. Her body was much more tired than she'd realized. It would be late morning before Venice and Sidney would get up. The guys all got up around nine o'clock and went their separate ways. Mrs. Taylor made sure they had breakfast before they left.

They all decided to go to the club that night. Venice was excited that she'd probably see some of her friends she hadn't seen since she left for college. They all lounged around the house most of the day. Venice talked to Chanelle and discussed what they were going to wear. Galen and Craig left, going no telling where, and Venice and Sidney chilled out at the house. They relaxed the rest of the evening. Venice was surprised Craig didn't mention anything to her about Jarvis and Jarvis didn't say anything to her about Craig. She was wondering if it was the calm before the storm.

The club was filling up quickly as the partygoers arrived ready to shake their booty. It was the holidays and many were home from college and ready to release the stress of exams. Venice was happy that everything had been running smoothly the last couple of days. She just hoped it would last.

They finally arrived and not long afterwards, Chanelle arrived.

Immediately, Chanelle and Venice introduced Sidney around to some of their former classmates. Galen introduced Craig to some of his partners also. A couple of Venice's rivals gave her jealous looks. One in particular noticed Craig was a new face in the crowd and decided to inquire about him. She twisted over to Galen and said, "Hey, Galen! It's been a long time since I've seen you. You're still looking fine though."

Galen said, "Hello, Saundra. You look nice also."

She thanked him and tossed her weave with her fingers. She then looked Craig up and down and asked, "Who's your friend?"

"Oh, this is Craig. He goes to school with me. Craig, this is Saundra."

"Nice to meet you."

"So...you're visiting the Taylors?"

"Yes."

Saundra positioned herself between Galen and Craig, sizing him up. She said, "Well... Craig, if you're not doing anything tomorrow, I'd love to show you around or something."

The music was loud and it was hard to hear so Craig leaned down to her ear and said, "Thanks for the offer, but I don't think I'm available."

"Does that mean you're busy or that you're spoken for?"

"Both, but thanks."

Saundra looked surprised and said, "It's your loss."

"I'm sure."

As she walked away, she said, "If you change your mind, Galen knows how to find me."

Galen looked at Craig and shook his head in laughter. "Man...that chick is a trip! Venice can't stand her. She tried to break her and Jarvis up once."

Craig said, "That's a shame."

Galen and Craig got them a drink and found a table. The girls continued socializing. Venice occasionally asked Sidney if she was okay due to her pregnancy.

As the music played, the crowd danced to the beat. When the DJ slowed the music down, Craig danced with Venice for a couple of songs. The group was still enjoying themselves when Chanelle turned and said, "Venice, here comes your other man."

Sidney and Venice turned to see Joshua and Jarvis enter the room. They watched as the guys gathered, shaking hands with one another. Venice could see that Jarvis was scanning the room.

Chanelle said, "You might as well go on over there and tell him hello."

"He'll find me."

Chanelle said, "Look at you trying to be hard. I'll bet you're shaking in your shoes."

Venice gave Chanelle a look and said, "I'll be back in a minute. I'm going to the restroom."

Sidney and Chanelle laughed and said, "Don't run!"

Venice walked across the room, stopping to talk to several people as she made her way to the restroom. She noticed Jarvis was no longer talking to Galen and wondered where he'd disappeared to. As she approached the hallway, he grabbed her from behind, pulling her body against his. "I'd know those hips anywhere."

The heat from his body was electrifying. Chills shot up her arms as he held her tightly to his muscular chest.

"Hi, Jarvis."

He turned her to face him and gave her a gigantic hug, lifting her off the floor. Venice hugged him back, trying not to react too affectionately. Jarvis leaned in to give her a kiss, but she turned her head and he ended up kissing her on the cheek instead of on the lips.

He said, "Oh... You gonna do a brotha like that?"

"Jarvis, be cool. You know Craig is in here."

He smiled and said, "I know he's here. What? He's gonna try and beat my ass or something?"

"Quit trippin' and behave."

"I'll be cool for you, but that man ain't got a claim on you. So, when are you gonna dance with me?"

"If you wait right here, I'll dance with you when I come out."

He leaned against the wall and said, "All right. I'll wait, but not long."

"What do you mean by that, Jarvis?"

"Never mind, hurry up, Niecy." When Venice came out of the restroom, they proceeded to the dance floor.

"Venice, like I told you in Michigan, I don't care who you hook up with. You're gonna always belong to me and you know it. We've got a history that nobody can come between. I know I messed up in the past, but I promised you that I would never hurt you again."

Venice, seeing the seriousness in his eyes, said, "Jarvis, I don't feel like talking about that tonight."

"You can avoid talking about it tonight, but you can't avoid it forever. You know I'm telling the truth."

Damn he feels good!

But things were complicated now since Craig had entered her life. Jarvis was always popular and everybody liked him. He was a gifted athlete and honors student. They matched and she knew it.

There was only one storm in their relationship. Jarvis fell under the spell of peer pressure and Venice caught him messing around on her. She was devastated but it ended up hurting him more than it hurt her. For three months, she'd given him the silent treatment as he tried to get his beg on. It was driving him crazy to know that she'd found comfort in the arms of his best friend's brother.

Michael always flirted with Venice but she'd never taken him seriously because they all grew up together. Michael was a year older than Galen and he was Joshua's older brother. He had his own condo on the other side of town and worked third shift at a local company while going to college during the day. It started out innocent, but eventually their relationship took off. Galen wasn't too happy to hear about the relationship and would occasionally crack on Michael about it. It was perfect for Venice to hook up with him after school and it almost cost her the relationship with Jarvis.

Venice knew Jarvis was going crazy knowing she'd given it up to Michael. She felt Jarvis deserved to be hurt just like he'd hurt her. Michael was a good listener and helped her eventually find her way back to Jarvis. He suggested she try to work things out with Jarvis since they all grew up together. Michael knew if he were going to remain friends with him, he had to end his relationship with Venice. She finally was able to forgive Jarvis and they were inseparable from that moment on.

Jarvis and Venice continued their dance and also danced with other friends in the club. The night was getting longer and Venice and her crew were beginning to tire out. There was a short-lived scuffle in the corner of the club. The bouncers hurriedly dispersed the situation to keep things from getting out of hand. It was always the same. Somebody had a little too much to drink and tried to fight somebody for stepping on their shoes or something. Venice noticed Jarvis watching her from across the room.

I wish you would stop staring. I hope Craig doesn't notice.

Jarvis was very handsome, with a smile that could melt butter. He was a dark chocolate drop of gorgeous with dimples and plainly irresistible.

Venice began to reminisce about their past together. She never told anyone, except for Joshua, that on graduation night, after their divorce, she ran into him on her way home from the graduation party. She left early due to a headache and heartache. They were trying to put a little distance between them, but it didn't seem to work. Jarvis also left early and was picking up some take-out food. They ended up back at his dad's house and made love all night. She was supposed to spend the night with Chanelle. They had tried to convince everyone that they were going to be just friends since college was going to be separating them soon. No one believed them, knowing how much they were in love. He thanked her for spending the night with him and when she left his house the next morning, he told her that he'd always love her, no matter what. Venice told him she'd always feel the same about him. They ended up hanging out all summer. They just couldn't stand to be apart and they knew it.

Back on the dance floor, he was staring at her again.

"So...is college life still treating you okay, Jarvis?"

"Are you really giving my stuff away?"

Venice was shocked by his questions. "Jarvis...stop. Craig is nice."

Jarvis ran his hands up and down her back said, "I want to see you tonight."

"You know I can't."

"We need to talk, Venice."

"Do you want to talk or do you have something else in mind?"

He leaned down and whispered, "All of the above."

Venice felt a little intrigued. "It sounds nice, but I don't think that would be cool." When the song ended, he brushed his lips against hers and said, "Maybe you're right. Thanks for the dance anyway. I'll call you tomorrow."

"Are you mad?"

"Just disappointed, Niecy. Goodbye."

Jarvis disappeared into the crowd, leaving her standing there feeling empty. Something inside her made her feel a little disappointed that he didn't push the issue.

It was about 11:30 p.m. when Venice asked Craig if he was having a good time. He said he was and asked her if she was. She told him she was having a great time seeing her old friends. They continued to party with the rest of them until Sidney came over and said, "Venice, Chanelle tore her pants. She wants you to ride with her so she can change."

"How did she tear her pants?"

"Girl, I don't know."

Venice leaned over and told Craig that she was going to ride with Chanelle to change clothes. She explained to him what had happened. Venice asked Sidney if she wanted to ride also. This gave her the opportunity to get out of the smoked-filled room for a moment and get some fresh air.

As Chanelle pulled out of the parking lot, they began to gossip about the many people in the club. Sidney was laughing about the way Craig looked when he saw Jarvis hug Venice. She said, "I thought the vein in his head was going to pop."

Venice asked, "For real?"

"Not really. I'm exaggerating a little. But, he was checking you guys out though."

Chanelle said, "Venice, I'm glad you went ahead and told Craig about you and Jarvis. Under the unusual circumstances of your past, he needed to know."

"I guess you're right."

As Chanelle turned down several streets, Venice realized Chanelle wasn't on the correct street leading to her house and asked, "Where are we going?"

"Venice, you're going to be pissed at me, but I'm doing a favor for a friend."

Venice asked in confusion, "What friend?"

Sidney laughed and said, "Oh my God! No you didn't!"

Venice hollered, "What have you done?"

Chanelle pulled into Jarvis' dad's driveway and came to a stop. Venice gave her a nasty look. Chanelle said, "Oh, quit acting like you didn't want to see him. You know you wanted to get with him tonight. I just made it happen for you."

Sidney was laughing her head off in the back seat.

Venice looked at Chanelle and said, "I'm gonna kick your ass, Chanelle."

"Yeah, right."

Jarvis came out with a serious look on his face and his hands stuffed in his jacket. Venice rolled down the window and asked, "What's up, Jarvis?"

He leaned down into the window. "Hey, Sidney. Thanks, Chanelle." He then looked at Venice and said, "I told you I wanted to talk to you. I didn't feel comfortable talking to you at the club."

Venice sat there for a moment, then got out of the car and said, "Make it quick, Jarvis." She looked back at Chanelle and said, "This wasn't cool, black people."

Chanelle shook her head, then looked at Jarvis and said, "I'll be back for her in thirty minutes, brotha."

He closed the car door as Sidney got into the front seat and said, "No problem." Sidney giggled and said, "Take care, Sis."

Chanelle backed out of the driveway and left them standing there in the cold. He looked at her and said, "Well, aren't you coming in?"

Venice walked into the house and asked, "What do you want to talk to me about Jarvis?"

He took her jacket. "Want something to drink?"

"No, what do you want to talk about?"

"Us."

They sat down on the sofa and he said, "Venice, you know I love you and I don't think I can deal with this arrangement any longer. Especially now that I've looked dude in the eyes. I just can't do it."

"So what do you want me to do?"

"I don't know. I just can't handle it anymore."

Venice was glaring at him. "Do you hear yourself? You and I are hundreds of miles away from each other. We get together maybe once a month. It's nice when we do, but I always feel guilty every time I come back to school and look him in the eye. Don't get me wrong, baby. I still love you, too, but we just can't be together right now."

He took a sip of his water and asked, "Why were you protecting him tonight?"

"What do you mean, protecting him?"

"Every time I touched you, it was obvious you didn't want to make him think something was still going on between us."

"I don't want to hurt anyone's feelings. I wish there was some way we could…"

Jarvis pulled her against his body and covered her lips with his. Venice kissed him back and allowed his hands to explore her body. He whispered, "Let me make love to you, Niecy."

"You know I can't. Chanelle is picking me up in ten minutes. Plus, it wouldn't be right."

He grabbed the phone and started dialing.

Venice asked, "Who are you calling?"

He smiled back at her and brushed her hair away from her eyes. Finally he said, "Hey it's me. Could you give me some extra time?" There was some hesitation as he stroked her chin, staring at her. He then said, "All right, I'll call you." He hung up the phone, stood up and took her by the hands, and said, "Come here."

"Where? Who did you call?"

"Your girl. She'll be by later. Now follow me."

He pulled her from the sofa and reluctantly she followed, saying, "This ain't right, Jarvis."

"Niecy, you know in your heart it's perfect." They walked into his room. He showed her those pearly whites and said, "You know you're only woman for me."

"You're crazy."

He pulled her to him and said, "Crazy about you."

He brought his lips to hers once again and they found themselves on his bed. Venice couldn't help herself. She hungered for this man twenty-four seven.

They hurriedly undressed and wrapped themselves around each other. Venice moaned as he kissed her all over her body. Jarvis whispered what he was going to do to her and how he was going to do it. Venice cupped his maleness and screamed out in ecstasy as he pushed into the moistness of her body. Tears begin to flow from her eyes as her nails dug into his shoulders. Venice shivered with every thrust of his hips, every beat of his heart. Venice pulled him down to her lips as he slowly slid deeper and harder into her. She took a deep breath and let out a loud, long moan as her body went up in flames. His bare skin against hers was hot and explosive. She screamed out in Spanish as she felt her body collapsed and disintegrated.

His fire engulfed body as he whispered, "That's my girl."

He had her right where he wanted her. He knew it and she knew it.

Seductively he said, "Let it go, sweetheart."

"Jarvis! I-I."

In a sexy whisper, he said, "Come on, Niecy. Ah-h, that's it baby."

"My God! Oh my God!

Moments later she shuddered, then he shuddered as his released into the depths of her body. He sucked her lips into his and took her breath away.

They laid there in silence attempting to catch their breath.

The silence broke went he angrily said, "Don't you ever give you body to him or any man ever again! Do you hear me!"

"Jarvis, I-I..."

"No! I'm not going to tell you again! I mean it, Venice Anderson!"

She rebelled, saying, "You can't tell me what to do!"

"If you won't tell him, I will!"

Venice stared at him and saw the red in his eyes and the bulging vein in his neck. She pushed him aside and said, "This was a mistake! Move!" She grabbed her clothes and said, "I know you're not at school being as innocent as you're pretending. I'm pretty sure you're getting your share of tail! I know you, remember?"

"If I am, I'm not flashing it in your face like you are!"

Venice was visibly upset. "Jarvis, I can't help it that my family asked him to drive me home. I also can't help it that you can't deal with the agreement of seeing other people."

"I don't give a damn! He's here! You've taken it to another level now."

"I can't handle this kind of stress. If you can't deal with this, maybe we need to just stop everything."

He walked up to her, tilted her chin to look him into his hurt eyes, and calmly asked, "Is that what you want?"

Stroking his cheek with her hand, she answered, "Of course not. I don't want to lose you, baby."

Not breaking his gaze, he said, "Get dressed, Venice."

He sat on the bed as she continued into the bathroom. Once inside, she tried to compose herself unsuccessfully. It was there she completely lost it. Crying aloud, she knew that if Jarvis would've brought someone home, she would've been devastated. His comments caught her off guard and made her a little nervous. She knew he wouldn't give a second thought about telling Craig how he felt. She tried to stop the tears. Her makeup was gone and she looked completely drained. Standing in the mirror, she tried to put her hair up, but was having some difficulty. She noticed her hands were trembling uncontrollably. About that time, there was a knock at the door.

She tearfully said, "Come in."

Jarvis walked in, still nude, and asked, "Are you okay?"

She looked at him through the mirror and replied, "No, I'm not. I shouldn't have come over here."

When he saw her struggling with her hair, he took the clamp and arranged it properly. After he finished, he wrapped his arms around her waist and said, "I'm sorry if I upset you, but I'm having a hard time with this. I can't stand to see you cry. Please stop."

She flinched at his touch, turned and started the shower, then climbed in.

Since she had no response for him, so he said, "I'll see you when you get out."

Softly she said, "You can join me if you want to."

He hesitated for a moment, then pulled back the curtain and joined her in silence.

They got dressed and Jarvis said, "I'll let Chanelle know you're ready." He was very quiet after that, then finally said, "Venice, I don't mean to hurt you, but I can't help the way I feel. I don't believe you know just how hard it is for me to see you with someone else. You say you want to be with me, but I'm having a hard time believing you. I need to believe you still want to be together. Do you understand where I'm coming from?"

Venice looked into his dark brown eyes and said, "Jarvis...look, I'm tired. I can't think about this anymore tonight."

He just stared at her while his heart was taking another punch.

It wasn't long before they heard a horn blowing. He stood up and said, "Well, your ride's here. Thanks for coming over. I really did just want to talk."

Venice walked over and hugged him. "Don't worry about it. I don't regret anything I did here tonight. I *do* love you. I'll see you later."

She tiptoed and gave him a peck on the lips. As she walked toward the door, he pulled her to him and kissed her deeply on the mouth for one more assurance of his love. He walked her out into the cold air and thanked Chanelle for bringing Venice over. They all said their good-byes and Chanelle backed out of the yard.

Chanelle said, "O-o-o. You are so nasty."

Venice snapped angrily, "Shut up, Chanelle!"

Sidney sympathetically asked, "Are you okay?"

Venice didn't respond. She just stared out the window, fighting back the sting in her eyes.

They drove back to the club and continued to party. The guys didn't seem to suspect anything, but were happy to see them return. After a little time passed, Venice was noticeably quiet.

Craig asked, "Are you all right?"

"I'm just a little tired. Thanks for asking."

"Are you ready to go?"

"Yes, I'm getting a headache."

Craig went over to Galen and told him that Venice wasn't feeling well. Galen looked at his watch and said, "It's time to go anyway. I'll get Sidney so we can leave."

When they entered the house, Mr. Taylor was asleep in the recliner. Galen woke him up to let him know they were home.

Craig asked, "Do you need me to get you anything before you go to bed?"

She laid down across the bed and said, "No, I'll be fine, thanks."

He leaned down, kissed her on the cheek, and said, "I'll see you in the morning. I hope you feel better."

"Thanks."

"No problem. Goodnight"

When he turned to walk away, Venice said, "Craig..."

He turned around and came back to her. She stood up and laid her head against his chest, embracing him.

"Yes, Venice?"

She looked up into his warm brown eyes and said, "Thanks for being so sweet."

Smiling, he brought his lips down to hers and said, "No problem, Taylor. Goodnight."

He closed the door and left her alone to come to grips with what she'd done earlier that night. Venice pulled her pillow to her and cried herself to sleep with guilt.

An hour or so had passed when her telephone rang. She was staring into the darkness and she answered, "Hello?"

The voice on the other end asked, "Are you sleep?"

It was Jarvis.

"Not really."

"Can I come over?"

"No! It's late Jarvis and I'm a little pissed off at you right now."

"Let me come over and make it up to you."

"No! I have to go. Goodnight."

He softly said, "Niecy, nobody will know and I'll be out of there before the sun comes up."

"You've lost your mind. I've already taken one risk with you tonight and I'm not going to do it again.

"Oh, I'm a risk now?"

"Look, I have a headache. I'll see you tomorrow."

"Venice, if I come over, are you going to open the window?"

"No! Stay home!"

"I'm on my way."

Venice rose up and said, "Jarvis!"

"See you in a minute. Goodbye."

The phone went dead. Venice sat up in the bed, nervous as hell. When they were in high school, Jarvis found a way to climb up to the second floor using their garage. Venice was always afraid they'd get caught, but it never stopped them. She still didn't know if Jarvis was kidding about sneaking over. Her heart was pounding as she laid there in the dark. He only lived a few blocks away.

A few minutes later, Venice heard a tap on the window. She jumped up and saw Jarvis at the window. Venice was in shock that he still was playing these games. He took a serious chance by coming over in the middle of the night. She paced the floor a minute before raising the window.

She whispered, "Damn you, Jarvis! I told you not to come over here!"

He laughed, climbed in, and said, "You knew that wouldn't stop me. It's cold out there and that climb has gotten a little harder on a brotha."

Venice backed away from him as he quietly closed the window.

"You thought I was kidding, didn't you?"

Venice went over and locked her door and whispered, "Be quiet. What is wrong with you? I told you that I was upset with you."

"I know. It's not the first time, nor the last time."

"Jarvis, what's wrong with you?"

With a devilish grin, he said, "Right now I'm loving the way your body is responding through your nightgown."

Venice folded her arms to cover the obvious hardening of her nipples. She pushed past him and got back into bed and noticed the time: two-fifteen.

She set the clock and said, "You better by out of here by four. You know Daddy gets up early and keep your hands to yourself."

He undressed down to reveal his nakedness and crawled into her bed, reaching for her.

She announced, "I said, keep your hands to yourself!"

He continued to wrap his arm around her waist anyway, pulling her to him. "Did he try to get with you tonight?"

Venice kept her back to him and said, "Mind your damn business. Now move! You're cold!"

Spooning his front to her hips, he said, "Why don't you warm me up then?"

He held her even closer to inhale her sweet, intoxicating scent.

Growing weaker to his touch and feeling his hardened desire, she whispered, "Jarvis, please!"

"Okay, girl, damn! Goodnight."

Within minutes, he was snoring and had buried his face into the back of her neck. Venice, however, was wide awake. She could feel his strength against the softness of her skin and it felt perfect.

The next hour she laid there in the dark thinking about everything that had happened. She turned and looked at him and was glad one of them could get some sleep. The time was now about three o'clock and Venice was still awake. Occasionally, Jarvis would stir and snuggle even tighter, pushing his heated body into hers. He wanted Venice to know what he knew, that they were meant to be together, forever.

Eventually he woke up and gazed into her tear-filled eyes as he touched her body and soul.

She wasn't supposed to be enjoying this since Craig was right downstairs. This was disrespectful, but she couldn't make herself stop.

"Jarvis…Jarvis….Oh, sweetheart!"

With his hands seeking her middle, he slowly and erotically soothed her.

Moments later, he claimed her and began his sweet torture. Her soft moans seemed to engulf her room. Jarvis smiled, knowing he'd never love or want anyone except Venice. He covered every inch of her skin with his kisses and his touch.

Venice moaned, "Oh, that feels so-o-o good."

He whispered, "You like that?"

"Yes-s-s."

He took his time caressing and stroking her with precision, igniting the fire deep inside her body. He kissed her intensely, driving his tongue deeper into her mouth as their tongues danced. Once again, he moved above her, pushing her knees as far back as possible to the headboard. In one swift thrust, he melted into her creamy body. He moved in and out, taking time to lick and suck her aroused tips.

He picked up his pace, needing, wanting to fill every inch of her silken canyon. He whispered, "Baby, I-I love you."

Multiple orgasms invaded her body as her eyes fluttered and her body jerked underneath him. He shuddered also as he buried his face into her neck, which was moist from perspiration. Venice could feel his hot love enter her body as he became stiff, then relaxed.

Exhausted, he pulled her on top of his chest and covered them with the comforter. After a kiss to her forehead, he said, "I'll never stop loving you, Niecy. We're meant to be."

She kissed him on the cheek and listened to her heart race.

The alarm went off at four o'clock. Venice cleared her throat and said, "Jarvis, you'd better get up."

He stirred out of his sleep slowly and pulled her closer to him. "I'm not leaving."

"What?"

He smiled and said, "I'm just playing. Come here."

Venice turned to Jarvis and wrapped her sore arms and legs around his body and said, "You know I can get in a lot of trouble for doing this?"

"From who?"

"My folks."

She kissed him deeply taking his tongue to hers and said, "I don't know what kind of spell you have on me, but this was wrong."

"It didn't feel wrong to me. You are my wife. Remember?"

He kissed her again and pushed his arousal against her leg. "Let me get out of here before I get started again."

She laid there watching him dress and before he went out the window, she said, "Call me when you get home and be careful."

He gave her one last kiss and said, "That's a bet."

Thirty-Nine

It was about ten o'clock and Craig went ahead and took a shower before coming to check on an exhausted Venice.

If he only knew.

After his shower, he sat in the den with Mr. Taylor, watching TV.

Venice's telephone rang and as soon as she said, hello, a voice asked, "Can you talk?"

It was Jarvis.

"Yes, what's up?"

"I don't want you to have any regrets about last night. I couldn't sleep when I got home because I was thinking about you."

"I'm fine, but we can't do that again while Craig is here. Jarvis...I do care about him. I love him."

"Bullshit!"

"I'm serious."

"Then you're confused. I know you better than you know yourself." Jarvis fell silent for a moment before saying, "Look, Niecy, I'll talk to you later."

"A lost for words? That's not like you."

The phone went dead. Jarvis knew Venice couldn't have the same passion for Craig that she had with him. There was no comparison. He knew she loved him more, much more. Hearing the dial tone, she hung up the phone.

Venice finally got up and joined the rest of the family downstairs. This was going to be Craig's last night in her hometown and she felt like she needed to concentrate on him.

She entered the den and her dad said, "The dead has arisen."

Craig laughed and Venice asked, "Do you want to get out of here for awhile?"

He smiled and said, "Let me change and then we can go."

Venice sat there trying to decide how to spend the day. Craig didn't take long and his smile brought the guilt back to her heart. Venice told her dad they'd be back later. She thought it would be a good idea to go by the mall first. Venice was realizing that she'd betrayed Craig. But could she live with it? They walked through the mall and she began to loosen up. It was weird, but when Jarvis was around her, it was like he really did have a spell on her. There wasn't anything he couldn't get her to do.

Craig teased her about the small town mall. They enjoyed lunch and did some shopping. Craig asked her if she wanted to catch a movie, which they did. Afterwards, she drove over to Bryan's house. No one was at home, so she let herself in. They went into the rec room, started watching TV, and played pool. Craig got them some sodas and she laid against his chest as they took a break. He smelled wonderful and she was really going to miss him the next few weeks, even though she'd been sneaking around with Jarvis. Craig was special and she really did love him. She rubbed his chest and arms as they watched TV. Sinclair was out of town on a two-day convention. Bryan and Crimson were over at the Taylors.

Craig started tickling Venice and she screamed trying to get away from him. They tumbled to the floor where and he was able to pin her down. His body reacted immediately to their contact. With both of them out of breath, he leaned down and kissed her soft lips.

Venice put her arms around his neck and said, "I'm going to miss you, Mr. Bennett."

"I'm going to miss you, Taylor."

Craig grabbed the remote control and turned off the TV. He playfully picked her up and carried her into the bedroom and closed the bedroom door and locked it.

Venice asked, "What are you doing?"

Craig pulled off his shirt and said, "I'm going to show you."

Venice got up off the bed and said, "Are you sure? I know you thought Bryan was going to bust us last time we were down here."

"We're alone, remember?"

Craig covered her body with his and kissed her all over her neck. Venice couldn't help but put her arms around his broad shoulders and state, "I miss you already."

"Show me how much, Taylor."

Venice giggled as he continued to kiss all around her lips and press his body against her. She asked, "What if Bryan comes to the door?"

Craig unbuttoned her blouse and unhooked her bra. "Let me worry about that." His hands immediately caressed her breasts as he kissed her nipples, sending an electric jolt throughout her body. Venice's body tingled to his touch, different from the way Jarvis made her feel, but still nice. As they continued to kiss each other's necks, chests, and earlobes, he pulled her to the floor and removed the rest of her clothes. He also pulled the pillows and comforter down to the floor.

Feeling the want in her as she arched her body into his, Craig dipped his lips between her thighs making all the air escape her lungs.

She gasped and moaned, "Craig, baby...oh baby..."

He used his tongue with expertise, covering every inch of desire. After opening the foil package, they were making intense love. Craig greedily kissed her swollen lips and confessed his sincere love. "I love you, Venice. You have to know. You just have to!"

Venice was breathless and paralyzed by his strength and love. He gripped her wrists tightly as his body drove in and out of her weakened body. He moaned her name as he climaxed inside her hot, sweat-drenched body.

They laid there in silence, listening to each other trying to recover their breath. He said, "I don't think I have the strength to play ball with your brother now and it's all your fault."

Venice threw a pillow at him and said, "You're the one who took advantage of me and I'm going to miss you after you leave."

Craig smiled and said, "Me, too."

Venice's heart was pounding as she got dressed. Craig was one of the sweetest men she'd ever met. How could she possibly throw all of that away without learning more? But, she didn't want to lose Jarvis either. Craig wanted to call Bernice, so Venice gave him some privacy.

She went upstairs to the kitchen and her pager went off. She looked and noticed it was Jarvis. Bryan had a separate line in his office so she hesitantly used his phone to return the call. When she called, Jarvis wanted to know what she was up to. Venice told him that she was over Bryan's house.

Jarvis asked, "Is he with you?" Venice did not reply so Jarvis calmly asked, "Did you think I was joking?"

Venice remained quiet on her end of the phone.

He said, "Never mind."

"Jarvis, please!

"Niecy, there's no way you could love him and make love to me like you do. There's no way in hell you can make me believe that."

She calmly said, "I have to go, Jarvis. I can't talk to you right now. Goodbye."

She hung the phone up and put her head down on Bryan's desk. She was totally confused. She'd just made love with a wonderful man that she'd fallen for. But she also made love to the only man she'd ever loved a few hours earlier. Something was truly wrong with this picture. It was a stressful situation and an accident waiting to happen. She had no idea what to do. She didn't know whether Jarvis would come over to Bryan's house or not. What she did know was that she didn't want them to have any confrontation.

I don't see how men do this shit!

It wasn't long afterwards that Bryan came home and picked Craig up to play basketball. It didn't take long for Venice to get back home. She sat in her car and thought about what she'd done that day.

Things were getting out of hand.

She got out of the car and went inside.

Venice was now struggling with the fact that Craig, Sidney, Galen and Bryan would be leaving the next day. She wouldn't see Craig for about three weeks. She shook her head and wondered how she was ever going to make it.

Venice snapped back to reality when Crimson said, "I'm hungry! Can we get some pizza?"

"I guess, but you'd better eat your dinner tonight."

When they got back, Mr. Taylor was working in the garage. Venice went into the garage and asked, "Daddy, what are you doing?"

"Oh, trying to fix the railing on the back steps. What are you up to?"

Venice played with his tools and sat down. "Not much. Just hanging out with Crimson."

"Baby, hand me that hammer." Venice handed it to him. "So, Craig's leaving tomorrow?"

Venice walked around the garage, looking at some of her old things. "Yes, Daddy."

Her father stopped working for a moment and said, "Is there something in particular you wanted to talk about, baby?"

"No, I just wanted to hang out with you a little. That's all."

He started working again and said, "You love him, don't you?"

"Who?"

He measured the piece of wood with his measuring tape and said, "Craig! Don't act like you don't know who I'm talking about. I have eyes. But, I also know you're still in love with Jarvis. You're my daughter and I'll tell you this. I think Craig loves you, too. So, you need to clear things up before this thing gets out of control. I don't want you to get hurt and I don't want to see either one of them hurt. I don't want to have to pop a cap in one of them. Just be careful, baby."

Venice smiled and gave her dad a kiss on the cheek. "Thanks, Daddy."

She went inside to change. Venice hadn't spent much time with her father since she'd been home and she'd enjoyed ever minute of their talk. They laughed about things they hadn't talked about in years.

Forty

The next day, Venice knew she had to talk to Jarvis before he lost his temper. When she reached his house, he was sitting out on the porch. He got in the car and they drove off.

Jarvis asked, "So, what do you want to talk to me about?"

Venice was changing the music in her stereo and said, "I'll get to that later."

He put on his sunglasses and reclined on the seat and smiled. Venice wasn't quite sure where she was headed. She just wanted to drive.

Jarvis rubbed her thigh and said, "You're looking as fine as always."

"Thank you, Jarvis."

Damn that feels good.

Venice pulled onto the high school football field and said, "Come walk with me."

"Of all places you wanted to bring me to, you bring me here? Girl, it's cold!"

"Yes, because this is where we first met."

They started walking and Venice interlocked her arm into his. She cuddled up to him trying to stay warm and he didn't mind it one bit. She said, "Jarvis, you're gonna have to stop freaking out on me, baby. I know it must be hard for you to deal with me and Craig, but I can't help that right now. We're not able to be together so am I begging you to please just chill. I'll still come visit you whenever I can. Right now, that's all I can offer you, baby. I know it would be hard for me to deal with this if the tables were turned, but please try to understand. Okay?"

Jarvis looked away and said, "I can't promise you anything,

Niecy, but I'll never accept you being with another guy. It doesn't seem natural to me. We were married for an entire year and I honestly thought it was going to be forever. The only man that is supposed to be getting loving from you is me!"

"Jarvis, do we still have our deal after graduation?"

Damn graduation, I'm ready to marry you now!

He looked into her eyes, more serious than she'd ever seen him, and softly said, "You bet, Niecy."

They climbed up the bleachers and sat down. Venice scooted over to him and put her arms around him and laid her head upon his chest. The smell of her perfume intoxicated him. He put his arm around her shoulders and said, "I know you love me, Niecy."

"Well, you don't have anything to worry about."

"I'm not so sure about that. You have a different light in your eyes."

Tears began to drop into her jacket when she said, "Jarvis, I'm sorry about everything, especially our baby. I should've been more careful."

He wiped her tears and said, "It wasn't your fault. You need to quit beating yourself up about it."

She rose up and looked at him and he reached into his pocket and found a tissue to wipe her tears. He looked out onto the field and said, "We've been through it all. So much has happened to us and we're not even twenty-one yet."

"I know my grandmother is probably turning over in her grave right now. If she was still here, there's no way I could get away with half the stuff I've done. She would've been so hurt about me getting pregnant so young."

Jarvis said, "We got married, remember?"

"Yeah, but…we're not now."

We'll see about that.

They watched a few kids run across the field.

Venice said, "You know, Jarvis. When I said 'I do', I meant it."

Jarvis looked into her eyes and said, "Me, too." He stood up and said, "Come on, it's cold out here." They got up and walked down the bleachers to her car. As they drove off, he asked, "Why don't you come by the house so I can make you some hot chocolate?"

"Okay."

* * * * *

Chanelle was having a house party and Venice wanted to get all the drama she'd experienced off her mind. While Craig showered, Venice put on her outfit, which Craig had never seen. She buttoned her red silk blouse and pulled on the black form-fitting pants that zipped up the crack of her butt. She had some black, two-inch ankle boots that really accented her outfit. When he came back into the room, he saw her trying to zip the pants, making sure the zipper was straight and where it should be. He stopped for a moment to admire the view, then asked, "You need some help?"

"I think so. I want to make sure the zipper is straight."

He put his things down and walked up behind her and pulled the zipper up slowly, making sure it was like she wanted. He caressed her stomach as he stood behind her. She could feel he was aroused as he pressed his body against her hips.

"Damn!"

"What's wrong?"

"It's a shame when a man can't even come near his woman without wanting to jump her bones every chance he gets."

"I don't see anything wrong with that, baby."

She turned and saw him with only a wet towel covering his trim waist. Her gaze went from his feet up to his freshly shampooed hair. She sucked in her bottom lip and tried to swallow, but her throat was dry.

"Craig, baby, hurry up and get some clothes on. Please!!"

Approaching her slowly, he asked, "What's the hurry?"

Inhaling the soap he'd showered with, she pressed her hands to his broad chest caressing his body, and kissed him tenderly.

"That was nice, Taylor. Keep that thought until we get back here tonight. You're looking so delicious, I hope I don't have to fight any of your homeboys tonight. One in particular."

Venice closed her eyes and softly said, "You don't have to worry about anything like that."

Finally, they were dressed and ready to go. Craig, dressed in tan pants, was looking fine as always with his black dress shirt. He trimmed up his goatee and mustache and was really looking sinful. Venice looked at how fine and sexy he was and had a feeling she was going to have to keep women from pushing up on him. Venice realized she really was torn between the two men. One was new and so sweet and attentive. The other was loving and secure.

Hell, I may just have to flip a damn coin.

When they got to Chanelle's house, there were already a few cars there. The party was in her parents' recreation room downstairs. Her parents were having a card party upstairs with some of their friends. The basement was beautifully decorated with a Christmas tree and sparkling gold and ivory bows and ribbons. The music was already blasting and some of Chanelle's guests were kicking it out on the dance floor. Galen and Sidney were sitting over on the sofa sipping on some punch. Craig went to join them as Venice went upstairs to say hello to Chanelle's parents. After an hour passed, Venice noticed that Jarvis had arrived and she started shivering. He was talking to Craig and Galen and then started dancing with Chanelle. Joshua arrived with his girlfriend, Cynthia, and the crew really partied. Venice was happy to see all the people she loved in one room.

Joshua came over to Venice and said, "Venice, I can tell you've been up to something. What's up?"

She looked at him surprised and said, "Where have you been? I've been trying to reach you for two days!"

"I had to take Momma to the country. Don't change the subject. I saw your car over at Jarvis' house today."

"You think you know me, Joshua."

"I do, girl!"

Venice looked at him seriously, then asked, "Joshua, am I a hoe?"

Joshua laughed and asked, "Where is that coming from?"

"Seriously, am I?"

Joshua looked around the room to make sure the coast was clear and said, "No way, girl! You're only sleeping around with two of them. I could see if you were messing around with a different dude every night. I know some chicks like that, too."

"Thanks, I was beginning to wonder."

Joshua laughed and said, "Why?"

"I sleep with both of them the same day."

He strangled on his drink and said, "What?"

She slapped him on the back and said, "Jarvis got Chanelle to drop me off at his dad's house early last night. I didn't know what she was up to, but we ended up…well, you know. Then after we left the club, he called me about 2 a.m. and asked if he could come over. I thought he was playing."

Joshua was laughing out loud and asked, "You mean to tell me that you got with Jarvis twice in one night?"

"Well, yeah!"

"Wait a minute. You were bumping and grinding with Jarvis in your room and Craig was right downstairs?"

"I didn't mean to."

Joshua took a sip of his drink and said, "Yeah, right! Venice, you're a freak!"

She punched him on the arm and said, "Don't say that!"

"Well, you are! When did you get with Craig?"

"Later that evening."

"Damn! You've got a lot of nerve."

"You better not tell anybody."

"You know I won't."

Venice was left alone for a moment to think about her inappropriate behavior.

During the evening, the room of friends talked and danced far into the night. After awhile, they were ready to say goodnight. But, before they left, Jarvis came over and asked for one last dance.

He held Venice as tight as he could without causing a fight. When they finished the dance, Venice courageously gave Jarvis a kiss on the lips and said, "I'll talk to you later."

Jarvis stared at her for a moment and finally let her hand slide slowly from his grasp. His touch was magnetic and heated. Everyone said their good-byes. Venice and Craig rode silently back to Bryan's house.

Venice took a shower while Craig packed the last of his luggage. Venice was a little quieter than usual. She was having a hard time shaking the hurt look in Jarvis' eyes when she'd left with Craig. She was also coming to grips that it was going to be three weeks before she saw Craig again. It was about two-fifteen in the morning when Craig asked, "Are you all right?"

Venice didn't respond. She just laid there, looking at him without any expression on her face. It was a blank stare and she felt perspiration beading on her face.

Craig again asked, "Venice, are you all right?"

She finally nodded, signaling that she was, but she felt like she was having an anxiety attack. The situation was beginning to take its toll on her both physically and emotionally. Craig snuggled closer and Venice immediately scooted over and put her head on his chest.

While putting his arms around her, he said, "These next few weeks are going to fly by. You'll see."

Within about twenty minutes, they were asleep.

Several hours later, Venice woke up to find herself still lying on Craig's chest. Venice rose up and saw that he was sound asleep and slightly snoring. She snuggled up to him and put her face against his neck, gently kissing it. She felt him slowly begin to stir out of his sleep and move his hands up and down her soft body. He opened his eyes to look at her. Venice stared back and rubbed his face as she gave him a small kiss, then another and another. For some reason, this felt final to her. They began to caress each other's bodies without speaking. Venice's breathing was a little deeper and slower, as Craig hit her hot spots.

She closed her eyes as he kissed her neck and shoulders and pulled her tighter, whispering, "You're so hot."

"So are you, Bennett."

"Do you feel that?"

"M-m-m-m. How could I not?"

"More?"

"Much more."

Needless to say, they didn't get much sleep the rest of the night. Venice had fallen for him or was it infatuation? Whatever it was, Venice felt like this was the calm before the storm.

The sun seemed to come quicker than it had before. Sinclair had to work so Venice had the honor of driving everyone to the airport. Bryan was trying to give Venice some instructions of things he needed her to do for him until he got back into town. But, she was too occupied with clinging to Craig.

He leaned down and whispered, "Venice, we're gonna see each other soon. You'll see. The days will go by faster than you think."

Burying her face into his neck, she responded, "Not fast enough for me."

"Taylor, is it going to be safe for me to leave you here? I feel like I'm at a disadvantage now."

"Craig, whether you believe me or not, I want you to know that what I feel for you is real. I never in my wildest dreams thought another man's love could come between me and Jarvis, but it has and I have no regrets. I don't have a clue what to do next. What I do know is that I love you both with all my heart and soul. If I choose you, I feel like I have broken every vow I took with Jarvis. If I choose Jarvis, I feel like I've thrown away every whisper of love I've spoken to you. I don't want to feel like I've used the word love in vain. I pray that whatever happens, you and Jarvis will not hate me or become bitter with love."

He tilted her chin up and, through her tears, saw the sincere pain and confusion that she carried.

Craig lowered his lips to Venice's mouth and kissed her hot and demandingly.

"Venice, like I've said so many times before, I'll always love you and I'll always be here for you, no matter what. I could never hate or be bitter toward you, sweetheart. Remember that and trust your heart."

It wasn't long afterwards when the pilot announced that it was time to leave. Venice gave Sidney, Galen, and Bryan one last hug. Then Craig walked Venice back to the truck. He pulled her tightly to him and gave her one last fiery, breathtaking kiss. As he turned and walked away he said, "I'll call you later."

"Okay."

He ran back to the plane and she sat in the truck and watched it take off. Within minutes, it was out of sight. She stared into the blue sky as tears streamed down her face. From this moment on, things would never be the same.

Venice spent the next few days running the list of errands Bryan had left for her to do while he was out of town. She also did some last minute Christmas shopping with Chanelle. Jarvis called or came by almost every day, usually with Joshua. She was trying to remain neutral, but it was hard. Especially since she also talked to Craig on a daily basis.

It was the day before Christmas Eve and the Taylor family always had a family gathering on that night. They invited Chanelle and her family over, as well as Jarvis' and Joshua's families. Everyone was there, even her loud, drunken uncle who kept things very lively.

Jarvis, Joshua, and Cynthia arrived together. Chanelle and her family also arrived in a cheerful mood. There was finger food, desserts, and plenty of drinks and eggnog to go around. While the grownups celebrated in the living room, Venice and her guests relaxed in the den. They were having a great time reminiscing on their days together in school. Joshua's brother, Michael, walked into the room. After greeting everyone, he walked right over to Venice and planted a big kiss on her, right in front of everyone.

Venice was stunned and nervously said, "Michael! I'm glad you made it."

"Hey, V! You look fine as ever, girl!"

Michael couldn't help but admire Venice in the green straight skirt that was hugging her curves. Her V-neck sweater revealed perfectly rounded breasts that Michael couldn't help but stare at and Jarvis was fuming.

Venice was happy to see him. He looked sexy and sinful as usual. He had women all over town chasing him. While he'd had his share of affairs, his main concern was graduating from college and working. She remembered the man had the biggest penis she'd ever seen in her life and he really knew how to use it.

Michael acted like he couldn't keep his hands off her as he wrapped his arms around her tiny waist. She was getting a little uncomfortable and she could see the muscle in Jarvis' jaw twitching. She knew he was getting pissed and was ready to explode. There was definitely no love loss between them. It went back to the time Venice caught Jarvis cheating and they briefly broke up. She unexpectedly started messing around with Michael, which ended before it got started.

Holding her hand and looking her up and down, he asked, "Why haven't you come by the house and hollered at me?"

Venice smiled and said, "I've been busy since I've been home. I'll come by before I go back to school."

When she said that, Jarvis looked at her like he wanted to snap.

Joshua watched his brother play mind games with Jarvis and quietly sipped his drink.

Chanelle mumbled, "Oh my God."

Venice allowed Michael to hold her close to him as he whispered something in her ear.

Jarvis got up, walked over to them, and said, "Damn, Mike. What are you doing, man?" Michael laughed and said, "I'm just talking to my old girl."

Jarvis sternly said, "She was *never* your girl!"

Joshua walked over to them and said, "Fellas, chill! This is supposed to be a party."

Venice grabbed both of them by the arm and said, "Look, you two. Stop it! That shit's old! Come on, Michael, behave and Jarvis, cool out baby."

Joshua said, "Ya'll are acting like a bunch of damn kids."

Venice made them apologize to each other. As she walked off, she asked Chanelle to help her in the kitchen for a minute. Once in the kitchen, Chanelle asked, "What was that all about?"

"I don't know. Jarvis acts like he's never going to get over what happened between me and Michael."

"He needs to be cool. If his ass hadn't been cheating, you and Michael wouldn't have ever happened."

"I know."

Changing the subject, Chanelle asked, "So, what's up with my boy Craig?"

Venice turned and attended to the food. "It's crazy! I have no idea what to do since I've fallen for Craig. It's special, but it's not like what I have with Jarvis. Our relationship is new and I haven't really given it a chance yet. My relationship with Jarvis has so much history. I just don't know, Chanelle."

"Well, one day, they're going to get tired of sharing your ass."

"We'd better get back in there before they kill each other."

Giggling, Chanelle said, "Let me carry that tray for you."

The two left the kitchen and returned to the den. They talked, listened to music, then decided to play cards and dominos.

Craig called a few hours later and after a brief conversation with him, she hung up the phone. When she turned around, she ran right into Jarvis' hard chest.

"What are you doing in here?"

He walked over to her and angrily asked, "What the hell was that in there with Michael?"

"Nothing! You know he was just messing with you. Why are you tripping? It was just a kiss."

"Everything's so trivial to you. Isn't it, Venice?"

"That's ridiculous! Michael's my friend and that's all!"

Venice went into the pantry to get some more cups. Jarvis closed the door behind him and locked it. Venice turned with a pack of cups in her hands and said, "Open the door, Jarvis!"

Walking toward her, he asked, "Have you been messing around with Michael again?"

Venice tried to go past him. "No! You heard him. I haven't even seen him. Now open the door."

"Venice, I'm beginning to think I can't trust you or believe anything you say."

"What's wrong with you, Jarvis?"

He stood there for a minute, then put his hands over his face and said, "I'm sorry, Niecy."

"You need to get a hold of yourself. Nothing's going on between me and Michael. You need to quit stressing whenever he's around. You've had your share of rendezvous that you don't think I know about, but I do. You want to talk about trust? Do you really think I only know about the one I caught you with? I knew about Lisa too, Jarvis. Now, the one time I was with somebody else, you want to trip after all you've put me through. Well, get over it. It was *you* that I married. Remember?"

Venice tried to push past him but he blocked her and pulled her into his arms.

"I'm so sorry, baby. I really can't blame you for being pissed off. I don't deserve you."

He held onto her for a moment but she wouldn't dare gaze into his sad, sexy eyes. He wiped a tear, which had run down her cheek.

"I love you, Niecy, and I don't know why I go so crazy. This thing with Craig has emotionally drained me."

She laid her head on his chest and said, "We'll be okay, Jarvis."

She became hypnotized by his cologne, which happened to be a bottle that she'd given him a few months prior. He was wearing some navy blue dress pants, a white shirt, and a navy jacket.

Still holding Venice, Jarvis said, "I need to see you tonight. I want to give you your present."

"I want to give you yours, too."

Venice parted her lips and kissed Jarvis hungrily because she really was weak to him. She always had been and always would be. Their bodies melted into each other and it felt right.

They left the pantry and joined the others in the den. As soon as they walked in, Chanelle looked up at them and started smiling. When Jarvis sat down on the sofa, Joshua looked at him and asked, "When did you start wearing lipstick?"

The room burst into laughter as Jarvis wiped Venice's lipstick from his mouth and said, "Forget ya'll."

It was tradition for the Taylors to have their party the night before Christmas Eve. Everyone exchanged their gifts on this night. The party was winding down, but the grownups were still going strong. Everyone hugged, kissed, and said their goodnights after having a great time. Jarvis helped Venice clean the kitchen and the den. He again invited her to join him at his dad's house for the night. Venice was a little reluctant, but decided to go anyway. She went upstairs and packed a bag, then told her folks where she would be. They weren't strict on her when it came to Jarvis since they still considered them spiritually married. Jarvis' dad told him that he was staying with his mother and wouldn't be home. Even though Jarvis' parents were divorced, they were in the process of reconciling. They told everyone goodnight and headed out into the snow.

When they arrived, they did exchange their gifts. She'd bought him a leather jacket that she knew he'd been admiring. He was very excited and surprised to get it. He bought her two outfits she'd been eyeing. Chanelle helped him since Chanelle knew what Venice had been shopping for.

After they talked and thanked each other for their gifts, Venice decided to go ahead and take her shower. Her feet were hurting and she wanted to get out of her clothes. When she came out of the bathroom, music was playing and Jarvis was standing there grinning. As she came closer, he held out his hand and asked her to dance with him. She was wearing a silky, gold spaghetti-strapped nightgown and she accepted without hesitation. Toward the end of the song, Jarvis pulled something from his pinky finger.

"Give me your hand, Venice."

"What are you doing?"

He brushed her lips with his and slid a large marquis cut diamond ring onto her finger. Venice's legs gave out on her and she dropped to the bed, stunned. She stared at her hand, then up into his nervous, desire-filled eyes.

He calmly said, "Venice, I've loved you since the first day I laid eyes on you. I don't want to live my life another day without you. Please, please be my wife again. I love you more than life itself."

"Jarvis, I-I love you too, but...."

"Baby, I don't want to wait until we graduate. I want to get back together now."

Venice was surprised with his statement. "You mean to tell me that you want to get married, now?"

He laid back on the bed and said, "Yeah, what's wrong with that?"

Venice closed her eyes briefly. "Jarvis, you know I love you, but I'm seeing someone else and I have feelings for him also."

"You've only known him a few months, but we've been together for four years. There's no way you can compare the two."

"It has nothing to do with the length of time, baby. It has to do with our feelings. Things are a little different now. We're on two different ends of the country and we barely get to see each other."

"Venice, I understand where you're coming from, but I still want you to marry me."

She stared at the ring, then at him, and asked, "Are you really serious about this?"

He brought his lips within inches of hers and asked, "Do I look like I'm joking?" Before Venice could answer, Jarvis covered her lips with a long, tender kiss. After breaking apart, Venice got up and walked across the room, admiring the ring. "I'm speechless."

He walked up behind her, put his arms around her waist, and lovingly kissed the back of her neck.

"Are you asking me to marry you because you want to marry me or are you asking me just to get me away from Craig?"

Jarvis turned her to him and said, "You know I've always wanted to be with you. You also know that I've always been in love. I'll admit the situation with Craig has shaken me pretty bad, but I don't want to go back to school without you. I can tell you've wandered away from me a little, but I feel like we still love each other enough to do this. If you need some time to think it over, I'm willing to wait.

You're the only one I want. There's not much else I can say to convince you."

"What about Dawson?"

He smiled, gave her a kiss on her neck, and said, "I just know everything will work out."

She leaned back against his chest.

Now what the hell am I going to do?"

"I've been holding onto this ring for a couple of months now. I didn't know when the time would be right to give it to you. Something told me tonight was the night. I think that's why I went so crazy about Michael earlier. I guess I was nervous."

Venice did love this man and she'd been married to him once before. It shouldn't have be hard to say 'yes' again, but it was. Craig was new in her life, and she didn't want to hurt him as if he'd never meant anything to her. She loved him, too.

They spent the reminder of the night reminding each other why they loved the other so much. The heat their bodies generated was enough to engulf them in flames. After many hours of making love, Venice fell asleep nestled in Jarvis' arms, still dazed on the events of the night. Looking at his satisfied face as he slept, she had no idea what she was going to do.

She whispered, "I love you, Jarvis."

Jarvis didn't hear Venice but stirred after she gave him butterfly kisses on his lips and neck. Molding her sore body closer against his, she eventually fell asleep.

Forty-One

It was Christmas Eve morning and Jarvis was awakened by Venice throwing up in the bathroom. He ran into the bathroom and asked, "What's wrong, Niecy?"

"I don't know. It must be nerves and this sinus headache is killing me."

He got her a cold towel and placed it on her head as he held her in his lap.

"Thanks. That feels nice."

Jarvis gently wiped Venice's face with the cold towel. "Come get back into bed. I'll get you some 7-up and sinus medicine."

Jarvis helped her back into bed and as he walked out of the room, he leaned back in and asked, "You're not pregnant, are you?"

"No!"

Venice knew it was only nerves. She wasn't pregnant because she'd just come off her period. The 7-up helped settle her stomach slightly. She was still worried about breaking the news to Craig. He was important to her and she didn't want to give him up. He'd been a wonderful lover and great friend over the past few months.

Venice woke up a few hours later and felt a hundred percent better. It was still snowing when Jarvis drove her home.

When they walked in, Mrs. Taylor grabbed Venice's hand to look at her ring and asked, "So what's the verdict?"

Venice looked at her mom in shock. "You knew about this?"

She said, "Oh yes! He asked us if he could propose to you the other day."

Venice shook her head in disbelief and went upstairs. Her mother turned to Jarvis and asked again, "What did she say?"

"Nothing yet. I don't know if she wants to do it. She's not feeling well and she was throwing up earlier. I think she's just nervous about Craig and all."

Mrs. Taylor looked concerned and asked, "Lord, she's not pregnant, is she?" Jarvis was hanging up their coats and said, "I asked her and she said she just came off her period."

Venice's mother asked Jarvis to wait in the den. She was partial to Jarvis while her husband liked both Jarvis and Craig. Mrs. Taylor followed Venice upstairs and knocked on the door.

"Come in."

When her mother entered, Venice was unpacking her bag. Mrs. Taylor asked, "Are you feeling all right, baby?"

Venice looked at her and said, "Yes and no, Momma! I'm not pregnant."

Her mother sat on the bed and said, "Girl, don't put words into my mouth and watch your tone."

"I'm sorry, Momma. I'm just tired. I can't believe you and Daddy knew what Jarvis was planning. I just don't know what to do. I love him, but I also have strong feelings for Craig. How could I possibly tell him about this?"

Venice was holding up her left hand displaying her ring. Her mother told her to come sit next to her.

She then said, "Baby, if you love Jarvis and you know he loves you, then you should be together. I like Craig and he seems to be a nice young man. He cares about you and I know you care for him. But, if you're in love with Craig, you need to take your time with this. There's no rush. You guys are only nineteen and have college to finish. I'm sorry I helped create the problem when we made you get a divorce. Look, sweetheart, whatever you decide to do, your father and I will stand by you."

Venice hugged her mother. "Thanks, Momma."

After their mother left the room, Bryan angrily barged in and said, "Venice, you've got to be out of your damn mind if you're considering doing this! You just started college? Did you let Jarvis intimidate you into doing something you're not ready to do? I could kick his ass for trying this right now. You know why's he's doing this. Look, baby girl, don't get me wrong. I like Jarvis a lot and I know how you feel about him. But, you need to chill on this issue. Once you turn twenty-one and finish college, I might be willing to look at this in a different light."

Venice was quiet as Bryan continued to pace the room lecturing her.

Finally she said, "Bryan you don't have to go off on me. I know how old I am and I'm not stupid! I'm not going to do anything I don't want to do, okay? I haven't given Jarvis an answer anyway because of Craig."

He walked over to her, put his hand on her shoulder, and said, "Venice, I just don't want to see you mess up your life."

"Thanks and I'll think about everything you've said."

About that time, Jarvis knocked on the door. When he walked in, Bryan stood up and sternly said, "Come by my house sometime today. I want to talk to you. Got it?"

Jarvis started playing with Venice's stuffed animals and said, "No problem, Bryan. I'll be by."

Bryan just stared at him and told Venice that he would see her later and to remember what they talked about. Venice went over to the window and watched Bryan pull out of the driveway.

Jarvis jumped on the bed beside her. "What was that all about?"

"Us."

"I guess he wants to have a man-to-man talk with me."

Venice didn't respond. She just crawled back on her bed and fluffed her pillows.

Jarvis asked, "So, are you going to marry me or what?"

"Jarvis, I just can't...."

At that time, they heard Mrs. Taylor call out. They both ran downstairs and found her crying at the kitchen table. Mr. Taylor was on the phone. Venice and Jarvis could both see that something was terribly wrong.

Venice felt sick to her stomach. She just knew something had happened to Galen. When her dad hung up the phone, he said, "Guys, Joshua's been in an car accident and it doesn't look good."

That's all Venice heard before everything went dark. The next thing she knew, her parents and Jarvis were standing over her on the sofa.

"What happened?"

Her mom responded, "Venice, you fainted. We need to get to the hospital. Can you sit up?"

Venice remembered and screamed, "Joshua!!"

They found Joshua's family in the waiting room. Venice had pulled herself together for only a moment. When she saw Michael's worried face, she broke down again. He hugged her tightly as she stood cradled in his arms, crying. Cynthia, Joshua's girlfriend, was sitting there staring into space. Joshua's mother was in the room with him; so was the minister of their church. Venice asked Michael through tears, "Is he going to be all right?"

Michael attempted to sound confident when he said, "We're not sure, V, but I think you'd better see him."

Venice continued to cry.

Michael grabbed her and said, "Venice, you can't go in there upset. You've got to pull yourself together. Joshua needs you right now!"

Venice tried her best to get herself together. Michael prepared her for what she was about to see. He told her that Joshua was hooked up to a lot of tubes and that he was swollen and didn't look like himself. When she entered the room with him and walked over, their mother looked up at Venice with tears in her eyes. When Venice looked at Joshua, she became nauseated and nearly fainted. Michael steadied her. Joshua's mother got up, hugged her, and then they both left to give Venice some privacy with Joshua. It was hard for Venice not to break down, seeing him so messed up. Michael was right. Joshua didn't look like himself and she wasn't prepared for what she was looking at.

Venice sat down next to him and rubbed his arm. "Joshua, what are you doing laid up in this bed? You know you have no business in this hospital."

All she could hear were the noises of the machines, which were helping him breath and monitoring his heart and other functions.

"Boy! Don't you know it's Christmas Eve! I haven't even given you my gift yet." She wiped some tears away, held up her left hand to reveal her engagement ring, and said, "Jarvis proposed to me. He wants to get married on New Year's Eve. I just can't consider it without talking to you. You need to get better so you can help me out. Otherwise, I can't go through with it. I need your advice on what to do because I don't have a clue because of Craig. You've held all my secrets for me for years and I can't trust them with anyone else, so get your ass out of this bed. Do you hear me! You'd better be fighting, Joshua! I love you!"

Venice couldn't take it anymore. She was starting to lose it. She stood up, leaned over, gave him a kiss, and hurried out the door.

When Venice reached the hallway, Michael was standing by the door talking to Jarvis. She stood there for a moment and just collapsed. Joshua was in a coma and Venice was devastated. Jarvis was trying to be there for her, but it was hard. Joshua was his boy and he also had to find the courage to go see him. Michael and Jarvis buried their differences. It was sad that it took a tragedy like this for them to settle things. It was a Christmas Eve to be remembered.

It was a restless night and the snow was still falling but tapering off. There were about six inches on the ground. It was hard to tell there was a crisis going on inside room 321. About four a.m., Venice woke up and found everyone asleep. She went inside Joshua's room and found a nurse checking on him. She sat down, held his hand, and began to stroke it. Joshua's mother had fallen asleep in the chair on the other side of his bed.

Venice began to softly whisper to Joshua so she wouldn't wake his mother. As tears streamed down Venice's face, she saw Joshua move his finger. She whispered again into his ear. Once again, Joshua moved his finger. Venice went over and excitedly woke up Joshua's mother, who ran over to watch as Venice did it again.

They called for the doctor who came in and checked on Joshua. The doctor said it appeared that Joshua was going to be okay, but he wasn't completely out of the woods. It was going to be some time before Joshua would be off the critical list. They were going to have to make sure there wasn't any permanent damage. Venice hugged Joshua's mother and left to tell everybody else the news.

Back at home, Venice saw that she had messages on her answering machine. She was totally exhausted but knew they must be from Craig. As she played them back, she had message after message from him. She picked up the phone and told him what had happened to Joshua. He asked Venice if she was all right and she explained to him that she was fine, except that she was exhausted from being up all night.

"Do you want me to come up?"

"No, Craig. There's six inches of snow on the ground. I'll be okay. Thanks anyway and I'll keep you posted."

"Okay, Venice. You call me the minute there's any change. I know it's going to be hard to enjoy Christmas."

You don't know the half of it.

Craig wasn't satisfied with Venice's answer and decided to try and get a flight out anyway. It was Christmas Day and he knew it was going to be hard, but she was worth it.

Venice took a shower and crawled under her covers. Little did she know, Craig was flying up to see her. Before she went to bed, she cut the ringer on her phone off so she wouldn't be disturbed. She knew if there were anything wrong, her parents would get the call on their phone line.

Forty-Two

It was about five o'clock in the afternoon when Venice's mother knocked on the bathroom door. Venice had finally woken up from her nap and was taking a shower.

"Venice, are you expecting any company today?"

Venice pulled the shower curtain back and curiously asked, "No. Why?"

"Well, Craig's downstairs."

"What? Craig's downstairs?"

"Yes, ma'am. He said he flew in to be with you through this crisis with Joshua." "Tell him I'll be down in a minute."

"Have you told him about the ring yet?"

Venice looked at the ring on her finger and said, "No, Momma. I wasn't concerned about anything but Joshua."

As Venice exited the bathroom, her mother said, "Well you'd better get ready to tell him something, baby. I'll let him know you'll be down in a second."

Venice toweled off and put on her robe. She had no idea what she was going to do since Craig had surprised her. She sat inside her room and felt her heart pounding in her chest. She took off her engagement ring, put it in the pocket of her robe, and went downstairs.

Craig was sitting in the den watching TV with her dad. When Venice walked in, Craig stood up to gave her a hug and kiss.

Venice said, "Merry Christmas, stranger. What a surprise! Why'd you come all the way up here in this weather?"

"I thought you might need some company. I know you and Joshua are close." Venice was feeling guilty. "I'm glad you came, but you shouldn't have wasted your Christmas traveling."

"Getting to see you is not a wasted day. Plus, I need to talk to you."

Venice stood up and said, "Well, come on upstairs so we can talk."

Craig told Mr. Taylor he would see him shortly to finish watching the football game.

Venice's dad was half asleep in his recliner, but he was able to say, "All right."

Craig followed Venice upstairs to her room. Her mother watched them go upstairs and had no idea what Venice was going to tell him. Whatever she decided was going to make someone very unhappy that day. They entered the room and Venice closed the door behind them. Craig laid back on the bed as Venice crawled back under the covers.

He grinned and asked, "How's Joshua doing?"

"He's showing signs of improvement, but he's not out of the woods yet. I know you want to see him."

"That's great news, Taylor. I knew he'd make it."

There was a pause, then he asked, "Venice, are you naked under that robe?" Venice smiled, pulled the covers up to her, and replied, "None of your business."

He tried to pull the covers back and said, "Let me see."

Venice laughed and tried to stop him, but she couldn't. She was trying not to be loud so her parents wouldn't come upstairs to investigate. He sat on top of her, pinning her arms down.

Venice giggled. "Stop, Craig. My mom and dad are downstairs."

"They're not coming up here."

Venice struggled to get loose. "How do you know?"

He leaned down to kiss her and whispered, "I just know." Craig kissed his way down to Venice's neck and added, "You smell good. What are you wearing?"

Venice couldn't answer him. She just closed her eyes as he ran his hand under her robe.

Venice was breathless as she moaned, "Craig…"

He smiled and said, "Sh-h-h-h."

Craig was getting a little bolder as he kissed her from head to toe causing Venice to moan even louder. She pulled a pillow to her face to muffle her moans. He stopped at certain areas, which made her arch her back to the touch of his lips.

Venice whispered, "Craig, stop."

He gazed into her eyes. "Are you sure?"

"Yes, you're so nasty."

He laughed and said, "Girl, let me get off you before I take advantage of you."

He helped her close her robe and the ring fell out onto the bed. She didn't see it, but he did.

Craig picked up the ring and asked, "What's this?"

Venice looked down at the ring. "Damn! I was planning on talking to you about that." Craig held the ring and leered at her. Venice went on to say, "Baby, Jarvis gave the ring to me last night and asked me to marry him."

Craig placed the ring in the palm of her hand and got off the bed. He walked over to the window in silence.

Venice stood next to him and said, "Craig, I'm sorry. I didn't know you were coming up and I'm not emotionally prepared to deal with this right now. I can't handle this and what's going on with Joshua at the same time. I don't want to lose you and I don't want to lose Jarvis."

Craig walked away from her and paced the room.

"Craig, please say something."

Craig shook his head, closed his eyes for a moment, and asked, "Venice, do you love me?"

"Yes, I do."

Venice sat on the bed and stared at the floor.

Craig sat down next to her. "Venice, I've always felt that you loved me. I just didn't know you were this serious about getting back with him."

Venice laid her head on Craig's shoulder and held his hand.

Craig hesitated, then asked, "Do you want to marry him, Venice?"

She had tears running down her face as she replied, "I don't know what I want. I told Jarvis that I needed more time."

Craig said, "You know, I can make this easy for you and it's really ironic. I flew up here to be with you through this crisis and to tell you some news. I had no idea I was going to be played this kind of hand."

Venice asked, "What's news?"

"I was given the option to go to Japan for two months. I leave the second week in January."

Venice clearly looked hurt as she asked, "For what?"

"My company always sends a student over to their parent company each year. The person who was scheduled to go had to drop out. They asked me if I wanted to go. I told them I would get back with them. I was worried about breaking the news to you. That's the other reason I came to see you. I don't want to leave you. But, I guess I have no reason to stay now. Huh?"

Venice was stunned. "Japan? Two months?"

"I'll be out of your way by tonight, if I can get a flight out."

Venice grabbed Craig's arm. "You're not going anywhere tonight and you don't have to leave. I want you to stay because we still need to talk. Nothing has been decided and I don't want to make a hasty decision. I don't want you to make a hasty decision either."

"So what are you saying?"

She stood up in front of him with tears flowing. "I'm not sure, but I know we need to talk some more.

Craig stood up and gave Venice a hug. "Venice, I want you to know that I sincerely love you."

Venice looked into Craig's distraught eyes and said, "I know. I love you, too."

He wiped her tears with his hands and sadly replied, "Let me get out of here so you can get dressed. We'll talk later. I want to go see Joshua."

"I'll be right down."

Craig closed the door behind him and stood there for a moment before heading downstairs.

When Craig came down the steps, Mrs. Taylor asked, "Is everything okay?"

Craig smiled at her and said, "Venice told me about the ring."

"Craig, let me talk to you for a moment."

They walked into the kitchen and sat at the table where she'd made him a sandwich.

"Craig, Venice is my baby and I love her very much. I want you to understand that what she's going through is very stressful. She's been confused about her relationship with you and Jarvis for a while now. You need to understand, she doesn't mean to hurt either one of you. I do know she loves you and I believe you know it. If she didn't, this would've come easy to her. I also know she loves Jarvis. Venice does have a breaking point, just like everyone else, so I hope you and Jarvis go easy on her. Jarvis and Venice may make it to the altar and they may not. I don't want you to be upset with her if she decides to marry him. Whatever the outcome, please remain close to her and look out for her. She's going to still need you in her life. She will be depressed for a while because she's never been able to hurt anyone's feelings. Do you know what I'm saying, Craig?"

"Mrs. Taylor, I don't think we have to worry about that. It looks like I'll be one less problem for Venice. I'll be spending the next two months in Japan on a co-op program, if I take them up on their offer. I just found out the other day, but I didn't want to leave her. I love your daughter very much and I hoped that I was going to get a chance to show her just how much. Thanks for talking to me about it."

Mrs. Taylor held his hand and said, "Craig, don't you make any rash decisions right now. If Japan is something you really want to do, then I think you should do it. But, if you're having second thoughts, then you might need to reconsider it. It sounds like an opportunity for you, but I'm sure there will be other offers. Don't let Venice be your reason not to go. I don't want you to have any regrets if things don't work out for you two. Okay?"

Craig agreed and Mrs. Taylor gave him a hug and kiss and told him that he was welcomed in their home anytime and could stay as long as he wished. He told her that Venice had also extended the invitation to stay. Mrs. Taylor was pleased her daughter handled the situation like a real woman. Craig finished his sandwich, then told Mrs. Taylor that Venice was taking him to see Joshua. She told them to please be careful because the roads were still icy. He assured her that they would and waited for Venice in the den.

In the meantime, Venice was upstairs getting dressed. She had no idea her mom had just had a heart-to-heart talk with Craig. All she knew was that someone would probably end up hurt before it was all over. It was turning into the worst Christmas she could imagine. Venice gathered her purse and coat, hesitated for a moment, then slipped the ring back onto her finger. She didn't want to offend Craig by wearing it and she didn't want to offend Jarvis by not wearing it. She'd accepted it and she was going to wear it until she decided what to do.

Craig went inside for his visit with Joshua while Venice stayed outside and chatted with the family. Craig prayed over Joshua and talked to him about his feelings for Venice. He wasn't sure if Joshua could hear him, but it was a comfort to be able to talk to someone. As Craig talked, he noticed an occasional twitch of Joshua's finger. After talking to him a few more minutes, he decided to let him rest.

When he came out of the room, Venice asked, "Are you okay?"

He told her that he was fine. Venice went in to check on Joshua, and she also talked to him about the situation going on between the threesome. She stroked his arm for a few minutes and then leaned over as usual and gave him a kiss.

Before she left the room, she whispered into his ear, "I love you, Joshua. Hurry up and get well."

Venice had become a little stronger since the initial shock of the accident. She was able to visit Joshua without breaking down with emotion.

After Joshua's family decided to go home and get some sleep, Venice said, "Let's go back inside with Joshua."

Craig agreed and followed Venice into the room.

Only about thirty minutes had passed when the door opened and in walked Jarvis. Craig stood up and greeted him as friendly as possible, considering the circumstances. Venice was caressing Joshua's arm when Jarvis walked in, but she didn't skip a beat. She looked up and softly said, "Hello, Jarvis."

He walked over and kissed her on the cheek and asked, "How's he doing?"

"About the same."

Craig asked Jarvis if he wanted his seat, but he declined saying, "Thanks, but I'll stand."

Venice asked, "Did Portia have a good Christmas?"

"Yeah, she's got stuff everywhere."

Venice explained to Craig that Portia was Jarvis' eight-year-old sister. She also asked Jarvis if he'd had dinner yet. He told her that he wasn't hungry and that he'd probably get something later.

Venice said, "You're welcome to have dinner with us later, if you want to."

"We'll see."

About that time, Jarvis turned and asked Craig, "What brings you back to town?"

Meeting his gaze, Craig answered, "Venice called and told me about the accident, so I thought I'd come up to be with her."

Jarvis looked over at Venice and said, "That's cool."

As Craig and Jarvis continued to talk, Venice occasionally cut her eyes over at them to check their facial expressions.

There was silence in the room for a moment, then Jarvis asked, "Craig, do you want to go down to the cafe for a drink?"

Venice froze, looking at Craig and waiting for his response.

Craig boldly said, "Sure, I could use a drink. Venice, do you need anything?"

She shook her head, declining.

Jarvis winked at her and said, "We'll be back in a little bit."

Craig said, "I have my phone on if you need anything."

"Thanks, Craig. Jarvis…"

"Relax, Niecy. We'll be back in a minute."

Venice had no idea what was about to take place, but she figured the two of them were about to discuss the present situation. She couldn't worry about it. All she knew was that she didn't want things to get out of hand. Joshua was the only issue important to her right then.

Jarvis and Craig rode the elevator to the cafeteria. When they entered the room, the aroma of chicken and dressing hit their nostrils. Immediately Jarvis grabbed his stomach and said, "Now I'm hungry. How about you?"

"I think I could eat a bite."

They went through the line and piled on their lunch. After they found a table, Jarvis looked at Craig and said, "You know, man, you make me nervous."

Craig was sprinkling pepper on his dressing and asked, "How's that?"

"Because Venice is in love with you."

Craig took a sip of his water and said, "From where I'm sitting, it looks like you're the man." Craig hesitated for a moment, then added, "I saw the ring."

"It's not important to her right now. I don't think she wants to do it."

"Why do you say that?"

Jarvis stopped eating for a moment, looked into Craig's eyes, and said, "Because of you."

"So, when did you decide to do this?"

Jarvis looked down at his food, then back up at Craig. "I never wanted the divorce in the first place."

Craig sat back in his chair and said, "Well, whatever Venice decides, no hard feelings. I'm going to be honest with you. I don't want to lose her and I want you to know that I love her, too. It bothers me when she flies out to see you. She's going through hell right now and I don't want to upset her. Whatever happens, happens. "

Jarvis said, "I don't' want to pressure her either. I've known for awhile that I've lost a part of her to you. I just felt like I needed to be a man and talk to you about it. I don't know what Venice is going to do. Her only concern right now is Joshua. Mine, too."

Craig said, "I appreciate you coming to me about it. Venice is special to me and I'm not going to just let her walk away easily, if she decides to do it. But, I feel like I can deal with it, if we don't work out. Regardless, we'll always have a special connection."

"I feel the same way. But, you're a better man than I am. I almost lost Venice once and I don't plan to lose her again."

"What do you mean?"

"Remember Joshua's brother, Michael? You met in the family room."

Craig nodded and Jarvis said, "I sort of pushed her into his arms. She caught me adventuring out with someone else. I was stupid and curious and she dropped me like old news."

Craig shook his head in disbelief. He thought Jarvis was the only one Venice had in her past.

Craig listened to Jarvis attentively before responding, "I realize that you and Venice have a long history together, but I'm trying to build one with her. It messed my head up when Venice told me that she'd flown up to visit you. She didn't have to tell me, but she did and I admire her for that. It showed me that she wasn't one of those women who creeps around behind your back. She made it clear that she was still into you. She also told me what happened to you guys with the baby and all. I'm sorry for that, but I want her and I'm man enough to deal with whatever happens."

"Look, Craig. Whatever happens, I'll always think of Venice as my wife."

Craig didn't respond. He just stared Jarvis in the eye. Craig didn't want Jarvis to know that he was considering going to Japan for two months. He kept that to himself. The two men were able to release some of their anxiety about each other. In a way, they bonded. Both of them laid their cards on the table. The bell had rang and the best man would ultimately win.

They finished their lunch and silently rode the elevator back up to Joshua's floor. When they went back into the room, Venice was asleep laying on Joshua's arm. Jarvis went over and woke her up and told her he was getting ready to go.

She asked, "Is everything okay?"

He smiled and kissed her on the cheek. "Everything's fine. I'll see you later."

As he walked across the room, Jarvis shook Craig's hand and said, "I'm out of here. Take care of Venice out in the snow. Those roads are pretty bad out there."

He said, "I will. Thanks."

Jarvis left the room and Venice asked, "What was that about?"

"Nothing."

Forty-Three

Joshua was improving as each day went by. The doctors were starting to take him off some of the machines and he had regained consciousness. He was still a little swollen, but everyone was glad that he had woken up and that there didn't appear to be any brain damage.

Craig stayed until four days after Christmas. He told Venice to call him and let him know where they stood. He didn't know if Venice was going to get married or not. Neither did Jarvis. It was only a few days before New Year's when Jarvis came over for a visit. Her mom and dad left the house to visit Joshua at the hospital. When she opened the door, he immediately pulled Venice into his arms and kissed her with deep affection and desire. She enjoyed the love he was making to her mouth.

Finally breaking free, she said, "Hello to you, too."

"Venice, what's up? What are you going to do? You're wearing my ring, but you haven't given me an answer yet. Joshua is doing a lot better now, so you can't use him as your excuse anymore."

"You're right. You do deserve an answer, baby, but I just can't right now."

"It would be nice to know something before we go back to school."

Taking his hand into hers, she led him into the den and said, "I can't promise you anything, Jarvis."

The holidays came and went by faster than in the past and Joshua was finally able to go home. A couple days before Venice returned to school, she walked over to Joshua's house for a visit. He had a lot of therapy ahead of him, but he was doing well. The doctors expected him to make a complete recovery. Venice walked into his room and crawled into bed next to him and took the remote control.

He said, "Girl, don't come up in here being bossy."

Venice smiled, leaned over, and gave Joshua a big hug and kiss.

"Girl, get off of me, traitor."

"What are you talking about?"

"I already know you're going to marry my boy. Thanks for deserting me."

"You don't know that!"

"Yes, I do. Have you given him your answer yet?"

"No."

"What are you waiting on?"

She fluffed her pillow and said, "Craig."

They didn't talk about it anymore. Venice was always amazed that Joshua could read her so well. Joshua took the remote back from her and said, "Venice, everything will work out. You'll see."

They watched TV for the next few hours before they both fell asleep.

Hours later, Venice turned back over and started watching TV again. It wasn't five minutes later when Jarvis walked into the room.

He gave Joshua a handshake and jokingly asked, "Man, what the hell are you doing laying up with my woman?"

"I'm just filling in for you, dogg."

Venice said, "Ya'll are crazy." She got up from the bed and asked, "What's up?" Jarvis sat down and said, "You forgot, we're supposed to meet with Pastor Green in fifteen minutes."

"Dang, I did forget. Do I look okay?"

Joshua said, "You're fine. Just wash your nasty face."

Jarvis added, "You look beautiful, Niecy."

"Thanks, you two."

Venice went into the bathroom to freshen up.

Jarvis asked, "Man, how are you doing? That drunk ass fool almost took you out of here, dogg."

"Sure did. I didn't even see him coming."

"You're lucky, man."

"I know."

Jarvis asked, "Venice, you ready to go?"

"I guess. Joshua, I'll be back tomorrow. Tell Cynthia hello for me."

He said, "All right."

Venice gathered her purse and gave him a kiss goodbye.

Jarvis shook his hand again and said, "Later, man."

They told the rest of the family goodbye and were out the door.

Jarvis and Venice met with the pastor, who talked to them for about two hours. He'd counseled them before, so he was familiar with them. He covered several issues with them, then asked if they had any questions or concerns. Then from nowhere, Venice began to tell him about Craig. Jarvis was frozen in his seat. He had no idea Venice would bring Craig up during their counseling session. Venice admitted that she loved Craig and that she was still confused and didn't know what she wanted to do. Pastor Green listened attentively, as did Jarvis.

After she finished getting this off her chest, Pastor Green asked, "Venice, do you love Jarvis?"

She glanced at Jarvis. "With all my heart."

He asked, "Do you love Craig or are you in love with him?"

Venice answered with, "It's hard to tell."

"Let me ask you this way. If Jarvis wasn't in the picture, could you see Craig sitting here with you right now?"

Venice was stunned and looked into the reverend's eyes. "I guess so."

Jarvis didn't say a word. He just sat there listening.

The pastor asked, "Jarvis, is there anyone in your life you feel strongly about outside of Venice?"

"No, sir."

Pastor Greene looked at the two of them and said, "I want you two to sit down tonight or tomorrow and talk about this, before we go any further. I feel that there are still some unresolved, serious issues to overcome. I don't think ya'll are ready. But, if you decide to get married, I need to know that all of these unresolved issues are settled before I perform any ceremony. Okay? Venice, you did the right thing by expressing your feelings here tonight. Jarvis, don't you hold anything against her for doing it. It's better that we discuss this now than have to deal with it later."

Jarvis said, "Thanks, Pastor."

In the end, he prayed with them, and told them that he wanted another session with them before they returned to school.

They drove away in silence and Jarvis finally asked, "Are you all right?"

"I'm fine. I just have a little headache."

Venice still had some packing to do, so she asked Jarvis to drop her off at home. They sat out in the car for a few minutes before going inside.

He asked her, "Venice, I've been thinking. If you decide you want to marry me, we don't have to do it any time soon."

She looked at him and softly said, "Thanks. I needed to hear that."

"Is that what you want? I have no problem putting everything on hold for as long as you want."

"I'm sorry, Jarvis. I'm just tired. We'll talk tomorrow. I feel like I'm talking in riddles."

He rubbed her leg and asked, "Why don't you spend the night with me so we can talk?"

She said, "Not tonight. I'll call you later."

Venice exited the car and Jarvis walked her inside before heading home.

The next day and a half went by fast. Venice continued to be confused and in a daze, even though she hadn't given Jarvis an answer yet. Her mother and Sinclair were secretly making plans for March, since they knew March would be their next school break. Bryan still wasn't happy about the entire situation and often showed it. He hoped Venice would wait until she graduated from college before she considered marriage to anyone.

Mr. Taylor felt the same way and told Mrs. Taylor they should've left the situation alone a year ago. At least she wouldn't be going through this stress about Craig if they'd stayed out of it. Galen was sort of shocked with the news. He was trippin' because Craig was his friend and he didn't want any hard feelings between them.

Venice and Jarvis met with Pastor Greene again. This time, things went a little better. He still sensed that Venice wasn't completely ready. He vowed that he'd continue to talk with them by phone over the next few weeks.

Venice drove Jarvis to the airport before heading back to school. He told her that no matter what she decided, he would continue to love her. Jarvis told her to call him the minute she got back to campus and to be careful. She agreed and gave him a hug and kiss, then laid her head on his chest.

"Venice, don't worry. Everything's going to be fine."

Venice nodded in agreement and hugged him again. "Jarvis, bear with me. Okay?"

He lifted her chin up to gaze into her eyes. "Girl, you know I'll do anything for you. I don't want you to feel pressured."

"Thanks and I'll call you went I get in."

"That'll work. I love you."

"No, thank you for being patient. I love you so much, Jarvis."

Jarvis put his arm around Venice's waist and said, "I love you too, Niecy."

He gave her one last sensual kiss, parting her lips with his tongue and greedily tasted before boarding his plane.

It was going to be a long ride back to Dawson but she had Chanelle rolling with her this time. They had a great opportunity to talk about the stressful Christmas and the love triangle. Venice knew Jarvis had faith that she really did want to marry him. She just had to decide if she wanted to do it now or after graduation. Bryan was still riding Venice hard on the issue, too. He even called her on the cell phone as they drove back to school. Venice just listened and took everything he said to heart.

Arriving back on campus, the two women headed to their respective rooms. On the elevator, Chanelle asked, "So, did you tell Jarvis?"

"Nope! I haven't given him any kind of answer. I'm going to call Craig later. For some reason, I feel like he's given up on me. He'll be leaving for Japan in two weeks. This is still going to be hard, Chanelle."

Chanelle said, "I can't even imagine. I'm glad I'm not in your shoes."

Venice paused for a minute. "I don't have a clue, Chanelle."

The rest of the ride was quiet as she said goodbye to Chanelle and exited the elevator.

When Venice reached her room, she saw that Monique wasn't back yet. She did have a couple of messages. One was from Monique—who said she'd be in tomorrow—the next message was from Jarvis and the last one was from Craig. Venice put her things away before returning any of the calls. She called Jarvis first to let him know that she'd made it back. He told her again that he loved her and would talk to her later. Next, she called Craig and told him that she was back in town. She could tell by his tone that he already knew. It was something in his voice. She asked him how things were going in preparation for his trip to Japan. He told her things were going fine. He asked her if she was up to coming over. She told him she'd be over in about an hour. This was really it.

Venice showered, then dressed in one of her long skirts with a split up the back and a cute blouse to match. When she arrived, she found Craig's room somewhat cluttered. He had his suitcases scattered around the room and clothes stacked in several piles on the floor. She asked if he needed any help. He thanked her, but told her he pretty much had a system going.

He went on to ask how Joshua was doing and also about her family. She sat on the bed and filled him in on everybody. He stood in front of her and grabbed her hand and said, "I see you're still wearing the ring. I don't see a wedding band, so I guess you haven't got married yet."

"No, I didn't."

He sat down next to her. "I need a break. I've been at this for a couple of hours now."

Venice looked around the room and said, "I can tell."

She wrapped her arm around his arm and laid her head on his shoulder.

He said, "Venice, you don't have to say anything. Baby, I already know why you're here. To tell you the truth, I knew what you were going to do when I came up for Christmas. Don't stress yourself out over this."

The tears started falling when he said that.

He put his arm around her and said, "I told you that I wasn't going to just let you walk away from me. What would it take for me to change your mind? Huh?"

Venice couldn't answer him.

He stood up and said, "You know I love you and I know you love me. I can't see how you could go through with it. So, when's the wedding?"

She walked across the floor and got a tissue to wipe her eyes.

She sat back and said, "I haven't decided what I'm going to do yet. I haven't given him an answer."

He had a relieved look on his face and said, "I still can't believe you're considering it. You're just going to act like we didn't exist?"

Venice continued to wipe her tears as she stood up again.

He stood up and angrily said, "Say something, Venice!"

"I don't know what to say, Craig! I do love you, but I've been in love with Jarvis for a long time. I'm emotionally connected to him. It's hard to explain."

He took her hand into his and asked, "Is that the best you can come up with?" Venice looked up into his dark brown eyes. "I can't explain it any better than that, Craig. I've always been in love with him."

Craig sat back down on the bed and calmly said, "I just can't let you go through with it. I've had an unbelievable time with you, Venice, and I can't dismiss us as easily as you can. You're a special lady and because I know you love me, I just can't let you go."

He took the tissue from her and wiped her tears.

She said, "I should've never let you on my emotional roller-coaster in the first place. You've been great to me and you've being nothing less than wonderful for me."

He slid his arm around her waist, pulling her into his lap. "Baby, you mean the world to me. You always have and always will."

After he said that, she broke down hysterically on him. It took all he could not to shed a tear himself. As he held her tightly in his arms, she released all her emotions in loud sobs. It took several minutes, but finally she was able to calm down a little.

She stood up and said, "Let me get out of here. I've caused you enough problems already."

She grabbed her jacket and hurried through the kitchen and into the garage. She opened the door just as his palm slammed it closed.

He grabbed her and pulled her to him. "Venice, I love you!"

At that moment, he lowered his lips to claim her mouth, feeding off her desire. Venice dropped her purse and jacket on the floor as they continued their passionate kisses.

He broke free and said, "Venice, I don't want you to go. Please stay so we can talk this through."

She pushed away and went back into his bedroom in silence. Craig followed her and once he entered the room, Venice started unbuttoning her blouse.

He grinned and asked, "What are you doing!"

She stared back at him with a blank expression on her face.

He asked again, "Venice, what are you doing?"

She finally smiled at him as she continued to undress. He was frozen as he watched her do what he wanted to do to her. He took a couple of steps toward her and reached out to touch her nakedness. Her body responded as she slowly pulled him toward the bed and started undressing him. It was obvious, at least for the night, that he didn't give a damn about her engagement. He wanted her for himself and he wasn't about to give her up.

Craig began to do things to Venice that he had never done before while kissing her body from head to toe. Lacing his fingers with hers, he kissed her in places that drove her wild. He took his time delicately tasting her body. Venice trembled uncontrollably as she whispered for him not to stop. She stroked his head as he continued to kiss her.

Venice hollered and moaned to every touch of Craig's hands and lips. Venice welcomed him and moved her hips until he could no longer stand it. After rolling her over onto her stomach, he pushed himself into her so deep that it took her breath away. He held onto her hips tightly as he pleasured her with great force and intimacy. He turned her over on her back and kissed her harder on the mouth, drugging her with his taste. He penetrated her body again and again as she wrapped her legs around his trim waist. He rose above her grinding deeper as he moved around inside her hot body.

Venice screamed out, "Craig! Oh, baby! I love you!"

Venice screamed so loud, it seemed to echo throughout the house. Her body trembled as he worked her over thoroughly to her core.

He also moaned as he pleasured her calling out her name, "Venice! Baby!" Finally he looked her in her passion-filled eyes and let out a deep groan as she shuddered beneath him and he filled her with the essence of his love. Delirious and breathless, he pulled strands of her hair away from her angelic face.

Craig held Venice tightly in his arms and said, "I'll never let you go through with it. I love you and I wish I could take you to Japan with me."

Venice didn't respond because she knew he was serious. She just laid there enjoying his caresses and inhaling the scent of their love-making. She then kissed him, told him that she'd always love him, and said, "I'd better go."

Craig again asked Venice to spend the night, but she declined. She got dressed while Craig sadly watched her with a crushed heart. Venice sat back down on the bed and jumped because she had sat on something hard. She reached under her and pulled out a small box.

"What's this?"

Craig took the box from her and said, "Sorry about that. It's my cuff links."

He tossed the box in his suitcase and paced the floor as she continued to get dressed. He followed her into the garage and said, "Venice, please stay with me tonight. We need to talk."

She turned to him and said, "Craig, I can't. I need some time to myself. I'm so sorry."

They almost started up again as he held her against the car giving her deep, sensual kisses.

He said, "Baby, please, and I'm not a begging man."

Again, she said, "I can't, Craig. I just can't. I have too much on my mind."

He held her firmly by her shoulders and angrily said, "Venice, I'm not going to let you marry him. Do you hear me!"

Venice pushed away from him and started crying as she got inside the car. She said, "I have to go!"

He bent down into the window and kissed her again. "It's not so easy for me to let you walk away from me. I'm telling you now, it ain't over." Venice gave him a concerned look. "I'll be here waiting for you, if you change your mind and want to come back over. Okay?"

She nodded as the garage door went up. He started to pull her from the car, but he didn't. He stood there and watched her possibly drive out of his life. He slowly walked back into his room and picked up the box of cuff links. When he opened it, he revealed, not cuff links, but the ring he'd planned on giving her on New Year's Eve. The difference was that Craig really did want to plan their wedding once she graduated. Sadly, Jarvis beat him to the punch. He stared at the ring for a while, then put it away in his dresser. Her scent still engulfed his room, his body, and his soul. At that very moment, he decided what he was going to do.

When Venice got about two blocks away, she felt her body begin to shiver uncontrollably. She had to pull over to the side of the road where she lost it emotionally. The scent of his maleness covered her body. She finally made it back to campus, showered, and crawled into bed, but she could still smell him. She laid in bed, in the dark, to think. She had a lot to consider and her head was pounding.

An hour or so later, Joshua called her to check on her. He asked her if she had talked with Craig. She explained to him that Craig expected her to break up with him but that he said he wasn't going to let her go. Venice was sounding very depressed and it disturbed him.

After talking for a little while longer she said, "Joshua, I'm not crazy. I do love them both."

"I know, Niecy. You'll be all right. I'll check on you tomorrow."

They said their goodnights to each other and hung up the phone.

Forty-Four

The next several days, Venice did her best not to be alone with Craig. They often met in public and talked on the phone a lot. He constantly tried to get her to come over and spend the night with him, but she didn't think it would be a good idea. He told her it wasn't fair to avoid him.

He said, "Venice, believe it or not, I feel like my heart has been ripped out of my chest."

Venice told him she was really sorry and wished there were a way that she could make it up to him. What he wanted, she couldn't provide right then. He wanted her to spend the night with him before he left for Japan. Venice told him it wouldn't be a good idea and he didn't like it, but he tried to accept. They did, however, continue to talk on a daily basis and Craig didn't want to give up on her.

Venice talked to Jarvis every day, but still wouldn't give him an answer; especially since Craig was going to be leaving later that night for Japan. Over the previous few days, he didn't put any more pressure on her and this really helped her cope. He asked her if she would drive him to the airport. Bernice had to work and it was going to be too sad for her to see him get on the plane. Venice was hesitant but finally agreed. Craig's plane wasn't leaving until eleven-thirty, but he wanted to get to the airport early to check in.

The ride to the airport was quiet and Venice was starting to get nervous. After Craig checked his bags, he still had an hour before takeoff. He asked her to join him in the restaurant to talk. They found a booth and ordered some appetizers. Venice wasn't very hungry. She just wanted to get through the sad moment, but Craig was noticeably cheerful. Venice assumed he was excited and nervous all balled into one. He scooted closer to her, put his hand on her thigh, and said, "I guess this is it."

Venice looked at Craig sadly and said, "I guess it is."

"Sweetheart, it doesn't have to be."

"For now, it has to be."

He stroked her face with his hand and said, "I love you, Venice LaShawn Taylor."

"I love you, too."

Tears ran down her cheeks as he brushed his lips against hers. They fed off each other's emotions as they deepened the kiss. Her heart pounded in her chest as he pulled her even closer to his body.

She removed her swollen lips from his mouth and said, "I would love it if you stay in touch with me while you're in Japan."

He kissed the corner of her mouth. "I wouldn't have it any other way."

They talked for a while longer and before long, he received his boarding call. Venice held his hand tightly as she walked him toward the gate. When they got there, he held her tightly in his arms and hugged and kissed her senseless. He reached into his pocket and pulled out a small box. He told her not to open it until she got back to campus.

She said, "You shouldn't have bought me anything."

"It's just a little something something."

She wrapped her arms around his neck and kissed him again and told him, "Craig….always baby. Whatever I decide, please don't hate me for what I've put you through."

"I could never hate you and if he ever does anything to hurt you, I'll kick his ass."

Venice smiled and said, "Thanks!"

"I'll call you when I land."

"You'd better."

She stood there and watched him walk down the hallway and possibly out of her life. Or was he?

When Venice got back to her room, she pulled the small box from her purse. After staring at it for a moment, wondering what could be inside, she finally opened it. She took a deep breath and opened the lid. Inside was a beautiful gold charm bracelet. Tears welled in her eyes as she read the included note:

"Venice, you're the love of my life. I'm going to miss you terribly. I wanted to get something for you to remember our time together. Each charm represents places we've been or things we've done together. I hope that each time you wear it, you remember how special those times were. I wish you all the love and happiness your heart can hold. Love Always, Craig."

She put the letter down and began to look at each charm. Each one did exactly what he said; it told the story of their time together. Venice couldn't have received a more priceless and precious gift. She lost control of her emotions for hours as she cried into her pillow until morning.

A week later, Venice called Jarvis and told him that she'd marry him the week of Spring Break. He was a little surprised since he'd told her that there was no rush. She knew she was letting go of someone very special, but she also knew Jarvis was the one who truly owned her heart. Bryan went ballistic because he felt Venice should at least wait until she graduated. Sadly, she called Craig and told him about her decision to get married. He didn't take the news well, but told her that he'd never give up on her love. She told him that she needed him to be at the wedding. He told her that if he made it back from Japan in time, he'd be there.

Forty-Five

The wedding day was getting closer and Venice's mother and Sinclair were stressing. They had approximately two weeks left and Venice visited Jarvis every other weekend to look for somewhere to live. They'd narrowed it down to a nearby condo and on-campus housing and had to make a decision that weekend. They laughed together about their parents freaking out over the wedding plans. Venice allowed Sinclair to handle everything. On this particular visit, they spent the day at an Italian Festival. This was one of Jarvis' favorite foods and they stuffed themselves with food and drinks. When they got back to the hotel, they couldn't do anything but sleep.

After about three hours, Venice woke up to go to the bathroom. Once she sat up in the bed, she felt it. She ran into the bathroom and "called Earl." She didn't want to wake Jarvis so she closed the door. She knew she'd eaten way too much and was paying for it. Jarvis ate more than she did and she just knew he'd do the same when he woke up.

Every time she tried to leave the bathroom, she got sick again. She sat on the cold floor for about ten more minutes and was finally well enough to get back into bed. Jarvis woke up as she crawled back into bed. She told him that she'd gotten sick.

He jokingly said, "I hope it's not food poison."

"Do you feel okay?"

"So far, so good. Here, take this."

He gave her something to settle her stomach. She took it, then laid across his chest for the rest of the evening.

The next morning, Jarvis got up before Venice and went jogging.

When he returned, he found Venice with her face in the toilet again.

"Girl, you're still sick? Maybe I need to take you to the doctor. You must have food poisoning."

He felt her forehead to see if she was running a fever, but she wasn't. She was just was sick to her stomach.

"I'll be fine. I think my sinuses are draining and making me feel this way."

He sat down next to her and held a cool cloth to her head. She laid back against his steel chest and absorbed his warmth. Jarvis held her in his arms until she felt a little better. He brought her a 7-up and crackers and put her into bed.

He said, "Don't be trying to play sick to get out of marrying me."

She turned over and said, "You're silly. I'm not playing."

Jarvis held Venice and rubbed her stomach, hoping to help make it better. Venice eventually fell asleep and Jarvis got up and took his shower. He called home to see how his mother and sister were doing and they discussed the wedding.

The weekend had come to a close and they had decided on the condo. It was going to be convenient for both of their schedules. Venice was able to get her credits transferred and was blessed to recover her scholarship.

When Jarvis took her to the airport, he told her, "Venice, I'm going to do everything I can to make you happy. I don't want you to ever regret marrying me."

Lacing her fingers around his neck, she said, "You just show up at the altar."

"I told you before, you don't have to worry about me. I'll be there."

They kissed each other breathless and she boarded the plane.

It was Venice's last week on the Dawson campus. Bryan and Gator drove down and picked up all her things except for a few suitcases. She spent the last few days on campus telling the many friends she'd made goodbye. She was really going to miss Monique. They had really become close, through the good and the bad. Venice hoped Monique would take care of herself and not fall into the wrong hands. Her last task was to visit Bernice. She was really going to miss their "girl talk" sessions.

Bernice let Venice know that she didn't blame her for ending the relationship with Craig. Bernice told her that she understood her difficult position. She let Venice know that she was welcome anytime. Lastly, she thanked Venice for making her brother so happy.

"You better come back down here for my wedding in June."

"I wouldn't miss it."

Bernice said, "Make sure you bring your new husband. Craig will be fine with it, I'm sure. It's not like he hasn't met him."

Venice thanked her and said, "Bernice, you know I love your brother?"

"I know, Venice. Craig knows it also. It just wasn't time for you two."

Venice was about to get emotional. "Well, I guess I'll see you at my wedding. I'd better go."

"I'll see you next week. Craig told me to tell you to always remember that he loves you."

"Thanks, Bernice."

They hugged and said their good-byes.

Forty-Six

Wedding Week

Venice and Jarvis were home and in the middle of frantic last minute wedding plans. Venice received a call from Craig and missed it, but he left her a touching message on her answering machine. Sinclair was bossing everyone around as Venice and her mom went in for her last fitting. The wedding dress she'd selected was gorgeous. It was a beautiful diamond-studded, ivory, strapless gown that came down to the knees with a detachable train.

Venice decided to wear her hair up with trestles hanging down around her face. Her veil would have a halo around the upsweep and hang down her back. Her bridesmaids were also wearing strapless lavender gowns. Sinclair had done a wonderful job organizing everything and Venice was grateful. Jarvis also met with his boys for their last tuxedo fittings. Venice was happy Joshua was able to be in her wedding. She wished he could've been her man of honor. He was very deserving of the title. Venice and Jarvis didn't want a large wedding. Just something nice and small. Sinclair got out of hand with the plans because it had turned into a large wedding. Venice wasn't happy about it, but she could live with it. Venice tried to return Craig's call, but was unable to reach him. The time difference and his busy schedule made it difficult at times.

It was two days before the wedding. Venice and Jarvis were planning on shopping for gifts for the bridal party. Venice woke up with a headache and when she sat up in bed, she felt sick again. Her nerves were really getting the best of her. She had no idea it was going to affect her like this. It took her a minute to get herself together, but the shower helped. Jarvis picked her up around ten a.m. When she got into the car, he noticed she looked flushed.

"Are you feeling okay?"

"Just nerves."

"Are you sure?"

She leaned back in the seat, closed her eyes, and said, "I'll be all right."

He backed out of the driveway and headed to the mall. As he drove, he asked, "Are you going to stay with me tonight?"

"No!"

He laughed. "Oh, you're going to make me wait?"

"You'd better know it."

After shopping, they took the items over to Bryan's house to wrap them in private. Joshua came by and offered to help. Before they could finish wrapping, Jarvis had to leave and run some errands for his mom. Joshua told Bryan that he would take Venice home. Before Bryan left, he gave Venice a kiss and said, "I'll catch up with you later."

"No rush. I'll probably be over here for a while."

After he left, Joshua said, "You look terrible. What's going on with you?"

She sat down next to him and said, "Joshua, my nerves are so shaken, it's making me sick. I can't sleep, I can't eat, and I'm tripping."

He patted her on the leg and said, "You don't have anything to be nervous about. What's wrong? Are you thinking about Craig again?"

She got up and picked up some ribbon. "Sometimes, but not like I used to."

"Well, you should be cool then."

She got unusually quiet as she wrapped another gift. "Joshua, I'm late."

He was switching channels with the remote. He looked at his watch and said, "Late for what? Where you got to go?"

She looked at him seriously and said, "Not that kind of late!"

"I know you're not talking about what I think you're talking about."

"Yes, and I don't want to know the truth right now."

Joshua looked her in the eyes and asked, "Does Jarvis know?"

"Oh no!"

"Why not?"

"Because I don't want to upset him right now. He's getting curious because I've been sick."

Joshua fell back on the sofa and said, "That's messed up, Niecy. What are you going to do?"

"Nothing and you keep your damn mouth shut."

"How could something like this happen?"

"I don't know. The last time this happened, my doctor increased the dosage of my birth control pills and said one of us is unusually fertile."

Joshua stared at her. "For your sake, I hope you're not pregnant. Talking about deja vu. Your family will go off. Venice, you need to get a pregnancy test."

"I can't handle that right now."

"Don't say I didn't try to help you." There was no response. "Niecy?"

"Yeah?"

"If you're really pregnant, could it be Craig's?"

Startled by his comment, she looked up and said, "We always used protection."

"Just checking."

She held his hand and said, "I know. I appreciate your help, Joshua. I may decide to take a test. I just don't want to right now. Look, I don't want to talk about it any longer. Okay?"

He agreed and helped her finish wrapping the gifts.

Forty-Seven

It was the day before the wedding and the rehearsal was scheduled for that evening. Venice hadn't been sick all day, but she did let Joshua pick up a pregnancy test for her. At least if she got up the nerve to take the test, it would be available. She still hadn't heard from Craig. She hoped that he was on his way. Sinclair was running rehearsals smoothly as Venice sat up front to watch Jarvis and the others get their instructions. Crimson was bopping around having a good time. She told everyone that she was going to look like a princess the next day. Venice sat there and stared at Sidney, who was now six months pregnant. She was glowing and Galen was a changed man. Jarvis was visibly excited and occasionally looked over at Venice winking or blowing her kisses. Venice checked her watch and saw that things were running on schedule. Sinclair was touching up the decorations in the church. She wanted to make sure every "t" was crossed and every "i" was dotted.

After about thirty more minutes, the rehearsal was over. They had the rehearsal dinner at a local restaurant arranged by Jarvis' parents. As they ate, Mr. Taylor became emotional as he told everyone about his feelings to finally get to walk his baby down the aisle. He praised Jarvis for being who he was and for taking care of his daughter. Once he sat down, each person stood up and said nice things about the two. Joshua made it a point to be the last one. He told the story about his relationship with Venice over the years. He explained he wasn't blessed to have a sister, but she was the best sister anyone could ever wish for.

Next, Joshua told the story about how he almost died in December and could've missed the event. This brought tears to everyone's eyes in the room. He went on to tell of his closeness with

Jarvis and how they'd had their brotherly ups and downs. He ended with, "No two people deserve to be together as much as Jarvis and Venice. I believed they were destined for this day the moment they were born. You two are my closest friends. I wish you nothing but love and happiness and a couple of little Venices and Jarvis' running around one day." Everyone laughed, then Joshua finished with, "Seriously, I love you two very much and I'll always be there for you." Venice, with tears flowing, got up and hugged Joshua tightly. "Thank you!"

He said, "You're welcome."

She laughed, kissed him, and said, "I love you, Joshua."

He took a sip of his drink and said, "I know."

After everyone had finished eating, Jarvis and Venice gave out their gifts. Jarvis went out with his friends, but Venice didn't feel well, so she went home.

Before Venice knew it, the sun had come up. She had an early hair appointment so she had to get moving. Venice hid the pregnancy test in her suitcase and dressed. Before she could finish combing her hair, the sickness hit her hard. She tried her best to hide this from her mother, who was downstairs waiting on her to go to the beauty shop.

Venice needed more time to get herself together. She hollered for her mom to go ahead. She told her that she'd meet her there in a few minutes. The wedding was six hours away. Venice had no idea whether she'd be well enough to walk down the aisle, but she had no choice. As she held a cool towel to her head, the doorbell rang.

Who could this be?

When Venice got to the door, a delivery person was standing there with a large flower arrangement. She told him to put it inside the den. She was wondering who could've sent them. When the delivery person left, she read the card:

"To the most beautiful bride in the world. I just wish you were going to be standing next to me instead. I wish you much happiness. With eternal love, Craig."

Venice stood there and held the card to her heart, then grabbed her purse and headed out the door. She read the card again as she drove to the beauty shop. She stuck it in her purse for safekeeping.

Venice was quiet at the beauty shop. The beautician had closed her shop for the day to fix all the ladies' hair. Venice was still a little sick so she drank another 7-up. She was afraid to put anything in her stomach besides crackers.

Her mom asked, "Venice, are you ill?"

"I'm just nervous, Momma. That's all."

Mrs. Taylor pushed the issue and said, "You don't look well at all. Patricia, how soon will you be ready for Venice?"

"About an hour."

Mrs. Taylor asked, "Would it be all right if Venice went home and laid down? She's not feeling well. We can call her when you're about ready for her."

Patricia told Venice it would be fine. Venice only lived five minutes away, so she took her up on the offer.

When Venice walked back inside her room, she had a message on the answering machine. She pushed the button and heard, "Hey, Niecy. I know I'm not allowed to see you before the wedding, but I had to call. I want you to know that I love you more than you could ever know. I'm going to do everything in my power to make you happy. I also want you to know that I don't care about the football, the money, any of it. I'd rather be poor and have you in my life, than be rich and without you any day. I can't wait to see you come down that aisle to me. I love you. I'll be waiting for you at the altar, sweetheart."

Venice smiled, removed the tape, and locked it away in her hope chest. She laid down on the bed and waited for her call from the beauty shop.

The countdown had started. Venice was at the church, dressed and ready to have her pictures made. The men weren't scheduled to be there for another fifteen minutes. The wedding was in less than an one hour. Venice was hoping she could make it without getting sick. Her makeup was flawless and she looked like she'd stepped right out of Bride's Magazine. Her mother cried when she saw the finished product of her baby girl. Mrs. Anderson cried also, which started a chain reaction from Sidney to Chanelle on down to Sinclair.

After all the pictures were taken, Venice took off her dress and laid down on the sofa to relax before the ceremony started. It was Joshua's job to keep her company while she waited.

They sat there in silence for awhile, then Joshua looked over at Venice and said, "You clean up really good."

Venice laughed and said, "You're silly. Thanks for always being there for me. I couldn't have made it without you. I love you."

He looked lovingly into her eyes. "Thanks for being the sister I never had and you know I love you to death."

Venice hugged him, laid back down, and continued to try and relax. "Joshua, I'm going to rest my eyes for a moment. I'm a little tired."

"Okay, I'm going to dim the lights for you."

Being really tired from the past few days, Venice closed her eyes and smiled. "Thanks, Josh."

Forty-Eight

About fifteen more minutes passed, Venice was awakened by Joshua softly saying, "Niecy, Craig's here."

She sat up and asked, "For real? Oh, Joshua, please go get him. I want to talk to him before I do this."

"Have you lost your mind? Jarvis ain't gonna kick my tail."

She grabbed his hand and said, "Please!"

He had never been able to tell her no, so he did as he was told. As soon as Joshua left the room, Venice put her wedding dress back on. A few minutes later, Craig entered the room looking as handsome as expected. He was wearing a black suit with all the matching accessories.

When he laid eyes on Venice, he leaned against the door and said, "Well, Taylor, I knew you were going to be gorgeous, but I didn't know you going to be breathtaking."

She just smiled, walked over to him, and laid her head against his chest. His heart was racing inside his chest. He paused for a moment, then finally closed his eyes and embraced her lovingly.

She looked up into his warm brown eyes and said, "Craig, I want you to know that I never lied to you. I do love you."

He tilted her chin upwards and said, "I'm glad to hear you still love me, but witnessing this is pure hell, baby."

"I'm so sorry."

"I know Taylor. So am I."

"Can I have a kiss?"

"Do you think that would be proper?"

She leaned against his broad chest and pressed her lips to his tenderly. A soft moan escaped her mouth before Craig broke free of her lips.

Still holding her, he asked, "Are you feeling okay? You look a little flushed."

"I'm a little nervous and I've had a nagging sinus headache for a few days."

"Maybe you should take something."

"No, I'm afraid it might upset my stomach."

Looking up into his misty eyes, she said, "Craig...you're so special to me and I'll never ever forget you."

"Venice, I really believe you're my soul mate, and I'll never forget you for the rest of my life."

Her eyes filled with tears and they continued to embrace each other for what seemed like hours.

Venice said, "Thank you so much for coming. I really needed you to be here." He kissed her tears away as they ran down her cheek and said, "I had to come." She leaned up and they gave each other the most sensual and loving kisses.

A minute later, Joshua came in and said, "Craig, you'd better go. Venice's dad will be here to get her in a few minutes."

"I'll be right out."

Joshua looked at Venice, then closed the door as he left the room again.

"Venice, I want you to know that I would never want to hurt you or embarrass you or your family. My heart is telling me to do one thing and my mind is telling me to do another. I don't know if I'm going to be able to sit back and let you go through with this. Especially after I've held you in my arms again."

Venice didn't blink an eye. She knew he was hinting about stopping her wedding. He pulled her to him tightly. "I'd better go. I guess I'll see you upstairs. I'll always love you, Taylor."

"I'll love you too, Bennett. Goodbye."

It was difficult to release Venice from his embrace. Craig knew it would probably be the last time.

After Craig closed the door, Venice felt nauseated again and started massaging her forehead. She said, "Lord, please help me get rid of this headache and help me get through this day."

Joshua and Craig chatted for a minute in the hallway. They shook hands and Craig said, "I'll see you guys upstairs."

Joshua agreed, then reentered the dressing room and found Venice unconscious on the floor.

He ran over to her and tried to wake her up. When he was unsuccessful, he ran to get help. Immediately, Jarvis' mom, who was a nurse, ran to Venice's side. Joshua went to get Jarvis, along with Venice's family. Mrs. Anderson attended to Venice as worried family stood close by. Bernice had gone to the restroom and when she saw Sinclair looking upset, she asked what was wrong. Sinclair quietly told Bernice that Venice was unconscious and that they were calling paramedics. Bernice hurried into the church and told Craig, who sprung up from his seat and ran downstairs.

When he got to the room, it was full of family and the wedding party. Bryan asked everyone to move out into the hallway except for those who were seeing about Venice. Bernice, also being a nurse, joined Mrs. Anderson who was still trying to revive Venice. Jarvis stayed by her side and looked like he was going to become hysterical at any minute.

Joshua pulled Craig to the side and asked, "What happened in there with you two?"

"Nothing! We just talked and I kissed her and I told her I'd see her upstairs."

"Did she give you any indication that she didn't feel well?"

"She just said that she wished she could get rid of her sinus headache."

Joshua put his hand on Craig's shoulder and said, "Don't worry. She'll be fine." For some reason, Craig didn't believe him. Joshua told Mrs. Anderson that Venice had been complaining about a headache. Jarvis added that Venice had been sick to her stomach for several weeks. The paramedics arrived, started working on her, and discovered that Venice's blood pressure had skyrocketed to almost stroke level. They immediately readied her for transport to the hospital. Jarvis was holding her hand and was visibly upset. Joshua whispered to the paramedics that there was a possibility that Venice could be pregnant.

Jarvis was shocked at the news and gave Joshua a pissed off glance.

Craig also heard the news and looked at Joshua in total surprise.

The family knew they had to let Pastor Green make some type of announcement to everyone in the church. While he tried to collect his emotions and thoughts, the rest of the family followed the ambulance to the hospital. Pastor Green announced that Venice had taken ill and was being taken to the hospital. He told them to proceed to the reception hall for dinner and they would be updated as soon as they could.

Everyone seemed stunned and before the minister dismissed the church, Pastor Green held them for a short prayer for Venice's recovery. At the hospital, everyone paced the hallway. Jarvis sat on the sofa with his face buried in his hands. He didn't hide the fact that he was scared to death. He was worried that he was going to lose her. Craig and Joshua stood together in silence as everyone waited for some type of word on Venice's condition. Jarvis and Craig's eyes met several times. They knew they were both in love with the same woman and were now faced with possibility of losing her.

Finally, the doctor came out and told the family they were able to get Venice's blood pressure to start declining. He went on to tell them that she was conscious, but that she was very weak.

Jarvis jumped up and asked, "Was there a baby?"

The doctor sadly nodded. "I'm sorry. We weren't able to save it."

Jarvis sank back into his seat and covered his face in pain. His mother tried to comfort him, but he requested to be left alone. Craig dropped his head also, because he secretly knew there was a slim possibility that he could've been the father. The doctor told the family that she would have to stay a few days until her blood pressure was back to normal.

Mrs. Taylor asked, "Can we see her?"

The doctor gave instructions that she could have two visitors at a time for only ten minutes.

Jarvis looked at the Taylors and asked, "Can I please see her first?"

The Taylors agreed and Jarvis entered the room. When he reached her, he practically collapsed on the bed in tears. He couldn't hold them back any longer.

Venice was weak, but was able to caress his head and softly said, "Hey, stop that. I'm fine."

Jarvis continued to cry, which also made her tear up.

She said, "I'm so sorry I messed everything up today."

He continued to lie across her body. "I'm not worried about any of that, Venice. I was worried that I was going to lose you."

"You're not going to get rid of me that easy."

Jarvis smiled and said, "Baby, it's all my fault. I'm sorry I put so much pressure on you about getting married. We don't have to get married right now, if you don't want to. Maybe we should stick to our original agreement and wait for graduation."

Venice's eyes overflowed with tears. "Thank you, baby. I needed to hear that."

"Baby, I have faith in what we have. There's no doubt in my mind that you'll be my wife. I love you more that anything. Just trust me."

"I do trust you, sweetheart ,and there's nothing more I want in this world than to be your wife. I have no problem marrying you right here tonight."

"Venice, I'd love to take you up on your offer, but we need to get you well first. I don't want you to say that you married me under the influence of medication."

"I'm sorry I didn't get a chance to tell you about the baby. I just wasn't sure."

"Stop apologizing and get some rest. I'm going to stay with you, all right?"

She nodded in agreement and he gave her one last kiss and said, "Well, I'd better let the rest of the family have a chance to come check on you. I'll be right outside, okay?"

"Okay."

One by one, each family member came in to see how she was doing. Craig and Bernice were the last ones to come in. After Bernice checked the medical equipment and gave Venice a kiss, she allowed Craig and Venice to have some privacy.

He looked at her and asked, "Did I cause this?"

She reached for his hand and motioned for him to sit on the bed. "Of course not. It was nobody's fault but mine. I should've gone to the doctor when I couldn't shake that headache weeks ago."

Craig hesitated because he didn't want to upset her. "Was that my baby you were carrying?"

"We used protection, remember?"

Craig sat down and held Venice's hand tightly. "Well, Venice, the last time we were together, it didn't hold up. But all that is meaningless now."

Venice was stunned, then turned and said, "I'm sorry to put all of you through this drama. It also looks like the wedding is off for now."

Craig wanted to scream words of joy, but felt like he shouldn't. He asked, "Have you told Jarvis yet?"

"He was the one who suggested that we probably should wait and he apologized for pressuring me. Anyway, why don't you go on to the reception and get something to eat?"

"I really don't want to leave you, especially now, but I know you and Jarvis need some time alone right now." Venice smiled as Craig brushed her tangled curls from her face. "Taylor, I love you." He then leaned down and kissed her as hard as he could. Before leaving the room, he said, "If you need me, just call."

"I will and, for the record…I love you, too."

After Venice got out the hospital, it was Sinclair who made sure that all the guests were sent special cards of thanks with their returned gifts. Jarvis returned to school in Michigan and Venice returned to her life at Dawson University. Craig and Venice were hanging out again. Meanwhile, Venice and Jarvis decided they should not discuss marriage again until after graduation. Things basically went back to normal. They all decided not to put any demands on each other and just to let things flow. Venice did not commit to either one of them to the full extent. At the moment, all were in agreement and felt that they would live with this arrangement, especially after what they'd all just endured. Life was too short.

Forty-Nine

Knock, knock, knock. The loud noise startled Venice. She had to collect her thoughts and finally realized that she had fallen asleep. She looked at herself and noticed her wedding dress hanging up. She finally realized she had been dreaming. But how much of it was a dream? She couldn't tell.

Again, there was a knock on the door. Venice, still somewhat delirious, said, "Come in!"

"Baby, it's almost time and you don't even have your dress on."

"Daddy, I fell asleep. Just give me a minute."

Mr. Taylor had come for her. He hadn't seen her in her dress and when he finally saw her in all her glory, tears welled up in his eyes.

Venice was still a little fuzzy and confused when she said, "Daddy, don't get me started. You're going to make me ruin my makeup."

He grabbed her and gave her a big kiss. "Baby, you look beautiful!"

"Thank you, Daddy."

"Are you okay? You look a little dazed."

"I'm fine. I had a weird dream, but I guess I'm okay."

"Jarvis is a nice young man, Venice. I trust him with you. But if you feel in any way that you want to call this off, just say the word. Your mother and I will stand by you because we recognize that you have feelings for Craig..."

Venice kissed her dad on the cheek and said, "Thanks, Daddy, but I'm fine. Let's go. Jarvis is waiting on me."

He smiled and led her into the hallway.

Venice hadn't been able to figure out if Craig really came to her or whether it was in her dream.

They made it to the church doors where Venice took a series of deep breaths, praying the sickness wouldn't return. She was still baf-

349

fled about her dream. The music began to play and when the doors swung open, the first face she saw was Craig's. He was sitting near the back with Bernice and J.T. When she saw him, she almost lost it. He had on the exact same clothes he had on in her dream and he looked wonderful as expected. Venice almost stopped in her tracks. When she passed him, she read his lips, which said, "I love you." Venice smiled at him as she walked on down the aisle. She then turned and looked toward Jarvis who waiting for her at the end of the long aisle. He was smiling and visibly misty-eyed. When she finally made it to the altar, she could hear sniffles from people all around her. She didn't want to turn around to see who was crying for she was afraid she would start crying herself.

The ceremony went on as planned. Venice didn't know whether Jarvis realized Craig was in the audience or not. Her heart started pounding when the minister got to the part stating, "If anyone here can show just cause why these two people should not be married, speak now or forever hold your peace." That's when Venice nearly fainted. A part of her wanted Craig to speak up and proclaim his love for her. A part of her didn't want him to.

Jarvis felt her trembling and gave her hand a comforting squeeze. Bernice looked over at Craig, who had his head down and eyes closed. She reached over and held her brother's hand. Bernice knew his heart was breaking at that very moment and there was nothing she could do to help him besides holding his hand. He finally stood up and left the sanctuary.

Venice felt like Pastor Greene paused just a little too long at that particular part of the ceremony. Once they got past it, Venice felt a little disappointed, yet relieved. She really believed Craig would stand up and proclaim his love. She still was a little troubled about her dream. Could it have been a premonition?

Pastor Green finally got to the end where Venice and Jarvis were pronounced man and wife. He kissed his new bride and they exited the church.

The photographer took the rest of the wedding party pictures. A few people stayed behind to watch. Bryan had a limousine out front to take the happy couple to the reception. Jarvis asked the driver to take the long way.

As they rode around the city, Jarvis said, "Niecy, when you came down that aisle, I thought I was going to pass out. You looked like an angel. You're so beautiful!"

Venice snuggled against his neck and replied, "Thank you, baby. You're looking fine yourself."

He held her in his arms and asked, "Did you see Craig?"

"Yes, I saw them."

"Are you cool with him being here?"

"I invited him, remember? You're still okay with it, aren't you?"

"I'm fine. I have everything I need right here."

He lowered his mouth to her lips and gave her a deep, demanding kiss.

Venice enjoyed his embrace and kisses for the rest of the ride.

When they reached the reception hall, Venice was amazed at the results of Sinclair's hard work. The room erupted in applause as they entered. They went through all the formalities for the photographer. Crimson ran over to Venice and gave her a hug. She really did look like a little princess.

Sinclair came over and Venice gave her a big hug and a kiss and said, "Thank you, Sinclair! Everything is beautiful! I love you."

Sinclair teared up and said, "You're welcome, Venice. I love you, too."

After finishing all the pictures, Venice and Jarvis danced their first dance. As they danced, Jarvis couldn't help but confess his love for her over and over. They affectionately kissed each other throughout the song. Venice also confirmed how much she loved him into his ear. She finally felt contentment and peace.

The reception was going along fine when Venice asked Jarvis if he would object to her dancing with Craig. He told her it was fine by him and Venice started scanning the crowd.

She found him coming out of the bathroom. "How about a dance, mister?"

He grinned at her and said, "You look unbelievable. Did you get the flowers?" She grabbed his hand. "I sure did. Now come dance with me."

She pulled him onto the dance floor and Jarvis was no longer worried. He had finally married the love of his life.

Craig held Venice in his arms and confessed, "I almost stopped your wedding today. I just couldn't do it."

"I love him, Craig. I tried to dismiss it when I came to Dawson, but it was too strong. I had to face the fact that it wasn't going away. I never meant to hurt you and my love for you is just as clear and permanent in my heart. I don't ever want to lose you."

"I'm never going to get over you, girl. I guess under different circumstances, you would have been mine."

"Without a doubt."

"Taylor…I mean Anderson…"

"Venice will do, Mr. Bennett."

"Sweetheart, I would love nothing more than to have you in my life in whatever way I can. My broken heart will eventually heal, I hope. I guess if you hadn't fell in love with me, it would have been some other poor soul."

"Craig, I'm glad it was you. I'll always love you, baby."

"I love you, too."

The song ended and she gave him a tender kiss on the lips. "Save me another dance."

Craig slowly let her hand slide out of his and said, "You bet."

After their dance, Venice made her way back over to Jarvis and attempted to eat her food. She was afraid to eat because she didn't want to get sick. Jarvis convinced her to at least try the fruit. She did and it didn't upset her stomach. They finished up with the ceremonial cutting of the cake and throwing of the bouquet. The hours passed and the reception was winding down. Venice was exhausted and after a long night of dancing, she was ready to call it a night. Venice saw Galen and Joshua talking to Craig as they got ready to leave. Venice and Jarvis gave their parents hugs, kisses, and many thanks for all they had done, then left the reception.

When they reached their room, she lay down on the bed and let out a deep breath. Jarvis took off his jacket and crawled over next to her. She wrapped her arms around his neck and pulled him down to her for a long, passion-filled kiss.

"That was nice, Mrs. Anderson."

"I'm glad you enjoyed it, Mr. Anderson."

He continued to kiss her neck and lips as their bodies became enflamed.

She whispered, "Let me get out of this dress. I want to try out that Jacuzzi."

He helped her up and unzipped the dress for her. She slipped out of it and he hung it up for her in the closet. Since her veil was held in her hair by so many bobby pins, he had to help her out of the veil also.

Venice slipped into her lingerie as Jarvis opened the bottle of champagne. She entered the room with a long, white satin gown with spaghetti straps. The neckline plunged deep between her breasts and the back was out down to her firm round hips.

He said, "Damn, baby, that's sexy!"

She blushed. "Thank you!"

He sat beside her on the bed and handed her a glass of champagne. "Thank you, Niccy, for making me complete. You have always been my girl and I feel blessed that you allowed me to make you my wife. Again."

They laughed together and Venice said, "Thank you for not giving up on me and for having faith that we would be together again and forever this time. I love you."

They kissed each other then took a sip of their champagne.

Venice asked, "Are you ready to test drive the Jacuzzi?"

He smiled and said, "Right now, I'm aching to feel my body inside your body. You're all I want."

"I'm aching for you too, baby. Make love to me…now."

"My pleasure."

Back upstairs at the reception, the guests were still partying. Joshua and Craig were sitting at a nearby table talking about Japan and school. Joshua had had his fair share of champagne and was talking a mile a minute.

"Craig, you know I'm really going to miss my girl. So, I can only imagine how you must feel. I don't see how you handled it today. If I were in your shoes, I don't know if I would've been able to deal with it. Hell, I probably would've gotten me a few drinks and stepped up and stopped the wedding."

"Don't think I didn't have that very thought."

"Hey, you know Venice really cares about you. She was torn and I think she wanted you both, but realized she couldn't have it that way."

"Joshua, I don't think I'll ever get over her. She's special. It almost killed me when she told me she was getting married."

"I can imagine."

Craig played in his food and said, "Well…what's done is done."

Joshua smiled and glanced out on the dance floor at Chanelle and some of the others. He then asked Craig, "So what are you going to do now?"

"I'm going back to Dawson to graduate and then I am going to attempt to move on. I'm not going to be in any hurry to start another relationship anytime soon."

"You don't mean that."

"Yes I do. I thought Venice was it for me. She was the one."

"Well, if it's worth anything, I think she felt like you were the one also. Under different circumstances, you two would be together."

Craig finished off his drink. "Whatever, man."

Joshua paused for a moment and asked, "Hey, man, when was the last time you and Venice got together?"

"What do you mean?"

"You know…together. Hit the sheets."

"The day she came back to school after Christmas break. Why?"

"Look, don't repeat this. I've never, ever betrayed Venice and this will be the first time I did something she told me not to. She will kill me if she found out I told you."

"What is it? Is Venice okay?"

"She's not sure right now, but her period is late. Real late."

Craig fell back in his chair. "Is she pregnant?"

"It's possible, but she's not sure yet. Nobody knows, not even Jarvis."

Craig leaned toward Joshua and asked, "She hasn't told him yet?"

"Nobody! I'm the only one who knows. I bought her a test but she hasn't taken it yet. I don't think she wants to. If she is pregnant, it's deja vu for her. She was pregnant the last time she married Jarvis. Her doctor up'd the strength of her birth control pills cause the first ones weren't strong enough. It's a trip cause she's been on the pill for a while. I hope she's not pregnant cause she needs to get out of college before she starts a family."

"Damn! That's messed up."

"I know. Look Craig, I'll holler at you in a minute. I'm going to hit the dance floor."

"Okay."

Joshua hit the dance floor just like he said, not sensing the storm about to erupt.

A baby? I might be having a baby. Talk about luck.

Jarvis and Venice enjoyed the warm waters of the Jacuzzi after a heated session of making love. Straddling his lap, she wrapped her arms around his neck and kissed him as he caressed her back. His body renewed itself and he was anxious to consume her once again. She took a deep breath as he slowly entered her heat.

Venice tightly wrapped her legs around him and continued to push her tongue into his warm mouth while saying, "I love you, Jarvis."

He smiled and stared into her eyes, noticing that he was hitting her hot spots. Venice closed her eyes and threw her head back and let out a series of moans as he moved deeper inside her.

He groaned, then whispered, "Baby, you feel so good."

Jarvis continued to work her body slowly and erotically while covering her hardened nipples with his mouth. He felt her body tremble as he emptied his seed into her enflamed cavern. She released a loud moan as she clung to him lovingly, feeling him shudder with his release.

"I don't want this night to end."

"Who said it has to? I'm just warming up, baby."

He toweled her dry as he whispered his love in her ear. She closed her eyes, feeling her body tingle and shiver from head to toe. He wrapped a towel around his waist and they fell upon the bed. He covered her body with his and immediately parted her lips with his tongue aggressively. Soft whimpers escaped her throat as she savored the taste of him. His roaming hands and lips devoured her soft body as his desire pushed against her leg. Then, in a surprising move, he started kissing her between her thighs.

Venice moaned out loud, "Oh-h-h, Jarvis!"

He didn't answer as he kissed, licked, and devoured all her sweetness. This was a total shock to Venice since he had never done that to her before. She breathed loudly and moaned to the pleasure. She trembled and moaned even louder as he orally made love to her forcefully, yet tenderly. Venice began to speak in Spanish as Jarvis worked his tongue and lips over her body. He finally stopped and thrust himself into her and made love to her plunging deep and hard into her moist cavity. Venice held onto him securely and felt a little lightheaded from the session. He was burning with hot desire and love until his body was hit with explosive spasms. He exploded inside her body as Venice screamed out in erotic moans.

"Baby, where did that come from?"

He smiled, kissed her, and said, "Women aren't the only ones who have things they want to save for their wedding night."

"I can't argue with that, baby. Thank you for making me feel so…loved. I thought I was going to cry."

"You are my life, Niecy."

You also might have another baby on the way, sweetheart.

He pulled her over to him and wrapped his arms around her. She buried her face into his neck and they quietly fell asleep in each other's arms.

Fifty

The next morning, Jarvis and Venice found themselves still cuddled under each other. The Andersons planned a family brunch at eleven o'clock. Jarvis turned to look at the clock. It was already past nine. Venice was still unconscious, but Jarvis had no problem waking her up. He began to push his aroused body against her hips and without saying a word, they found themselves going at it again.

Venice felt like she was on top of the world as she rode his body like she had never done before. Jarvis turned his attention to Venice's firm breasts as he cupped them with his hands. She was with the man she loved and it felt wonderful. Jarvis' head was spinning as he tried not to wake the neighbors with his moans. He was unsuccessful and hollered out as Venice finally finished her assault on his body. Jarvis gripped her hips as he unleashed into her heat. Venice had to scream herself as she felt him explode inside her.

The morning seemed to fly by and they finally started to get dress for the breakfast.

"Jarvis, I am so sore."

"Sorry about that, baby. I'll fix you up later."

Venice had invited Craig and his family to join them. As they continued to dress and get their luggage together, Venice solemnly sat down and said, "Jarvis, I have something to tell you."

He stopped what he was doing and asked, "What's up?"

"My period's late."

"What! How late?"

"Six weeks!!"

"Six weeks! Is that why you've been so sick lately?"

"I don't know. I don't think I'm pregnant, but something's wrong. I didn't want to worry you."

He angrily said, "Venice, don't ever hold anything back from me again. We have to be able to talk."

"I'm sorry. I have a pregnancy test to take, but I haven't gotten around to it yet."

Jarvis sat down on the bed next to her. "Don't worry about it. If you are, we'll just have to deal with it. Okay? At least it won't be the first time."

"Is there anyway Craig could be…"

Venice strongly replied, "No! I've always used protection with him. There's no way!"

"I hope you're right."

"I'm sorry I didn't tell you sooner. But, if I am pregnant, you're my baby's daddy."

"I'd better be."

Jarvis gave Venice a comforting hug before they left the room and headed for the restaurant for breakfast. The newlyweds entered the reserved room and found that almost everyone was there. The only ones missing were Bryan and Sinclair. While they waited on Bryan, everyone hugged and talked about the beautiful wedding. Venice greeted Bernice, J.T., and Craig with warm hugs.

She gave Craig a kiss and he whispered, "I'm happy for you, girl, but I'll never get over you."

"I'll always have a special place in my heart for you also, baby. I love you."

Craig gave Venice another kiss as Joshua and Jarvis watched from across the room.

Joshua asked Jarvis, "You cool?"

"I'm cool."

Within ten minutes of the newlyweds' arrival, Bryan and his family entered the room. Once everyone was seated, Jarvis' dad stood up and gave a short speech on how elated he was to have Venice as a daughter-in-law and how blessed Jarvis was to have found someone as special as her. Jarvis reached over and held her hand as his dad continued to talk. He gave her hand a soft squeeze and planted a kiss on her cheek as they listened to the nice speech.

Once his dad finished, Jarvis' mom also offered some words for the couple. She couldn't finish her speech after she broke down into tears. As Jarvis' mom tried to regain her composure, Venice noticed

Craig staring from across the table. She smiled at him and he winked back at her.

After all speeches were made, the families enjoyed a wonderful buffet. The breakfast was a success and it was time for everyone to go their separate ways. Venice and Jarvis were going on a four-day honeymoon to a nearby resort, then on to Michigan.

Everyone gathered in the lobby for their departures. Venice noticed Galen, Joshua, Jarvis, and Craig talking near the checkout counter. Galen and Joshua walked off leaving Jarvis and Craig alone.

Jarvis said, "Look man, I know it must've been hard for you to come here and I just want to say thanks. It meant a lot to Venice that you came." Jarvis went on to say, "You know, Craig, I realize Venice still has strong feelings for you. She really does care about you. I'm telling you this because I don't want you to be mad at her and think she was just playing you."

"I never thought Venice was playing me. I knew she had feelings for me and I also knew she was still in love with you. I just hate that I didn't get a chance to get to know her better. I'm not going to lie to you, Jarvis. I love her and I believe I always will. It's not going to be easy getting her out of my system. I just hope you take care of her and make her happy."

Jarvis put his hand out to shake Craig's hand. "I'm going to do my best. Thanks." They shook hands and Craig walked away to gather his luggage. Jarvis went to load their bags into the car.

Venice told Jarvis she wanted to say goodbye to Craig. He told her it was fine with him. She caught Craig walking to the elevator. He was going back up to make sure he wasn't leaving anything.

She hollered, "Hold the elevator!"

"Where do you think you're going?"

"With you."

He laughed and said, "Your husband's going to be looking for you."

"He knows where I am."

The elevator door opened and they walked down the hall to his room.

As Craig searched the room, Venice sat on the bed watching. He was acting somewhat nervous. Venice asked, "What's wrong with you?"

"What?"

"You're acting nervous."

Craig leaned against the wall and said, "What do you expect? The woman I love just got married and is alone with me in my hotel room. Yes, I'm nervous because all I want to do to is kidnap you."

"I'm sorry. I don't want you to be upset with me. I still love you."

"I hope you guys have a great life together. Keep in touch with me. I'd like to know how the Sports Medicine thing is going."

Venice walked over to Craig and put her arms around his waist. He reluctantly did the same.

"Baby, I will never, ever forget all the love you've given me. You're the most thoughtful, sweet and loving person I know and I will always love you for that."

"Thanks, baby. That means a lot to me. It's going to take a while for me to get over you."

She grinned at him and asked, "Can I have a goodbye kiss?"

"Is your husband going to mind?"

"Come here, Bennett."

She leaned into him and they gave each other the sweetest, most sensual kisses. Craig found it hard to stop, but he knew he had to. He didn't want to let her go.

As they rode the elevator back down, Venice smiled and said, "You know, our first kiss was in an elevator. How about our last kiss being in an elevator?"

Craig immediately grabbed her and planted a long, juicy kiss on her lips.

Venice giggled. "I'll never forget our last night together, Craig. It was incredible."

He leaned against the wall of the elevator and came out of nowhere with the question. "Are you pregnant with my baby?"

"What! Where did you get that from?"

Craig calmly walked up to her and asked again, "Well, are you?"

Venice felt all the blood leave her face. She stopped the elevator, got off a couple of floors up from the lobby, and walked down the hall to a sofa before she fainted. Craig followed and hovered over her.

Venice asked, "Who told you that? Oh, you don't have to answer that. Joshua's no good ass."

"Don't be mad at him, but I am kind of disappointed I didn't hear it from you."

"Look, Craig, I don't even know yet. Anyway, if I am, it couldn't be yours. You know we were always extra careful."

He dropped his head and said, "The last time we were together, the condom broke."

"What? Why didn't you tell me?"

"We were both upset. I felt like it didn't matter."

Venice played back the events of that night in her mind and recalled being emotionally upset.

"How could you not tell me, Craig?"

Craig stood up and said, "I was also upset at the time, Venice. I didn't think it mattered and I would never have mentioned it to you if I hadn't discovered you were late."

Venice sat down and covered her face with her hands. "How can I tell Jarvis? I promised him there was no way you could be the father."

"So when will you know?"

"I don't know."

"Will you call me?"

She stood up and started walking toward the elevator. "I'll think about it. I'm kind of in shock right now."

Craig grabbed her arm. "Venice, don't play with me. I'm serious. That could be my baby."

Venice was practically a zombie when she replied, "Okay. I'll let you know."

Craig thanked her before they got back on the elevator and continued the quiet ride back to the lobby.

When they got off the elevator, Jarvis and Joshua were sitting in the lobby talking. Venice walked over to Joshua and stated firmly, "Get over here! I want to talk to you."

Jarvis asked, "What's wrong, Niecy?"

"Nothing!"

Joshua shook his head and immediately knew what was up. "Damn!"

They went outside to the parking lot where Venice lit into him. She got in his face and said, "Why in the hell did you tell Craig about me? I thought you were my damn friend? It wasn't his business to

know that. Now he tells me his condom broke our last night together. Now I have no idea who the father is if I'm really pregnant.
Thanks for nothing, Joshua."

Joshua reached for Venice's hand. "I'm sorry, Niecy. I didn't
mean to upset you. I guess I had a little too much too drink last night
and spilled my guts to Craig. But, I'm a man and I just think Craig
should know what's up. It's not like it was impossible for him to be
the father. He was hitting it on a regular basis, Venice, and you just
never know. First, I hope you're not pregnant. You and Jarvis need a
fresh start. Can you forgive me?"

"What I need to do is to kick your ass."

Joshua hugged Venice and asked, "I know and I'm sorry. Do you
want me to talk to Jarvis?"

"No, you've done enough talking. I'm not telling him anything
right now. You just pray I'm not pregnant."

"That's a bet."

They walked back to the front of the hotel and Jarvis had put the
last of their possessions in the car. She gave Bernice, J.T., and Craig
one last hug as they got into the car. Craig looked at her, smiled, then
drove away.

What have I done?

As soon as they got to the house, Jarvis asked, "Where's that
pregnancy test?"

"In my bag."

"You need to go ahead and take it. Why were you're pissed at
Joshua?"

She slammed the kit down. "Because he ran his damn mouth and
told Craig that I might be pregnant."

"So, what did Craig say?"

Venice solemnly said, "He told me the last time we were together...his condom broke."

"What! Damn, Niecy! Go take the test!"

She went into the bathroom to take the test. Jarvis was under-
standably upset as he started packing his clothes for their trip. Venice
took the test and the results came out positive. They didn't know
how to react to the results. She wouldn't be able to get to the doctor's office until they got back from their honeymoon. She was hoping this news didn't ruin the trip. She was going to do what she could

to make their honeymoon a happy one. They would just have to wait and worry about everything else later. Venice still could not forget the dream. Should she have waited to get married? It was too late to worry about that now. There was no doubt that she loved Jarvis, but it would take time to stop thinking of Craig.

Once at the beach, they put all their worries behind them and were able to really enjoy the trip. They spent a lot of time walking in the sands, especially for sunset walks. The days flew by and before they knew it, they were back home. Venice didn't waste any time getting to the doctor's office. Jarvis went along with her to find out the results. Once the blood test was conducted, it revealed that Venice was indeed pregnant. Jarvis and Venice didn't want to stress their parents out about the news, so they decided to keep the news to themselves for a while.

They finally said their good-byes and were on their way back to school. Venice couldn't imagine what life was going to be like from that point on. She was married to the love of her life and possibly pregnant by the other love in her life. Jarvis and Venice jumped back into their classes without skipping a beat. The situation did put a lot of stress on her marriage. Venice wished that she could change things, but she couldn't. Weeks later, they finally told their parents about the baby. They decided not to divulge the possibility of Craig being the father.

Another month passed and Venice began to show. Jarvis got over the initial shock and programmed his mind to believe he was going to be a father. He did his best to reassure Venice that everything was going to work out fine. Venice wanted to believe Jarvis, but she couldn't. Jarvis noticed that Venice was in a state of depression. He tried his best to keep her spirits up, especially in her current condition.

A couple weeks passed before it happened. Venice began bleeding and Jarvis had to rush her to the emergency room. Once again, she lost her baby. Once again, Venice and Jarvis were devastated. Jarvis wanted to know if Venice was ever going to be able to have children. The doctor explained that Venice didn't have any physical problems preventing her from carrying a child to term. She would just have to remain stress free during pregnancy. Jarvis revealed the sources of Venice's stress and added that college didn't help the situation any. The doctor asked Jarvis if he wanted to know if he was the baby's biological father. He said it was irrelevant to the current situation and that his main concern was to take care of Venice. He asked the doctor to reassure Venice that she didn't have a physical problem. The doctor promised that he would take care of it and release Venice the next day.

Jarvis called their parents and filled them in on everything. He also tucked his pride away and called Craig. Craig was hurt and asked if Venice was okay. Jarvis told him that she was obviously upset and said Craig could call her tomorrow. Craig expressed sincere gratitude for the call. Jarvis spent the night in the hospital room with Venice, then took her home the next day. They never discussed the paternity of the baby. Venice also never revealed her psychic dream about the situation. They were going to attempt to put everything behind them and get on with their lives.

Epilogue

Two years passed and Venice and Jarvis were both in their junior year. Galen and Sidney were doing well raising their two-year-old daughter, Gayla Cheyenne. Galen had been drafted and was playing for the Carolina Panthers. Sidney was busy teaching kindergarten and loving it. Venice and Jarvis were busy with their classes as the year came to a close. Jarvis had excelled even more on the football field that year. Venice had been co-oping with the football team the past season as a team doctor. All of the teammates knew Venice was Jarvis' wife. At first he had a hard time watching her put her hands on the other guys as she taped their ankles, massaged their sore muscles, and much more. It was an adjustment for all of them. Being their first female trainer, Venice was clearly a distraction for the players. The coaches made it clear that she was to be respected as a team doctor, as Jarvis' wife, and as a woman. Venice didn't pay any attention to the half-naked men when they walked around the locker room. It was a job and she was good at it.

Chanelle told Venice that Craig had accepted a job in Philadelphia and even though he was doing well with his career, he was not seeing anyone seriously. Craig traveled a lot and avoided any possibility for a relationship. Venice hadn't had any contact with Craig in almost two years, but hoped their paths would again cross one day. Joshua and Chanelle were still sharing an apartment at Dawson. Chanelle and Spoonie were also still together and discussing engagement. Joshua was still dating Cynthia, who was back at home running her own beauty shop. They had wedding plans soon after graduation.

Jarvis was drafted at the end of his junior year in the first round of the NFL draft. He did become the instant millionaire Bryan said he would become and was, fortunately, drafted by the Detroit Lions. This would allow Venice to finish college without transferring. She had another year ahead of her and she was determined to finish. Jarvis promised that he was going to work on completing his degree in the off season.

It was late summer and before he left for training camp, Venice informed him that he was going to be a father. This time, there were no surprises and this time, Venice was going to make sure nothing happened to their baby. Things were really looking up for them after all the trials and tribulations of the past. Venice often thought of the dream she had on her wedding day. She never mentioned her dream to anyone, not even Joshua. She knew in her heart that she'd made the right choice marrying Jarvis. Life was good and they were more in love than ever.

Venice, Jarvis, Joshua, and Chanelle had come a long way together. Each of them had a path they were traveling and it seemed they were all on the right road. Good friends are hard to come by. Everyone should be happy to have at least one true friend in their lifetime. When you have three, you are truly blessed beyond life's expectations. It's all good because life is all that and a bag of chips.

About the Author

DARRIEN LEE, A NATIVE OF COLUMBIA, Tennessee attended Tennessee State University in Nashville, Tennessee, which is where she picked up the love of writing. Her experiences on the college campus, was the inspiration for **All That and A Bag of Chips**, her first novel, published by Strebor Books Int'l. Majoring in Business Administration, she started out writing various works of poetry for her friends to help them "get the one they loved or get over the one they loved and lost." She is a member of African American Authors Helping Authors.

It wasn't until recently that Darrien began to take her writing serious after feeling unfulfilled with her present job at United Parcel Service. She found writing was the perfect setting which to unwind in while entertaining her friends.

Darrien lives in LaVergne Tennessee with her husband of 10 years and their two daughters. In her spare time she loves reading, sports and listening to jazz.

Dear Readers,

I hope you have enjoyed Venice's unique and adventurous love story. I would also like to thank all of you for your encouragement and support. While writing this story, it reminded me of the fun and minor drama that took place on my college campus. I hope in some way that I was able to entertain you and provide you with a thirst for reading. Some of you may have been able to relate to one or more of my characters. If so, I hope in some way I was able to move you either with tears, laughter, or love. Please write and let me know your thoughts and opinions.

And for those of you who are wondering, a sequel to *All That and A Bag of Chips* is in the works. Craig Bennett is too handsome and sexy not to find love also. Look for the sequel in the near future by checking my website. I look forward to bringing you Craig's story and many others.

Take Care,
Darrien Lee

Readers can contact me via my website at www.DarrienLee.com and at www.luvalwayz.com

Been There, Done That

By Darrien Lee

In merely seven years, Craig Bennett has managed to become one of the most successful architects in Philadelphia, PA. Labeled as one of Philadelphia's most eligible bachelors, Craig has had his selection of beautiful, intelligent women. Unfortunately, since his breakup with Venice, none have come close to fulfilling his passions and desires the way that she did. Having removed himself from any and all contact with her, Craig has built a wall around his heart, vowing to never risk falling in love again.

Jarvis and Venice could not be happier as the proud parents of their five-year-old son, Brandon. While Jarvis is relishing his fifth season in the NFL, Venice is enjoying her career in Sports Medicine with the Michigan State football team. Like all married couples, they have experienced their ups and downs. However, nothing could possibly prepare them for the unforeseen tragedy awaiting them. Will love enable them to overcome the unexpected turn of events? Only time will tell.

Been There, Done That

by Darrien Lee

The Detroit Lions won the Super Bowl and Jarvis was the MVP. The entire family was excited and happy for him, but Venice noticed Joshua was unusually quiet.

She asked, "Hey Josh! You okay?"

"I'm cool. Just happy Jarvis finally got that ring."

Smiling she said, "So am I, Josh."

Later that night, after hours of celebrating, Venice laid in Jarvis' arms after making hot, steamy
love.

"Jarvis, I'll love you forever."

Tilting her chin up so he could look into her eyes, he said, "Till death do us part, sweetheart. I'll
love you forever and don't you ever forget it."

A single tear rolled out of her eyes as he lowered his lips to hers and stole her breath with his
hot kiss. Making love to her this night was necessary and special as he joined his body with hers.

* * * * *

Philadelphia was blanketed with several feet of snow. Not many people showed up for work, either because of the weather or because they had one drink too many at a Super Bowl party. Craig came in that day, not having anything else to do. The newspaper was at the door when he arrived. Once in his office, he opened it to see the headline: *Detroit Lions Win the Super Bowl!* On the inside was a picture of Jarvis, holding the MVP trophy and kissing the still breathtakingly beautiful Venice. He didn't expect to have to lay eyes on her, but it was too late now. She had begun invading his dreams on a regular basis lately anyway and it unnerved him. He used to only think of her on rare occasions over the past few years, but lately it had increased for some odd reason. Now he'd laid eyes on her for the first time in seven years. Throwing the paper into the trash, he angrily shouted, "Damn!"

Months Later

The month of July seemed to be an unusually wet one. The late night storm woke Venice up as it rolled through. Venice watched as the lightening lit up the room. Worried that five-year-old Brandon might be afraid, she decided to check on him. Finding him sound asleep, she returned to bed and snuggled up to Jarvis and kissed him on the lips, but it felt strange. She stroked his face and his skin felt different.

She whispered his name to wake him to make sure he was all right. After no response, she started to

shake him, first softly, then frantically.

"Jarvis! Baby, wake up!"

He still did not respond. Venice's heart was now pounding as she reached over to turn on the light.

He was still breathing but was unresponsive. She reached for the phone and dialed 911 as tears streamed from her eyes.

She screamed, "Jarvis! Don't do this to me! Please!"

Luckily, Ms. Camille has spent the night. Venice ran to wake her so she could tend to Brandon.

She didn't want to alarm him that something was wrong with his daddy. The paramedics were there in no time and Venice dressed hurriedly while trying to stay calm.

"God please don't take Jarvis away from me."

ORDER FORM

Use this form to order additional copies of *Strebor Books International* Bestselling titles as they become available.

Name:_____

Company _____

Address: _____

_____

City: _____ State_____ Zip _____

Phone: (_____)_____ Fax: (_____)_____

E-mail: _____

Credit Card:❑*Visa* ❑ *MC* ❑ *Amex* ❑*Discover*

Number _____

Exp Date: _____Signature: _____

ITEM	PRICE	QTY
1. *Blackgentleman.com*	$ 15.00	
2. *Shame On It All by Zane*	$ 15.00	
3. *Luvalways by Shonell Bacon & J. Daniels*	$ 15.00	
4. *Daughter by Spirit by V. Anthony Rivers*	$ 15.00	
6 *Turkeystuffer by Mark Crockett*	$ 15.00	
7. *All That and A Bag of Chips by Darrien Lee*	$ 15.00	
8. *Nyagra's Falls by Michelle Valentine*	$15.00	
9.		
10.		

SHIPPING INFORMATION		Subtotal	
Ground one book	$ 3.00	shipping	
each additional book	$ 1.00	5% tax (MD)	
		Total	

Make checks or money orders payable to
Strebor Books International
Post Office Box 1370
Bowie, Maryland 20718